The

Lost Dragon Isles

William
Zackery
VanderHorst

Book 1 of
The Guardians of Nalawren Series

ISBN 978-09799834-9-8
Library of Congress cataloging in progress.

Cover Art by Zackery VanderHorst

Published by

LAUREL
Mountain
PRESS

PO Box 1973, Clayton, Georgia
www.laurelbooks.com

Dedicated to:

My Grandmother

Donna Ellen VanderHorst
1942 - 2011

A diamond in the rough

The Lands of Nalawren

The Lost Dragon Isles

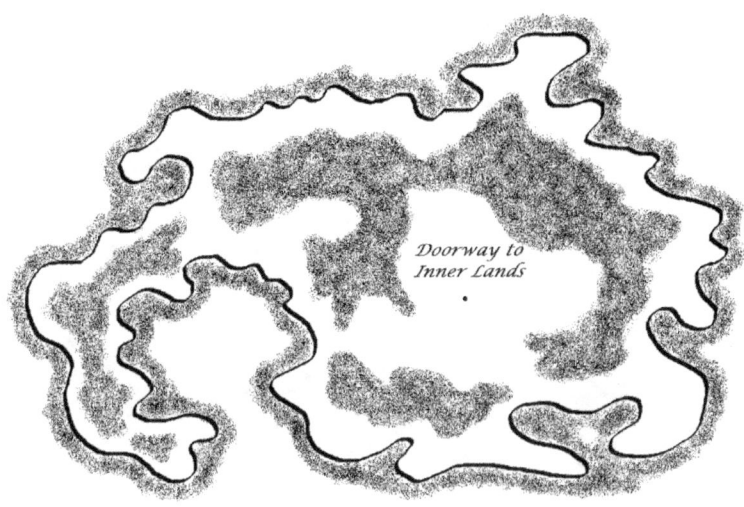

The Inner Lands of the Dragon Isles

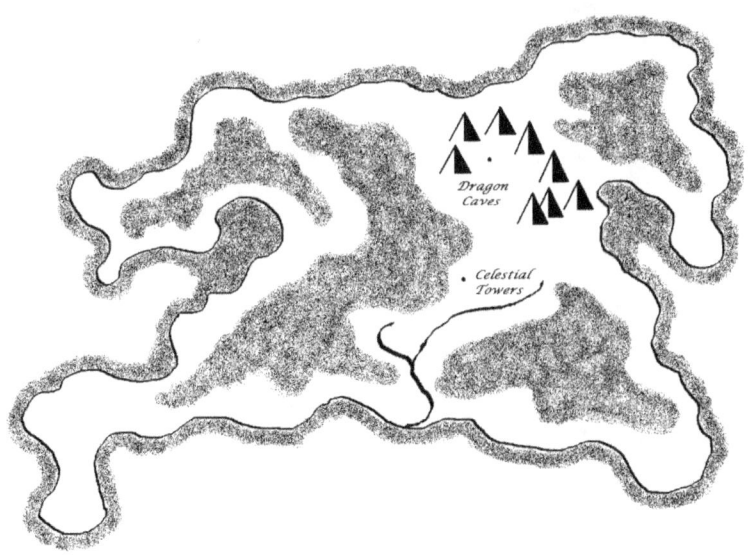

Prologue

The Early World

Few can remember the lands before the aftermath of the Chaos Wars and the turmoil brought to those involved. The races of Nalawren had lived together with little reason to fight and trade had flourished. At its peak the Human empire held close to five hundred thousand people. The Wood Elves held similar numbers while the High Elves boasted numbers nearing one million. Last were the Dwarves, whose total could never accurately be known because most of the Dwarves rarely ventured from their underground cities in the Tvan mountains. Those who did guess would say between two and five million, making them the largest race that was never seen. The three major races lived peacefully with most of the smaller races until a fourth contender was introduced, one that would challenge the rest for superiority throughout the lands of Nalawren.

The southlands had always belonged to the Humans, with the Elves, both High and Wood, holding from the extreme east to the far western reaches with a movement into the northern lands. The Dwarves had taken full ownership of the most northern reaches of Nalawren known simply as the Tvan mountains and all the earth below the peaks. The division of lands had always sat well with the races as they worked to maintain a balance of peace and harmony. Things changed forever on one brisk winter morning when pillars of black smoke could be seen rising out of the horizon behind the southern forests. Curiosity soon drove the Elves to investigate and they sent a small party of soldiers into the Human lands. A week passed, and then another but the soldiers did not return. The smoke intensified over the next few days and the Elves' curiosity turned to worry. The ruler of the High Elves dispatched another group to the southern lands, this time better prepared and well armed. A third week slipped by and at the eve of the first snow, the remnants of the Elves returned. Along with them came what was left of the Human army. Tattered and exhausted, they told their story.

A month prior to the mysterious fires and smoke pillars, ships began arriving on the southern shores by the hundreds. Soon, thousands upon thousands of odd creatures known as Goblins began ruthlessly assaulting the Human villages and towns surrounding the city of Qwaz, capital of the Human empire. They laid siege to the city and prevented any and all communication with the outside world. The Human soldiers that had arrived with the Elves were a third of the force dispatched to fight their way through the horde to find help. The news became increasingly concerning when the Humans told of more ships arriving daily, bringing thousands more of the horrible creatures to the battle. As the day grew to a close word was sent to the Wood Elves in the east to ensure the armies of the Elves would be ready for war. Within three days time, the two races of Elves rallied their armies and prepared to march to the south to lend what help they could to the shattered Human resistance. As they departed, they sent messengers to the Dwarves, praying the elusive race would leave their mountains and join in the efforts to eradicate the new threat. The vast armies of the Elves crossed the lands swiftly and on the fourth day of travel, the scouts reported sightings of the creatures.

The Goblins were short, no taller than five feet at most, with grayish blue skin. They wore very primitive armor and were armed with weapons that appeared to be made of bronze or stone. When the Elves first met the menace in the forests several were killed and brought back to the Elf encampments to be studied closer. They found the new creature was strong even though it lacked size. The large eyes gave it great sight in the dark forests but in full sunlight their vision was greatly reduced. Along with their weapons, the Goblins had a set of pointed teeth that could be used when all else failed. For all the differences of the two races, the Elves found that the Goblins were just as easy to kill as any other creature that called the lands home. The lack of efficient armor gave the Elven archers larger targets and their cheaper forms of weaponry were easy to break or damage past the point of being usable.

When the Elves arrived in the fields outside of Qwaz, the mass of the Goblin army was ready for the imposing attack. What followed was the bloodiest battle in history between the Elves and Goblins. In the first three days of fighting, nearly ten thousand Elves were killed with as many or more of the Goblins sharing the same fate.

The Elves found themselves faced with yet another creature they had never before seen. The new menace stood close to eight feet tall and seemed to be pure muscle with the exception of an obvious gut overhanging the waist. They had jagged teeth like the Goblins but it was their size and strength that made them a nightmare for the combined armies of Elves. They were known as Ogres, and the impact they made on the battlefield was felt all across the allied forces.

After a straight week of fighting the Elves were forced to pull back into the forests. For a while the Goblins and Ogres focused on destroying and raiding the city of Qwaz but the Elves knew that in time they would be forced to face the invading armies once more.

As the creatures remained in the south, happily pillaging the city they had fought so hard to gain control of, the Humans who had survived and escaped from the battle pushed north in an attempt to find safety with the Elves. The former King of the Humans had been captured and was brutally executed as an example for those who fought against the new races. What was left of the Human race, including the former Prince and newly made King, lived within the largest city of the Elves known as Pentegarn, ensuring some of their once great race would survive.

It was deep in the heart of winter when a surprisingly strong offensive was launched against the Wood Elves of Swanhaven. Like the Humans had done, the Wood Elves used their army to hold off the enemy long enough to get their people out of the city, leaving behind as few as possible. The High Elves came to the aid of their brothers and pushed the creatures back from the ruined city.

Battles became more frequent and unpredictable and the Elves began to wonder if the horde of destruction would ever ease. The answer came as the snow stopped falling throughout the Elven lands. With the city still on high alert, a monstrous surge of Goblin and Ogre forces could be seen at the edge of the plains outside of Pentegarn. They moved like a wave in the ocean towards the city walls, countless falling from the hundreds of Elven archers that lined the battlements. They crashed against the defenses time and time again with no success as an endless supply of arrows rained hell down on the foolish attackers. Ogres battered the gates with all their might but the sturdy defenses held against all that came their way. The catapults within the city cut through the lines of attackers with ease but even with all their success, it soon looked as if a successful siege was in place. Day and night the Goblin armies battered the city walls, constructing their own crude catapults from the forests from which they had emerged. Just when things started to appear their worst, a welcome surprise arrived in the form of a full Dwarven army. From the north arrived what seemed to be an endless supply of small soldiers who had traveled day and night to help their allies to the south. They charged the fields, fresh and ready to spill the blood of those who had caused such pain and suffering in the lands below their mountains. A week of intense fighting saw no clear victor but as the Elves joined the fight once more, they found themselves successful at pushing the armies back into the southlands. When the armies fell into full retreat the Elves chased them back to Qwaz where the enemy had apparently made its capital city. The allies of the north gathered themselves and tallied their losses. Since the beginning of the war against the Humans more than a month prior, nearly two hundred thousand Elves, Dwarves, and Humans had lost their lives. Their future and that of the lands of Nalawren were forever changed.

The New World

The Chaos Wars redefined the lands of Nalawren. Freedom was no longer taken for granted. With the Goblins and their armies pushed back to the southlands where they had conquered the Humans, the rest of the races struggled to return their lands to their original glorious state. The Dwarves returned to their mountains, continuing to mine the earth for the precious gems and ores that lay buried in the ground. Every day they dove deeper into the earth, creating a network of tunnels and cities that only seemed to exist in the dreams of the other races. Their massive army would forever be on call as they knew no free breath would ever be drawn if not fought for first. With the ravaging of Swanhaven, the Wood Elves sought to rebuild their city deep in the heart of the Elven forests. The reconstruction of the elaborate city was swifter than expected as many of the other races, both large and small gladly offered their expertise to the Elves. For two years they worked, and when the construction was finally completed, even the swans that had originally lived in the first city returned, finding the new city as good as the first. The remaining numbers of Humans and their new King moved out of the Elven city to an area three days north of Pentegarn where they too began to rebuild their city. Abandoning the name Qwaz, their new King Calyn opted for a new name. He decided to call his new city Cisalia after his sister who had been slain when they had fled Qwaz. The duty to defend the north now fell on the High Elves as they became the buffer between the southern armies and the northern races.

When the wars had finally ended, the vast armies of the south began a massive buildup of soldiers and weapons, waiting for their chance for another invasion. The city of Qwaz had become a breeding ground for odd creatures and pure evil. No longer were the southlands hosts to only Goblins. Out of the swamps came the fierce Lizardmen, large creatures who believed the new ruler of the south would lead their race to a triumphant victory over those who had stood over them for so long. The ruler of the armies was a mysterious sorcerer by the name of Valsera. With the help of his Goblin armies and the protection of a fearsome and powerful shadow Demon known as Infus, he soon began construction of his personal city. His will to dominate the other races drove him to the point of madness as his numbers soared beyond those of the Elves and Dwarves. He sought to recruit any race not bound to the three northern enemies to serve him.

Nearly thirty years had passed since the end of the Chaos Wars. South of Qwaz a new fortress named Nomaria was nearly complete. With it, the southern armies had secured a powerful foothold, pressing their numbers north again. They took a little more land with each passing week as the northern races tried to avoid another all out war. The armies had grown over the years as more and more of the reclusive creatures of the lands found a home behind Valsera's banner. Soon his numbers doubled that of his last invasion and the tension was ready to erupt into bloodshed once again.

Scouts from the north began returning to Pentegarn with news of massive armies threatening to move into the northern lands. The aggressive nature of Valsera's armies pushed the northern races to form their own buildup on the borderlands. For the next three years, the Elves spent nearly every day enhancing their border defenses as well as building up their armies. Stronger weapons were imported from the finest crafters the Dwarves had to offer as the Elves sought to find something they could use against their enemy. The tensions between the north and the south grew and the Elves prepared their armies at the borderlands for an invasion. At the close of the fourth year, the uneasy truce was threatening to come to a violent end. Skirmishes became common on the borders as the races clung to their old hatreds. The south's introduction of new and more powerful creatures gave the Elves a taste of the fears that were still to come with the imposing war. Not even in their nightmares had they imagined an army as large or as terrifying as the one they were faced with. Resistance across the border turned to bloodshed as the start of a new war began. Soon, an elite group of the Elven army known as the Order of the White Eagle began a hard fought campaign against the encroaching armies in the south. With Pentegarn and the might of the Elves behind them, the borders braced for war.

A World on the Brink

The sun emerged on yet another ravaged battlefield on the borders between the Elven and Goblin armies. The once green fields that separated the north and south were now stained red from the constant bloodshed between the two. The Elves regrouped in the forests of the north, awaiting the first sign of their enemies who hid amongst the gnarled and twisted trees of the south. Standing just inside the tree line was the captain of the Elves, his shield resting against a stump and his sword still in his hand from the past skirmish. He wiped his eyes on the edge of his sleeve as the lack of sleep was taking a heavy toll. A group of Elves passed by, heading down the line to reinforce the fatigued and injured. Erzel looked into the gnarled forest but saw nothing.

"My Lord Erzel, news for you from Pentegarn," an Elf said as he handed the captain a rolled piece of parchment.

Erzel took the scroll and read it to himself without blinking and then read it a second time. He peered up at the soldier who now stood awaiting orders. The captain read the scroll one last time before rolling it up and storing it under his cloak. "It seems that my Order has been summoned to see the King at once. A force should arrive from Pentegarn to replace those who are leaving. Please send for Elerith."

The Elf hurried off to his task, eager to please the captain who had a new light gleaming in his eyes. The thought of finally returning home was enough to put a smile on Erzel's tired face. He strolled quietly down the camps of soldiers, stopping among those belonging to the Order of the White Eagle and letting them know the new orders he and his soldiers had received. Among the masses were several branches of the Elven armies who had fought together for the past three years. The largest collection of soldiers wore black tunics with a golden lion centered across the chest and were known fittingly as the Order of the Golden Lion. Below them was a fair sized group wearing white tunics with a cluster of red stars; they were known as the Order of Blood Elves. Lastly were Erzel's soldiers. They wore dark blue tunics with a white eagle, its wings spread across the fabric. They were known as the Order of the White Eagle. With the exception of the King's royal guard, they were the most elite of the Elven armies.

Footsteps behind the Elf caught his attention and he turned to find Elerith approaching. Elerith was in command of the Golden Lions and together they had fought the hordes of the south for years. Erzel sheathed his sword and extended his hand to his fellow Elf who took it and greeted his comrade as if he had not seen him in many days. They turned to the tree line and studied it together as the sun rose higher in the sky. Realizing his friend was about to leave, Elerith was noticeably saddened.

"I suppose you know that my soldiers and I have been called back to Pentegarn?" Erzel asked without looking at the Elf.

"Yes... after all this time we've fought alongside one another, bleeding evil creatures to protect our homelands I never believed you would leave this border unless carried away on your shield."

"I'd be thankful for that... I like being alive. I've no intention of dying here, Elerith, and neither do you. We'll be serving the King in Pentegarn before the end of this war... his personal guards in the castle itself."

Elerith nodded to the idea, not sure if he was ready for a life without the outside world to guide him. "I don't know Erzel. My whole life is out here in the wilds. All I have done has been in the service of the King. I've grown accustom to the life out here and I can't see that I will be able to give it up any time soon."

"I understand my friend. Well, I must depart soon. Reinforcements should be arriving any time to replace what the border is losing. I will pray for your victories," Erzel said, shaking his head once more.

With the last few words, Elerith turned to leave the captain to his own soldiers that had begun to gather around the two. Word had spread of their chance to return home and the excitement showed in their eyes. As he gathered the fighters around him, the speech he had planned seemed to simply slip from his mind and he stood in the center of the mass without a clue as to what needed to be said. He pulled the scroll from under his cloak and held it above his head, like a prize earned after a triumphant victory.

"This piece of parchment holds the words that can change our lives after all these years of fighting. More than just telling us we are being recalled to the city of Pentegarn, it also states that our Order has been chosen for a mission of importance by the King himself, a task that requires our personal attention. Make no mistake, it will be no easier than what we've done here at the border for the past three years, but the honor of serving our King makes it much more important to me and to you. We leave as soon as you are packed and ready!"

The Elves gave a resounding cheer that echoed around the trees as the Order of the White Eagle began packing their supplies, weapons and other belongings into various wagons and carts. Erzel secured his weapons to his horse and watched as the rest of his soldiers prepared to leave. The line that headed away from the border was filled with happy Elves who could hardly wait to see the walls of Pentegarn once more. Erzel waved goodbye to the soldiers left behind at the border and fell in behind his Order. As the Knights belonging to the Order crossed into the plains that would eventually lead them to Pentegarn they passed an extra four hundred Knights from the Golden Lion who were sent to replace them. As the two Elven forces passed by one another, they shared nods and waves, each knowing their place and duty in the world around them.

As the Order of the White Eagle left the border for the first time in three years the forests of the south came to life. Elves peered into the shadows of the trees, trying to catch a glimpse of what lay hidden within them. Once every few minutes the form of a Goblin would appear outside of the trees but before an archer could take a shot, it would disappear once again. The Elves waited patiently, knowing the creatures could only wait so long before they revealed themselves. Scouts raised the alarm and soon the entire border army was ready to defend its homelands. Elerith stepped out of the trees with his sword and shield ready for whatever the army hiding in the forest brought forth. Behind him came the entire Order of the Golden Lion that was stationed on the border, their weapons ready to once again meet their enemies to the south. The Elves stopped in the clearing between the two forests and watched the disorderly armies of the south emerge from their cover. The surge of Goblins shot forth from the corrupted southern forests with no distinct discipline or formation throughout their ranks. The Elves locked their shields, one overlapping the next to form a powerful wall. As they waited for the foolish creatures to charge headlong into their superior soldiers, the Elves behind the wall drew back their bows. Elerith raised his sword and watched the enemy closely.

"Now!" he yelled, slashing the air with his sword.

Every other soldier in the line of shields turned to the side, revealing holes that were in turn filled with archers. The bows were quickly fired, dropping the front lines of Goblins in mid step. The archers continued picking the foolish creatures off as they still lacked any form of discipline to their ranks. Soon the trees coughed forth the hulking forms of Ogres who charged at the lines, some trampling their own soldiers in the process. The Elven archers fired on the enemy until the Ogres and Goblins were literally steps away. They then fell back and let the Elves with shields step up. As soon as the Elves locked their shields together, the Goblin mass crashed violently against the wall of shields in a fury of metal against skin, spears and swords crossing once more. The Elves held their ground well, stabbing and slashing at the creatures repeatedly until the Goblins were definitely on the losing side of the fight.

The first of the monstrous Ogres lowered its shoulder and charged through the wall of shields, sending Elves flying backwards as it used its sheer size and weight advantage to create large gaps in the defense. Several of the creatures demolished places in the Elven wall until the archers took up the slack, covering the Ogres with arrows and slowly bringing them down. The damage to the lines was substantial, however, and it left the Elves struggling to fortify the weakest spots with their reserve soldiers. With the holes plugged as best they could, the Elves once again resumed their attempt at holding the creatures back. The fallen Goblins began to pile high in front of the shields, making the battle more of a shoving match between the two armies. Elerith had worked his way to the front of the lines, dodging a spear as he kicked and stabbed his way into an opening. He saw the rear of the Goblin lines falling back, leaving the front lines to follow or face their doom at the hands of the superior Elves. As the body of an Ogre fell to the ground engulfed in arrows, the Goblins realized their fight was lost this time. With the retreat intensifying, the Elves climbed the piled Goblin dead and gave chase to their opponents. They worked across the dead and dying as they slashed their way through those foolish enough to continue standing their ground.

"Forward Elves! Drive them back to the forests from which they came!" Elerith shouted, driving his sword into the stomach of a foe.

The Elves could taste victory as the Goblins retreated back to their forests with the Ogres following unhappily. The Elves halted their advance halfway across the field as they began slaughtering any enemy left behind or wounded. Elerith knocked one opponent to the ground with his shield and stepped on its chest, cutting its throat with a quick swing of his sword. The blood added yet another stain to the already crimson ground and the Elf stepped across the dying creature with his eyes set on yet another fight. The last of the Goblins had disappeared but Elerith stepped up beside the shape of an Ogre lying face down on the ground. It struggled to crawl away from the massacre with arrows jutting from its body in every direction. He raised the blade of his sword and then thrust it down with all his might, severing the head from the body. As it rolled to a stop, the Elf turned back to his soldiers and held the bloody sword aloft to a cheer of victory that erupted from his lips.

"Elerith my Lord, the Goblins are in full retreat through the southern forests. Shall I give the order for our forces to pursue them?" a Knight asked as the Elf started back to the tree line of the north.

"No, pull the Order back to our forests and collect our dead and wounded. I need a messenger ready to travel to Pentegarn. The King will want to know that the creatures are becoming more and more daring and our borders are far from being secure if the battles intensify."

"Yes sir!" the soldier replied.

Elerith walked back to the forest, stepping past mounds of dead Goblins as he cleaned his sword on the edge of his cape. A gnarled hand raked against his boot and he spun around, delivering a viciously swift kick to the skull of the Goblin. The creature rolled away and was instantly finished by one of the many Elves of the Golden Lion following the captain. Inside the trees the leader found rows of fallen Elves on the ground, their weapons laid across their chests. The rows stretched through the trees and he knelt next to the end of it to pray for those who had died that day.

"How many were lost?" he asked, stepping back from the bodies.

"At last count sir, sixty four. There are also many others who are wounded past the point of healing and may not even make it through the night, but I will say that our numbers of dead and wounded are nothing compared to those who died serving Valsera this day."

"Gather our dead and send them home to their families so they may be buried in proper surroundings. Then I want any available archers to take up positions in the trees overlooking the clearing. I think they will find it a more strategic area for them to view the battle. Also, take any who are wounded past the point of being useful and send them back with the dead. Perhaps if we spare them another battle they will heal and fight again beside us one day."

"Yes my Lord. I will see it done at once," the soldier replied as soon as his orders had been given to him.

The Elves moved quickly, loading their dead and dying

onto wagons to be sent home where they would be buried with their families who had passed before them. Fire leapt from the mounds of dead bodies left in the clearing as they burned the dead of their enemies. The battle had hardly spanned an hour but in that time more than two hundred Goblins and Ogres had been slain. The Elves' superior fighting skills and desire to keep their homelands safe from the grotesque intruders had once again cost the south an embarrassing loss. The rage it would bring Valsera would more than likely force him to send even greater numbers of his seemingly endless supply of soldiers at the Elves.

Elerith watched as two fresh units of spearmen marched to the edge of the tree line, staring across the clearing and waiting for their chance to kill more of the southern creatures. Fresh soldiers arrived all throughout the camp for the remainder of the day and those who were beyond exhaustion were finally permitted to take leave. Elerith entered the barracks at the edge of the encampment where he spent most of his time plotting out the best way to face the forces in the south. The guards saluted him and he took his seat at the long table in the main room of the barracks. He leaned his shield against the wall behind him and rubbed his tired eyes. A servant brought a pitcher of fresh water and a large bowl for the Elf to wash his face and hands. Once he was finished and free of the blood and grime, the guards admitted an Elf in a white traveling cloak. He gave a half bow and took a seat at the left of Elerith.

"You asked for a messenger sir? I am at your service," the Elf noted.

"Are you rested and have you a fresh mount?" Elerith asked, receiving a nod from the Elf. "Good, your journey will take you to Swanhaven to warn King Tanis of the heightened number of attacks lately and then to Pentegarn to inform our King of the border situation. Let him know that we will need additional reinforcements as soon as they are available. Also, be sure to tell him that our enemy has begun mixing its forces, and that we no longer face only the Goblins."

"Yes my Lord," the messenger replied as he stood from the table.

"Leave right away. The sooner King Elendil knows how

aggressive our opponents have become, the better our situation will be. I wish you safe journey," Elerith said with a quick salute.

The messenger returned the salute and disappeared outside. Elerith remained in the main hall of the barracks for the remainder of the day, looking over maps and drawings of the surrounding lands. He knew that somewhere in the rolls of parchment was hidden the information he needed to gain the upper hand over his enemies. He searched endlessly for a soft spot in the southern border defenses but it just wasn't as evident as he had hoped. Around an hour before sunset a soldier rushed into the room, his face drained and void of any color.

"My Lord... my Lord... they are making another assault on the border! They've brought help!"

"Help? Show me!" Elerith ordered, jumping from the table and grabbing his shield from the wall.

The two Elves hurried out of the barracks, through the camp, and then into the trees that led to the clearing. The bulk of the border guards who were not already stationed at the front lines followed the two Elves into the trees, lining up with their fellow soldiers wherever they could find a spot. Elerith pushed his way to the front lines and looked out across the clearing at the wave of opponents. The Goblins and Ogres stood centered in the clearing with a little more discipline to their forces this time as their formations were packed and in general lines. The number of Ogres and Goblins hadn't really increased but a new opponent brought a hushed murmur to the lips of the Elven forces. On either side of the Ogres were large groups of muscular creatures known as Lizardmen. The creatures stared the Elves down with their hollow eyes, ancient hatreds still brewing between the two races. The Lizardmen were better armed than their smaller companions, each using short swords or spears and they carried a large, round shield. Each Elf knew that the weapons of the Lizardmen didn't stop at what they carried in their hands and that their tails and teeth were just as deadly.

Elerith watched as more Lizardmen and Ogres lumbered out of the forests to reinforce their already monstrous numbers. The new additions to the southern armies made the field one sided in their favor but the Elves were not ready to back down and hand their lands over without a fight. Even though they were visibly shaken, the north stood firm. Elerith drew his sword and nodded to the soldiers behind him.

"This is going to be a very long night."

Erzel and his soldiers marched all day and then all through the night without stopping once to rest. The large moon in the sky above supplied light for their trek north, the idea of seeing home keeping their spirits high. They marched on into morning as the sun's first rays began to appear. The army entered the vast fields where Pentegarn stood and though it was still more than a mile away, the Elves felt like they were already home. In the distance they could see the tall outer walls and towers that encircled the entire city. Behind the first wall were the houses, shops, stables and buildings where the trade and economic empire flourished. A second wall separated the city from the fortress which stood almost twice as tall as the outer wall. Someone traveling through the area could easily mistake the city for a mountain in the distance. Pentegarn had become the center of the Elven lands, both militarily and economically and even the great race of Dwarves admired the advancements of the Elves. At any given time there were between two and three hundred thousand Elves behind the walls of the city, not counting those in the surrounding lands.

The captain and his soldiers reached the first gate where the bulk of his army separated throughout the city to rest and catch up on all they had missed for the past three years. Erzel and his highest ranked Knight Aric passed through the second gate and into the fortress. The two traversed the many corridors and staircases held within the mountainous castle until they found themselves at the throne room doors. Two twelve foot tall oak doors were pushed wide as they walked into the room.

"Greetings Captain Erzel," the guards addressed him with a salute.

The captain nodded as he and his Knight entered the room. Inside the doors were another dozen Elves belonging to the elite group known as Elendil's Winged Knights. They wore plated armor from head to toe and were identified by the curved eagles wings located on either side of their helmets. They watched the two Elves cross the room to where the King sat upon his throne. Erzel and Aric knelt together before the King until they were told to stand.

"Rise Erzel, let us talk as old friends do. Come, let us walk," the King said as he stood from his throne.

"My King, this is my head Knight Aric. He is one of the most trusted soldiers I have under my command and he has served you proudly. Now, I understand our Order is needed. What can we offer you my King?" the Elf asked as he and the Knight stood with Elendil. The King placed a firm hand on the captain's shoulder.

"I have a task for you and a selection of your best Knights that will require you to leave as soon as possible. Tanis, the King of the Wood Elves, has decided his daughter will be safer if she is brought away from the borders and into our city. Our armies here in Pentegarn would provide the protection he seeks in the event that Swanhaven is attacked again. At the rate things are progressing, it seems like only a matter of time before the city is no longer safe."

"What would you have me do my King?" Erzel asked, stopping next to him at the railing to the balcony.

"As I have said, I want you and your finest Knights, around fifty of them would suffice, to travel to the city of Mihlann where you will await the arrival of the Princess and her royal guard. If you leave tomorrow morning you should arrive there a day ahead of them and you are not to leave her side until the caravan is safe within our inner city. She is of the utmost importance and this is a duty I trust you can accomplish."

"As you wish my King. I will personally guarantee that the Princess will arrive safe and unharmed. We will send word to the soldiers and mobilize first thing in the morning," Erzel replied with a bow.

"Good then. Now please forgive me for I have business to attend to elsewhere. I wish you and your soldiers a safe trip and await your return," Elendil said as he left the balcony.

Erzel and Aric bowed their heads as the King left and

then followed him back into the throne room. The two Elves left the room and walked in silence through the halls of the castle as if searching for the way out. Erzel felt a tickle at the back of his neck as the details of their assignment rolled through his head over and over. They entered a large chamber leading to the massive door at the front of the castle and the Knight and his captain moved to one side of the doorway. A patrol of archers hurried past on their way out to the many towers on the inner and outer walls. Erzel stopped just outside of the gate and turned back to Aric.

"Go on and enjoy the evening. I will make the selections of those accompanying us to Mihlann and we will be ready to leave before midday tomorrow. Get some rest away from the border wars."

"Thank you my Lord," the soldier replied as the Elf walked away.

Erzel walked slowly through the streets, peering into the shops and buildings as he looked ahead to a familiar one. It stood three stories tall and was as wide as any two buildings within the city put together, excluding the barracks and castle itself. The sign swayed gently in the breeze as the captain entered the Morning Moon Inn and Tavern. The room was filled with Elves and Humans drinking their fill and feasting in front of the large fireplace. The smell of cooked meat and ale invaded his senses as he took a deep breath. The captain spotted several soldiers on the opposite side of the room with a group of the Golden Lion. He nodded to the barkeep and continued on to the group with a pitcher and tray of glasses. The captain took them to the corner where his troops sat alongside the others.

"My Lord!" the soldiers addressed him together, standing from the table. One of the Knights from the Golden Lion poured the glasses full and each of the Elves took one, holding them aloft.

"A toast to our King Elendil!" Erzel called out.

There came a resounding cheer from all round the bar and soon the pitcher was gone. The Elves swapped stories of the many battles they had shared on the borders and how they had each made it out alive. Erzel sat at the edge of the table in silence, watching and listening to the tales of bloody skirmishes and valiant deeds accomplished by the brave soldiers. Another pitcher of ale arrived and the captain poured the glasses full once more, catching the attention of the group.

"I remember the first battle I ever drew a sword in. A long time ago, before the battle for our lands began, before Valsera thrust his armies upon us, I was young and in the wilds of the woods below where Qwaz once stood proud. I remember camping on a ridge just north of the swamps, thankfully out of reach of the smell. Anyway, the flicker of the campfire must've drawn something's attention because just before I was about to fall asleep, I heard soft movements through the trees."

"What was it my Lord?" one soldier asked.

"I could hear something dragging behind it. The trees parted and from them came the form of a Lizardman. It dove for me at the edge of the fire, apparently thinking I was asleep, but it was fooled and I rolled away, drawing my sword from its sheath. I can remember it crashing headfirst into the coals of the fire, howling and thrashing in pain as I closed in to finish the beast off. It swiped at me but missed, leaving my cloak torn. A quick swing brought the blade of my sword down across its neck, sending the head rolling back into the fire." Erzel said as he reminisced about the encounter that had taken place long ago.

"So... that was before you saved Elendil?" one of his soldiers asked, draining his ale and setting the glass down on the table.

"Wait... what! You saved King Elendil's life?" one of the soldiers from the Order of the Golden Lion asked surprised.

"Well, that too was long ago."

"No... come on Erzel. Tell them about it," one of his Knights urged.

"Fine. It was during one of the campaigns against the Lizardmen tribes in the heart of the southern swamps. Somehow, the bulk of his forces became separated from him and with only a handful of soldiers defending him, it was clear the King was in trouble. I used the art of surprise to gain the upper hand and it gave his soldiers the time they needed to overcome the creatures. With the King safe, I was able to lead them out of the swamps and reunite them with the bulk of their soldiers further north. Afterwards, I was asked to join the ranks of his soldiers and after several more battles, I was put in charge of my own Order."

"Wow... I had no idea. It's not exactly something you hear about in everyday conversation," the soldier said thoughtfully.

Erzel continued, "Speaking of such, you Knights within my company have been given a task. I need the best of our soldiers prepared to leave for Mihlann in the morning on an errand given to us by the King himself. It has been deemed one of the most important duties we have ever been asked to perform. In our absence, I want what remains of my Order to join the defenses here in Pentegarn."

"Yes my Lord," the soldiers replied. Two solders left to spread the news of their orders.

"What is the mission my Lord?" another asked, filling his glass once more.

"Escort someone of great importance back to Pentegarn and see that no harm befalls them no matter what. We needn't take the entire order as we have to move swiftly and only the Knights will keep up with us. The remainder will stay behind here. Think of it as an extended leave. It shouldn't take but a few days. Now if you will excuse me, I need to rest for tomorrow's journey."

The captain left the table and trudged sleepily up the stairs to a spare room made available for him. The Elf leaned his shield against the wall beside his sword. He hung his tunic over the edge of the chair and let his chain armor form a pile a the foot of his bed. The blankets were soft and inviting and Erzel quickly fell fast asleep. He was soon swallowed into a world of dreams and nightmares.

The rays of the early morning sun peeked through the thick trees on the eastern forests and came to life as the elusive Wood Elves moved throughout the forest securing the land around Swanhaven. The road to the city was now reinforced with heavier protection than ever before as the Princess prepared for her long journey to Pentegarn. She had been up since before the sun appeared, nervous about the trip but excited to see the different world outside of her home. An army of servants had labored through the sunrise, helping her pack her clothes and belongings for what would be an extended stay at the capital of the High Elves. In all her life, she had never spent that much time away from her home.

Tanis, the King of the Wood Elves, stood at the other side of her bedroom door, wondering if his decision to send his only daughter away was the best choice for her. The southern armies had not intensified their attacks on the forest border of Swanhaven for over a year but Pentegarn remained the largest and most heavily defended of cities in the north, with the exception of Tvan, homeland of the Dwarves. Tanis knocked gently on the door as he heard footsteps crossing the floor on the other side.

"Rhen, are you decent daughter?" he asked through the door.

"Just one second Father!"

The King waited patiently and after a minute the door opened. One of the servants moved out with a bag of the Princess's belongings and hurried down the hall and out of sight. Tanis stood next to the door, watching his daughter fasten her cloak over her shoulders. She was, in his mind and that of almost all other Elves and Humans, beautiful. She had long, wavy red hair, fair skin, emerald green eyes and a glow of innocence that radiated around her. She smiled at her father as she finished buttoning the cloak.

"Father, why such a sad face? Are you worried about the trip? Is there something wrong?" she asked, running her hands down the front of her dress.

"Wrong? Of course not my dear. I was just thinking about how this is the first time you've left without us. The first time you've been away from home for such a lengthy period of time. I have to trust that someone else is going to protect and look after you and it just makes me a bit... sad."

Rhen walked up to him and threw her arms around his shoulders, hugging her father tightly. "Father, I will be fine. Pentegarn is the strongest city of any race and I know that the High

Elves won't allow anything to happen to me. I'll be fine, really. It might be interesting to see a different part of the world. These forests are all I have ever really known. If you want me to go somewhere safe, then I know that is where I should be."

Tanis nodded and held the door open for her. They walked together down the hall slowly, savoring the time they had left. The last few servants followed them down to the lower courtyard where the carriage and nearly all of Swanhaven waited to see off the Princess. Standing beside the carriage was the Queen and the head of the army. The head of the army bowed to the King and Queen and took a few steps back to allow them privacy with their daughter.

"Narissa, you came down?" Tanis asked in a shocked voice.

The Queen nodded. "As much as I hate watching you send our only daughter away to a city she isn't familiar with, I had to come see her one last time before she left."

Rhen hugged her mother, a single tear falling down the side of her cheek. "I didn't think you would come down. I won't be gone forever you know, just until it is safe to come home."

The King and Queen stepped back and allowed the servants to finish putting their daughter's belongings away. The Princess gave them both one last hug goodbye and turned away, lifting her dress and climbing into the carriage. She turned back and looked out the window as her father approached the side of the carriage.

"You will be safe Rhen. Your escort is well armed and you will be meeting up with an even heavier armed force in Mihlann to take you the rest of the way. Once you reach the fort city you will be surrounded by the best soldiers Pentegarn has to offer. Send word once you arrive in the High Elf capital."

"I will Father."

With the Princess secure and comfortable in the carriage, the King waved to the Elf at the reins and the convoy of soldiers started out of the city. As they began their journey into the forests, the city waved their farewells as the Princess passed by, her wave and smile telling them all she would be just fine. As the carriage and the last of her escort disappeared from view, the city of Swanhaven returned to its everyday duties.

The road twisted and wound through the trees and across the creeks and rivers. The Princess stared out the window for a while, admiring the beauty of the surrounding wilderness. The journey to Mihlann would take a day and would send the convoy south before cutting back to the east. The armed escort had concerns about how close to the borders their route would take them but it was the quickest one. She leaned back and smiled to the younger Elf sitting across from her. The blonde Elf had been selected to accompany the Princess to the city and care for her needs while they were in Pentegarn.

"Are you nervous?" Rhen asked.

"Yes, somewhat nervous. I've never dreamed I'd be going to the largest city the Elves have ever built. What is it like?"

"Big... if you see it from a great distance, you'd probably confuse the city itself for a mountain. I've only seen in once, but I've read so much about the history. There is one I am particularly interested in meeting there. I've heard stories of his bravery and I want to put a face with what I've read," the Princess answered, half daydreaming as she spoke.

"Really... who is that?"

"His name is Erzel. He is the captain of the Elven armies and leader of the Order of the White Eagle. He wasn't even born into nobility. No, as I have read, he was found by the Elves battling against Lizardmen alone in the southlands. When he had healed from his wounds, King Elendil of the High Elves gave him the Order to command and since then he has proven his worth in battle after battle."

The blonde Elf looked at the Princess with a smile all her own. "Is it love you feel?"

Rhen turned her head quickly with the start of a blush on her face. She fought in her head for a response to the question but nothing was coming to her. Seeing the troubled look on the Princess's face, the servant quietly apologized.

"Begging your pardon, it wasn't my place to ask such. He does sound like a fine man, even without the title of nobility."

"Yes... a fine man indeed," she replied. Rhen rocked in

her seat as the carriage bounced with the road and less than half an hour into the journey the Princess was fast asleep.

Morning had brought with it a horrible massacre on the border lands as the size of the Ogres coupled with the ferocity of the Lizardmen created immediate problems for the armies of Elves. The initial charge from the north had proven fatal as the Ogres used their sheer size and strength to trample through those not on horseback. The only break for the Elves came as the archers began to concentrate their fire on the Ogres and their accuracy helped bring the beasts down quickly. Those who survived the deadly volleys of arrows fell back to the forests, but the Lizardmen refused to retreat. They wove their way across the battlefield, carrying with them a line of death and destruction. It took a coordinated charge from the mounted Knights to finally end the bloody skirmish.

Elerith sat in the barracks, a wet cloth held in place across his face as the servants prepared to tend his wound. The gash he had received ran from the bottom of his ear to the side of his jaw and though the pain had been excruciating, he never made a sound. A new cloth with fresh water was brought to clean the wound further. During the battle he had been knocked from his feet to the ground and managed to turn in time to miss the deadly swing from one of the Lizardmen. Instead of the fatal blow, the sword sliced cleanly through his ear and face He now sat bloody and angry, waiting for the servant to stitch the wound closed. He looked up to find that a soldier had arrived and was waiting to be addressed.

"Yes?"

"Pentegarn has sent the reinforcements you asked for. Another two hundred Elves arrived moments ago and we are waiting for your orders my Lord. Where would you have us stationed?" the Elf asked, eyeing the wound on the Elf's face.

"Take them to the border and dispatch them through the tree line. Relieve those who need to rest or who are injured and build up the weakened section in our eastern defenses where the Ogres did the most damage."

"Yes my Lord."

The soldier left the barracks quickly to carry out the duties that had been given to him. He marched the reinforcements to the border where the number of fallen had jumped to over three hundred in the last battle alone. The fresh footmen and archers immediately filled the gaps in the defense that were showing the worst signs of stress. The exhausted Elves from the previous battle were finally able to leave the border in search of something hot to eat and a place to rest for a while.

The captain struggled to wait patiently as the servant stitched his wound closed. The Elf winced as the thread was pulled tight and cut, allowing him to wash his face once more and then dry it on a fresh towel. Elerith waved the servants away as he picked up his bloodstained shield and walked heavily out of the barracks. Exhausted and injured soldiers were still filing into the encampment as the leader of the Golden Lion headed out to the border once again.

The fresh and rested soldiers made a noticeable difference as they took their new positions. Another battalion of archers positioned themselves in the trees as the footmen fell in with the lines of soldiers. Elerith arrived with the soldiers and looked over the field. From the left he heard an Elf shout.

"My Lord Elerith, we've a soldier approaching!"

"Where?" the captain asked.

"In the clearing sir, a single cloaked soldier. Shall I give the order to fire?"

"No, have the archers stand down. I will deal with this."

The captain hefted his shield and walked cautiously out of the trees. He kept his shield close to his chest as he eyed the creature in the center of the battlefield. It was cloaked in black and appeared to carry no weaponry at all. Elerith stopped a dozen paces short of the creature, eyeing it with great suspicion. The Elf shifted on his feet, his free hand resting on the hilt of his sword. The cloaked creature opened its robed arms, revealing it was in fact armed.

"What is it you want?" the captain asked, unwilling to relinquish his grip on his sword.

The hooded creature did not respond to the Elf's question. Its black cloak and robes swirled around its feet the way smoke would in the wind. Nothing could be seen in the darkness of the hood and no form of armor was apparent. It took a single step forward, causing the Elf to take several steps back and to draw his sword quickly from its sheath. Elerith steadied himself but kept his sword erect.

"Stay your blade master Elf," the creature hissed. "I've come not to quarrel with you this day."

"Then what do you want?"

"It is a very simple concept. In three days my army will control all of your borderlands from east to west in the name of Valsera. A choice you have… leave, and allow us this land or every one of your Elves will die here, I promise you that!" the creature threatened as it turned to leave.

Elerith felt his anger swell in his chest and quickly advanced on the creature. With his shield raised to protect him, the captain of the Golden Lion swung his sword with all his might, aiming for where he believed the creature's neck to be. His sword sliced cleanly through the dark cloak without resistance, emerging on the other side with only a wisp of smoke following the blade. The damage he thought he had done was obviously absent as the creature turned once more. The hollow darkness within the hood sent a chill down Elerith's back as he realized he had swung his sword completely through his opponent without causing a scratch.

"Three days Elf… three days," it hissed a warning, whirling around and heading back into the forest.

Elerith barely moved until the cloaked creature had disappeared into the shadowy forest to the south. He walked slowly back to the lines of soldiers that had witnessed the event unfold in the clearing. The captain finally sheathed his sword and looked over the rows of concerned Elves as they all stood anticipating an explanation. He tapped the hilt of his sword nervously, trying to find the right words to describe what he had just witnessed.

"What happened my Lord? What was that about?" one Elf asked after the long silence.

"Assemble the army. I want every available soldier who isn't injured awake, armed, and ready for battle at once. It claims we have three days before they invade... so I want everyone ready in two."

"Invasion?" the soldiers whispered in confusion.

Elerith ignored them as he made his way back to the barracks. Word had quickly spread through camp of the upcoming battle and before the Elf had a chance to enter his barracks, the majority of the camp and army surrounding it had heard the news. The soldiers able to fight quickly began to mobilize and moved to the border as the captain had ordered. The quick mobilization of the Elves gave Elerith more reassurance that the north still had a firm grip on the borderlands. He sat in the barracks alone, wondering what form of creature he had encountered earlier in the field. Evil had so many forms, but never had the Elf faced an opponent that seemed as invulnerable to harm as the one he had just seen. A small group of soldiers entered the room where Elerith sat, the looks on their faces telling the reason they were there.

"My Lord, may we have a word?" one asked as they stopped at the edge of the table.

"If that is what you have come for then please, sit down," Elerith replied.

"When you met that creature in the clearing, the robed one, why did you not kill it?" one soldier asked as he sat down across from the captain.

"I tried. When I swung, my sword seemed to pass straight through the soldier as if it were only smoke under the robes. Even the robes themselves sustained no damage. I've never before seen an evil as powerful or dangerous as this one appears to be. Apparently it believes that in three days, they will control the borderlands."

"Impossible my Lord, no army could ever take our border in three days. Our soldiers are far superior to those of the Goblins and their numbers. Why, we have fought here for years and they're no closer to taking our lands than they were when they first started this war."

"I'd like to agree with you there. No army could take our lands that fast... but then again, no army we have ever faced has been invulnerable to harm. None of our Elves have the ability to receive a blade and continue walking as that creature did. So what we thought to be impossible has just been turned around on us, wouldn't you say?"

The captain ran his fingers across his chin as he wondered if the words the creature had hissed could be true. Perhaps if there was a way it could influence the rest of the Goblins with the strange ability it possesses, then the reality of taking the Elven lands would be all too real. Or if there was something yet to be seen, some sort of force that the shadowed creature controlled that it planned to unleash on the battlefield. The thoughts bounced through Elerith's head as he struggled to find a feasible answer to his own pressing questions. He gave the soldiers a false smile and shook his head.

"I have no doubt that our forces will be enough to hold the borders. You are dismissed."

The soldiers disappeared outside of the barracks, leaving the captain alone once more to wrestle with his thoughts. He looked over a map on the table, focusing on the lands just north of the border he currently controlled. If his soldiers were to fail at holding off the enemies and lost the borderlands to the south, Mihlann would surely fall with Swanhaven soon to follow. The next closest city was Pentegarn and every Elf knew that with the military backing and impenetrable defenses it possessed, the capital city would never fall. Even if the borders were lost, the disciplined ranks of the Elves of Pentegarn would surely hold strong against any invasion until the Dwarves could arrive to help. The captain of the Golden Lion remained in the barracks as the afternoon drug by.

The border was packed with soldiers waiting for the slightest sign of life from the southern side of the borders. Elerith had emerged and patrolled the lines of Elves with his sword drawn and shield ready. Not a single campfire was visible on the lower edge of the forest where the enemies were surely waiting for the Elves. Two days remained before the threat issued on the Elves would be carried out. The soldiers on the north locked their shields together and prepared for the night.

As Elerith's soldiers watched over the border, Erzel and his group of elite Elves were just arriving in Mihlann. They had left early in the night and arrived as the sun crested the mountains. The fort city was alive with soldiers as they hurried to greet and offer assistance to the famed captain and his Order. The mass of men and women that appeared surprised the captain as he dismounted from his horse and greeted the Elves with a warm smile. The reins were taken and his horse was led to the stables as the captain stretched. It took nearly half an hour for the crowd to disperse. The captain wandered the streets in search of the commander of the city. At last he found him, huddled over a map in the war room of the castle. He waited as the guards searched him and then allowed him in.

"Thank you for your hospitality thus far commander. I regret we shall only be staying a short time," Erzel said as he entered.

"You are most welcome to stay as long as you see fit captain. Please, call me Raziel. Now, what further service can we be to you and your soldiers?"

"I believe you have given us all that we require Raziel. For that I am grateful. I need to be notified of the arrival of a convoy from Swanhaven the moment it enters the city though."

"Of course Erzel, now please, quarters have been made available for you and your soldiers, so go and rest. You will find your room here within the keep and another for your officers."

"Thank you again," the captain said, turning to leave the room.

As the Elf left the war room he was met by Aric. They were led through the keep to a small pair of rooms where they would stay for the remainder of the morning to rest after their long ride. Erzel watched Aric vanish into his room before closing his door behind him. The room was small but elegantly furnished. It had a bed in the corner, a wash stand, a rack for clothing, a chair, a large trunk at the foot of the bed and even carpet. The captain removed his weapons and armor before collapsing onto the bed. The moment his head hit the pillow, Erzel was fast asleep.

After what only felt like an hour of sleep, the captain woke. He rolled over in bed and peered out the narrow window on the far wall. Sunlight struggled to appear through the slit and the Elf rolled over, putting his back to the window. A knock at the door jarred him awake and he rolled back over and squinted through the morning light.

"Enter…" he muttered.

The door creaked open and a young servant entered carrying a pitcher of what was probably fresh water. He poured the liquid into the bowl on the wash stand and folded a towel over the chair. The boy then began straightening the captain's tunic, armor, and weapons. Erzel sat up on the edge of the bed, watching the Elf work.

"That will be plenty," he said, standing from the bed and walking to the wash stand.

"Yes my Lord," the servant replied as he straightened the bed.

Erzel dried his face and hands on the towel and tossed it to the edge of the wash stand, grabbing his shirt and armor. The chain ran across his undershirt smoothly as he fastened it down snugly. The servant handed him his tunic and waited for the Elf to fasten the belt down across the fabric. Erzel nodded, took his sword, and left the room. As the door closed behind him, the one next to his opened and Aric stepped out. The captain and head Knight walked through the keep on their way back to the war room. After being admitted into the room, the two Elves sat at the table and waited. A short time later Raziel entered and took his seat with the soldiers from Pentegarn.

"Good morning once more. I trust you slept well. Now what can I do for the two of you?" the commander asked.

"As I told you earlier, my soldiers and I are awaiting the arrival of a convoy headed to this city from Swanhaven. It has in its possession the Princess of the Wood Elves who we are to intercept and escort back to Pentegarn. I am sure they've yet to arrive but as we wait, is there anything my soldiers or I can do to help out around here?"

"Well, we've yet to have a convoy arrive. Several traders came through earlier this morning but no royal caravan. As for helping out, I believe the city is fairly well protected. I will be in touch the moment I have any information about the caravan you seek."

"I thank you commander. I believe we should be out of your way by nightfall, assuming the caravan has not been delayed."

Raziel walked them to the door and stood in the open space. The two Elves stopped and turned just outside the war room. The commander assured them both that he would let them know if there was anything they could do to help out around the castle but in the meantime, just to relax, rest and eat a good meal. Erzel and Aric nodded and the two Elves departed.

Outside the keep was a large, heavily guarded building, with many soldiers going to and from it. They filed in behind a large group of archers and upon entering the building, looked upon rows and rows of weapons. They had found the armory. The pair looked over the hundreds of swords, spears, bows, and daggers stored on racks against the walls. Erzel pulled one of the swords from the rack and ran his fingers up the length of the blade, admiring the craftsmanship. One of the guards stopped next to him.

"Can we help you with anything my Lord?" he asked.

"No... thank you though. We were just looking through the armory. Quite a collection of arms you have acquired," Erzel replied as he slid the sword back down into its rack.

They moved through the weapons and into an adjacent room filled with armor and shields. There were bins of chain mail along the wall and racks of plated armor throughout the room. The two Elves walked from piece to piece, looking at them all before exiting the building. They spent most of the day on the walls, watching for any sign of a caravan exiting the far tree line. As the sun started its usual downward trip into the trees, Erzel began to wonder in the Elves of Swanhaven had been delayed or encountered problems. He wondered if the Wood Elves had secretly decided not to send their daughter and had neglected to give the High Elves any sort of notice.

The captain made another loop through the fort city, stopping to speak with his soldiers before continuing back to the wall.

Once back atop the battlements, he kept a sharp lookout across the clearings and into the forest for any sign of movement. Several times an object caught his attention but he quickly dismissed it as it had no resemblance to a caravan of any sort. With the night fast approaching, the captain began to worry, knowing that the caravan of Elves would surely have made it by now had something not intervened with their progress. He left the wall and hurried back down into the castle with Aric at his heels. There they found Raziel waiting for them on one of the upper balconies.

"Erzel... catch your breath," the commander said, seeing the Elf's troubled face.

"Thank you sir. The caravan never made it to Mihlann and it should have been here by now. I fear the worst and it is my duty to protect the Princess so that is why I must leave at once to find the answers. I will rally my soldiers and we will begin searching the forests. I appreciate all that you have done to help us in this matter."

"Wait... captain, would you like if I send scouts out ahead of you while you pull your soldiers together?" Raziel asked as he crossed the balcony to return to the war room.

Erzel stopped. "Yes commander that would help greatly. Do so at your own discretion as if something has happened, there may still be danger to deal with."

"I will send them at once. Notify your soldiers and be ready to leave if anything is found."

The commander quickly spouted out his orders and in less than ten minutes a dozen scouts rode out of the city and into the forest in search of the lost caravan of Elves. As the scouts disappeared into the dark trees, the soldiers under Erzel's command rallied outside the gate. Aric pulled his horse in next to Erzel's and the two sat silent as the different possibilities of what might have happened bounced through their heads. Perhaps it was nothing. Perhaps the Elves were just running behind schedule and were just beyond the trees on their way out. Perhaps their enemies had learned of the transport and planned to take the Princess as an example to the resistance of the northern lands. Erzel secured his sword at his waist and shield on his arm before snapping the reins of his horse and taking off to find the scouts.

Raziel watched the captain and the Order of the White Eagle disappear into the forests. As the soldiers left, all of the city prepared its defenses in case something unexpected came from the forests.

As Erzel and his Elves wove through the trees, he pushed the thoughts of what he feared from his head. The Princess would be fine and his mission, another success. All he had to do was ride further into the forest and he would find the royal caravan being escorted by Raziel's scouts. He knew it to be true... all he had to do was ride further.

Each turn in the path brought another fearful moment to his head as he began to wonder if he had waited too long to act. What if he were sitting in Mihlann while the caravan was being attacked. The thought of being close by while something bad happened to the caravan made him almost dizzy. He shook his head and snapped the reins again, spurring his horse far ahead of the mass following behind him. He stared ahead, praying they would find the Elves safe.

A Traitor in the Midst of Allies

The forest was thick and the pace of the search slowed as the Elves looked on the roads and through the brush. The light cavalry had moved ahead of the Knights, combing the forest for any sign of the caravan. The dark of night made the search harder and the soldiers were forced to light torches when the moon disappeared in the tangle of treetops. An hour before sunrise, one of the scouts returned to the captain.

"My Lord Erzel... my Lord we've found the carriage."

"What of the Princess?"

"Gone my Lord... you need to see this with your own eyes."

The captain spurred his horse into a swift gallop as he chased the scout to the scene. A quarter mile up the road the forest opened into a long clearing where the trees parted and the remnants of the moonlight shone on the forest floor. Erzel could see the carriage without its horses and as he studied the scene closer, he noticed bodies scattered around the wreckage. He dismounted and handed his reins to one of the scouts as Aric dropped in next to him and did the same. They walked together through the massacre, looking at the bodies of Elves on the ground. Aric held his feelings in check, looking away at the trees and their surroundings.

"What happened here my Lord?" Aric asked as they approached the carriage slowly, swords drawn and ready.

The captain ignored the question as he stopped at the front of the carriage. All around his feet were the bodies of slain Wood Elves but thankfully none were the body of the Princess. The closest had a cluster of four arrows in his chest and Erzel knelt to examine one. He pulled the arrows from the dead Elf and examined the bloody tip with a face that showed both surprise and confusion. He passed it to Aric who looked at it equally as close.

"Aric, do you see what I see?" the Elf asked as he checked the next arrow.

"No... not possible. This is a Human arrow!" Aric exclaimed, realizing the horrible truth he held in his hands.

"Exactly... they are all Human arrows. Why would there be an arrow from our ally in the bodies of our fallen Elven brethren?"

The two Elves stood silent as each pondered the question. The arrows were all crafted by Humans and used by the Human archers, but the two races had always maintained a strong alliance. Why had they killed the Elves and where was the Princess? These questions ran through their heads as they examined the dead. Also odd was the fact that all of the bodies on the ground were Elves, killed either in the overwhelming volley of arrows or in the brief skirmish that followed. He looked to his left to a clearing through the trees.

"The arrows came from that direction. Probably most from that clearing not counting any that may have been shot from the trees. Aric, take the trackers and look for signs in that area," the captain ordered.

As his head Knight hurried through the trees to the hill, Erzel moved to the door of the carriage and peered inside. Erzel found himself shocked by the sight behind the damaged carriage walls. All across the walls he could see the tips of arrows visibly coming through the wood but it was the floor of the carriage that saddened him. On the floor he found the body of a young blonde Elf, stripped of clothing, raped, and then killed from several stabs to the chest. His grip on his sword tightened as a tear appeared in the corner of his eye. Such evil that could allow something so vile and horrid to take place was not known to the Elves and he cried out in anger, punching the door to the carriage which hung precariously on its hinges.

As he turned to avoid the sight on the floor of the carriage, a sparkle in the first rays of the rising sun coupled with his torchlight caught his attention. He looked to the back of the carriage and under one of the benches he saw the object sparkle again. Erzel reached across the cold body of the Elf to retrieve it. As he stepped back in the light he realized that in his hands was the crown belonging to the Princess of Swanhaven. It had been bent slightly in the struggle but it still retained its original beauty. At once the anger swelled inside of him again.

"What sort of thief leaves behind such an item of value?" Erzel asked himself out loud.

The answer was in fact very simple. Only someone who knew how valuable the Princess was would care so little for a piece of jewelry, someone not looking for valuables such as gold or gems, someone who was there to take the only thing missing from the scene. The Princess had been the target and it was apparent that she had been taken alive. The blood in the carriage belonged only to the young servant girl and Erzel was almost sure that wherever the Princess was, she was alive for the time being. There was still a chance to save her.

He spun around quickly. "Alright, I need three messengers to leave right away. Who are my volunteers?"

Three scouts from Mihlann walked their horses up to the captain and stood together as they awaited their orders. "We're ready my Lord."

"Ok, you ride back to Mihlann and alert Raziel as he will lend what help he can spare to clean up this massacre. In the middle... you are to ride to Pentegarn and warn King Elendil of these events and ensure him that my soldiers and I will be traveling after those responsible for the Princess's abduction. Be sure to tell him this attack seems to have been carried out by Humans, for some reason."

"What of my duty sir?" the last scout asked.

"Unfortunately the task of informing the King and Queen of Swanhaven falls upon you. Tell Tanis and Narissa that we are doing all we can to locate and rescue their daughter. We are sure she is alive and we will not stop searching until we have Princess Rhen back with us. Give them this," the captain said softly, handing the damaged crown to the soldier.

The scout took the crown and stored it safely in a pouch

on his saddle. Each soldier rode off in the direction of their destination as Erzel turned back to the bloody scene behind him. While Erzel was addressing the scouts, the soldiers of the Order had prepared most of the fallen Wood Elves for their journey home. Erzel unfastened his cloak and laid it over the naked body of the young Elven girl. He said a prayer and turned back to his soldiers.

"Listen up Knights. Finish preparing those who have died here for the journey home. Cover the dead with cloaks, blankets, anything you can find and let the Wood Elves claim their bodies. We will not bury them here."

Behind the captain appeared Aric and the rest of the scouts and trackers. "My Lord... I have a bit more news."

"What did you find?"

"These," Aric replied as he tossed another handful of arrows and a torn section of fabric to the ground at the angered captain's feet. "That's not all either. There appears to be a large number of tracks leading away from the battle to the north. Possibly Human, but the tracks are not fresh."

"Get ready to leave at once!" Erzel shouted to the Elves.

"Not to worry Erzel. The abductors appear to have been traveling heavy so I guess their progress through the forests will be slow. With the added struggle of a captive, we can probably catch them faster than I expected."

"What do you make of the fabric?"

"Possibly from the Princess's dress. It is a very fine fabric, not something a commoner would posses."

"Alright, mount up. We ride for Cisalia!" the captain ordered.

"Uh... Erzel? Did you not hear me. These tracks indicate that the attackers are on the move and pursuing them would probably be best done immediately rather than waiting a while."

Erzel shook his head. "No Aric. This may seem an odd decision to you but I do not trust those tracks to lead us to anyone responsible for the attack. We will head to Cisalia where we may uncover the truth as to why something like this was allowed in the ranks of our Human allies. As well, we may catch those responsible there, though for some reason I doubt it. After all, if

Humans really did attack the caravan then Humans might know something about it. It seems logical."

"Yes my Lord... forgive me. I became caught up with revenge and didn't stop to think the tracks could be a diversion. If we allow ourselves to wander from the task at hand, we may very well lose the Princess for good."

Erzel and Aric took the lead of the Knights and rode back out of the forest and across the plains above Mihlann without stopping at the city. They had their sights set on a certain destination and nothing was stopping them. Dawn passed them and soon they were looking at the early hours of the evening. Purples and oranges filled the sky and the sun danced with the horizon when the captain finally ordered a rest. The Elves tied their horses and dropped to the ground around the many campfires, some falling asleep instantly. Erzel and Aric sat off alone, listening to the woods around them.

"The Elf in the carriage... the blonde... she was so young. She didn't ask for this war, for this torment. She only came to serve the Princess. How could one be so evil to take her body and then her life?" Erzel asked, rubbing his hands together.

"If it is truly the Humans who have committed such a horrible act upon our race I will see that they are punished in ways far worse than what was inflicted on that young girl. I promise you that Erzel," Aric replied, his voice shaking with anger.

The Elf looked up suddenly at the captain. "My Lord, what if this runs deeper? Is it possible that all of Cisalia is involved?"

"I don't know Aric. For their sake I hope not. If it were not for the Elves help in the Chaos Wars, all of the Humans would have fallen long ago. The Goblin invasion would have swept across them and there might not have been a single Human left alive. If I know our King and the King of the Wood Elves, they will reduce the Human existence to ashes if the Humans are behind the abduction. Now get some sleep, we ride at first light."

Aric rolled over and quickly fell asleep but Erzel remained awake, worried that if they did not act fast enough at uncovering the truth, the Princess might disappear forever. If the Humans had taken her, what could they possibly hope to gain from their actions? The Elves would pay no ransom but instead, would destroy the traitors and all of those who stood behind them. Something inside the Elf told him that there was a deeper evil behind the event and that the Humans were merely pawns. He hoped that the Humans were not to blame, knowing the overwhelming numbers of Dwarves combined with the High Elves and Wood Elves would crush all Human life.

Before the sun even started to rise the Elves were in their saddles and riding north, bent on reaching the Human city before nightfall. Normally the journey would take three days but with the frenzied pace the Elves were putting forth and choosing not to stop, it was possible that they could arrive in two days time. Using the terrain to their advantage meant cutting a little further east to avoid the thickest parts of the forests between Cisalia and Pentegarn. They pushed their horses harder than they felt comfortable at times, knowing the horses were just as tired as those riding upon their backs. Erzel remained out in front, searching for signs that they were coming closer.

Cisalia backed up to the foothills of the Tvan Mountains with its gate only a hundred yards from the forest. Constructed between the fortified nation of the High Elves and the mountains of the Dwarves, the Humans believed they were safe from most any harm. The small army they had managed to raise never left the city for fear that the Elves and Dwarves may one day fail in holding back the horde in the south, the memory of the torture many of the Humans had suffered in the south before escaping to the safety of the northern lands having never faded.

Erzel and Aric sat on their horses just inside the forest, looking out at the city from their hiding place. The rest of the Elves had made camp a few miles south of Cisalia, allowing the captain and head Knight to enter the city without arousing suspicion at why such a large mass of Elves lay in wait outside the walls. If the Humans were in fact behind the abduction, the Elves wanted to attract as little attention to their presence as possible. The ride had close to drained the two Elves but they could not relax until they had some answers. They rode slowly through the gates, looking up at the high walls. When they passed into the city they paused at the gate for a moment to find information as to where they would find the King. With their directions clear, they continued on. The Humans regarded the Elves as just simply passing through and seemed to care little about their presence. They wound through the small city streets and stopped in front of the castle.

"Halt! What business have you with the King?" a guard asked as he approached the pair of Elves.

"We need to speak with your King at once regarding the war in the south. It is of the most important matter and is meant for only your King's ears," Erzel replied.

The Humans looked at one another and then back at the two Elves. "We will escort you, follow us please."

The two Elves followed the guards with another four Humans falling in behind them. The city was very small compared to Pentegarn and Swanhaven and after only a few turns and stairs they were standing outside the throne room. A trio of elite soldiers appeared, lowering their spears to prevent the two from entering.

"You shall not be allowed inside armed in such a way. Hand over your weapons and shields."

Erzel and Aric handed their swords and shields to the soldiers and waited as they were checked hidden weapons. When they were finally cleared, the two doors were pushed open and the pair was allowed in. The King was not in the throne room but around the walls were six to eight heavily armed guards watching every moved the two Elves made. They heard the door behind them close loudly and the King entered, heading straight for his throne and sitting without acknowledging the pair.

"Erzel... how do you start this conversation without accusing the Humans?" Aric whispered, kneeling before the King.

"I'm not sure yet. All I need to know is how he reacts when we tell him about the Princess's abduction," the captain replied as he too knelt.

"Alright, stand up. What can I do for the two of you?" the King asked as he left his throne and crossed the room.

The Elves did as they were told but waited until the King

was standing in front of them before rising. "Your majesty, my name is Erzel and this is Aric. We are here on behalf of the High Elves of Pentegarn and the Wood Elves of Swanhaven. Might we speak a little more privately?"

"Sure... out here."

The two Elves followed the King out onto a wide balcony overlooking the city of Cisalia and the lands beyond it. The King seemed somewhat irritated that the Elves were interrupting his day and avoided looking directly at them. He leaned against the railing and waited for an explanation to their presence.

"So... you had something important you needed to discuss?" Calyn asked, turning to the Elves at last.

"As you are an ally of the Elves I have come to alert you to a situation that has taken place in the lands just above the borders."

"If you've come to tell me that your races have lost control of the borderlands, then I must say this day could not get much worse. I received news that the battles were becoming more intense. What will you do if Valsera's forces are free to invade?"

Erzel looked to Aric and then back to the King with a mixture of confusion and concern at the news he'd just heard. "What are you talking about? The borders are secure and the southern armies kept in check. I was referring to an event that happened not three days ago. The Princess of the Wood Elves was abducted in a violent raid between the cities of Swanhaven and Mihlann. The truly disturbing fact was that the carriage and the bodies of the Elves were both pierced by the arrows of Humans. Would you have any knowledge as to why this is?"

The Human King stared past the Elves with a face of surprise. "Are you accusing me of abducting a Princess?"

"No... no my Lord Calyn, we're not. I just wondered if you have any idea why the Elves were killed with Human weapons. I was sending no blame in your direction. I just need to know anything you know if we are to save her before something happens to her."

"Well, master Elf, I do know that there are many pockets of races that follow no flag and kneel to no King, feeling they are better off without. Perhaps your search should take you to them. As for myself and the people of my city, I can not, and more likely will not be of any help. I suggest you look elsewhere for what you've lost. They will show you out."

Erzel and Aric looked at one another as the King walked away in a hurry. The guards waited until Calyn was gone before giving the weapons back to the two Elves and then followed them to the castle entrance where their horses waited. The King's words echoed through Erzel's thoughts as they passed back through the city. They crossed town quickly, tying their horses in front of the inn for a quick stop. The building was desolate inside with the exception of a few men at the bar. Erzel approached the bar and motioned for the waitress.

"What can I get ya?" a middle aged lady behind the bar asked as she cleaned a glass with a rag.

"I have a few questions for you if you don't mind. We are looking for a group of Humans who don't follow the banner of Cisalia... possibly a resistance of sorts. Would you know anything about men like that?"

"Well now, what would ya want with them folks?" she asked, avoiding a direct answer.

Erzel leaned against the bar and looked into her eyes a bit more sternly. "It is of a personal matter. Now I would appreciate it if you could tell me whether or not you know anything about such a group. Would it be worth a gold piece?"

She took the gold from the counter and examined it, sliding it into a pocket. "On the outskirts, rough group they be. Always raiding wagons and such to keep themselves going. Lots of folks afraid of them. Most of the time we just ignore them and go on about our business. You should do the same."

"Wait... hey come back." Erzel called out as the barmaid walked away.

Behind him he heard a commotion at the door and a group stumbled in, some already drunk and looking for more to drink. They were all dressed alike in crude leather armor, very different from that of the soldiers of Cisalia. The two Elves watched as they walked towards them, their conversation loud enough for all to hear.

"...if we can you mean. Claxis said we hold her a week and then the bitch goes south."

"What about them Lizardmen? You trust them enough to..."

"Shut up... damn Elves, look."

Erzel turned around so his back was to the bar and Aric steadied himself in beside the captain. The group headed for the other side of the bar but a few stumbled back towards the two Elves. Erzel's hand instinctively fell to the hilt of his sword as the men stopped a few paces away. The captain looked across his shoulder to the barmaid who gave a nervous nod and continued on around the bar.

"Is there something we can help you boys with?" Erzel asked in an almost mocking tone.

"Think they'd let any of them races in here but Elves? This is our city Elf... get out!"

"What did you say Human?" Aric replied.

The Elf took a step towards the men and squared off with the mouthy Human. The other two took one step and Erzel joined his Knight, ready to pull his sword from its sheath if needed. The scene became worse when the rest of the drunken party noticed the commotion and started towards the Elves to assist their fellow Humans. As the men boxed the two in against the bar, a large group of Cisalian guards entered the building, their swords and spears ready to fight.

"Stand down at once!" the leader of the guards ordered loudly.

"You'd let scum like this in our city but you want to turn on your own race. You are a disgusting excuse for a Human and I..."

"I said stand down or I will see to it that you spend the next month chained in the dungeon. You have been given an order, disperse now!"

The rabble of Humans slowly began a halfhearted march to the door where the guards waited for them to leave. The last of the Humans stopped face to face with the head guard and sneered at him. "Only our leader can give us orders, not your King. You're just a pawn."

Erzel and Aric followed the guards out into the streets and untied their horses. They lost sight of the Humans in the crowd but the information had slipped and they had at least an idea of who was behind the abduction. It wasn't the Humans within Cisalia after all. They mounted up and rode from the city before anything else could happen. They stopped at the edge of the forest and watched as the group who had threatened the Elves rode clear of the city to the east. The captain turned in his saddle to the Knight next to him.

"What is going on around here? First the King and now a group of Humans who apparently know something that we need to know more about. What odd behavior they have shown given the circumstances." Aric said.

"Human arrows in the carriage, King unwilling to help or even show any sign of concern, and now a resistance group of Humans I didn't know existed with an obvious hatred for our kind. A very suspicious turn of events we have uncovered."

They rode together through the trees on their way back to the camps of Elves that waited to the south of the city. The day had passed very quickly and they were faced with another sunset by the time they reached the clearing where the Elves had made camp. The shadows of afternoon had passed and nightfall was stretching a blanket of darkness across the lands. At the tree line they were met by one of the Knights standing watch.

"Halt! Who goes... Oh, my Lord Erzel, forgive me."

"No matter, though we might appreciate you lowering the bow now soldier. Any news from Pentegarn?" Erzel asked.

"None sir."

"Fine, help me by rounding up the soldiers. We have news and a lot to discuss with very little time left in which to do it."

"Begging your pardon my Lord but something happened while the two of you were away. Shortly after you and Aric departed for Cisalia we captured two Humans of interest."

Erzel and Aric dismounted and left their horses with one of the Elves on the edge of the camp, following the Knight to a large clearing in the center of the tents and fires. Many of the Elves were already there and waited as the captain studied the scene. In the middle were two tall stakes and tied to each was a Human soldier. They were both dressed in similar clothing as those the Elves had encountered in the tavern. Erzel crossed his arms and stared at the two Humans. One of the guards approached the captain.

"Soldier... why are these two men gagged and lashed to these poles?" he asked.

"Well my Lord, we intercepted these two as they tried to smuggle information to the southern lands. Here, this is one of the things they had in their possession that we thought you might find interesting. Read for yourself my Lord."

The Elf took the crumpled letter and carefully unfolded it. He eyed the two soldiers as he read the page, wondering if they were there when the Princess was abducted or if they were responsible. He read through it slowly, going back over certain spots several times before reading parts of it aloud for the soldiers to hear.

"... we have her... reinforcements sailed in north of Cisalia... Human city weak and... reinforcements? Untie one of them!" Erzel shouted suddenly, passing the letter to Aric.

The soldiers untied the prisoner on the right and removed his gag but left his hands bound at the wrists. The Human wobbled on his feet and the Elves held him to keep him upright for the captain. Erzel approached slowly, his face flustered and his fists balled and ready to strike.

"Look at me! Listen close... I want information about that letter and about the Princess of Swanhaven, and the one of you that tells me what I need to hear lives. The runner up... well let's face it, there is no runner up. Now, where is the Princess?"

The Human stared defiantly at the Elf for a second before turning his eyes to the ground at his feet. Erzel waited a moment but when the man said nothing, he brought his knee up into the stomach of the Human. The man doubled over and the Elves let him fall to the ground.

"Ah, well then let's untie the other one."

"Don't tell the bastard anything!" the Human shouted at his partner.

Erzel whirled back around and punched the Human across

the temple, making the man fall back to the ground. He started to get back up but Erzel grabbed him by the collar and forced him down face first in the mud. After hitting him twice more, the Elf threw him onto his back. The Human was nearly unconscious.

"Now where is she?"

"I... I don't know," the second man stuttered.

Erzel nodded and kicked the man on the ground in the ribs twice. "You know this is going to be you next if you won't tell me the things I need to hear. All you have to do though is tell me what I need and I will simply tie you back up to the stake. That doesn't sound so bad does it?"

The man on the ground squirmed as the pain worked through his body. Erzel put the heel of his boot against his chest, holding the man against the ground and drawing his sword. He slid the tip of the blade up under the throat of the trembling man, cutting him just barely so blood trickled down his chest. He got a better grip on the handle and looked to the kneeling man once more.

"This is the last time I will ask. If you will not tell me what I want to know, I will kill him and then you will be forced to endure the punishment for his silence. Now, where... is... she?" the Elf growled angrily.

The man on the ground clenched his jaw shut willing to die to keep the location a secret, but the one on his knees shook with fear as he knew he had to save himself from such torment that his comrade had gone through. "Wait! I know where she is!"

"Shut up soldier or I swear I'll..."

Erzel kicked him across the jaw, splattering blood at the ground in front of the kneeling Human. The Elf kicked him again and then turned to his soldiers. "Tie the foolish one back to the pole and bring the other one with me. I will soon find out everything I need to know one way or another"

The Elf led the captive through the camp to his tent. He excused the guards and ordered the captive inside at the tip of his dagger. The Human sat and the Elf tied his hands and feet to the chair. The remnants of a fire remained at the center of the tent and Erzel quickly brought it back to life once more with a few small logs of wood. Looking up, the man could see the sky out the hole in the top of the tent. Erzel pulled another chair up next to the fire and took a handful of unknown objects wrapped in a brown cloth out from a bag. As he removed the cloth, the Human's eyes became wide with fear. The Elf shoved the tips of two tools into the coals of the fire and turned to the man once more.

"Do you know what these tools are used for?" Erzel asked, holding up different shaped blades, scissors, and other pieces of metal.

"Yes... I'll tell you whatever you want, I promise..." the man squirmed, trying to avoid the instruments of torture.

"I know you will. Now let's start with an easy one. Where is the Princess and who is in charge of her abduction?" Erzel asked as he pulled one of the tools out of the fire, the tip glowing orange from the heat.

"Uh... the cloaked creature... he told my master he'd trade her for immunity to the wrath of Valsera. We trade her away in one week..."

"What cloaked creature?" Erzel asked, bringing the glowing piece of metal close to the Human's arm.

"I don't know... really! You have to believe me, I don't know!"

"Have to believe you? Ha... that really is a good one. Now who is this cloaked one you spoke of?"

"I don't know! He serves Valsera... his right hand Knight! Claxis claims he is the most fearsome of enemies."

Erzel hesitated for a few minutes, pondering the words the man had uttered in fear. "Claxis is your master? Claxis is the one who organized the abduction and the one who killed all those Elves in the forest?"

"Yes. The Princess is safe... she is safe..." he repeated.

"Good, now we are getting somewhere. Where is she?"

The Human looked to the tools of torture in the fire and the ones on the table beside the Elf and realized there was no escaping telling him what he wanted to know. If he didn't tell Erzel, there was no telling what kind of pain he might be forced to endure from the tools. "She is being held, um... in a temple to the east of Cisalia. About a day of riding in the thickest part of the forest. There are many levels and I think she is on the lowest, but the guards and many soldiers. You'll never make it into the temple, let alone get to the Princess."

Erzel ran the curved scissors under the bonds holding the man to the chair and cut them, watching as the man stumbled away. "I wouldn't be so sure about that. I will find the Princess, I will save her, and I will kill anyone and everyone who dares to try and stop me. Now get out."

The man turned to flee but was immediately caught and held by a trio of guards who had been waiting for the captain to emerge. They held him as Erzel approached and then followed the Elf through the encampment until he stopped back where the bulk of the army was still gathered. He clapped his hands together to get their attention and grabbed the prisoner by the restraints on his hands.

"I need an escort to see these traitors back to Pentegarn at once. I want a group of ten. Who are my volunteers?" he asked.

No sooner had he finished the statement than a group stepped forward, ready to do the Elf's bidding. They gathered their weapons and possessions and loaded everything onto their horses. The prisoners were tied firmly and a rope run from their hands to the saddles of two of the Knights, forcing them to walk the distance back to the city. Erzel stepped up to the prisoner who had been so resilient earlier and placed a firm hand on his collar. When the man refused to look at the Elf, Erzel shook him violently and turned his head with a slap.

"It would have been better on you to have cooperated when you had the chance. Now you've got no chance. I'm only letting you live so the King can do as he wishes with your traitorous hide."

The man reared back and spit into the Elf's face, earning a sharp kick to the skull from the Knight on the horse beside him. As the man staggered, Erzel pulled his dagger from his belt and stabbed the man in the hip, twisting the blade back and forth before jerking it back out. The man cried out in pain as blood ran down his leg. Erzel cleaned his face and the blade of his dagger and walked away laughing out loud. "Enjoy the walk Human."

"One more thing," Erzel said as the group turned to leave. "Inform the King that the remainder of my forces and I will make an assault on the area where we believe the Princess is being kept. We can not wait for reinforcements if we expect to find her in time. Get whatever information out of these two that you can."

The Knights started off through the trees with the Human still slinging insults and curses at the Elves. The Elves laughed at him as they continued cleaning the camp up and prepared to move once again. Erzel and Aric had not rested in almost two days but their promise to return the Princess drove them to keep going. Through the heart of the night they worked to get on the move, knowing a direction and some of what to expect when they got there. Erzel was on his horse and weaving through the trees with the bulk of his force behind him. The rest of the soldiers had remained behind to finish packing. Aric had been by Erzel's side through the worst of the night and now found his way there again.

"So… he claimed east of Cisalia? I don't suppose he mentioned about how far did he?" Aric asked as he ducked a low branch.

"Neglected to mention where, though he claimed it would be a day of riding into the thickest part of the forests. It can't be that far though. The men in the city were not supplied for long range travel and if I had to guess, I'd say that we could be there faster than the Human claimed."

"Of course, but I am not aware of any abandoned temples east of Cisalia, or anywhere near Cisalia for that matter. Are you sure he wasn't just setting you up to ride into a trap of some sort?" Aric asked in concern.

"Well I really don't know either way. At the time he was at risk of losing his fingers and being branded with scalding hot iron so I figured he would be apt to let the location slip to keep from feeling the pain. In his panic I think he told me what I wanted to know before he realized that he was saying it. He wanted to live… and the other one didn't care either way."

The Elves rode on through the night and into the morning with a single destination in mind. Somewhere east of Cisalia was a hidden temple or cave and somewhere hidden within it was the Princess of Swanhaven. She had become the most important person to the Elves of Pentegarn in the last few days as her rescue would strengthen the races that had been slowly drifting apart. Only time would tell what races had remained loyal and which were to blame for the horrible betrayal.

The room was cold and the only form of light was a single torch on the opposite wall. The Princess squinted in the flicker of the torchlight and struggled against the ropes holding her wrists above her head. They were rough and her pulling had resulted in painful scrapes and scratches on her wrists. She looked around the room again and lowered her eyes to the cold stone floor, crying softly in the darkness.

"Keep quiet over there! I swear I can give you a reason to cry if you really want one you stupid Elf," a man in the shadows said angrily.

"Wha... please, where am I? Who... who are you?" Rhen asked fearfully.

"You don't seem to be hearing very well huh?" the man asked as he appeared from the corner. "You do as you are told, understand?"

The man was right in front of her, staring at her in the dim light. She could smell the foul odor of his breath and she quickly turned her head to escape it. The man smiled, looking down the front of her dress into the shadows. He grabbed her by the jaw and turned her face back to him, easily overpowering her.

"You're lucky our master wants you unharmed cause I could make you my little Elf whore. It wouldn't be hard at all, just like that little blonde one back at the carriage. She was good, but I bet you'd be better." he said, running his hand down the front of her hips.

Rhen stared past the man with a face of shock as his hand dipped lower. Her body shook with fear and she quickly clenched her teeth together to keep from insulting him, for fear it would invoke greater harm. As his hand came back up the dress between her legs, Rhen brought her knee up into his groin as hard as she could, making him fall back in pain. He writhed in agony as tears dropped down his face. Rhen fought against the ropes once more, trying desperately to free herself but to no avail. After ten minutes on the floor, the man stood and drew a whip from his belt, snapping it against the wall beside the Elf's head. As he prepared to strike a second time, a figure emerged from the doorway and grabbed the whip from his hand. He jerked it back and shoved the man against the wall, striking him across the face with an open hand.

"Do you dare go against our orders from the master you fool?" the second man shouted angrily. "She is not to be touched!"

The man stumbled out of the room still holding his groin from the vicious kick the Princess had delivered. The second stranger turned and took a step or two towards her, putting the whip on his belt. She looked at the man who had protected her but saw nothing more than shadows and darkness. She pulled against the ropes once more but quickly gave up as her wrists were becoming raw. The man turned to leave her but the Princess called out to him.

"Wait... please... let me go! I won't tell anyone where I've been. I won't even have them look for you."

He stopped but he did not turn around. "You will be here only a short time and then you will be leaving. Until then the best thing you can do is stay quiet and save your strength."

The man disappeared and she was left alone once again, the ropes stretching her tired arms up towards the dark ceiling. Scared and confused, the young Princess closed her eyes and pictured her home, the gardens and swans and everyday life that surrounded her there. The memories came with a price as the thoughts brought with them tears and she cried softly once more, praying that one day she would see her home again. She hung her head and stared into the darkness that engulfed her.

The Elves of Pentegarn spread through the trees as the morning sun began to slowly rise. After scouting ahead all through the night, the Elves had located what could possibly be the temple the prisoner had spoken of. It appeared to be what was left of temple ruins and was very well guarded. There was a small army around the mouth of the entrance and also a patrolling group of swordsmen moving around the clearing in ten minute intervals. The behavior showed that they had something to hide or something important to guard. Either way, the Elves were ready to expose the secret.

The captain stared out at the mass of Human soldiers in front of the temple, counting the opposition once and then a second time. He knelt and waved Aric up beside him to have a closer look. They sat motionless as the Human patrol marched by, completely unaware of the army waiting in the trees. The Humans had between twenty and thirty soldiers outside the temple with unknown numbers within and Erzel looked to the side at the Elf next to him. They carefully made their way back into the trees where a number of Knights waited to hear what they planned to do.

"So what do you think our best approach would be? They have close to thirty soldiers out there waiting for intruders. Who knows what is in the temple."

"We have the element of surprise, our superior fighting skills, and a degree of anger on our side for the loss of our fellow Elves. All the same, this won't be very easy. We've faced hard before, but we are fighting on their grounds against unknown numbers. My worst fear is that they may realize we are here and harm the Princess before we can get to her." Erzel whispered.

The two Elves pulled the scouts back into the deeper part of the forest and the soldiers gathered around to hear more news. The area where his soldiers had gathered was busy with Elves preparing their weaponry and securing their armor in the event that they attacked soon. Erzel walked through them with a few comments until he came to a group of Elves dressed differently from his. They were between twenty and thirty strong and all wore dark green cloaks over dark brown leather armor with chain mail sleeves. They all carried longbows with swords strapped at their hips as a reserve weapon. One of the Elves approached Erzel with a nod.

"Greetings, how can I help you soldier?" Erzel asked.

"If you are Erzel then my soldiers and I are here to join you in your efforts to recover the Princess. We were dispatched from Swanhaven by King Tanis the moment we received news that Princess Rhen had been abducted. So I guess the question is how can we help you?"

"Hmmm… you must be Thalun. I am familiar with you and your soldiers. I guess it makes sense for Tanis to send the best soldiers that Swanhaven has to offer. I'm glad to see some sort of reinforcements to help us deal with this matter. Perhaps you should come see what we are up against for yourself."

The Wood Elf and the High Elf snuck back to the edge of the trees where they could watch the Humans around the entrance. They peered out at the Humans who were completely oblivious to the Elves watching them so intently. The patrol rounded the corner of the clearing and stopped when they met the guards at the font of the temple. Added to their patrol was the form of a tall Lizardman and five Goblins. They spoke for a few minutes and then the six were allowed to enter, leaving the Humans at the entrance, lightly guarded and vulnerable. Thalun nodded and the two made their way back to the soldiers. The groups pulled together as Erzel went over his plan to storm the temple.

"As you can see they are well defended with the patrol, but once it leaves to make its rounds, there are only a handful of soldiers left to guard the entrance. If the guards are taken care of we will be free to comb through the tunnels in the temple at our own pace, assuming we can hold the patrol off once it returns. It will have to be quick, and as Thalun and I were watching, the Humans were joined by a Lizardman and five Goblin soldiers. They are somewhere in the temple."

"My archers will serve as a new guard to the temple once their Human soldiers are down and if the patrol returns, our combined strength outside the temple should be more than enough to allow us ample time to find her." Thalun said with certainty. "If the patrol returns faster than expected, our soldiers will be able to handle them easily. My Wood Elves are ready whenever you are."

The captain went over his plan one more time in his head and then again with all of the soldiers in the clearing. It would have to be quick; everyone rushing together and no soldier left behind in the fray. The Knights of Pentegarn moved through the woods, preparing for the attack that was only minutes away. Those responsible for abducting the Princess were about to pay a heavy price for their betrayal. The Wood Elves settled in and waited, watching the patrol appear and stop to check in with the guards at the entrance. As the Elves paused, they realized the patrol was staying much longer this time. While they waited, the Wood Elves drew their bowstrings back; their nerves were solid as they watched the patrol head to the left out of sight. Erzel and Aric drew their swords and the rest of the Knights did the same.

"Whenever you are ready Thalun, you and your Elves take your shots. Let's get this over with before those soldiers return."

Thalun and his force aimed through the trees with their bows ready to fire, each choosing a different target around the entrance to the temple. The Humans were completely unaware of what was about to take place and stood with little protection against the attack. Thalun lined up on the closest soldier and released his arrow, following the deadly projectile as it sliced through the air. The rest of the Elves released their arrows as well, watching as they flew like a swarm of wasps towards someone attacking the nest. The first arrow buried deep in the soldier's chest, knocking him back against the temple entrance where he slid down the pillar slowly. The Humans had only seconds to wonder what was happening before the rest of the arrows began striking down the confused guards. Erzel watched for just one moment before turning and nodding to the mass of Elves behind him.

They burst forth from the trees on their way to the temple where the Humans lay dying. The Elves finished off the soldiers and the first step of the plan was complete without the slightest problem. Not even a warning had been sounded as the last of the dying Humans was stabbed through the chest and the Wood Elves joined the High Elves at the temple. Erzel pulled his sword from the chest of an enemy and took the first step into the temple, raising his shield as he moved through the dim light. Wood Elves and High Elves together secured the outside as the remainder of the Elves swarmed the tunnel behind Erzel and Aric. Passages branched off in different directions and the captain split his forces, sending groups down each one as he continued down the main tunnel.

As the tunnel became stairs, Erzel, Aric, Thalun, and just under half of the remaining Knights hurried down the steps two at a time. The sounds of battle suddenly erupted on the floor above them but the Elves continued searching the numerous rooms. The door to the last room opened and a handful of Human soldiers rushed out to see what the commotion was about. They were instantly met with a fury of swords and arrows as the Elves engaged them on sight, driving the enemy back into the room.

"Come on, we have to keep moving! Keep moving!" Erzel yelled over the clash of sword against sword in the room to his left.

Thalun took the lead, combing through the rooms at the bottom of the stairs with his bow drawn and arrow ready to meet its target. The Wood Elf peeked around a corner and then continued down another flight of slick stairs with Erzel and a handful of Knights hot on his heels. The stairs ended again and the tunnel formed a large cavern and the Elves were faced with an equal number of Humans and the five Goblins. Behind the Elves appeared Aric, his face splattered with blood from the battle that had erupted above.

"Take them... no survivors." Erzel ordered.

The Humans charged at the Elves with their weapons drawn and ready. Just before the two races met, Thalun fired his arrow, catching one of the Goblins just under the neck. Erzel quickly spun off the man closest to him, slicing him across the shoulder and turning to the last tunnel. In the confusion of the battle between the Elves and Humans, the captain bolted down the last passage alone. Aric watched him go and tackled a Goblin as the creature turned to pursue the Elf. Erzel moved with stealth, hardly making a sound as he walked. The passage ended and he looked into the dim room. On the far wall he found the Princess tied and gagged; she appeared unconscious.

Thalun ducked under a sword and kicked the Human in

the rear, making him stumble across the room into the wall. The Elf drew an arrow and fired, only to watch the shot miss just above the man. The Human ducked low and came back swinging, trying feverishly to hit the quick Elf. Abandoning his bow, Thalun drew his sword and caught the Human's weapon against his own. They fought back and forth between the other soldiers in the small room as killing blows were dealt from either side. The Wood Elf ducked under another swing and thrust his blade forward into the man, stabbing him squarely in the chest. He fell backwards to the floor and Thalun watched as the sword fell to the ground.

Aric ran towards the Wood Elf with his sword raised but he would not make it there in time. From behind the Wood Elf came the form of a soldier with his spear lowered and ready to strike. Thalun felt the weapon pierce him from behind and his sword fell to the floor. Aric cut to the right and swung down on the soldier, cutting him from the stomach to the jaw with one long slash of his sword. As the Wood Elf fell to the ground, Aric pulled his sword free and dropped in next to Thalun. His grip was weak and before he could speak a word, the life left his body. The Knight picked up his sword as well as Thalun's and stared down a cluster of three Goblins, charging at them.

Erzel lowered his guard and hurried across the room to where the Princess was bound and gagged. He dropped to her side and leaned his sword against the wall beside her, running his hand through her hair. "Princess... please Princess wake up. We're here to get you out."

Erzel pulled the gag from her mouth and pleaded further, touching her cheek gently with his gloved hand. She was breathing but very faintly. As he tried to wake her a noise behind made him freeze. It sounded of faint footsteps and a soft shuffle, making a prickle rise on the Elf's neck. He reached up, grabbed his sword, and quickly rolled to his left just in time. Seconds after moving the sound of metal striking stone echoed through the room and the Elf stood slowly, looking at the spot he had only moments earlier knelt.

In the dim light stood the figure of a large Lizardman he had seen earlier in the clearing. It held in its right hand a large broadsword and a round shield in the left. The place where Erzel had been sitting moments earlier was now missing a chunk out of the floor. The Elf realized he was without help. He stood his ground and raised his shield as the creature took the first step towards him. The Lizardman suddenly leapt from where it had been standing into the air, its teeth glistening in the torchlight as it raised its sword above its head. Erzel sidestepped the attack and moved to the other side of the room. The creature was now between him and the Princess and Erzel advanced on the beast. It swirled around and stared the Elf down with malice burning in its eyes.

As Erzel moved around the room the creature slapped its tail against the cold stone floor, making a loud crack echo through the small room. The Elf knew that the Lizardman was not only dangerous with a sword, but also its teeth, claws, and tail could be deadly as well. Erzel jumped this time, crossing the room in two steps and swinging his sword at the creature but only hitting the sturdy shield it held. It recovered fast, whirled around, and struck the Elf with its tail, slinging him back against the wall where he crumbled to the floor. Erzel climbed to his shaky legs and pulled his shield up in front of his body once more, seeing the size and speed of the creature as more than a match for his own. The beast took a step forward with a hiss of delight, seeing the wounded Elf and his inability to fight. Erzel supported the shield and dodged left as the Lizardman lashed out with its tail, but it was only a diversion.

When it turned, the creature swung its sword hard and struck Erzel's shield with the wide blade. The sword shattered Erzel's shield easily and the Elf dropped to the floor gripping his arm tightly. The shield fell away in three pieces and he dropped his sword, wincing as the arm throbbed wildly from the pain. The creature advanced quickly, shoving the tip of its sword up under the Elf's chin. Erzel felt fear for the first time as he saw the sword slowly draw back. He watched the blade hesitate in midair and then the creature attacked.

Erzel closed his eyes and covered his face with his arm, expecting to feel the pain of the sword piercing him through to the floor. Instead, he heard the blade strike metal and the pain never arrived. Erzel slowly opened his eyes and found Aric standing beside them with his sword up under that of the Lizardman, holding off the attack. The Lizardman slithered back a few feet and the new fighter squared off between the captain and the beast. Erzel crawled to the Princess's side as Aric and the creature stared one another down, each daring the other to make the first more. Neither seemed ready to chance the attack, but Aric's anger was pushing him further.

Erzel put his hand on the Princess's forehead and shook her again, hoping to wake her from her sleep. He reached down and pulled his dagger from his belt to cut her free. From the entrance came another Elf and now they had the upper hand on the beast. Aric and the soldier charged together, both swinging together to bring the creature down. Aric's sword was blocked by the creature's shield and the second Elf found his weapon stopped by a quick swing of the Lizardman's sword. The three danced back and forth as Erzel cut the ropes holding the Princess, catching her across his lap and holding her with his good arm. He looked up in time to see the Lizardman smash the second soldier across the face with its shield, dropping him to the floor unconscious but also giving Aric an opening to strike. He took one step and thrust his sword just under the creature's left arm, driving the blade deep through its ribs. A shrill hiss escaped the creature as pain spread through its side.

The Knight pulled his sword from the body and watched the shivering Lizardman fall to the floor, blood squirting from the wound. It made one futile effort to swing at the Elf before falling back to the floor, dying in a puddle of its own blood. Aric helped his companion up from the floor and together they crossed the room to check on Erzel and the Princess. With Aric's help the captain carefully laid her on the floor, wincing in pain as his arm throbbed. He leaned over her face and checked to make sure she was still breathing. Thankfully, she was still alive. Aric cleaned the blade of his sword on the edge of his cloak and sheathed it, placing a hand on Erzel's shoulder.

"Erzel… is she still alive?" Aric asked, looking at her pale skin in the torchlight.

"Yes. I am no healer but I am pretty sure she is going to

make it. She seems very dehydrated and suffering from exhaustion. I wonder if these creatures were here to transport her... to the southlands." Erzel said as he looked at the body of the Lizardman on the floor.

Erzel tucked his left arm in against his chest tighter as the pain intensified. Aric sent the Knight back out to secure the passage and knelt next to the captain, examining his arm that had been injured severely. "Erzel... your arm is hurt badly. Can you use it my Lord?"

"It may be broken... it hurts... but the Princess is our first priority. We take care of her first... and worry about the arm later."

"Yes my Lord, what should I do?"

Erzel didn't seem to hear the question as he shook her a little harder, seeing the first signs of life from her limp body. He supported her back and rocked her gently until she brought her shaking hand up to her face, brushing the hair from her eyes. She struggled to see in the dim light, making out the shape of two figures but not realizing right away that her hands were free of the rough rope.

"Princess, rest easy. We are here to take you home." Erzel said softly.

Rhen reached up slowly to run her fingers across his face and ears, making sure the one she spoke to was an Elf. When she realized she was truly safe, Rhen's eyes sank to a close once more. Her vision blurred and slowly disappeared and she slid back against him with a deep sigh of relief leaving her body. She whispered softly. "Thank... you..."

As the sun rose for Erzel and his soldiers, the borderlands were alive with life as the soldiers prepared for the onslaught that had been promised if they refused to abandon their defenses. Three days were all the creature had said it would wait before it would take the border by force. Every available Elf had been armed and sent to the border to help hold off the invasion that loomed in the distance. The soldiers awoke to find a very welcome surprise arriving at the encampment in the form of one hundred heavily armed Knights fresh from Pentegarn. Elerith immediately warned them of the danger that had been threatened upon the borders but the Knights eagerly rode into positions with the rest of their comrades. They took the front line and waited as Elerith made his way to the border. He was fearful of the battle to come. The morning resulted in no signs of life from the opposite side of the clearing but he knew not to underestimate the enemy.

At last the beginnings of the opposing army began to appear from the gnarled forests. They moved together with discipline and poise, something the Elves had not seen in the years of fighting. The south had countered the Elven Knights with a massive swarm of Ogres and Lizardmen backed by a seemingly endless number of Goblins. The two armies squared off, staring one another down as each was ready to draw first blood. The center mass of Ogres parted and allowed the stranger cloaked in black to enter the battlefield. It carried in its left hand a long sword as dark and deadly as the creature itself. The back of the sword was serrated, giving the creature the appearance of a merciless fighter who lived for the kill.

"So it begins." Elerith whispered.

The cloaked enemy walked across the field and stopped roughly in the middle as Elerith did the same. The Elf stood next to the creature for a few minutes, his hand resting on the hilt of his sword as if he hoped it would help him this time. He remembered how the blade had done virtually nothing to the creature the last time he had tried but he knew that giving up was not an option. He looked the monster down, struggling to decide the best choice of action to his current situation without revealing his doubts to his opponent. Neither one moved but the creature spoke in a menacing hiss that gave the Elf and unwelcome chill.

"I see you've decided not to abandon your border posts. It's very valiant of you Elf... foolish, but valiant."

"Turn this army around and leave our borders now. I have not the need to quarrel with you and your kind. Surely you can see that the past three years of fighting has only resulted in massive losses to your untrained armies."

"Watch your words master Elf. It would be a shame to have to kill you before you are given the chance to watch your soldiers die all around you, and they will die. You should've left when you had the chance. I will find you on the battlefield."

"What are you?" Elerith asked suddenly before he had time to realize what he was saying.

"I am Infus, right hand of the great Valsera and Demon from your worst nightmares."

Elerith turned away and headed back to his soldiers, ignoring the last words the creature had spoken. When he turned around to face those to the south, he found the cloaked creature had not moved from the spot where it had been moments earlier. It waved the sword to the lines of solders and the mass of the south took a few steps forward, all moving together as one. Elerith watched patiently as they marched across the field to meet their leader. The rumble of the march echoed through the trees and the Elves looked to one another, wondering for the first time if staying at the border was a clever move. The massive army stopped short of their commander and waited silently for an order to be given. Realizing what was expected, Elerith drew his sword, raised it, and the soldiers of the north locked their shields and prepared to charge.

"Well, I guess it's a bit late to consider leaving. Come on, no turning back now!" Elerith yelled, taking the initial charge into the clearing.

The Elves charged into the open clearing, weapons drawn as they eagerly pushed towards the mass of creatures. The Goblins broke their lines and ran at the opposing army, murder gleaming in their eyes. The Knights on horseback moved ahead, lowering their spears as they formed a wide line across the field. The Goblins slowed their approach when they realized they were up against the armored cavalry, a hopeless match for the enemy charging on foot. As they tried to scatter, the Ogres moved up to intercept the Elves. The line of Knights met the Goblins in a thunderous crash that pierced the air around the forests. Bodies were thrown in every direction as the Knights led a massacre through the unprepared Goblin ranks but when the mass of Ogres arrived, the odds were leveled greatly. Like the Knights moments before, the Ogres charged forward and broke the line of Elven Knights in the middle of the field. With the bulk of the army engaged in the clearing, the archers vacated their trees and joined the other soldiers on the battlefield, their arrows striking Goblins down by the handfuls. In the frenzy of the battle, Elerith had lost sight of the cloaked leader and found himself searching back and forth for the beast, hoping to be the one that killed it.

The Elf dodged a spear thrown from the left and moved on, stabbing and slashing the creatures around him. He watched as the groups of Lizardmen finally made their way into the battle, destroying the left flank of the Elves with little effort. The soldiers fell back into a mass and charged again, fighting the reptiles back and forth across the clearing. Throughout the field, the Elves were losing the battle at the hands of the Lizardmen and Ogres. The only hope they had was in the form of the mounted Knights who had almost decimated the Goblin forces and were now spreading their way through the masses. The captain of the Golden Lion took a step to the left and lunged out, stabbing a Lizardman from behind to save an Elf who had been knocked to the ground. He reached down and helped the soldier to his feet.

As the Elf whirled around in the midst of the chaos, he found the cloaked creature standing no more than ten paces away, staring him down and waiting for the Elf to make his move. The two leaders squared off, each wielding a long sword but only Elerith held a shield. They didn't move and soon soldiers from either side around them stopped to see what the two would do. Elerith took one step up and pointed his sword at the cloaked creature, staring it down with eyes of hatred.

"Here I am, now let's see what you've got!"

They both broke into a swift sprint, weapons ready to draw blood. Cheers rang out from either side as they watched their leaders battle fiercely. Elerith knocked the enemy sword away, swinging his own but missing wide of Infus's cloaked head. The Elf kept swinging, fearful to ease off of his attacks and give the enemy a chance to get a stroke of its sword in. He raised his shield to block what he thought was an attack but was fooled as the creature kicked him across the knee with its plated boot. He fell on the knee that had been hit and quickly received a strong backhand from its armored gauntlet. Elerith fell to the ground and rolled, jumping back to his feet fairly quickly.

"I told you I was going to kill you, foolish Elf. You and your soldiers will die here having accomplished nothing." Infus hissed.

A trio of Ogres quickly charged the Elf from the battle and Elerith raised his shield, brandishing his sword at the beasts. Before they could get into range to attack the Elf, the Demon raised its clawed gauntlet and they stopped, turning to find someone else to kill in the fray of the battle. Elerith watched intently, gripping his sword tighter.

"Come on then!" he yelled, charging at the cloaked Demon.

The two crossed swords and then pushed away. They danced back and forth, ducking under the attacks and spinning across one another. Elerith caught the creature's sword with his shield and quickly lunged forward, driving the blade of his sword through its shoulder. As before, the weapon passed through the enemy without causing any visible damage. He swung again but found the same result as the sword sliced through its wrist. After a third swing and another failed attack, he realized he couldn't damage his opponent and he took a few steps back, watching the creature advance.

"My turn," it hissed, lifting its sword to attack.

The creature leapt at Elerith with a powerful overhead strike that missed by inches as the agile Elf dodged to the right. He spun away, swinging wide with his sword but missing completely. The cloaked opponent closed in swiftly and their swords crossed again with a loud clang. The two stared one another down as the Elf looked deep into the darkness of the cloak only to see a hollow blackness that no detail could escape. Elerith gave his sword a jerk and shoved the creature back, trying to devise a plan to dispose of the enemy. He raised the tip of his sword and pointed it to the creature's chest but instantly dropped it when a sharp stabbing pain ripped through his shoulder. The Elf fell to his knees and struggled to keep a grip on his sword, knowing the enemy would take advantage of the moment of weakness.

While he was looking at the creature, a daring Goblin approached and thrust a spearhead into him just below his shoulder blade, bringing excruciating pain to his body. He felt the pain but also a degree of rage surged through him. Now injured, he knew he had even less of a chance of beating his opponent. Infus lowered its sword in line with the Elf's neck and walked swiftly towards him. Elerith tried to raise his sword but it fell back beside him as the pain rocked him violently. He looked up at the enemy who strangely walked right past him and stopped in front of the Goblin. Elerith turned his head, watching the creature grab the Goblin around the throat and lift it into the air. As it choked slowly, the Elf fought his way back to his feet, jerking the tip of the spear from his shoulder with a painful cry.

"Foolish coward... stay away from him! This Elf is mine!" the creature ordered, squeezing until the Goblin had lost all signs of life.

It threw the body into the mass of his own soldiers, making sure they understood that no one other than the cloaked leader was allowed to fight the Elf. Elerith could feel the warm trickle of blood running down his back under his armor but he had found renewed strength, standing his ground for the imposing attack.

The Elves managed fairly well against the Goblins and even stood their ground against the Ogres, but the Lizardmen had carved a path of death across the battlefield. Their strength coupled with their agility made them hard to hit and even harder to avoid. Having the ability to leap high into the air and get behind the Elves they used their tails to knock down their enemies. They were formidable opponents. The archers managed to bring down a group of them but shortly afterwards the Lizardmen became wise to the tactics, some carrying the bodies of fallen Elves above them like a second shield guarding them above and in front. The arrows did no damage as they sank into the lifeless flesh now supported by the reptiles. Even the regrouped Elves and their shield wall began to fall back a step at a time as the Lizardmen led the Ogres and Goblins in for what they believed to be a triumphant victory.

The mounted Knights had somehow found their way to the other side of the field, battling in and amongst the gnarled southern forests. They easily picked through those not smart enough to take cover or those who were just too slow to get away. The Elves worked through the trees, storming the lines of Goblins with a battle cry that made many of their enemies turn to run but the might of the Elves followed. Their mercy had been forgotten, and now all they could see was the next kill, the next victim to bleed with their swords and spears. Tired and struck with fear, the lines of Goblins began falling back deeper into the recesses of the forest, desperate to find somewhere the Knights couldn't pursue.

Where the Goblins had failed and retreated, the Ogres and Lizardmen were making a stand that gave the light footmen of the Elves a horrible thrashing. They had destroyed the left wing of the Elves and pushed back what was left into the center where the shield wall still stood strong. They grouped together and in one massive charge, the wall of Ogres crashed through the wall like a battering ram against a weakened fortress door. Bloodshed spread across the field like a firestorm as Elves suddenly became the weaker race. At the center, Elerith and the shadowed opponent continued to battle one another.

The Elf shook away the pain in his shoulder and rushed the creature to show he was still very much able to fight. He missed with his swing but stopped to turn and block the attack in return. They battled back and forth between the crowds of soldiers who were eager to praise the victor. The Elf swung hard at an opening and watched sadly as his blade passed through the creature's head, once again dealing no damage and exiting with a wisp of smoke. It whirled away and blocked the next swing with its sword, punching the Elf under the jaw with its sturdy gauntlet. Elerith fell to the ground face first and watched helplessly as his sword bounced out of his reach. He tried to push himself back up but the creature shoved the heel of its boot down onto his back, pinning him to the ground.

A handful of Elves broke the crowd and rushed towards the fallen captain but were quickly cut off by a wall of Goblins and Ogres and the battle erupted between the two sides once again. The Elves cut through everything they could but it became apparent that they would never reach their captain in time. The Ogres pushed the soldiers back and soon they fought to save themselves instead of saving the Elf on the ground. Like the rest of the battle around them, the Elves were slowly losing their grip on the borderlands and a new power was coming into focus. With their hopes dashed, the Elves began to fall back.

Elerith felt the boot lift from his back and he crawled slowly towards his sword, stretching out to reach it. The creature shadowed his every move, its sword poised to deliver the final deadly stroke. His fingertips grazed the hilt of his blade and the creature kicked him sharply in the ribs. It picked up his sword and kicked him again, rolling him onto his back. Everything that followed seemed to move in slow motion as Infus took a step across him and lowered the Elf's sword to his own throat.

"I told you there would be no victory here. Your race will fall, your lands will burn, and you shall not be alive to see any of it." Infus hissed, watching the expressions on the Elf's face.

The creature drew back Elerith's sword and stared down at the Elf, pausing for a moment to take in his fear. The look it received said everything; the Elf had given up hope. The Demon quickly thrust the Elf's own sword down through his chest, driving it through his fallen opponent with ease. As it let go, the sword remained erect. The light slowly left Elerith's eyes but the hopeless expression never left his face. The Demon looked up to the forces surrounding him.

"Don't stop until the border is in our control... and kill everyone."

The armies of the north had fallen back completely, holding their defenses at the edge of the northern forests. They tried to regroup and prepare for the onslaught that was bound to come again very soon. Their leader had fallen, the bulk of their Knights had been trapped and destroyed in the southern forest, their remaining forces had been shattered. Somehow their enemies had become so much stronger. The pride of the Elves had been washed away, their strength shaken to its core. The battered northern army locked their shields and prepared their defenses, fearful of the events that were to take place during the night to come.

The Safety of the Elves

The morning sun streamed through the windows into the eyes of the sleeping Princess. She cracked one eye and rolled onto her side, squinting through the rays of light and finding herself in an elaborately decorated room with what could have been the softest bed she had ever felt. She pushed herself up onto one elbow to get a better look at her surroundings, finding the furniture crafted by the Elves with designs and emblems of Pentegarn and the High Elves on the rugs and banners. As the confusion of sleep began to clear, Rhen remembered the events of the past few days. Just when she was ready to leave the bed to investigate her surroundings further, the door to her right opened and a woman entered carrying a stack of towels and bed sheets.

"Oh... oh my... you are awake! It's ok, please just lie back and I will send for your father at once," the servant said quickly, trying to bow and carry out her duties at the same time.

"My father?" the Princess exclaimed as her eyes shot open with excitement for the first time. It was only a few minutes but for Rhen, the time between the servant leaving and her father arriving felt like an eternity. She stared at the door forever and soon she heard footsteps echoing up the hall. The door burst open and Tanis rushed in, wrapping his arms around his daughter with tears in his eyes.

"I thought I'd lost you Rhen. If it had not of been for Elendil's soldiers... I may very well have never seen you again. Are you ok?"

"I guess I'm fine... but where am I? How long have I been here? All I can remember is a dark room and the damp air."

"My dear... you are in Pentegarn. You arrived yesterday afternoon escorted by the remnants of the Order of the White Eagle, its captain, and a handful of our archers from Swanhaven. The soldiers who came for you suffered many losses, as did those I sent to help. Thalun lost his life in the temple where you were held prisoner and the one who initially found and rescued you didn't leave your side until about an hour ago. He appeared to have been injured pretty severely in the skirmish but he refused to leave or accept treatment until he knew you were safe."

"I would very much like to meet him Father... I owe him so much," the Princess said, kicking the covers back off of her legs.

"Slow down my dear. You will meet him soon enough. Right now you need to rest and recover. So relax and if you need anything at all ask one of these ladies in the room. They are here to care for you," Tanis said as he stood to leave. He stopped at the doorway and looked back at the Princess. "I'm so glad you're back."

The King of the Wood Elves closed the door behind him, leaving the Princess and the servants alone again. Rhen leaned back into the bed again, happy to finally be somewhere away from the dirty temple and horrid Humans. She closed her eyes and in only a few minutes the warm sheets and soft bed snuggled her into a land of dreams.

When Rhen woke again she found the sun had already begun its downward fall that allows night to claim the sky. She saw her father sitting at the foot of the bed conversing with two other Elves. She recognized the Elf on the left by the crown he wore. He was Elendil, King of the High Elves. The Elf on the right however she didn't know, though he did seem somewhat vaguely familiar. He wore a blue tunic with no emblems and had his left arm wrapped in crisp white bandages supported by a sling around his neck. He held it close to his body, giving the impression that the injury still caused him pain. She sat up in the bed, keeping the sheets up close to her body to hide the nightdress she wore. The movement caught their attention and Tanis turned around to see how she felt.

"Awake again my dear? How did you sleep?"

"Well, I think. Is everything alright?" she asked, looking over the three Elves curiously.

"Of course everything is fine Rhen. These two wanted to meet you when you were awake so if you don't mind I'll introduce them. I believe you already know this is the King of Pentegarn, Elendil. He was in charge of the forces that were sent to rescue you from the depths of that temple."

Rhen nodded politely to the King and turned to the second Elf.

Tanis followed her gaze. "This is Erzel. He is the Elf who found you in the temple and the one who fought to save you. His soldiers of the Order, along with the archers I sent to help, fought the Humans throughout the temple until they were able to free you. He initially found you and has hardly left your side since you arrived."

The Princess stared at the Elf as if she was seeing the ocean for the very first time. Her eyes sparkled and she mouthed a thank you, finding that she had not the ability to speak the feelings she had inside. Now she knew why he looked so familiar. In the flicker of the light she could make out very little detail but now, the details she remembered were apparent. Though she had only caught a glimpse of his face in the darkness, she could remember him now. To top it off, she had met the one Elf she wanted to meet in a way that she would never forget. Erzel gave a half bow to the Princess and stepped back behind the King of the High Elves.

"Good evening dear. I know you have been through so much lately but I must ask you a few questions about your experiences as their captive. What can you remember?" Elendil asked the Princess.

Rhen took a deep breath, hesitant to recall her experience. "It happened so fast. I remember the start of the attack on the carriage and then a Human tied my hands and they drug me to that cave. I can't remember anything about that dark room or the people in it."

Elendil looked from Erzel to Tanis and then back to Rhen.

"Do you know if any of the Humans had ties with the Humans of Cisalia? Were they traitors or some sort of rogue group acting on their own?"

"I... uh, I don't think so. I don't remember anything about Cisalia. They didn't have markings or flags with emblems," she replied. "Their leader said something about trading me to the South for something... though I know not what they sought."

"You didn't hear who they were going to trade you to?" Tanis asked angrily.

"The Demon Infus..." she whispered, her voice trailing off as she thought about what she had escaped in the rescue.

The two Kings looked at one another and Elendil turned to the Princess. He crossed his arms and spoke firmly. "You needn't worry my dear. I will see that everything is taken care of. Now, when you are well rested, feel free to enjoy all that the castle and city have to offer. I am sure that Erzel would be more than willing to accompany you as a guide for your walks through the grounds."

"Of course my Lord, I would be honored." Erzel said as he stepped forward.

"Then it is settled. Your father and I have business to attend to so I welcome you and hope you will make yourself at home. Know that you are safe from harm within these walls, I swear it."

Tanis kissed his daughter atop the forehead and patted her hand. The Kings left the Princess and the captain alone, knowing that her safety had been the number one priority of every Elf in the realm. Rhen looked up at Erzel, trying to think of what she wanted to say but words continued to escape her. She motioned to the end of the bed where her father had been sitting earlier and Erzel hesitantly sat down, continuing to favor his arm. Rhen folded her hands and bit her bottom lip, looking at his injury and knowing it had been caused while he had tried to protect her in the temple.

"Is your arm alright? Does it hurt much?" she asked as she saw him wince slightly.

"In time it will heal. Princess. It isn't something I won't be able to live through I assure you. How about you... are you going to be ok?" he asked, meeting her eyes with his for the first time that evening.

"I am still a little tired, but I too will heal and please, call me Rhen. When I hear Princess it makes me feel like everyone around me is afraid they are going to insult me. I'd rather just be Rhen."

"As you wish... Rhen."

"I want to thank you Erzel. When I was in the carriage and they attacked, I had no idea how I would ever get back to see my parents. They were rough and threw me around regardless of who I was and what I represented and it was there I realized the title of royalty meant nothing. What happened to the young blonde girl, the one they sent with me as a servant?" she asked suddenly.

"She uh... she didn't make it. The Humans killed everyone except you in the attack and she was no exception. We sent the bodies back to Swanhaven to be buried with their families," Erzel answered, leaving out the details of what had actually happened to the servant girl.

Rhen shook her head sadly as she heard the answer to her question. She sat with her head down, wishing that she could've saved the young girl. The Princess reached down and pushed the blankets and sheets back, revealing her nightdress to the captain who instinctively turned his head to the window to avoid seeing her body. She quickly covered herself back up when she realized how uncomfortable she had made him and giggled to herself.

"I think I'd like to take a walk, maybe see some of the castle. Are there gardens here amongst the towers and walls?"

"Of course. I'll just step outside until you are dressed," the Elf said quickly, leaving her to dress. Rhen stepped out of the bed, testing her shaking legs and numb feet. Her bare feet curled against the cold spots of the stone floor as she quickly walked to the large rug only a few steps away. She found a variety of dresses mixed in with some she had not seen before in the large hutch against the wall. She pulled a green dress out with a pair of shoes to match and after fighting with her hair for a few minutes, she joined Erzel outside the room. The captain looked at her with a different respect now that she had changed and was presentable, fighting the smile that sought to spread on his face.

"You look... good," Erzel said quietly as they walked up the hallway. "So what would you like to see tonight Princ... uh, Rhen?"

"Gardens remember? The ones back home were my favorite place to spend my time. So quiet and peaceful, I'd sit for hours surrounded by the flowers. If you sat long enough, it felt as if you were a part on the garden itself."

"Very well then, right this way."

Erzel led her through the halls of the castle which seemed to form an intricate maze. If someone did not know the castle they could easily get lost in the network of tunnels and stairs. Several groups of Elves, both servants and soldiers stopped in the halls to bow and pay their respects to the Princess who nodded back, amazed to see that almost everyone in the castle knew who she was. The captain led her down one last set of stairs and to the left through a large arch which opened into a grassy courtyard. Rhen was amazed at the colors and the numerous flowers that surrounded her. The path they walked wound through the trees and plants, ending at a large pool and fountain. The Princess sat down on a bench next to the water and stared at the walls of flowers.

"So... are they anything like you had expected?" Erzel asked, picking a single yellow flower from the plant next to him.

"Yes and more, there are so many more than I expected to see. I figured being a war torn area that beauty would be sacrificed for the might of your armies but someone takes the time to tend these regularly. I am very impressed. There are so many I have never seen before, like these. What are they?" Rhen asked, motioning to several different plants.

Erzel looked at the different flowers and plants. "Well this one is a Dragon Lilly. See how the wings resemble the curve of a Dragon's wings? These are a strange type of flower called a Sword Tongue, possibly because the flowers look almost like a tongue mixed with the fact that the leaves are sharp enough that they could be mistaken for a sword. I'm really not sure the reason for the name."

"What about this one? Why does it not bloom?"

Erzel looked at the plant covered in pods from the top to the ground but not one had a single flower. "That is a rare plant indeed. The Elders call it a Moon Flower. They will only grow near the freshest of water and will only bloom in the light of the moon. It has beautiful petals alternating between cream colored and white and a deep red center."

Rhen sat in awe as she stared at the splendid array of life around her. Erzel sat down next to the Princess, watching the ripples in the pond. They could feel the mist of the fountain against their skin and it gave Rhen a shiver. The captain handed her the flower he had picked with a smile and she looked at it, in awe that something so small could be so beautiful.

"Thank you Erzel. This is so overwhelming to me. I owe everything to you and your soldiers and yet I have nothing that I can offer in return."

"My dear Princess, I did not help you for profit or prize. I helped you because the blood running through your body is just like mine. We are Elves and what would we gain by not helping one another, especially someone of our own kind. You need never worry about a debt of any kind."

Rhen nodded to him with a smile and rolled the stem of her flower between her fingers wondering what she could give the Elf as thanks even though he asked for no reward. She spent the next two hours in amongst the flowers and trees, taking time to look upon each one, as they all had different forms of beauty. She had lost track of time but it didn't matter. She was in paradise. The sun had disappeared and the two became quiet as the first rays of moonlight met the land. As the radiant glow swept across them it found the mass of Moon Flowers growing around the edge of the pond. When the light fell on the pods, they instantly cracked and began to curl open.

"Look... just like I told you. The moon brings them to life and it only takes seconds for them to reach full bloom," Erzel said, pointing at the pods that were opening.

As he spoke, the blooms spread wide and the last of the petals pulled themselves open, revealing the red center. When the plant had finished, its dark green leaves and stems had nearly disappeared underneath the cascading mass of blooms. It was an amazing sight, and Rhen stood from the bench and walked over to the closest of the plants. It reached her mid thigh and she stopped next to it, reaching down to one of the blooms with her delicate fingers. Erzel turned and called out to her suddenly.

"No Princess, you mustn't pick the blooms!"

Rhen pulled her hand back, startled. She looked up to him. "I'm sorry, I didn't know. Is the plant dangerous?"

"No, but this plant is very, very sensitive and taking a flower from it would be like having a finger cut from your hand. It would never be the same again, one of the reasons it is so hard to find in the wild."

She walked back to the bench and sat down again, feeling horrible that in her ignorance she had nearly damaged such a beautiful plant. "I'm sorry Erzel, I never wanted to hurt it. I had no idea it was so tender of a plant."

"It is fine. No harm done to it, look. Happy as can be."

Rhen nodded and picked the stem from her yellow flower and set the bloom in the water of the pool, watching as the flower bounced and rolled with the motion of the ripples. It floated until it became tangled in a cluster of lily pads where it danced against the leaves, trying to free itself. Rhen leaned out over the water and plucked the flower away from the lily pads, setting it back away and letting the water push it around once more. Erzel watched intently, enjoying the quiet for a change and the company as well. As they watched the flower dance with the ripples Erzel took the chance to sneak a look at the Elf sitting beside him. Even in her tired state she was gorgeous. When she straightened he quickly looked across the garden.

"Uh… we should probably head back inside soon. We can have another walk tomorrow when the sun is up. Let's not put too much on you at one time, don't you think?"

"You're right, I am still tired. I never realized one could sleep so much and still be tired. Thank you Erzel."

Erzel reached down with his good hand and helped her to her feet, leading her away from the pool of water. They walked side by side through the garden and into the castle on their way back to her room. The halls were deserted and their only light came from the torches spaced down the walls. After five minutes of walking they arrived at her room. She stopped and turned to Erzel.

"Thank you for showing me the gardens Erzel, and thank you once again for what you did back in the temple."

"As I told you before Princess Rhen, it was my duty to protect you. Perhaps you would like to continue our little tour tomorrow? That was only one of the numerous gardens Pentegarn has to reflect in."

"Sure, of course. Well then, goodnight." Rhen replied, disappearing behind the door.

Erzel stared at the door for a few minutes before continuing on to his personal quarters. He walked slowly through the hall, amazed at how the night had turned out and that the Princess enjoyed their time together as much as she did. Then again, being anywhere other than that putrid temple had to be a relief. He pushed the door open and walked into his room, collapsing in a chair as he too was still exhausted.

Over the next week Rhen saw nearly every room in the castle with the exception of the dungeons. She visited the two other gardens within the city walls, finding them equally as amazing but it was the garden from the first night that captivated her. Each night she and Erzel would sit on the bench and watch the Moon Flowers bloom and then close back up as the moon disappeared. By the end of the week she was tired of the stuffy castle and wanted to see more of the city. Early in the morning she woke, washing and dressing and before Erzel could get up and out of his room, the Princess was waiting outside his door. Just after breakfast they left the castle and together they walked to the city outside of the inner wall.

Erzel and Rhen looked from shop to shop, speaking with everyone they met and admiring the crafts and goods for sell. She stopped in front of a small shop filled with jewelry of all sorts but it was an inexpensive object that caught her attention. Strung across a set of shelves were necklaces handmade with tiny white and blue shells. Some had shades of pink mixed in but all were new to the Princess. Outside the forests of Swanhaven was a very different world. Erzel watched her intently as she tried one on and then a different one, turning to the captain for approval.

He smiled. "They brighten your eyes."

Rhen turned back to the shelf and tried on a third necklace and whirled around so Erzel could see it. The shells were a mixture of dark green alternating with crisp white. She ran her fingertips down the string of shells and smiled, enjoying the way they felt against her neck. Erzel nodded to the third necklace, liking the way it looked around her neck.

"That one... it looks very nice. The shells are not too large and the colors really accent each other."

"I know, and it will match my favorite dress. Green and white were just meant to go together. Like a fresh snow on the limbs of the tallest pine trees," she said, turning to the woman in the corner. "Ma'am, how much?"

The lady looked at the necklace and nodded. "My daughter makes those herself. Quite a talented pair of hands she is. Saera, come here please."

From the back of the shop came a small Elven child. She wore a dress similar to that of the Princess and had her hair pulled back out of her face. She blushed the moment she saw the two customers and hid next to her mother who gave her a light shove towards the two. The captain laughed to himself and Rhen knelt down next to the girl.

"Do you make these all by yourself?"

"Yes ma'am. Father sends back all the shells he finds and I sell them."

"Your father? Where does he get such beautiful items?" the Princess asked, turning back to the woman.

"Her father, my husband works in Murm, the port city a little north of Cisalia. He finds them and sends them back with the traders so that she has something to do. Saera takes the shells and strings them together and people who've never seen such things are more than willing to pay her for them. Where are you from?"

Rhen looked to Erzel who nodded, letting her know it was safe to trust the woman and her daughter. "I live in Swanhaven. My name is Rhen, Princess of the Wood Elves."

The mother fell from her seat to the floor, pulling her daughter with her as they both stopped on their knees. "Please forgive us. I didn't know we were in the presence of royalty."

"Please, get up. Now, Saera was it? How much do people buy these for when you sell them?"

"Uh... a copper, but you can have it," the girl replied nervously.

Erzel reached into a pouch on his belt with his good hand and pulled a handful of coins out into view, thumbing through them. He kept them out of sight of the girl and shrugged. "I don't have any copper dear, would a gold do?"

The look on the little girl's face was more astonished than Rhen's when she had seen the gardens for the first time. She held out a shaking hand and took the coin from the captain, examining it closely. She'd never held gold before and it showed as she clutched it close to her body with a wide smile. She didn't speak, but her thanks came in the form of a tear that streamed down her cheek.

"Come on Rhen, let's keep going," Erzel said, extending a hand to help her back up.

As they left the shop, the mother stopped them just outside, letting the door close behind her. She was still reeling from the shock of what had just been given to her only child, something that one of the higher priced pieces of jewelry might bring.

"I can't thank you enough sir. You've no idea how happy that made her. She's gotten nothing but a few coppers here and there but now she has something she can show her father when he comes home. Thank you."

Erzel nodded as they continued on towards the front gate. The presence of the army was more obvious the closer they came to the outer walls. The soldiers saluted the captain as they hurried past to their posts. The general public and their goods became mostly markets of food and blacksmiths. Erzel walked out of the city a few steps, looking out across the plains that led to the forests past the clearing. Villagers from all over were moving about the fields, some coming to Pentegarn with their goods and some leaving to return home. Rhen stepped up next to him and joined his stare at the busy area.

"Why did you do that back there? I mean, you had several copper in your hand. Why did you lie to her and give her a gold instead? You could have bought twenty necklaces for what you paid for this one."

"I didn't want twenty. Besides, did you see her face. What she does is very hard and she gets very little in return. The look on her face was more than worth the gold and I really have little need for mountains of gold. I serve the King so I will always have a home, always have food and always have a means to come upon more gold. By doing this little good, I have done myself a great. I feel better knowing that I made her happy."

Rhen pondered the words carefully, realizing that the Elf she stood next to was not only a battle hardened warrior, but a very generous and loving person as well. Buried beneath his bloody past was a gentle person that sought to make peace with the people as well as bring peace to the lands. Standing out in the open, she felt so small. All her life she had lived under the massive trees of the forests but now, having nothing to hide beneath showed her how small her world really had been. A trio of soldiers approached the pair and Erzel nodded, waiting as they bowed to the Princess.

"My Lord Erzel, the Kings of Pentegarn and Swanhaven have requested your presence in the throne room as soon as possible. We will escort you if you would like."

"That will not be necessary, thank you. Princess, I am afraid this is where we must part ways for a time. I will find you again later after the meeting."

Rhen shook her head. No Erzel, I want to come with you. I know my father, he will not mind, trust me."

Erzel looked at her for a few minutes and then hesitantly nodded. She walked by his side back through the city and into the castle where they climbed the stairs and wove through the halls on their way to the throne room. Several times his hand brushed against hers which made her look sideways at him. Erzel would move to the side a little but the Princess followed him, keeping as little space between them as she could. They finally arrived at the throne room and the guards opened the doors, allowing the pair into the room. Tanis and Elendil turned when they entered, each surprised to see the Princess.

"Erzel... Rhen... we were expecting, well we were expecting one of you. Please sit with us," Elendil said, moving to his chair at the head of the table. He waited for the two Elves to take their seats.

"Dear this isn't the place for a young Elf like yourself at the time. Wouldn't you be much happier in the gardens?" Tanis asked her, hoping to persuade her to leave for a little while.

"Well, I guess so. I'll just be in the gardens then." Rhen said softly, a little surprised that she wasn't allowed to stay.

After she had left, Erzel looked up at the Kings. "Yes my Lords?"

"Erzel, we waited for a while to mention this because we know that you and the rest of your men have been through a traumatic experience, not to mention the pain the Princess has been through. I think it is time we take care of it though." Elendil said bluntly.

"Take care of what my Lord?"

"The prisoners you sent back... they've yet to be interrogated and no information has been learned. We locked them in the dungeon the moment they arrived and let them sit this long. I think it is time to see what we can get out of them. We are going to need to know everything we can if we expect to figure out just what is going on."

"Ok, let's go."

Elendil, Tanis, and Erzel made the long trek to the bottom of the castle a few floors underneath the ground where the prisoners and captives were held under strict and close guard. The soldiers moved aside as the Kings and captain walked in and pulled the door to the cell open for the three, joining them inside the cell. A single torch cast a dim light and the guards lit four more, illuminating the musty cell and its occupants. The two Humans were huddled in either corner, each trying to stay away from the Elves. Erzel looked at the one he had stabbed in the hip, seeing the bloodstains still on his pants. The other recognized the captain and turned his face to the stone wall, thinking it would keep him from being seen. The King pointed at the one who had been stabbed and ordered him unchained and brought to the group.

The Human prisoner drug his leg limply behind him, staggering on the better of his limbs and staring at Erzel with gleaming hatred. He noticed the arm wrapped in bandages and laughed to himself happily, hoping that more of the Elves had been killed in the battle. Elendil opened the room to a small chamber and the guards brought the Human in, chaining him to the chair in the center and dropping back to the door leaving the Kings and captain to interrogate the prisoner. Tanis approached quickly but Elendil held up a hand to stop him, knowing the Wood Elf would seek vengeance first and information later. Elendil crossed his arms and walked across the room in behind the prisoner who tried to turn his head to follow the Elf.

"So, are you ready to tell what is going on in the Human lands? Who was responsible for the Princess's abduction?" Elendil asked firmly.

"Piss off Elf, I'm not telling you nothing!" the man shouted, still defiant.

Elendil nodded to the guards who brought in a box of items. Elendil opened the lid and started pulling things out one at a time: lengths of rope, knives, sharp hooks, hammers, wedges. The Human seemed less than surprised as the box was emptied and tossed to the floor. Tanis walked to the edge of the table and gave an evil smile, knowing what was in store for the Human. Elendil picked up a length of rope and walked back behind the prisoner once more, keeping calm as he asked more questions.

"So... you're sure you can't tell us anything we might need to hear? I have to tell you, that's going to be bad on your part."

Before the Human could reply, the Elf wrapped the rope around his throat and pulled back towards him firmly, choking the man. He struggled, but with his arms and legs tied down he had no way to defend himself. Elendil remained emotionless as he pulled the rope tighter until he finally let it go, shoving the mans head forward. The man coughed and sputtered with a face blood red but he could do nothing to stop the Elves and their anger. He glared at the Wood Elf angrily, continuing to choke. Tanis nodded to Elerith and smiled again.

"This scum doesn't know anything. Just slit his throat and get the other one."

"Now Tanis, we must at least give him a chance to speak. There's no reason we can't be civil." the High Elf said, picking up a wooden hammer and looking at the man's wrist. "Then again, he doesn't need his arm anymore does he?"

The man whipped his head around so fast that Erzel almost missed it. The cocky attitude had disappeared and his face now held a shocked look. "You can't be serious. You can't do this you damn Elves!"

Elendil lifted the hammer and lined it up with his elbow, his eyes narrowing to slits. He smiled and lowered the hammer slightly, hoping to have scared the man into talking. "Can't do this? You are tied down and helpless in a room full of Elves just dying to get a stab in on you. I think the odds of us being able to do what we want to you are pretty good. Unless of course, you have something to tell us."

"Yeah, I got something. Screw you Elf!" he snarled, spitting at the King.

Elendil raised the hammer and brought it down hard on the bare area just below his elbow, crushing the arm with a sickening crack. The man's scream echoed in the halls and dungeon and Elendil tossed the hammer to the table, picking up a sharp hook and a jagged dagger. He held them out to Tanis and nodded.

"Which would you prefer Tanis?" the Elf asked, looking at the Wood Elf.

Tanis smiled and took both weapons from the Elf and waited for the High Elf King to step to the side. He walked to the door and excused the guards, taking Erzel with him so Tanis could be alone in the room to take his revenge. Erzel looked at the King confused. Seeing his face, Elendil nodded to the cell down the hall and shrugged.

"Well, Tanis needs a measure of revenge to clear his head and there is still one more prisoner to interrogate. He seems to be the weaker one."

"He was the one that let the information slip about where the Princess was being held. I'm sure he will give you what you need, but are we not supposed to show some sort of discipline? This is as barbaric as the Humans."

"Sometimes Erzel, even the most disciplined of soldiers are allowed a moment of barbarism. To keep him from revenge over those who took his daughter and threatened to have her traded to the most barbaric of rulers would be inhumane. I'm sure you understand."

Erzel nodded sadly, not convinced completely that it was the right move but knowing that the King was a very intelligent person and that his reasoning was sound. They heard the Human scream from within the sealed room and then only a gurgle, followed by silence. They waited patiently and soon the door opened and the King of the Wood Elves walked out, blood on his hands and face. He stared straight ahead as he walked past the two Elves and continued on to the cell where the second man was being kept. The pair followed him in and watched as he grabbed the Human by the neck and forced him up onto his feet.

"Do you see this?" he asked angrily. "The blood on my hands, the blood of your partner that used to take up that corner. He isn't going to be talking ever again so what do you want to do? Do you want to talk, or do you want to join him?"

Erzel took a step into the cell but Elendil placed a hand on his shoulder, stopping him at the entrance. "Wait."

"My Lord, he is the only other prisoner we have. Don't allow him to take the information to his grave."

"He won't I assure you. Just watch."

The Human gagged and choked out a response, trying to get the Elf to release his grip. Tanis softened his grip and the man collapsed to the floor, gasping for air. The Wood Elf took a step back and crossed his arms, watching the pathetic Human crawl about the floor. Just before he lost his patience, the man on the floor cried out.

"Ok! Ok… what do you want from me?! You've got her back, you beat Claxis… what do you want?!"

"Did the Humans of Cisalia betray us? Are they traitors?" the Wood Elf asked.

"No, we were banished from Cisalia long ago and wanted revenge."

Elendil took over. "I want to know who is in charge. Give me the names, give me their alliances, and maybe you will live a long life in this dungeon. Otherwise, he is going to finish what he started with your friend in the other room."

The man looked at the Wood Elf who was busy cleaning his hands of the blood and then back to Elendil. "Claxis was in charge. We all reported to him. We didn't have an alliance yet."

"Yet? Ok then, who were you trying to ally yourselves with?"

The Human looked up at Elendil for the first time, still gasping softly for air to cool his burning lungs. "Valsera of course. He will sweep across these lands and claim them for his own and there is nothing you can do about it. He is gearing up for a massive..."

Elendil gave him a sharp kick to the chest, stopping him in mid sentence. The man growled and climbed to his feet to strike the King but the chains held him back against the wall. Elendil took a step towards him and the Human backed down, knowing he was on the losing end. The Elf King turned back to the guards and nodded to the room where the other prisoner had been killed.

"Clean that room, dispose of the body. Keep this one chained but keep him alive. We may have more questions for him later."

The guards bowed as the two Kings and Erzel left the dungeon, walking back up to the throne room where they took seats around the table. Tanis turned to a servant and asked that Rhen be found and brought back in. They sat in silence as they waited for the Princess to arrive. When the doors opened the three stood to greet her and she took a seat next to her father. Elendil tapped the table and everyone turned towards him.

"There is another matter we need to discuss with the two of you. Now that the prisoners have confirmed my fears that the South is building up for an invasion, Tanis and I have decided to send the Princess north.

"North? Where to?" Erzel asked, finding the information odd.

"Well, we've sent word to the Dwarves of Tvan and we

expect they will agree to help protect her. They have unlimited resources and deep cities. You see, Valsera's armies likely to strike Mihlann next and if it falls, Swanhaven will follow. Afterwards they will be able to move north and cut our alliances in half. Tanis will be returning home soon to secure his defenses and prepare in case the Elves at Mihlann fail. We have a duty to ask of you Erzel."

"What?! Wait a minute, I'm not leaving!" Rhen exclaimed suddenly, startling the table. "I don't want to be sent away again, I want to go home with you father!"

The Wood Elf looked at his daughter with a hint of surprise. "Please Rhen, calm down. I don't think you understand what is at stake. Just hear us out before you decide you won't go."

Rhen sat back in her chair and bit her lip, feeling foolish for her outburst. She looked down at her hands to avoid the looks from the Elves at the table.

The captain shifted his injured arm and looked from Tanis to Elendil. "What would you ask of me?"

Tanis looked to the Elf. "I wish to appoint you protector over my daughter. You will take her north past Cisalia to the Dwarven lands to keep her safe. Once you arrive, I will ask that you remain in Tvan."

"Erzel, how is your arm?" Elendil asked.

"Nearly healed my Lord. The cleric's magic is very strong. Shouldn't be more than a few days and it will be back to normal, I think."

"The task at hand should be appointed to you as it was your efforts that secured the Princess's freedom. We need someone to lead a small group north with the Princess into the Dwarven lands where she will remain as long as the threat from the south is constant."

"You want me to take the Princess north to Tvan? What about my soldiers my Lord? Who will lead them in my absence?"

"Your next in command is Aric, correct? I am sure he would be more than capable to lead them. Would that suit you captain?" the High Elf asked as he stood from the table.

"Yes, of course my Lord. I take it Aric will not be accompanying me to Tvan in that case. I trust him to fulfill the duties you will appoint to him."

Elendil crossed the room on his way to the balcony with Tanis and Erzel following him. Rhen watched them but remained at the table by herself, still recovering from the shock of leaving the city. Elendil leaned against the railing and looked out across the city. He seemed worried even though the Princess was safely defended by more than one hundred thousand Elven soldiers. Erzel rested against the rail next to the King.

"Erzel, by accepting this mission and for the safety of the Princess and those who will be traveling with you, you must now sever your ties with the Order of the White Eagle. Different clothing, weapons, everything. Are you willing to suspend your title as captain of the Order for now?"

"Yes my Lord, I will. If it is your wish that I lead the group on its journey north, then I will gladly accept the responsibility."

"That is what we wanted to hear captain. We will talk again later about the details of who will be accompanying you but for now, we only needed the assurance that you would take on the duty. Please feel free to equip yourself in any way you see fit from the royal armory. I will send for you when your companions arrive."

"Thank you my Lord." Erzel replied, turning to leave. He stopped at Rhen's side and smiled. "I have to go but I will see you again later this evening."

Rhen smiled back with a slight blush before leaving the room to join her father on the balcony. The captain left the throne room and headed for the royal armory which for easy distribution of arms was centrally located in the enormous castle. The Elf stopped outside the armory doors to have a word with the guards. He looked around the vast rooms at the walls of weapons. Virtually every design of sword, spear or bow was on the racks before him. He walked down the walls of weapons, looking at the broad selection. He passed into a second room where there was equally as much room but instead of weapons, it housed racks of plated armor and bins filled with chain and leather armor. He pulled out a suit of blackened chain mail, folding it over his good arm and carried it back into the room of weapons. As he entered a servant he had asked for approached.

"You asked for assistance my Lord?" the servant asked with a nod.

"Yes, could you hold onto this please. With only one arm it proves quite difficult to carry many items at once."

"Of course."

The Elf took the folded chain armor from Erzel and followed him around the room of weapons. Erzel examined numerous weapons but nothing really seemed to fit his style. He pulled a pair of short swords from a rack, examining them closely one at a time. Each had a blade roughly two and a half feet long with identical handles and hilts. The sheaths strapped on either side of the soldier's hips and could tilt up to be concealed within a cloak. He slid the swords into their sheaths and hung them over his shoulder, scanning through the walls of bows. The servant stopped next to him, shifting on his feet.

"If I may ask sir, why the sudden change in your equipment?"

"The duty calls for it. My King prefers that I carry nothing with ties to the Order of the White Eagle for our journey north so I am to honor that wish for our safety."

Erzel pulled a curved war bow from the rack and handed a quiver of arrows to the servant. Together they left the armory with his new arms and made their way up to his room where he leaned them against the wall for safe keeping through the remainder of his stay. He folded the chain mail on a chair and turned to leave his room. He walked back to a room above the armory where clothing was kept. The woman in the room greeted him warmly and walked him through the selection of tunics and cloaks. Every color imaginable hung on the racks and Erzel now had to choose what he felt suited him instead of what his Order wore. Taking his time, he decided on a sky blue tunic and a black cloak to match the armor. He carried them back to his room as well and folded them with his armor on the chair. Erzel walked back to the throne room after an hour of plundering and was surprised to find the Princess still standing on the balcony.

"I didn't expect to see you still here Princess. Where did Elendil and Tanis go?"

"I really don't know. I just wanted to stay and look at the view. It is amazing what you can see from this height."

"Do you mind if I join you?"

"Sure..." she replied, sliding over so the captain could lean against the railing next to her.

The captain settled in beside her and looked out across the rooftops of the busy city. They were quiet for some time, each with their own thoughts swimming through their heads. He watched a small group of soldiers headed through the inner gate, walls of archers making their patrols, and hundreds of townsfolk moving through the city. Life carried on as it always had. A scuffle in the heart of town broke out but a group of guards who were close by quickly broke it up. Rhen looked far out over the balcony, staring down at the gardens below. The flowers were in full bloom, all except the Moon Flowers. Erzel cautiously placed his hand on her shoulder to steady her.

"Please Princess Rhen, do not lean too far over the railing."

"Are you worried captain?" she asked with a smile. "Please, I wasn't leaning that fa..."

She never had a chance to finish the sentence as her right hand slipped on the railing and she fell forward. As quick as she fell, Erzel wrapped one arm around her waist and though his other was injured, he used it to catch her wrist, saving her from a deadly plummet to the garden below. He quickly pulled her back from the rail and steadied her, one hand on her stomach and the other on her back. Rhen looked to the side at the captain, her face growing just as red as her hair.

"Not... one... word," she mumbled, looking down at his hands.

He followed her gaze and quickly pulled his hands back. "I uh... I'm sorry Princess... forgive me."

She smiled and hid her eyes, still blushing with embarrassment from her foolish move on the railing. She turned away from the rail and walked back into the throne room. Just before she reached the opening she stopped and turned back to Erzel, giving him a gentle smile. She wasn't mad at all. As it turned out, she had her own way of expressing her gratitude.

Two days later Erzel stood on the same balcony. The bandages that had been wrapped around his arm were gone and he stretched it, happy to be able to use it once more. He looked out across the city as its people worked throughout their day. He spent more than an hour in the quiet surroundings, looking over his home and thinking about the young Princess. She was the way many Elves had described her, amazingly beautiful. Her skin was soft and her love of the lands as great as any other Elf. He would never have guessed he would be as close to her as he had become. Her emerald green eyes appeared in his head and he smiled to himself, admiring their beauty. Voices behind him caught his attention and he turned to enter the throne room.

In the room were Elendil, Tanis, and Rhen as well as four people he didn't recognize. They came in a variety of sizes, one topping close to seven feet tall. The captain stopped behind the group and waited as they talked among themselves. Elendil turned to his left and found Erzel standing alone in the back and gave a slight nod.

"Erzel, come and join us," he called, causing the group of four strangers to turn towards the Elf.

Erzel stepped past the strangers and stood next to Rhen. He looked over the group with an apprehensive glance, unsure of what to make of the situation. Elendil walked in between the group of four strangers and the captain, speaking quickly with one off them.

"Now, let me introduce you to the ones joining you on your quest north."

He started with the shortest of the group, a Dwarf from the foothills of Tvan by the name of Thorgrim. He was dressed in plated armor and held an entire armory on his belt; a short sword, blunt mace, several daggers, a small axe, and a short spear. Strapped across his shoulder was a large round shield. Next was Kail, a shadowy half Human ranger from the wilds below the Tvan mountains. He carried a long sword and a curved long bow.

The seven foot tall man was Rathe, a fighter armed with a belt of throwing knives and a monstrous two handed sword. The King didn't seem to know where the man was from.

The last of the four was an middle aged man. He wore dark green robes and leaned against a bleached white staff topped with a cluster of rubies. His eyes were pure white and his hair was kept short and as red as the rubies atop his staff. The wizard introduced himself as Ectle and extended his hand to Erzel who shook it. Erzel then shook hands with the others and waited as each of the group explained the skills he offered to the group. It turned out that the Dwarf was their guide as well as an accomplished fighter. Kail was an expert at stealth and tracking while Rathe was a powerful fighter. Ectle pulsed with arcane energies, showing his skills surpassed the other three. The group took seats with the Kings, Princess, and captain at the long table. They brought out maps to outline their journey north.

"When would you prefer we leave for Tvan my Lords?" Erzel asked.

"As soon as possible, tomorrow if you can. We are ready whenever you and the Princess are prepared."

The Dwarf turned the map in different directions, running his fingers across the path they would take. "I'd think it's safer to stay close to this shore, west of Cisalia until we are a day north. We can stay at the port city Murm overnight once Cisalia is safely behind us. From there it's a straight shot through the forests to the foothills of Tvan. I'm familiar with this area."

"That sounds decent. We should encounter the least resistance on this route. A small skirmish may not be a problem but if we meet a large force, it may be a serious problem."

"I am fairly sure that by using the forests and avoiding larger cities we should be safer. Then again, if we do meet up with a problem we can handle the problem," the Dwarf replied confidently.

Erzel reviewed the map and route for a while as the Kings became better acquainted with the four and the lands from which they came. Each had a different style of life but all were there for a common cause. They spent hours at the table discussing what was expected of the group. Their task was not a simple one.

The group had to travel north, eluding any remaining pockets of enemies around the Human capital. Once they reached Murm, a neutral city, they would travel through the wilds that separated the Humans and the Dwarves.

The captain handed the map back to Thorgrim. "It is somewhat risky but considering our other choices, this will be the best option. Thorgrim, I understand you have knowledge of the lands north of Cisalia. What about the rest of you?"

Rathe shook his head but Kail and Ectle both had history in the lands above Cisalia. "Yes, we've spent many years in the wilderness above Cisalia as well as some time in the mountains of Tvan. You are correct, this is the safest choice," the wizard replied.

The meeting was finally coming to a close as daylight began to dwindle. A fresh shift of guards arrived to relieve the days soldiers. Erzel and the four newcomers left the two Kings at the table. The captain followed behind as servants led them to their rooms. Ectle stopped at his door and turned.

"Are you worried about the journey Erzel?"

"No... well maybe a little. I guess I was given the task so quickly that I didn't really have time to consider what was being asked of me. I'm sure I can handle things though."

"You will. You have us to see you through it and further. Goodnight captain," the wizard said as the door closed.

Erzel continued on to his room where he sat on the edge of the bed, alone and in deep thought. He could see the map in his head and he pushed it away. He moved the chain armor and weaponry to the corner and stacked his belongings in the chair close to the door. Ready to leave, the Elf rolled into the bed. Even with the stress of the mission looming in the future, he fell asleep quickly.

Morning came earlier than usual it seemed. No sooner had Erzel opened his eyes than a servant arrived with a pitcher of water for him to wash his face. The captain cleaned up and pulled on the blackened chain armor, adding the light blue tunic over the chain mail. He strapped the two swords across his waist and the quiver of arrows across his back, carrying the bow with him. The halls were empty throughout the castle with the exception of a few guards here and there. He was surprised to find the throne room empty and he continued on. For half an hour he patrolled the halls until he made his way to one of the upper balconies. As he looked over the railing he could faintly make out the King and his royal guard in the main courtyard.

Erzel left the balcony and headed down the stairs two at a time as he hurried to meet up with the group down below. By the time he reached ground level he was nearly out of breath. The courtyard was filled with soldiers as well as the group heading north. The Princess was no where to be seen. He stopped next to the servant holding the reins of his horse and secured his bow to the saddle. The Elf holding the horse steadied the animal as a group of people hurried past. To keep from raising suspicion, the Princess would be riding her own horse with the group instead of using a carriage.

"Good morning Erzel." Ectle said as he led his horse in beside the captain.

"Same to you. Where is the Princess? I thought everyone would be ready by the time I made it down."

The wizard glanced out of the corner of his eye at the Elf. "It appears you have taken a fancy to the young Wood Elf."

"I suppose there is no need to deny it, especially to a wizard," Erzel replied quietly. "You'd know even if I were to lie about it."

"This is true, I'd know. Well, if you will excuse me I need to have a word with your King."

Erzel nodded as the wizard left and turned to look over the group. Thorgrim was dressed the same as he had been the night before, as was Ectle. Kail wore leather armor with sleeves of chain mail and a dark green hooded cloak. Rathe wore a scale breastplate over leather armor. He still carried his belt of throwing knives and leaned proudly against his two handed sword. As the captain waited, Tanis approached him. He stopped next to the Elf who bowed out of respect.

"Good morning Erzel, I have to ask another favor of you. When you are out there, I want you to personally look after Rhen.

Never leave her side. You have saved her life once, and now I want you to protect her further. Can I count on you Erzel?"

"Yes my Lord, of course you can count on me. I will not let her out of my sight, you have my word."

The Wood Elf clapped him on the shoulder and turned back to the castle, catching sight of the Princess for the first time. She looked beautiful as always; wavy red hair, curved body, adorable face. She was wearing the snug green dress with white trim, a matching hooded cloak, and the necklace they had purchased in the city. As she had said, it went perfectly with the rest of the outfit. Rhen hurried towards Erzel with a smile, her hair whipping around behind her. Erzel smiled as she stopped next to him, her face filled with excitement as the departure time neared. The captain led her to her own horse, helping the Princess up into the saddle before mounting his own steed. The only one not on horse was Thorgrim, who refused to ride and promised he could keep up on his own feet. Tanis and Elendil approached the Princess and the Wood Elf leaned against her horse, patting her leg softly.

Elendil approached. "You are going to be fine. You are in safer hands now than if you were with your own soldiers. They will see you safely north," Elendil said softly, moving on to Erzel.

Tanis approached as Elendil left. Rhen leaned down to hug her father. "It's going to be just fine father. I believe it this time. Don't worry."

They said their goodbyes and the six companions started out of the city. Thorgrim took the lead with Kail and Rathe in behind him. Erzel and Rhen followed and Ectle brought up the rear. They passed through the first set of gates into the city where they found thousands of people lined up to wish them farewell. At the second gate, flowers fell upon them from children on the wall above and the group rode out into the clearing with the forests in their sights. Erzel remained close to Rhen.

"Are you nervous?" he asked her, looking at her flowing red hair.

"A little. What happened before was terrifying, so yes I am a little nervous."

He reached down and touched her hand gently. "I promise that I will let nothing happen to you so long as you are by my side. I will give my life to protect you if it is asked of me."

Rhen looked to her right hand and smiled warmly at the captain. He had saved her life twice already and she trusted his abilities more than any other in the group. "I know you will Erzel, I know."

Back Into the World

*T*he borders of the two lands were alive with conflict as the armies in the south pressed their dominance farther. Two days after Erzel and his force of Elves left the fort city of Mihlann, a massive attack took place. The Elves suffered heavy losses all across the border but at the city of Mihlann they made an amazing defensive stand against the unruly Goblin armies. Mihlann was one of the most heavily fortified cities in the Elven realms, other than Pentegarn. The Goblin army was not in the least prepared for the siege it had begun. Without the form of siege weapons of any sort, the attacking forces had no chance of taking the massive fort city. On the fourth day of the siege, Raziel stood on the wall overlooking the enemy.

The commander smiled at the sight of heaped dead in the distance near the edges of the forest. Goblin camps came to life as the flames climbed higher in the ruined fields. The Elf commander squeezed the hilt of his sword, wondering how long it would be before they made the next foolish charge. A group of Knights stepped in around him, watching the mass begin to build once more. The Goblins were wary of the range of the Elven archers but as more of their soldiers piled into the clearing they were forced closer to the city. Raziel turned and left the front wall with the handful of Knights on his heels and they pushed their way to the war room. He drew his sword and set it on the table.

"How long until they try again?" one Knight asked as the commander paced to the end of the room and back.

"An hour, a day, a week, there is no way of telling right now. There is no pattern to their attacks. They just send everything they have at the walls until they've lost enough soldiers, then they back out. It is almost sickening to watch."

"What would you have us do?" the same Knight asked.

Raziel stopped pacing and looked at the Knight for the first time. "Start by rearming the catapults and ballista and make any repairs. The rest of you soldiers see that our gates and walls are secured for the next wave. Make sure the gate withstands anything they can throw at us."

The Knights hurried from the room with the tasks they had been appointed. The commander waited until they had left before crumbling into his chair from exhaustion. He stretched and yawned as he fought away the sleep threatening to set in. Just as his eyes started to slide together, the door swung open and a pair of soldiers burst in. They were red in the face and out of breath from running.

"What… what's going on?" Raziel asked, startled.

"They are marching… on the walls again… commander. Goblins, Hobgoblins, and Ogres, and they have giant ladders. They are more organized and definitely more numerous this time," the soldier exclaimed.

Raziel jumped to his feet as if he wasn't the least bit tired, grabbing his sword from the table. "Lead the way."

They arrived at the wall quickly and Raziel looked out across the fields below. The tale had been true. Large groups of Goblins, Hobgoblins and a mass of Ogres had begun a slow but steady march inward. They carried with them monstrous ladders to scale the city walls. A group of Ogres carried what appeared to be a thick, makeshift battering ram with a reinforced head. The commander quickly spread his soldiers across the walls, preparing their bows as the enemy closed in. Raziel pushed away the last of his exhaustion, preparing himself for yet another battle.

"Archers to the ready, load the catapults, make ready the cauldrons!" the commander ordered.

The soldiers followed their orders, readying the defenses for the newest threat. The enemy continued their march, speeding up as they came closer. The bulk of Ogres carrying the battering ram began moving faster, breaking into a hobbled run with the sturdy gate breaker ready to strike. Raziel watched the bulk of the army on its slow advance as the single group carrying the ram broke away from the rest, hoping to create a hole in which their misshapen armies could flood through the city. The Elf commander raised his sword and thrust it at the enemy.

"Fire!" he yelled.

The catapults launched their massive boulders across the walls of Mihlann and into the sky. Right behind them came a cloud of arrows from the archers on the battlements above. The Goblins below that were carrying shields locked them together, hoping to stop what arrows they could. It was semi effective as some arrows glanced off or stuck into the shields while others found holes not quite tight enough and stabbed the creatures behind the shield wall. The boulders flung from the catapults were a different story as they crashed into the lines of shields with catastrophic results. Bodies were thrown in every direction as the rocks bounced and rolled across the ground. With the Elves dealing the first blow, the Ogres rushed forward, driving the ram at the gate.

Raziel turned and pointed to the Elves at the cauldrons as the Ogres with the battering rams met the gate. "Burn them!"

The Elves dumped the two cauldrons of boiling oil over the edge of the wall onto the unsuspecting mass of creatures. Howls of pain and terror filled the air, louder than the sounds of the battle. One of the Elves threw his torch down to the gate, causing the oil to erupt into flames. The enemy fled in every direction as the flames rolled across the ground like a wave in the ocean.

Even with the gate defended, the ladders began to land against the city walls, covered with the forms of enemies as they scaled the siege ladders up to the battlements. The archers picked off those that they could until the enemy was flooding the top of the wall and the Elves were forced to fall back to using their swords and spears.

The first of the enemy made it to the battlements, engaging the rows of Elves. The battle atop the wall became fierce as the catapults continued to bombard the grounds outside the city. Bodies fell from the top of the walls as the Elves put their greater discipline to work, keeping the Goblins and Hobgoblins from spreading any further. The Elves pushed the enemy back to the ladders which cut off their only means of escape. The enemy on the ground continued to swarm up the ladders, while the ones on the wall tried desperately to get back down them. Raziel knocked a Goblin from the top of a ladder, sending several others falling to the ground. He swung and stabbed at the creatures left on the wall as the Elves took back the battlements.

"Forward!" he yelled. "Push them back!"

The commander dodged the thrust of a spear to his left and delivered a powerful overhand swing, splitting the Goblin's head with ease. He pulled his sword free and the body collapsed in a bloody heap at his feet. The largest part of the opposition had begun to flee, leaving behind small pockets of resistance that were still trying to get up the crowded ladders. In the massacre atop the wall, it was amazing to still see enemies brave enough to keep fighting. As the walls were cleared, the archers retook their positions, picking off the defenseless Goblins still on the ladders and in no time at all, the Elves had successfully repelled yet another attack.

The archers forced the last of the southern attackers back into the forests. The last to enter were a pair of oversized Ogres. They stared back at the Elves on the wall, confused and bewildered, then slid into the shadows and disappeared amongst the trees. Raziel wiped the blood from his sword and sheathed it, turning back towards the keep as the soldiers began clearing the walls of bodies. They carried their own fallen away to be cared for and tossed the bodies of their enemies over the edge to the ground below. The battle had spanned no more than an hour but the commander was near exhaustion again. He made it to the war room and closed the door, collapsing in his chair and falling asleep in minutes.

Nightfall brought with it another threat of attack. The guards arrived in the night and woke Raziel suddenly. He worked to get his eyes open as the soldiers stood around the table. "What... under attack? What's going on?"

"No my Lord, all is well. The forests are alive with activity but they remain well out of range of our archers. We only wanted to make sure you were alright."

"Oh, yes, much better now. I will be back out shortly. Carry on."

The soldiers nodded, leaving the commander alone once more. He wiped his eyes and stood from the table with his hand on his sword. His walk back to the walls took longer than usual as his body tried to keep him from waking. The wall had returned to its normal state, free of bodies and ladders but pools of blood still stood in several areas. Raziel's eyes fell upon the sight of distant torches moving about the southern forest. As the soldier had said, they dared not come closer to the defenses. Every so often an archer would fire to test the distance but none of the arrows ever found their targets.

"Did our messengers we sent to Pentegarn ever return?"

"No my Lord, not one. No news from King Elendil has been heard. Shall I send another while the enemy has fallen back?" one Knight asked.

"Send several this time. If more than one take the journey, maybe one will get through to the city. Perhaps Elendil will send us Knights."

The soldier turned and left to carry out Raziel's orders. The Elf in charge watched as three riders exited the city through a secret back gate. They moved slowly so they would attract as little attention as possible to themselves and entered the forests. He watched them until the trees had wrapped the three in darkness. When he was sure they had encountered no resistance, the commander turned to his soldiers who awaited further orders.

"Alright, clean everything up and lock down the city. They will be back and next time they may actually be smart enough to bring siege weapons to their siege."

"Yes sir," the Elves replied together.

The Elves loaded giant spears into the three ballista and aimed them at the forests as massive boulders were hefted into the catapults. Archers took their positions along the walls and in the towers, their eagle eyes piercing the darkness for any sign of opposition. All through the night they watched, sure the creatures would attack again under the cover of darkness. Several times the Goblins darted out of the trees long enough to get a good look at the city before hurrying back to the safety of the thick forest. They seemed to be testing the Elves' patience. The archers held their fire as more creatures braved the open ground to get a look at the Elves.

"What are they doing? Our archers could pick them off even as far away as they are."

"They want to know as much as they can about us. They want to see where we are weak and where we are the strongest without putting themselves in a clear shot from our archers. They know we can hit them from here but they love to push things."

The Knight looked out at the trees across the clearing. "Shall I give the order sir?"

Raziel looked at the increasing number of enemy scouts and nodded to the soldier beside him. "When the next group appears, give them a volley or two."

The archers drew back their bowstrings and waited for the creatures to make the foolish mistake of coming into view. The wait seemed to last a long time but finally a group of eight to ten Goblins appeared. The archers fired and twenty arrows soared through the air. The group of enemies hesitated in the clearing, trying to get every last detail but didn't seem to see the arrows beaming down on them. They struck their targets to the ground and after all the projectiles had met their targets, only one Goblin made it back to the trees.

Raziel looked to his soldiers, "Now they will surely come."

Erzel sat next to Rhen as they watched the current of a small stream take away the leaves they tossed into it. They had spent most of the night in the forests to the southwest of Cisalia to rest for the next journey. At their current rate, they could make it to Murm just after nightfall the next day. The Princess sighed and looked around the dark forest with sad eyes. Erzel looked at her with a fading smile, "What is it Rhen?"

"Oh... nothing really. It's just that I have never traveled away from my home and my family like this. I know it is for my own safety but at the same time, I am afraid that I may not see them again."

"What can I do?" Erzel asked.

Rhen picked up another leaf and tossed it into the water, watching it disappear from their limited light from the moon. She followed the leaf with a pebble, watching the splash ripple and disappear in the current. She didn't seem to know an answer to the question. Her slumped shoulders and saddened face made Erzel feel just as bad. He reached up slowly and ran his fingertips across her back, gently rubbing her spine and shoulders. Her head leaned forward and her breathing became softer and soon Erzel wasn't sure if she was even awake. She shuddered as a breeze penetrated the trees, sitting upright and looking to Erzel.

"Thank you. Father said you would take care of me. I'm glad it is you I have to protect me."

A noise behind them made the pair turn and look back as Ectle emerged from the trees. The wizard smiled as he leaned against his staff. "We've a small breakfast prepared if the two of you would care to join us. Afterwards, we will continue north even without the sun. The sooner we get moving, the sooner we can find Murm.

Erzel stood and extended his hand to the Princess, helping her to her feet. Rhen stood with a grateful smile, adding a low nod to the Elf captain.

"Thank you Erzel, I am glad to see that you have a gentle side as well as a battle hardened one."

"You are most welcome Rhen. Now please let us return to camp. I can see that you are most hungry."

They made it back to the campsite where Thorgrim had managed to cook a pan of crispy bacon and combined it with a loaf of bread from a pack to make a sort of biscuit. They ate in silence, the events to come in the day running through their heads. Rhen had rarely been accustom to the foods many adventurers were forced to improvise with in the wilds but found that there was absolutely nothing wrong with the meal. She and Erzel walked back down to the stream to wash up after the crumbs were eaten. As she splashed the cool water across her face and hands, Erzel tried not to stare at her. Even though she was not looking, he feared she would catch him.

With that taken care of they walked back to camp as the other four members packed everything together so that they would be free to leave at once. As they crossed through a thicket of berry bushes, Rhen stopped and knelt next to one, picking a succulent berry from the lower branches. She held it out to Erzel, rolling it back and forth in the palm of her hand.

"Erzel, what is this?"

The Elf turned back to her. "Ah, that is a dewberry. You found one of the last for today. See, they only form in the morning dew, but as the day progresses and it becomes warmer, they return to water and fall to the ground."

As Erzel spoke, the berries on the bush seemed to melt and fall to the forest floor like an army of raindrops. Rhen quickly popped the last berry into her mouth before it could do the same. There was a burst of sweetness in her mouth. She savored the taste as she swallowed the liquid.

"How is it?" Erzel asked.

"Sweet… very sweet indeed. It kind of bursts in your mouth when you press your tongue against it," she replied. "So, how is it that you know so much about the world outside of Pentegarn?"

"I spent all of my younger life out here until the battle of Dramdol where Elendil finally defeated the hordes of Lizardmen. Most were killed but many were driven back into the swamplands to stay. I fought alongside his soldiers without his consent but once the battle had ended, he inducted me into his Knights. Since then I have served him, but I grew up out here."

They continued on to the camp, finding everyone but Thorgrim on their horses and ready to leave. The Dwarf held Rhen's horse still as Erzel helped her into the saddle. He climbed onto his own horse and took the reins. The others gathered around and the Dwarf waited patiently in front.

"Well, lead the way Thorgrim," Erzel said finally.

The Dwarf took the lead on foot while the rest of the group followed on their horses. The stocky fighter made impressive time while the horses were walked or trotted but if pushed to a gallop, the Dwarf would be outrun. Erzel's group made its way through the forests, ducking and weaving through the underbrush to avoid the open roads. The mounted riders were forced to move slower as they pushed through the bushes and around trees while the Dwarf was nimble for his size, moving ahead with ease. Their route was a difficult one, but it was also the furthest from Cisalia. In case there was danger from the Humans, the group would stay well out of sight. With a wave of his hand, Ectle bent the branches and limbs back to create a clearer trail to travel on. Erzel and Rhen rode side by side, deep in conversation.

"So... what about your family? Parents, brothers, sisters, a wife?" the Princess asked.

"No siblings. I was an only child. My mother died giving me life and my father ten years later. He was attacked on the road to Qwaz by a group of Human bandits. At the time, it was still controlled by the Humans."

"I am sorry Erzel, I hope I haven't hurt you."

"No," replied the Elf. "As for a wife, I have never met the one. When you serve in the largest Order of the Elves, you never seem to have time to get close to anyone, emotionally."

Rhen looked down at her hands. "I do understand. Though I have my parents, I am hardly ever close to them. Before all this they were wrapped in war and diplomatic affairs, so I entertained myself. It is hard to love someone when you are not sure if they will still be here the next day. Do you think you will ever be settled enough to meet someone?"

Erzel looked out of the corner of his eye at the Princess before returning his gaze to the path ahead. "I suppose only time will tell. I guess when the wars end, the need for an army this size will diminish and perhaps I could take on a much calmer life."

They rode through the trees for what seemed like a day before the forest finally thinned. The thickest parts of the trees were replaced with sparse vegetation and rocky terrain dotted with masses of boulders. After the countless hours of riding in the thick forest, the group was happy to see the open fields. Thorgrim pressed on with Kail riding next to him. The other four decided to hang back a little in case the area was not safe to travel through.

"I understand you are counting on Murm being a neutral

city still. Is there an idea as to what we do if they are no longer neutral and do not welcome our kinds? What if the pockets of Humans no longer loyal to the alliance have turned them?" Erzel asked Ectle as the wizard dropped back next to him.

"Well, our initial hopes are that they have not turned against us. If they have, I guess we will figure that one out when we get to it. We have quite a collection of talents my friend. If things get ugly, we will do what we must to survive and protect the Princess."

Thorgrim and Kail stopped them as they came around a large stand of boulders. Kail had dismounted and tied the reins of his horse to a large log before waving them close to him. The rest of the group did the same and Erzel quickly joined Kail and Thorgrim at the edge of the outcropping of boulders.

"What is stopping us?" the Elf asked the two.

"Quiet! Look there, beyond those trees," Kail whispered.

As Erzel followed the gaze of the man, a group of creatures moved into view. He studied them closely, finding the poorly disciplined group was made up of Goblins. When they had all made it into the clearing, the Elf counted between twenty five and thirty of the creatures. His heart sank as he watched them stop in the middle of the clearing to set up camp. Erzel turned away from the clearing, sighing to himself at their ill luck.

"Well, it looks like we will be staying here for a while. There is a large party of Goblins some eighty yards north of us. Where they now sit, they would see any attempt to sneak past them and possibly any attempt to get back to the thickest part of the forests from which we came."

Rathe turned to the Elf. "Wait, is Ectle not a wizard? Why can't he just wipe out what he can and let us mop up the rest?"

"Wizard or not, we can not handle this. I am limited by how much magic I can use daily. We did not come this far to pick a fight with a force of Goblins so sit down, keep quiet and stay hidden," Ectle replied sharply.

The group settled in behind the boulders as Kail and Thorgrim kept watch to ensure none of the creatures accidentally stumbled upon them. The Goblins could be heard across the field clearly as their drunken complaints echoed up to the group. Kail kept an arrow notched in hand as he stood guard, watching a fight break out in the Goblin ranks. To settle the argument, the commander of the force quickly beheaded one of the two with a swing of its sword and ordered the one remaining to dispose of the body. It was an example of their barbarism.

Rhen rolled a smooth stone around the palm of her hand as she worried. Erzel sat down next to her, closing his eyes to rest. "Something troubling you?"

"No... well yes. Just a little nervous with thirty of them and only five of you. I don't want to wake up a prisoner in another dungeon somewhere. I'm just a little nervous."

"Don't worry. At nightfall we will move further west across the clearing into that stand of trees and sneak past them under the cover of darkness. Judging from the noise, they are too drunk to care who hears them and obviously have no idea that we are even here. I do not see them as a threat," Erzel assured her.

The group waited until the sun began to set. They ate dried meats and bread in place of cooking a meal. As Erzel took his turn at watch, he saw the Goblin camp fall still and soon they were quiet as well. He could see one figure still up and moving about, probably on watch. With the cover of darkness complete, the group was packed and ready to move out. They each took their horse and gathered around Kail and Erzel as the two explained the plan that would safely get them away from the group in the field.

"Alright, this is what we do. About twenty yards west of us is a large stand of trees that looks to stretch quite a ways. If we reach it we can travel north for about a half a mile before the clearing takes over again. We will walk the horses to make sure they are quiet. Stay close and be as quiet as possible," ordered Erzel.

Everyone except Thorgrim took their horses and led them in a single file line from the stand of boulders. They moved swiftly through the night. Several times Kail held up his hand to stop them as movement in the Goblin encampment caught his attention. When all was clear, they continued on, rushing the last ten steps into the cover of the forest. Kail was the last one to enter, watching the enemy closely to ensure they had made it without being spotted. The walk through the forest was much harder as they fought the darkness and dried leaves under their feet. When the trees thinned on the back side of the grove, Erzel poked his head out and looked down towards the camp to find increased movement. He stopped everyone and held a finger to his lips.

"What do we do now?" Rathe asked impatiently.

"Set up camp a little further in away from this front edge. When they leave we will continue on our way. No fires, and keep it quiet," Erzel replied, tying his horse and moving to the edge of the trees to keep first watch.

They did as they were told and most went straight off to sleep. Kail joined Erzel at watch, staring out of the trees into the dark clearing. The campfires still danced as dark figures moved around them. Even though sunrise was several hours away, the creatures were starting to wake and move about. Soon the small fires were roaring and several soldiers began patrols around the camp. Two passed where Erzel and the group had been hiding and the Elf breathed a sigh of relief.

"I'm sure glad we moved. Otherwise, we'd be fighting the lot of them by now," Kail whispered, watching the Goblins move back towards camp.

"No doubt there. I am willing to bet there are more patrols in these woods just waiting to stumble upon us. Next time it may not be simply Goblins."

"So why are we resting? We need to get to Murm where we can be sure the Goblin patrols have not reached. We shouldn't sleep until we are safe behind walls where their eyes can not see us."

"What makes you believe the city is out of their reach? For all we know Valsera has turned the city already. I do hope the city is safe though because I would give anything to sleep in an actual bed once more."

Kail laughed, knowing the difference between the captain and himself. Kail rarely spent time in a life of luxury. Castles and beds had been replaced by caves or forests and a sleeping roll. He occasionally stayed in a small town when it was available, but it was a reward he rarely gave himself. The Human lived the way Erzel had prior to joining the Elves and their armies. Erzel had spent three straight years in the wilderness at the borders but just as much time behind the walls of Pentegarn. Though he lived behind the walls of the largest city of the free lands, Erzel had seen plenty of caves and forests. He looked at the man beside him in the dark.

"So, what made you join up to help our cause?"

"I've traveled these lands with Thorgrim for quite a long time so when he came, I did too. We've always been here for one another because he was the first person I came across after I lost my parents."

Erzel started to ask but he knew the subject was not one to openly discuss. With Kail becoming silent, the Elf could only assume he didn't want to pursue the conversation any further. As the two watched, Thorgrim appeared behind them to take his turn at watch. He settled in beside Kail and nodded to Erzel.

"Go get some rest Erzel, we've got it."

Erzel thanked them and walked back through the trees and sat down next to a sleeping Rhen. He looked down at her hair spread around her shoulders on the ground. She seemed to sleep so peaceful in the middle of the war torn lands. He scanned around the others and found Ectle awake and reading a pair of scrolls in the dim light before sunrise. His pure white eyes now had a blue glare to them. Erzel stood and joined the wizard.

"Why do you not sleep?" Ectle asked, not taking his eyes off his work.

"I could ask you the same thing. What are you studying so intently? How do you see it in this dark wood?" the Elf asked.

"Using magic of course. These scrolls are from a time long before the invasion of Nalawren. They tell of beings that most of our races have never seen, Dragons They could be the key to turning the tides in this struggle, though they are very difficult to find."

"Oh not this again!" Rathe breathed, turning towards the wizard and Elf. "All he did the entire trip to Pentegarn is talk about the Dragons and finding them and how they are the key to our salvation!"

"That's because no one else will take the time to hunt these great creatures. They did not want to be found when they disappeared from their great lands to the furthest northern reaches across the seas. They may be hidden, but I seek to uncover their location." Ectle hissed at the fighter.

Erzel looked up into the sky as the black was turning to a light purple. "So what do those scrolls reveal about this myth?"

Rathe threw his hands up and rolled back over away from the two. Ectle didn't look at the fighter but spoke softly. "A power that even Valsera at one time feared. It seems the Dragons were his greatest adversary and he sought to wipe them out, and almost succeeded. This scroll tells of how the last of the Dragons escaped the mass genocide of their brethren. Apparently, they now inhabit an island that none have ever found to exist. It seems to get foggy after that."

"So... they inhabit an island that there is no proof of, and yet you are fairly sure they exist?" Erzel questioned.

"Well, I believe what I read when the records are kept correctly. These scrolls are older than many of the cities we now inhabit, and they tell the tale. If they are not accurate, it will not have cost me anything to study it."

Erzel sat silently as he tried to decide what to make of the wizard's odd claims. He had heard the myth long ago but in time, it had been forgotten. What good was an old myth anyway when the world knew nothing but war. A myth would not stop a charging enemy nor defend a city from an attacking army. Unless of course there was truth behind the myth. He rolled his thumbs together and watched the first smear of orange appear in the sky. Kail arrived with good news.

"The Goblins are moving out as we speak. Another ten or fifteen minutes and we will be clear to leave."

The ranger returned to his post to watch the creatures leave. After he left, Erzel knelt next to the Princess and shook her very gently. When her eyes finally cracked open the captain placed a finger against her lips, urging her to stay quiet. Rhen looked around and sat up slowly, brushing the leaves and dirt from her hair.

"What... what is it? Are we leaving?" she asked between yawns.

"Not quite yet. Kail says we have fifteen minutes before we are clear to leave. I just wanted to wake you so we could proceed as soon as possible."

When the Goblins disappeared from the clearing, Kail nodded to the rest of the group to assure them that the fields were empty. With the coast clear, they mounted their horses and started through the trees with Thorgrim out in front on foot. Erzel reached over to the Princess and pulled a strand of grass from her hair. Rhen grinned and took it from him, tossing it down. They shared a quick glance before Erzel spurred his horse up next to Rathe and Kail. He looked to his left at the ranger.

"So, how far would you say we are from Murm?"

"A few hours, three or four at the most. That is, assuming we do not encounter any more problems. Drop back in with the Princess and I will let you know ahead of time if anything arises."

Erzel waited for the Princess to move her horse up next to him. She brushed her hair away and behind it was the hint of another smile. Her flirtatious attitude brought a smile to Erzel's face but before she had the chance to notice he backed away. The game of cat and mouse continued as neither seemed brave enough to do or say anything more.

Elendil had indeed gotten word of the attacks at Mihlann and had sent a force to help. Just north of Mihlann was a mass of High Elves numbering between three and four hundred. Most were fresh infantry but a small group consisted of well trained Knights. They moved south into the fields of Mihlann where the castle came into clear view. The only thing that seemed to be missing were the giant hordes of Goblin and Ogre soldiers. The Knights led the infantry in through the gates where they congregated, waiting for the one in charge. Raziel appeared and greeted them.

"Welcome... welcome to Mihlann. You brave soldiers have been long awaited by my weakened defense. Come, gather round soldiers."

The leader of the Knights stepped up and gave a nod. "Thank you commander. The High King has sent us to reinforce your city. Please use us where you see the need."

Raziel returned his words with a gracious smile. Many were dispatched across the walls while the mass of Knights was positioned behind the main gate. What was left of the infantry was sent to the keep in case the walls were breached. If the gates ruptured, the keep would have to be well defended if we were to have any chance of surviving the siege. The leader of the Knights joined Raziel in the keep.

"How have they been coming? Their numbers, their formations. What do they bring?"

"It varies. They have yet to bring a single piece of siege weaponry but they did try a makeshift battering ram in their last attempt. Oh, and ladders, they've tried ladders. They rarely have any discipline to their formations but they always bring waves of soldiers. Sometimes they outnumber us ten to one but our walls have held."

"This is very good news. I saw the charred body of an Ogre in the fields outside and several around the castle. I must say, I wasn't expecting to see them here and it is a wonder they have not broken through with such strength on their side."

"Well, we've been using brains to their brawn and so far it has worked amazingly. They just can not seem to comprehend the importance of siege weapons during a siege. I do not expect that to last though and they will catch on soon. Until they do, we will continue to slaughter them without mercy," Raziel replied.

The commander led the Knight through the castle, showing him the strengths and weaknesses in case the enemy forces made it through the walls. Towards the center of the keep was a powerfully reinforced room used as the last stand. The room had one entrance to defend, with strong locks and plenty of room within for a skirmish. The Knight walked the room several times, looking over what the commander referred to as the Heart of the Keep.

"So basically, if the keep is breached you and what is left of your soldiers retreat back to this room and barricade yourselves here for one last stand?"

"Yes… basically that would be the idea. Never give up, never surrender."

The Knight stood quietly for a moment, pondering the thought of the rooms purpose. "Sounds like an honorable death, considering once you fall back to this point there is no escape. Why not go down swinging."

"Exactly, come with me so I can show you more of our defenses before they try another assault on the walls."

They crossed the outer battlements of the keep, looking at the catapults and ballista that dotted the defenses. Reinforced walls made any siege weapons the enemy might use less effective. The Knight seemed impressed with the defenses. They stopped in the war room where a few other soldiers passed through with reports from the outer walls and gates, all of which were clear. Raziel pulled a map to him and ran his hands across it, explaining the circumstances and how the creatures had acted so far.

"The first attacks were isolated on the southern walls but as the attacks have continued, they have spread around, trying to find any weakness they can exploit. Soon they will completely surround us and we will have to defend every direction. Our catapults are in these areas and are useful up to here, and then we have to rely on our archers," Raziel pointed out.

A soldier burst into the room, panting from his run. Raziel and the Knight stood, shocked at his appearance.

"Yes… speak up!" Raziel ordered.

"My Lord… soldiers gathering in the fields… one has a white flag."

"Show me."

The three hurried to the wall where they found the Goblins massed and waiting. Out in front was a single figure holding a white banner on the end of a spear to ensure the Elves would refrain from attacking. Raziel wondered why they wanted to talk when they clearly outnumbered the Elves. He marched down to the gates and out into the field, followed by about a dozen of the Knights from Pentegarn. Raziel raised his hand and the Knights stopped. He continued until he was a few feet away from the creature.

"Put away your white flag, you have no intention of peace," the commander said as he stopped in front of the odd creature.

It looked a great deal like a Goblin but was larger. Its body was very muscular and the commander could see some troll in it too. Its skin was similar in color to the Goblins but it looked rougher, almost like stone. The Elf squared off bravely with the creature, looking it in its squinty black eyes. He tapped the hilt of his sword and waited, knowing the enemy had something to say.

"I am Uljic. You and your soldiers can surrender now or die."

"Ha, perhaps you have yet to notice Uljak…

"Uljic!" the creature growled, tightening his grip on the spear.

"Who cares… my soldiers have done nothing but slaughter yours. Would you care to rethink your offer before you lose another battalion or two?" the Elf asked sarcastically.

"If you go back into your city, you will die there. I guarantee it Elf, you will die. Last chance to save your own life."

"A prisoner to your kind is as good as dead so I will find you when you get inside and I will kill you myself! Be gone!"

Raziel turned back and the Knights fell in around him as he walked confidently into the city. Most of the soldiers looked on with concern as he passed but the commander spoke to no one. His concern did not rest with the creatures outside, but with the morale of his own within the walls. With no end to the fighting is sight, the Elves were in for quite a long stay. This time fortunately, the armies of the enemy slowly fell back into the forest, leaving the Elves be for a time.

A World of Differences

The group of six sat at the crest of the hill overlooking the port city of Murm. The thought of a real bed, a good meal, and a safe place to stay was unanimously accepted by the entire group. They kept a sharp eye on the city to ensure the Goblin presence had not reached this far. After another ten minutes of watching and they felt it safe to continue on down the hill. Even as they moved closer, the group kept their eyes on the buildings and streets.

"Well, nothing here seems too out of place. Perhaps the lands between Tvan and Pentegarn still serve a little value to the races," Kail noted quietly as they entered the city.

"Find the inn. I want to get settled in safely and know for a fact that our presence goes undetected," Erzel replied.

They rode through the city streets with little regard from the rest of the townsfolk. At last they found the inn nestled in between the many docks and shops. It was by far the largest building of the town and the six stopped out in front of what appeared to be the community stable. In a heartbeat two young stable hands were next to the group waiting to care for the horses. As the rest of the group headed into the building, Erzel took a few coins from the pouch on his belt and paid the two. The outer appearance of the inn looked old and worn but after walking in, the Elf found it to be very clean and quite luxurious for such a small town. He saw the others at the desk talking with the owner.

"The rooms come with two beds, two silver a night for each room. Food and drink are separate and depends on what you want."

"We'll take three rooms and dinner later. Six silver it is," the Elf said, handing the man the coins.

The owner pulled three small brass keys from a box under the counter and handed them to the group. Kail and Thorgrim took the first room while Ectle and Rathe settled into the third, leaving the room in the middle for Rhen and Erzel. He opened the door for her and closed it behind him, looking over the small room. Two beds, a wash stand, one chair and a window. He put his bag on the bed next to him and looked up at Rhen.

"Perhaps I should pay for another room. Give you your privacy and all."

"No need Erzel, I will be fine."

"I could move the chair out into the hall and stand guard, just in case. I mean, it feels..."

"Erzel... is something bothering you about staying in a room with me? Surely someone as strong as you has nothing to fear from a Princess like me. You know, my father told you that you were not to leave my side. Would you disobey the King's orders?"

Erzel straightened some, finding that she had taken advantage of a loophole he wasn't aware existed. "Of course not. I live to serve the Kings of the Elves. I would never disobey their orders."

"Good then, make yourself comfortable. Remember, I'm not supposed to be a Princess while we are away from Pentegarn. You don't have to treat me like one."

Rhen reached behind her neck and pulled a pair of buttons loose, working down the back with surprising speed. Erzel turned his head and stepped back to the door. "I uh... I will step outside for a moment while you wash up. I'm sure your father wouldn't mind me being away from you while you are dressing."

The Princess gave a smile and blushed, holding the front of the dress to her chest until the Elf had disappeared outside of the door. Erzel waited with his back against the wall next to the door as pictures of what he had seen crept into his head. He fought them several times until the door cracked and the Princess walked out. He stood quickly and nodded to her, taking in her smile. Her dress was now a light blue and she had pulled her hair up out of her face. He smiled in return and led her down to the first floor. Everyone except the wizard sat at a long table in the corner.

"Where is Ectle?" the captain asked as they got settled.

"Studying those scrolls. Said he would be down later," Rathe replied, watching the waitress as she worked through the room.

They ordered dinner without the wizard and sat around discussing the rest of the journey. From the sound of things, they were planning on staying a second day in the city before leaving for Tvan. They all agreed that an extra day of rest would not harm them as they were only halfway clear of the dangers of the trip. Though the area north of Murm had not been settled by any race, that didn't mean the Goblins or worse were not using it to move about. Platters of food began arriving and as soon as they were all on the table, everyone but Rhen began eating. She cocked her head to the side and then looked to the group.

"Um... excuse me Erzel, what is this we are eating? It looks like... well, somewhat like a spider."

Rathe and Kail both laughed and Erzel wiped his hands clean. "No... not a spider Rhen. This is a crab. It is the common meal for almost all the port cities. They live in the ocean and can be caught dozens at a time so they are easy to catch and cheap to serve. What you do is take a leg, crack it like so, and pull it apart to expose the meat. It's very good, try it."

Rhen followed his example and after several tries she managed to pull a large piece of meat from the shell. Amazed by the taste she continued through the legs, ignoring the fact that it was quite a messy meal. When she stopped to wipe her hands for the fifth time, she noticed Erzel watching her.

"What?" she asked, tasting the juice on her lips.

"Nothing... just for someone who has never tried crab you have taken to it quite quickly. You've got a little here, and here, and a little more there." Erzel said, pointing around her lips.

Kail and Rathe exchanged a few more chuckles as the Princess tried to clean herself up. When the plates were finished, the waitress cleared them all and brought a pitcher of honeyale to the group. When the ale arrived, so did Ectle. The wizard joined them without a word and took his drink from the table. He seemed withdrawn, rocking in his seat and mumbling softly. When his eyes cracked open he set the drink back on the table. Instead of honeyale, there was now a sparkling green liquid that filled the cup.

"What is that Ectle?" Thorgrim asked nervously.

"Poison my curious friend," the wizard replied with a smile. "No... it is a potion I use to retain all the knowledge I have come upon. Without it, I could lose all I have worked so hard to learn. It must be consumed once a month."

"Seems like a waste of good ale to me," the Dwarf scolded, emptying his mug quickly.

They spent the next two hours around the table sharing stories of past battles, grand adventures and noble quests. Of all the tales though, all Rathe seemed to recall were the numerous women he had met, giving Erzel good reason to watch the man closely when the Princess was near. As the ale flowed freely, Rathe had a waitress in his lap and a mug in his hand, struggling to decide which to put to his lips first. Rhen took Erzel's drink from him and tasted of it, giving it back with a raised eyebrow.

"No good?" Erzel asked.

"Well, it isn't bad, but then again it really isn't good either. I think I am going to bed. If you will excuse me for the evening, good night."

Erzel stood with her, finishing his ale and setting the glass on the table. "I think I too am done for the night. See everyone in the morning."

Together they climbed the stairs and Erzel opened the door for the Princess. Just before he stepped into the room, he watched Rathe stumble up the stairs with the same waitress under his arm. She too had apparently had plenty to drink as her blouse was open, revealing her breasts to the Elf. Rathe winked at Erzel as he passed, giving the captain a boyish grin. It was quite obvious what he had planned for the night. The Elf closed the door and unfasten the belt holding his swords.

"Who was that?" Rhen asked.

"Rathe and... uh..."

"Rathe and who?"

"Rathe and that little blonde waitress from below. Apparently he aims to add another woman to his long list of journeys. It seems quite shameful if you ask me," Erzel replied, standing his swords in the corner.

"You are very honorable, and quite careful," Rhen said as she let her hair down and running her fingers through it. "You were the only one armed during dinner and Thorgrim usually carries around fifty pounds of weapons."

The captain stepped up to the window and stared out of it in deep thought. Throughout his life he had spent more time with a sword in his grasp than a woman next to him. All his time had been dedicated to serving the King, regardless of what his personal interests were. He had never before really sat down and thought about the things he had given up by always marching into war and not laying with a woman in love.

"I've seen too much bad in my life to not be prepared. Besides, Ectle is always armed, he's a wizard."

Rhen shrugged and undressed quickly while the Elf's back was turned and walked slowly to the bed where she would sleep. Though his back was turned, Erzel could easily see her reflection in the glass. He watched as the short, white nightdress swayed with her steps and wondered to himself if his constant service to the King was depriving him of love he had yet to experience. Rhen settled into the bed and when the covers were pulled up around her he turned, finding that the blanket came up short of covering her chest. He tried not to let her see it affect him but a light blush showed and she took notice of it. Feeling somewhat sorry for the Elf, Rhen decided not to pursue the matter. Erzel put his hand over the oil lamp, smothering the flame and sat down in the chair next to the window, looking out at the stars.

Rhen opened her eyes and found a long hallway stretching for about twenty or so yards. When she turned around she found only blackness behind her. She walked down the hallway, feeling cold stone on the bottoms of her bare feet. Where the hall ended there was now a doorway with light radiating from it. Cautiously, the Princess moved towards it. She wasn't sure where she was or how she had gotten there but forward was the only direction she could go.

She stopped at the edge of the doorway and peeked in, finding that the light was too bright to see past as her eyes fought to adjust. Her senses gave her no idea to what was in the room, no sounds, no smells, hardly anything to see other than the bright light. Even when shielding her eyes against the light with her hand, Rhen still could not make out anything in the room. With the last ounce of bravery she had left, the Elf took a shaky step into the room. The lights dimmed the moment she entered and she waited for her eyes to adjust. When they finally did, Rhen froze where she stood, her bravery failing her all at once. She tried to run back to the doorway but her legs didn't move, not even a quiver.

In the middle of the room curled against the floor was a monstrous Blue Dragon. It lifted its head, bringing it about to face the young Elf. The Dragon didn't have scales but instead had leathery skin covering its body. Its head was broad and it had two sets of horns, one set above where its eyebrows would be and another pair behind those but a little wider apart. The Dragon leaned closer and its mouth cracked open, showing the sharp, white teeth. Rhen tried to make her legs work to get away, just to get somewhere else.

"Do not fear me my dear Rhen... I am not going to harm you."

All at once Rhen had control of her body again and she suddenly fell backwards to the stone floor. She was in total awe at the sight of the Dragon. "How do you know who I am? Where am I?"

"My name is Alora, and I've know about you for a long time dear Princess. My kind has been watching very closely your world and what you are going through. You are on our island."

"The Dragon Isles? Ectle was talking about them, but I was just in Murm... asleep in a bed. How did I get here?"

The Dragon stood from the floor and stretched its massive wings out, tucking them back into its body as it took a step towards the other side of the room. Rhen stood cautiously, still unsure of anything she was seeing. "You are not here, but in a sort of dream. I brought you here to show you we do exist. I want to help your kind Rhen because my time is ending. When I go, there will be few who are willing to help the races of Nalawren. This Ectle is right, and he needs someone to believe in him now if he is to ever find this island."

The Princess further examined the body of the Dragon, finding curved talons and small spikes down its back to the bottom of its tail where it ended with a small leathery whip-like curve. She walked up next to the Dragon, seeing a set of scars on her side. "So this is real, but it is just a dream for now?"

"Yes, a dream for now. In time I pray that you will see us for yourself. I know you are young, but you must show your strengths now more than ever. We will meet again very soon."

Rhen looked into the eyes of the Dragon and suddenly felt a strong force pulling at her from behind. She leaned away from it, having so many questions yet to ask but no chance to ask them. Like a strong wind pushing her backwards she was forced to take a step back, steadying herself as best as she could.

"You must go now Rhen, but rest assured, you will come back."

"I have so much to ask you! Please, wait!"

The force suddenly strengthened and she was pulled from her feet back towards the darkness. She passed the doorway to the room with the Dragon staring back out at her. Tumbling and turning she continued to fall backwards, fighting as best she could to get back to the room. The moment she met the blackness behind her, Rhen's eyes shot open, finding herself back in the room in Murm. She sat up, seeing Erzel asleep in the chair. The Princess sank back into the bed, not sure if what she had just experienced was real or just a dream.

Morning was just like any other in a port city like Murm. Early ships came in bringing fresh catch to the markets and the earlier they arrived, the better chance of selling their goods. Rhen led Erzel through the little shops and markets, marveling over the many things she had never seen before. She had lived her entire life in the woods around Swanhaven. Cages of crabs and lobster, bins heaping with different fish and eels, which Rhen found to be similar to snakes. Even some land dwelling foods were found in the port markets including different meats such as deer, bear, boar and game birds like turkey and quail. She stopped next to a large bushel basket and peeked down inside.

"What are these?" she asked Erzel.

"Them be clams missy... best damn clams in the sea," an old haggler answered as he approached.

"Clams... what is a clam? Anything like a crab?"

"Sure... sure they be. Shells just like a crab they have. Good meat too, a bit chewy less you eat them raw."

Rhen stepped back away from the man, finding him somewhat rude and moved closer to Erzel. Seeing her discomfort, the Elf led her down the market a bit further to where bins of fruits replaced the odd foods she had not seen before. Apples, grapes, cherries, and pears filled the wooden crates and Rhen picked up an apple from the bin, admiring the deep red color. Though only looking, a gruff voice made her jump and nearly drop the produce.

"Hey! If you ain't buyin you best not be touchin!" an overweight man behind the stand yelled when he saw the Elf.

"I wasn't going to steal it, I just wanted to see..."

"Ya, ya, ya, just wanted to see, just wanted to touch, just you put it back less you want to lose a hand thief!"

Erzel stepped between the man and the Elf girl, his face warm with anger. "I think an apology would be the correct approach here. Then I will pay you for the apple since you so desperately need the coppers."

The big man climbed to his feet and shuffled around to the front of the stand, a wooden club in his right hand and an angry glare on his face. He had every intention of beating the Elf to a bloody pulp but when he got within striking distance Erzel pulled the pair of swords out of their sheaths, revealing his proficiency with such weaponry. The large man stopped, rethinking his steps and lowered the club, finding it best not to lose his life over an apple.

"Now... the apology was what you were planning, correct?" Erzel asked, taking a step towards the man.

"Yeah... er, sorry little miss. Can't be too careful rounds here. I'll, uh, I'll just go back round this way."

Erzel tossed a pair of coppers across the stand at the man and led the Princess away from the market with the apple in hand. She was still shocked at the turn of events. Never in her life had she been accused of stealing anything and that man was going to hurt her over a misunderstanding about an apple. She stopped and turned to Erzel.

"He had no right to talk to me like that! I can afford anything I want, I'm the Prin..."

Erzel quickly put his hand over her mouth, scolding her. "Not out here you're not, remember? This is a different world than what you are used to. People don't trust other people and for good reason. Let's go back to the inn where things are a little safer."

"Never before has anyone insulted me in such a way."

"I am sorry Rhen, but these people are much different from the ones back home. If you were in Pentegarn they probably would have just given you the apple but out here nothing is free. A different world."

Rhen walked through the door of the inn and sat down at the same table from the night before with Kail and Ectle, her temper still flaring. The wizard didn't look up from his scrolls but Kail watched her, wondering what had flustered the Princess in such a way. Erzel shook his head as he approached, trying to keep them from asking and sending the Elf back into an outburst.

Rhen looked down at the scrolls that Ectle was studying, seeing several different markings that were similar to Dragons and strange writings. "Are those about the Dragon Isles?" she asked.

Ectle looked up at the Elf with a raised eyebrow. "Yes... what do you know about them my dear Princess?" the wizard asked, folding his hands on the parchments.

Rhen battled with the idea of telling the group about the

dream she'd had the night before. She didn't want to be thought of as crazy, but if it was true that the Dragon waited for them then she needed to say something. "I uh, I had a dream last night. Well it wasn't a dream but it was, kind of an... out of body experience. I was in this hallway and the floor was cold. At the end of the hall was a room and when I got into the room, there was a Blue Dragon inside. It talked to me."

Kail and Erzel didn't seem phased by the description of the dream but Ectle was more than intrigued. "Was it an elder Dragon? A male or female?"

Erzel looked up at Ectle. "Does that really matter Ectle? It was just a dream after all."

"No Erzel... it wasn't just a dream. I've been in the same position before. It is what put me to searching for the Dragon Isles in the first place. This could very well be the break I have been searching for. Please dear, go on, what else happened?"

"Well, its name was Alora and I think it was a girl Dragon, I didn't ask. It knew my name and told me to believe you when you talk about the Dragons, but I didn't get chance to ask the things I wanted to. There was like a strong wind..."

"... and it pulled you backwards from the room into the darkness behind you. The moment you touched the black you woke up, right?" Ectle said, describing the events almost perfectly.

"Yes! Exactly like that!" she exclaimed.

Erzel and Kail looked at one another, suddenly amazed that the Princess and wizard had been having the same dream down to the details of the where they were and what they felt. Neither wanted to believe it was possible, but the evidence was strong to support it. The captain looked to Ectle and shook his head.

"So what does this mean?" he asked, trying to decide if it was good or bad.

"This means that I am not the only one who has visited their lands in my dreams. Someone else has been there and she actually learned the name of one of the Dragons. This could mean they want to be found at last, to help us against the south. All this work paying off at last."

Rhen looked to Erzel. "I'm sorry I didn't say something sooner, but I wasn't sure if I should or not. I felt foolish talking about a dream I had that made no sense to me either."

Erzel shrugged. "Not a big deal Rhen. What is our next move? I figure we will leave for Tvan around dusk so perhaps we should all get some rest for the journey."

Kail, Rhen, and Erzel stood to leave but Ectle remained at the table. "What? Oh, I can't sleep now. Too much new information to piece together. I will in time though, just not now."

The three headed upstairs to their bedrooms to rest for a while before they had to leave once again. Rhen didn't even change into her night dress before snuggling into the bed. Erzel sat down in the chair once more, looking out the window at the mountains in the distance. The new dreams she'd been having made him wonder just where they would end up. He pulled the curtains together to darken the room and closed his eyes, trying to manage a little rest while he could.

Under the Mountains of Tvan

*T*van was unlike the other major cities in many ways. To start, it was not ruled by a King but by a council of Elders, each in charge of a different part of the enormous city and mines. The council was made up of four Dwarves: one for the defenses above and below ground, one for the mines, one for the diplomatic affairs and one for the economic affairs. In times of war however, the four pulled together and created a War Council.

Though many of the outside races didn't realize, Tvan was actually made up of three cities in one. The first city was above ground and was more like a massive fortification, using mostly curtain walls, towers, and a fortified keep over the main mountain entrance. A bulk of the army was stationed on the above ground defenses, alternating with those in the underground cities regularly. The second city was below ground and stretched through underground tunnels and caverns for close to a mile. Anything one could imagine could be found in the city under the mountains, from shops to houses, great courtyards and even an underground lake. It was defended with numerous walls and a massive castle.

Lastly was the small city that served the mining community. It was mostly hundreds of houses with blacksmiths and carpenter shops, but no castle. The mines stretched down into the deepest reaches of the earth.

All and all, Tvan was a part of the world that would never be extinguished no matter what war came its way. Those that called the cities home numbered like the stars in the night sky, and not only Dwarves. Humans, Gnomes, Halflings, and even a few Elves lived among the Dwarves. Each race presented its own talents for the good of the community and for more than a hundred years the cities under the mountains had flourished. In the last ten years, the mines of Tvan produced tons of gems and gold, making mining a very prosperous profession. Not only was Tvan the largest of the cities, but it was by far the richest.

Nimir pushed his cart of tools down the tunnel to an available dig site where he had been the previous day. He passed numerous other Dwarves on his way and gave cheerful nods to each, hopeful to dig up another handful of the gemstones that lay hidden in the earth. The younger Dwarf steadied his lantern as his cart bounced down the tunnel, stopping against the wall with a bang. The other miners around him hardly looked up when he arrived, used to the hundreds of other workers that made a living in the earth. He angled his lantern so that the light shown where he was preparing to dig and pulled his pick from the cart, sinking it into the earth with force. He maintained a steady rhythm of swinging and prying, showering himself with dirt with each swing. Fifteen minutes into his digging, what appeared to be a small emerald was unearthed. He grabbed the stone and held it up to the light of the lantern. The sparkle it gave off made him smile and he tossed it into a padded box at the front of his cart.

"Got one already Nimir?" a Dwarf asked as he pushed his cart past the younger miner.

"Yep, and a good one she is. Bet you give me five minutes more and I will get me another one. Good digging today."

"Well I'm headed down to the gold veins, easier digging for older ones like me. Best of luck to ya."

"Watch your step Ghid, it gets steep on down a little further."

"Youngsters… I've been doing this for forty years… I know where I'm going…" the older Dwarf said as he pushed his cart along.

Nimir happily turned back to the dirt and dove right back in, slinging the dirt in every direction as he picked and pried his way deeper into the earth. His hope of uncovering another stone in five minutes faded as he dug on, not stopping for close to thirty minutes. With sweat running down his face and stinging his eyes, Nimir leaned back against the cart to take a break, catching his breath. He aimed his lantern around the loose dirt and three dull sparkles caught his eye. He grabbed them up, finding two to be emeralds and the third a small ruby. Even though he was sore, a smile spread on his face. He was back in business.

With his body rejuvenated from the find, Nimir started swinging once again. One more stone emerged and he tossed it into the cart with his others. Twenty minutes passed and he didn't see another gemstone. The Dwarf leaned back against his cart once more, throwing his pick into the earth with an exasperated sigh. He wiped the earth from his hands and moved the lantern across the loose dirt to see if anything shone in the light.

"Giving up already lad?" an old Dwarf asked from behind Nimir.

He turned and nodded. "Nah, just resting and thinking. Wonder why it is we kill ourselves in these mines instead of something else. Wonder why I can't just be a soldier, or a... something else. Guess there is just good living in gold and gems."

The old Dwarf leaned against Nimir's cart, listening to what the younger Dwarf had to say. Nimir used the lantern again, hoping to see something he had missed in the dirt but unfortunately, nothing but the dark earth was visible.

"Well, I'll leave you to your digging. Best of luck to ya lad," the old Dwarf said before he wandered up the tunnel to the mining city.

Nimir waved but did not turn from the wall. He picked up a shovel and began moving the piled dirt out of his way, tossing it to the side so he could reach the fresh dig area with ease. When it was cleared the Dwarf went back to digging, determined to find more of the precious gems. On the very last swing he was going to take, a particularly large mass fell free from the earth. Picking it up, Nimir knocked the extra earth from the clump, finding a ruby as large as a robin's egg. For a stone, this was a remarkable find. He gave a little dance and turned to his cart, dropping it in with the others, The moment his stone hit the padding, Nimir dropped his pick with a swell of anger. The small padded box was empty, except for the one ruby he had just put into it.

"That old... that thief! I swear to all that is... I'm going to kill him!" Nimir yelled, turning in every direction to see where the old Dwarf had gone.

When his back was turned, the old Dwarf had swiped the handful of gems in the box and made off with them. Nimir picked up his tools, pocketed his only gem, and shoved the cart against the wall out of the way. He hurried up the tunnel with murder gleaming in his eyes. When he reached the mouth of the mines he looked through the crowds of miners and peddlers, hoping to see the old Dwarf that had walked away with an entire days work. Realizing he had no chance of finding one Dwarf in the masses, Nimir walked through the crowds.

He made his way through the small mining city, his eyes adjusting to the daylight streaming through several cracks in the top of the cavern, to a building in the center where stones were sold to be polished, cut, and eventually turned into jewelry. It was heavily guarded and he stacked his tools on the left side of the door, brushing himself off as he walked in. The Dwarf behind the counter nodded and Nimir handed him the only stone he had, receiving a raised eyebrow and a questionable look.

"Only one today Nimir? You sure seem to be calling it quits early, don't ya think? Feel sick do you?"

"No... I had me five or six more that were very nice and then some old bastard swiped them while I wasn't looking. Just no heart in working any longer today. So what's that one going to bring me?"

The Dwarf in charge held the stone up to the light and set it in a bowl of water to wash it clean of any remaining earth. He dried it and set it on a scale beside him and nodded, scratching his head. "A large ruby indeed, good weight, no damage from a random pick or shovel, let us say it is worth... thirty gold pieces, a fair price I think."

"Yes, very fair, but I want forty." Nimir argued, hoping to get something more for his efforts.

"Forty? Very well lad, thirty five it is and next time keep a closer eye on your cart ya?"

Nimir took the coins and dropped them into a pouch on his belt, leaving the building less than pleased even though he had gotten more coins than he expected. The walk home took roughly twenty minutes on a good day but today wasn't one of those. He took his time, stopping several times to simply lean against the walls and think. The monstrous cavern where the mining community was housed stretched on forever. Rows of houses with the occasional market and blacksmith but most of the shops and venders were in the main chambers where the city of Tvan and its castles were located. He stopped in front of his house and tossed the tools next to the door, trudging in unhappily. For the last three years he had shared his house with his younger brother Gyllan, who through a string of misfortunes had lost his job in the mines.

When Nimir walked in the room he found Gyllan fast asleep in his chair across the room. With his day already having been so bad, the sight of the younger Dwarf sleeping when he should have been working made Nimir angry. Furious with his brother, Nimir crossed the room and kicked the Dwarf's feet out from under his prop on the table.

"Wha... what the... oh Nimir, why you have to wake me like that?"

"Why the hell are you not at work Gyllan? Don't tell me you got fired again. All you had to do was serve drinks to the people at a tavern. What happened, did you drink more than you served?" Nimir shouted angrily.

"No... thank you very much. I quit this morning. You always say things are my fault! I didn't..."

"Not your fault?! You quit you fool, of course it is your fault that you don't have a job! You'd do well to get your life together Gyllan!"

Nimir turned and stormed out of the house, his temple pulsing wildly as he quivered with anger. The door slammed behind him and he grabbed a torch from a steel rack on the wall and walked down the road. He walked down into the darker part of the city where no daylight shone. The flicker of the light from his torch cast an orange glow on the monstrous tunnels as he followed the other torches deep into the mountain. It was the only drawback to a civilization that existed almost entirely underground.

Nimir tossed his torch into the sand outside of the closest tavern and walked. He nodded to the waitress who looked up at him and walked to a table in the corner. It took a few minutes before the waitress arrived but she carried with her a pitcher of water and a small cup. Nimir raised his hand to stop her.

"No water this time dear... ale, strong ale."

"Nimir, you don't drink ale do you? Must have been a bad day."

"Yes, a very bad day, but that's what the ale is for. Come on, let's have it. Give me something to forget this morning."

"Right away..."

Nimir sat at the table by himself and waited for the strong drink to arrive. For it to be just a little past midday, the bar was surprisingly busy. Characters of all types could be seen around the bar drinking and talking. He saw the waitress approaching again, this time with a pitcher of ale. She sat it down on the table and gave Nimir an incredulous look as he grabbed his mug and filled it the second her hand left the pitcher.

"So, if you don't mind me asking Nimir, what's got you so out of shape? I've never seen you like this before," the waitress asked, taking a seat across from the Dwarf.

Nimir downed the drink in his hand and set it on the table, looking at the woman with deep eyes. "Horrid day. Gyllan quit work again and I worked my rear off in the mines all morning only to have everything I found swiped by an old codger while I wasn't looking. I just wish another life would open up and swallow me."

"Wow, that is quite a day. Just slow down a bit. Gyllan will straighten out in time, trust me. If you want another life that badly though, sometimes you have to make the first few changes yourself, for the rest to fall into place. I have to get back to work."

Nimir patted her hand as she stood, showing his appreciation for the talk they had shared and was amazed to find that he did suddenly feel much better. He poured one last drink from the pitcher and drank it slowly, watching the rest of the bar with a curious smile. One of the Dwarves in the corner slapped the waitress on the rear and the entire table erupted in laughter, teasing her as she walked away blushing. He downed the drink and left the mug and pitcher with a pair of coins for the waitress.

Once outside, he picked up his smoldering torch and lit it with one on the side of the cavern wall, giving him instant light once more. He wandered aimlessly, walking from street to street in search of something to help calm his nerves. He wasn't quite ready to head home so he walked further towards the center of Tvan where the castles and armies stayed. It was just shy of a mile following the winding tunnels and caverns but he didn't mind. Anything was better than sitting and brooding. He walked with his head held high.

The first sign of the city came when the corridor opened into a magnificent curtain wall with its own gate and soldiers to guard it. When he passed through the tall gate he found rows of buildings, all with something to sell or some kind of service to provide. The inner city was filled with shops and markets to cater to the massive population. A cluster of large buildings with numerous torches caught his eye. He walked up to the front, finding several racks of weaponry outside.

Nimir admired the steel blades one by one until a particular sword caught his eye. It had a wider blade than most and a longer handle, but the blade was short enough that it could be wielded with two hands or just one. The blade had carvings etched into it but Nimir was unfamiliar with the language. He held the blade out in front of him, testing the weight. The owner appeared at the door.

"You looking for something special friend?" he asked.

"Just looking. What have you inside the buildings?" Nimir asked.

"More weapons, some armors, just come and see when you are ready."

Nimir leaned the sword back against the rack and walked into the first building where racks and racks of weaponry amazed him. Every imaginable sword, axe, mace, spear and more could be found hanging on the walls. Nimir nodded to the man behind the desk and walked slowly through the rooms, looking at each weapon individually before moving into the room holding armor and shields. He spent little time in the room as he knew he could not afford any of the items on the racks or stands. He made his way back out to the racks outside and picked out the same sword he had chosen earlier and drew it back as if to attack an invisible opponent. The Dwarf approached again and this time he was set on selling that weapon.

"I see that you really admire that weapon friend. I can make you a good deal if you would like to own it today. What would you say to… thirty gold?"

"Sheath too?"

"Sure, thirty for the sheath and the sword. I've not had a sale all day so I don't mind dropping the price."

Nimir counted out the gold from the pouch on his belt and handed them to the Dwarf in charge of the shops. "This will do fine, thank you."

He continued deeper into the city with his new sword held over his shoulder. He saw several other blacksmiths and weapon shops along the streets as well as an uncountable number of food markets. He handed a man in one of the food markets a few coppers and grabbed a small sack of apples from his shelf. It was indeed odd for him to be this far away from the mines at this time of day but he rather enjoyed the change. Up ahead in the street was a large group of Dwarven soldiers headed towards him. He stopped and leaned against the wall of a building out of the way as the group hurried past.

Nimir watched them with a sort of envy that he had not felt before. To patrol with other armed soldiers was the kind of job he suddenly longed for. When he had a moment he strapped the sword across his back and carried the bag of apples with him on his way back to his house. Up till now, he had been content on living a life of digging for gems and hiding in the mountains but with the change of day, Nimir suddenly remembered the words of the waitress in the tavern. "Sometimes you have to make the first few changes yourself for the rest to fall into place." It made more sense now. If he wanted a new life, he had to start it himself. No one was going to walk up to him and offer him a new job, a new life, a new adventure. If he wanted it, he had to get it himself.

He found the house empty when he returned and quickly hurried to his bedroom where he dumped what was left of the gold and his sword onto the bed. He packed a sleeping roll and equipment for a camp and set it next to the door. With it he took the bag of apples, a loaf of bread, dried meat, and a skin full of water. When he was done packing, he wrote a note and left it on the mantel, telling Gyllan to keep the house up while he was gone. He strapped the pack across his back with the sword, grabbed his walking staff and down the cavern he went.

The walk was one of confusing nature. He felt happy to be finally getting out of the city and into the real world but at the same time, he felt sad for leaving the only home he had ever known. He knew his brother was lazy, but Nimir hoped that his absence would push Gyllan to straighten out his life. The tunnel ahead was suddenly enveloped in light and Nimir almost ran towards it, eager to see the outside world. The morning sun shocked his eyes and it took quite some time before he was able to adjust to the brightness of the outside world. When he had finally gotten used to the light, Nimir strolled confidently down the hill and through the outer defenses with a quick nod to the soldiers. A cool breeze touched his face and all at once he knew that no matter what the risk of the strange surface world, it would be well worth it all. Nimir took his first steps beyond the city of the Dwarves, looking out across the vast mountains.

"Good day new world… what have you in store for me."

Around the time Nimir was entering the forests at the foot of the mountain, Erzel and his group were doing the same on the opposite side. Though hardly ten miles apart, they worked towards one another without the slightest clue that the other even existed. The Dwarf moved slowly through the trees as it was his first time in the lands. An hour into the forest Nimir stopped for a short rest on a fallen tree. He hadn't been sitting more than ten minutes when footsteps in the brush caught his attention. At first he only heard one but a second and then a third figure could be heard in the trees. Nimir stood and turned in a circle, looking for who or what was around him. He became nervous, unsure of who or what could be just out of sight.

The trees on either side of him seemed to open and out

of them came three large Humans, each with an eager look on their faces. They wore cheap leather armor and wielded rusty weapons, one of which looked to be damaged past the point of effectiveness. All were part of a group that kidnapped and traded slaves away to other races and the sight of a lone Dwarf brought them the excitement of an easy target. They encircled him, staring at Nimir menacingly, their weapons drawn and ready for action. The Dwarf dropped the remainder of his gear and drew his sword from over his shoulder. He raised his weapon to defend himself as the first of the three charged at him.

"Get that Dwarf! Tie him up and drag him into the woods!" one shouted from behind.

Their swords met and they fought back and forth until Nimir swung with all his might, knocking the man, who had clearly underestimated the Dwarf's strength, off balance and to the ground. Wasting no time, he quickly made a swing at the Human, stabbing him through the chest.

Distracted by the first person he had ever killed, Nimir didn't see the second Human charge him. The force of the impact knocked the Dwarf to the ground and sent his sword flying far out of his reach. The Human landed with his knee on the Dwarf's chest and a curved dagger ready to strike. Nimir caught the man by the wrist as he struggled for his life. The knife grazed his cheek and a trickle of blood ran down his chin. He twisted the man's arm and slowly pushed him back.

"Give it up Dwarf... you ain't got a chance."

Just when things looked to be at their worst for Nimir, the Human suddenly fell back as if being pulled by some invisible force. The dagger fell to the ground beside Nimir and he grabbed it, confused as to why the Human had suddenly fallen away. He pushed himself up off the ground, finding the man on his back with a an arrow sticking up from his chest.

He heard something in the brush behind him and turned fearfully, finding an Elf with a bow standing just inside the clearing. The last Human hefted his axe and ran at the Elf but stopped short as the Elf quickly drew another arrow and jerked the bowstring back, aiming between the man's eyes. The axe fell from his hand and he stood rigid, waiting for the pain to come.

"Pick it up," the Elf ordered sternly.

The Human gave a hollow look of disbelief but did not dare move. A drop of sweat rolled down the man's cheek as the bowstring was pulled a little tighter.

"I said pick it up. I'll not kill one who is unarmed."

"Which is precisely why he wouldn't dare retrieve the weapon," a cloaked figure said as it appeared from the trees behind the Elf.

The Elf kept the arrow aimed at the Human for a moment longer, watching as his opponent barely dared to breath. He lowered the bow to the man's chest and waited. The string slowly slid back to the bow and he removed the arrow, taking a step towards the man. "Get moving before I change my mind."

The Human wasted no time in retreating back to the forest from where they had attacked, leaving behind his weapons and the bodies of his fallen comrades. The Elf leaned down and reached out his hand to the Dwarf who took it and pulled himself back up onto his feet. Nimir retrieved his sword and turned back to the two strangers who had just saved his life. The Elf walked up to the young Dwarf and stretched out his hand.

"Greetings young Dwarf, my name is Erzel and this is Kail. Feeling any better now?"

The Dwarf slid the sword back into its sheath and took a few careful steps toward the Elf, shaking his hand. "Nimir... and thank you Erzel."

They shook hands and suddenly more noises started behind the two, making Nimir instantly draw his sword once more. He looked around the two who seemed less than concerned with noises. Erzel turned and watched four more people appear from the trees, all of which were part of the group traveling with him. One by one, the Elf introduced them.

"This is Ectle, our wizard. The Dwarf is Thorgrim, this giant of a man is Rathe, and lastly is Rhen. Everyone, meet Nimir."

They each greeted the young Dwarf who spent extra time around Thorgrim, possibly because of their racial similarities. Erzel and Kail checked the bodies of the two fallen Humans but after finding nothing of interest, they rejoined the group behind them. They had taken the time to help him pull all of his gear together and Rhen handed him the last of it, his walking staff. The group started a campfire and sat around it with their newly made friend, getting a little more comfortable with one another. Ectle had not been sitting for more than ten minutes before he was swallowed by his scrolls.

It soon became evident that the Dwarf was abandoning his life in the city. "Quite amazing that we crossed paths the very day you leave Tvan while we are in fact on our way to that very city. So, why did you leave?" Ectle asked as he set his scrolls down long enough to join the conversation.

"Just got tired of the life inside the city there," Nimir replied. "Tired of digging in the mines and scraping together a living underground. I just wanted to know what it was like to live out here where the world is not confined between two walls."

"You've never been out of the city?" Rhen asked.

"Nope, been there all my life. I never even held a sword until now. I wanted to see just what it felt like to live by your own means in the wilderness, though only a half a day out and I've already needed help to survive. Not a good start huh?"

Rathe pulled the horses into the small clearing and each rider took the reins of their steed. Erzel gave Rhen a hand up into the saddle and followed into his own. Thorgrim and Nimir remained on the ground as the other five rode surrounding them through the forest. The young Dwarf followed close to Erzel, feeling that he owed the Elf a great debt. He knew they were headed back to Tvan and laughed to himself when the reality of not even being able to last a day without winding back up at the Dwarven city set in. Now that he owed someone his life, he had every intention of repaying that debt.

Soon after starting into the mountains, the surface gate of Tvan was visible. The Dwarves quickly closed the gate and soldiers were visible on the walls, preparing in case the strangers had ideas of causing any trouble. Nimir and Thorgrim approached the gate alone. When the guards saw that Dwarves were among the visitors, they opened the gate to allow a handful of soldiers out. One stepped up to Thorgrim, a stern look on his face.

"What business have they in the city of Tvan?" the Dwarf

asked, pointing to the other five adventurers.

"That is Erzel, captain of the High Elves of Pentegarn and Princess Rhen of the Wood Elves of Swanhaven. The rest including myself are here to help escort them. We are here to see the Elders."

"Here to see the Elders?" the soldier repeated.

"Yes, here... to see... the Elders. I thought it was clear the first time I said it but obviously not. Perhaps we need one of them to say it too," Thorgrim said with a nod to Erzel.

The guard felt annoyed as Thorgrim's comments cut him off. He waved to the soldiers at the gate and it opened for the strangers. Erzel led the horses and riders into the courtyard behind the wall. They all dismounted and the head guard stopped them.

"Perhaps the horses might be more comfortable out here. We will take care of them. Underground is no place for such animals."

The Elf nodded and the group pulled their weapons and belongings from the saddles. With their gear in tow they followed the guards through the massive tunnels on their way to the inner city of the Dwarves. The Dwarves could see in the dim torch light but had it not been for Ectle's magic, the rest of the group would have been blind in the darkness. The Dwarves moved swiftly through the dark tunnels as if they knew every inch of the floor and where they should walk. About the time Rhen's feet felt as if they could not take another step, the tunnel opened into a vast underground world. They stood in awe, marveling at the amazing feats of construction.

Massive stone walls stretched into the air with yet another well defended gate and plenty of soldiers to watch it. Towers on either side added protection with countless forms of Dwarves watching their every move. Inside the walls were buildings of every shape and type as far as one could see. The need for torches eased slightly as long cracks in the high cavern ceiling gave off slivers of sunlight, creating a sort of artificial sun at times. The guards led them through the winding city towards the mountainous fortress in the center. The people of the city stopped and stared as the group passed.

"Wow... very impressive indeed." Erzel said when they reached the foot of the castle.

The stairs that led to the mouth of the castle were white marble as were the pillars on either side of the two massive oak doors. The Dwarves pushed the two doors open and followed the group in. The Dwarves were barely five feet tall at best but the halls were three times that in height. The arched ceilings capped the monstrous hallways to perfection. Statues and paintings lined the halls but the group hardly had time to stop and admire the art. Five staircases later they were standing outside a room with a massive number of soldiers keeping guard.

"Here we are. The Elders are inside. Follow me please," the head guard said as the doors were opened.

The Dwarves pushed the doors open and the guard shuffled inside with the group behind him. "Most respectable Elders of Tvan, I would like to introduce Erzel of the High Elves and Princess Rhen of the Wood Elves. Forgive me, I must return to the outer walls."

The four Elders stood from the long stone table, each greeting the group and offering them food and refreshment. The Elder of the surface was Ardis, a stocky Dwarf with a long, brown beard. The one in charge of the underground city was Odar, a smaller Dwarf with a grey beard. The largest of the Elder Dwarves was Divos, the one in charge of the mines and mining community. The last was a blonde Dwarf with a shorter beard who stood over the diplomatic affairs for the Dwarven nation named Velex. They each had a different weapon at their hip and all wore ornamental plated armor. When they had settled into their seats, the Elders probed them for information. Out of the four Elders, only Ardis seemed to have any knowledge of their reasons for venturing to Tvan.

"So Elendil and Tanis decided you'd be safer here. I can't say as I blame them. Never an army made it below the surface. So Erzel, what can you do?"

The Elf looked at Ardis. "What precisely do you mean?"

"Well, one doesn't become the leader of the entire High Elf army without a set of skills. Where would you say your expertise lies?"

"Weapons, my sword and my bow. On top of that I was very experienced in the lands south of Tvan before joining with King Elendil and his Elves. Why do you ask?"

The four Elders talked quietly between themselves, discussing the Elf's skills and his past. Velex got up and with a nod to the group, left the table to attend to business elsewhere. The remaining three Dwarves turned back to Erzel and Ardis spoke slowly to him.

"Well Erzel, perhaps we could use your expertise in the fields of weaponry during your stay with us. I am sure that your group with talents of this caliber can really help out around here. No objections?"

"None..." Erzel replied, with a shake of his head. "Though I would prefer a position above ground if such is available. I find that I may not be very effective in these dark caverns, even if my eyes do adjust."

Ardis turned to Odar and spoke quietly. They glanced together at the Elf and smiled. "We will find something for you. Now, in the meantime, please make yourselves comfortable in the castle. We will send for you when we've need of you."

As they left the room, Ectle stopped and turned back to the Elders, crossing the room to speak with them. He gave the three Dwarves an inquisitive look and nodded. "Honorable Elders, may I ask where your records and libraries are kept? I have some research I would very much like to continue."

Odar nodded. "Two floors down, second set of doors after the marble archway. Everything you need will be at your disposal so take all the time you need."

"Thank you."

Ectle split away from the group and headed down the stairs, following the directions of the Elder. He walked into the library and marveled at the hundreds of shelves that were filled with books, scrolls, and maps. He found a table in the back of the library and leaned his staff against the wall behind him. With the help of two Dwarves and hours of looking he was able to find two books that pertained to the Dragon race. He sat down and whispered softly, using the same spell he had in the forests to allow him to see clearly in the dim light.

He flipped through the pages slowly, making sure to read every inch of each page before turning to the next. He walked back to the shelf where he had found the books, pulled down a pair of scrolls and walked back to his desk. With the mess of books, scrolls and maps spread across the desk, he studied for an hour, trying to find something to connect the Dragons to the rest of the myth. In one of the books, the symbols and words would have appeared more of a jumbled mess to someone who had not learned the old language.

The wizard set the book aside and produced a small leather one from under his robes. He flipped through the old tattered pages quickly until he opened to a page with similar writing. He compared each line to the one in his book and found the similarities to be remarkable. The book that he had studied for the past ten years had the same history as the records in the Dwarven city. He studied the two very closely and every few pages, something that he did not have in his book appeared on the scrolls. Ectle flipped through his book until he opened to a hand drawn map which he set down next to the larger map from the archives. Seeing what he expected to find, the wizard rolled the map and scrolls together and returned his book to its place under his cloak. He grabbed the books and hurried back to the stairs.

His feet barely touched the ground as he took the stairs two at a time. He hardly glanced at the first two doors he passed but slid to a stop at the third, knocking on it as he pulled it open. Scanning the room quickly, the wizard sensed the captain and Princess on the balcony.

"Erzel! Erzel, I need to speak with you."

"Out here Ectle," the Elf replied.

The wizard joined the two on the balcony, pondering to himself why an underground city would even have a view. The only thing visible other than the outlines of the hundreds of buildings were thousands of torches and candles lining the city. The limited sunlight streaming through the ceiling of the giant cavern seemed to soak only the castle in its light.

Ectle unloaded his scrolls and books on the table in the center of the room and waited for Erzel and Rhen to join him.

Once they were around the table, the wizard muttered inaudible words to himself. From the palm of his hand came a small ball of light no bigger than an apple but so bright that it gave the room the look of midday.

"Quite a useful spell Ectle," Erzel noted as he watched the ball of light split into two and hover above them.

"Thank you. This is quite an amazing find for just a few hours of research. You surely remember the myth of the Dragons that we spoke briefly of while we were in Murm and in the forests before the port city. Well, these Dwarven archives have much more information than I thought, and combined with my own, it is very useful indeed."

"Alright then, tell us what it is you've uncovered Ectle."

"It explains why the island that the Dragons is so hard to locate. The island has been recorded more than eight times… all in different places. This could mean the island disappears and then reappears or that the island floats so that it is never in the same place twice. Now, judging from these notes and drawings, taking in to consideration where the other sightings took place and when, I can possibly predict with some accuracy where to find it. Judging the length of time between encounters and the distance, I think I can locate the Dragons. What do you think?"

"I think some myths remain myths for a reason. Perhaps the Dragons are so hard to find for good reason. I think they want to stay hidden. Be that as it may, if you wish to further pursue this information, feel free."

"Thank you Erzel, I will. With this information I could have a destination within a few days. The language is old, and has to be deciphered first, but I will find it."

The wizard pulled his work and books together and headed out of the room, his ball of light leading the way. He stopped in the doorway and turned back to the two Elves. "If you have a need of me, I will be in the library."

Erzel gave a low nod and walked Rhen back out to the balcony. They stopped at the railing, admiring what view was available. The city had a very primitive look from the castle. The houses and shops were all carved stone with wooden roofs and the smaller stands and markets were simple wooden structures.

No real decorative design was put into building the city but with it being underground, away from the eyes of the world, it made sense to keep it as simple as possible. Erzel compared the simple Dwarven city before him to the elaborately ornate designs of Pentegarn. It made him miss home.

"Are you ok?" Rhen asked suddenly, seeing the obvious distant expression on his face.

Her voice brought him back to the balcony. "Huh? What did you say Princess... I mean Rhen?"

"It's ok, I was just wondering what was bothering you. You look like you're somewhere else. Is it what Ectle was talking about?"

"No."

"Then what is it. You can talk to me Erzel."

"Just thinking about home. I don't want to bother you about that because I know you long to be there as well. This is cozy though... for now."

"I know. I miss home too but there is nothing we can do about it here. We just have to keep our heads and hearts here for the time being. It's not that bad in the mountains. So what do you think about Ectle's research?"

"Honestly?"

"Well of course."

"I think it is a bit of a wild goose chase. If he can locate the Dragons and if we could make it to the island, there is still no telling what those creatures will do to us. They are isolated for a reason and they may prefer staying unseen."

Rhen took a few steps closer to him, touching his wrist. "So, you don't believe me when I told you and Ectle about that dream... or whatever it was?"

"No Rhen, I believe you. I'm not skeptical, I'm just concerned. We have so much going on around us. Is it safe to go after a myth that we're not sure of?"

The Princess was inches away from the captain and turned so her back was to the Elf's chest and leaned back. Erzel stood confused, not sure what had made her make the move that she had and not sure what he was expected to do now. She had her eyes closed and scarcely breathed as her weight slowly increased against his chest. He nervously reached up with his right hand and ran his fingertips through her long red hair, hoping not to offend her by doing so. He stroked her hair slowly, staring down at her.

"Why so nervous?" she asked, taking a step away and turning around to see his face.

"It's just... you're the Princess, and I'm... just a soldier. What chance would there be for love between us? It just doesn't seem possible," Erzel said sadly, walking back into the room.

"Love? Erzel... wait!"

By the time Rhen made it into the room, Erzel had closed the door and disappeared into the halls outside. She stood next to the table where Ectle had spread the maps and scrolls. She was stunned by his hasty disappearance, wondering if it was her sudden approach towards him that pushed him away or the mention of love that made him uneasy. She remembered how he had talked about love, like something he had never before had time to pursue. She walked slowly back out onto the balcony, rubbing her arms as a chill ran up her body. She chewed her lip, wondering how long it would be before the captain returned.

Bloodstains Along the Borders

The safety of the Dwarves sadly did not extend to the war torn region around Mihlann. The walls still stood at the besieged city but the defenses had received a massive amount of damage in the last assault. A long period of inactivity gave the southern forces time to equip their armies with crude catapults. The walls around the gate were missing chunks of stone and cracked but they refused to fall no matter how much pounding they received. Though their new weapons made a difference on the battlefield, the armies of the south continued to have no luck in swarming the castle. They were pushed back every time they got to the walls.

After twenty minutes of continuous bombardment, the Elves managed to strike the makeshift catapults with their own, destroying them for good. By the time the southern armies charging up the ladders to the wall realized the loss of their weaponry, the Elves had recovered and slaughtered everything coming over the edge of the wall. With the losses piling up, the Goblins began yet another hasty retreat into the forests. As the battle came to an end, the Elves accessed the damages and losses.

The gate itself had sustained noticeable damage and the Elves found themselves using wooden beams and poles to reinforce the massive wooden doors. Weakened, they could not withstand many more attacks. Many of the weapons the Elves used in their defenses had been destroyed, leaving one ballista and two catapults to hold off the horde and protect the city. With his numbers dropping and resources dwindling, Raziel stood overlooking the battlefield with a worried look on his bloodied face. Soldiers wearing the same look of despair joined their commander to watch for the seemingly endless enemies.

"Should we prepare to abandon the city my Lord?" an archer asked, wiping the blood from his brow with the back of his hand.

Raziel shook his head. "No. If we leave this city there will be nothing to prevent the southern invaders from laying siege to Swanhaven and Pentegarn. We are the buffer that allows them a chance to prepare."

"Great... we are going to die to give them a few days longer..." the archer complained as he walked away.

The commander watched as the soldiers locked the beams and braces behind the gate and returned to their posts. He looked upon half the soldiers he had started with and sighed, knowing there would soon be more Elves lost than alive. He picked up a spear at his feet and leaned against the shaft. The blade of the weapon was stained red with dried blood, much like the city. A gentle rain had started and across the walls raindrops could be heard as they splashed against the armor of the Elves. A chorus of rain against the metal filled the air. Raziel watched with a heavy heart as the first lines of the southern armies began appearing from the trees.

Once again it seemed that no matter how many of the Goblins and Ogres died trying to raid the city, new numbers took their places. The Elves on the other hand had not seen reinforcements in quite some time and the gaps in the their defenses showed just how desperate their efforts to hold the city had become. What remained of Raziel's soldiers lined up on the walls and prepared for yet another mess. The Knights urged their horses in behind the crippled gate with their swords drawn in case the defenses were broken. Morale was low as the Ogres moved closer, dragging with them several new catapults. As soon as they saw them, the Elves began adjusting their own weapons, hoping to strike quickly at the siege equipment. As all the times before, the Goblins and Ogres came to a stop and their leader Uljic appeared. The odd creature looked up to the walls and pointed at Raziel.

Ignoring honor, the Elf pointed back at it. "Archer, kill that creature!"

The soldier to his right drew an arrow from his quiver and notched it, pulling the bowstring back and aiming. He fired, watching it sail down at the creature. The creature, too, watched the arrow and before the projectile could find its mark, Uljic tilted his head to the side. The arrow hissed as it streaked by the creature's head and buried into the ground. Uljic pointed up to the Elf and drew his finger across his throat. The Elf tightened his grip on his sword and drew it from its sheath, brandishing it angrily. Soldiers all across the wall did the same.

"Archers, make ready!"

The Elves wielding bows pulled arrows and notched them to the bowstrings, pulling the strings back and aiming into the fields below. As the Elves prepared to fire, the Goblins shadowed their moves, drawing their own bows to fire. Raziel steadied his shield and took a deep breath. Even from the distance he could see the rusty tips of the Goblin arrows quivering, waiting for the chance to taste Elf blood. Knowing that it could be their last stand at the castle, Raziel locked his feet against the battlements, preparing to give his life with pride and honor.

"Fire!"

The order rang across the walls and through the field below as both sides released their arrows. Hundreds of arrows slit the sky. Some Elves fell from the wall to the field below but Raziel ducked behind his shield, hearing two strike the sturdy cover. From the edge of his shield he watched their catapults release their massive boulders.

Raziel turned to the soldiers on the wall and yelled. "Take cover!"

As the rocks struck the walls they shook the entire battlement and everyone on it violently. The last two catapults of the Elves fired back, scattering the bodies of Goblins across the field. Unfortunately, they landed short of the siege weapons. The two sides continued to exchange fire with arrows as the catapults were loaded for a second attack. Raziel looked desperately across the walls as Elves continued to fall from the hail of arrows and crossbow bolts. He spotted the ballista and pointed to the Elves manning it.

"Ballista, fire! Archers, fire at will! Drive them back!"

The oversized crossbow turned slightly and launched its giant spear into the mass of Ogres, skewering two of them before driving into the earth. The battle between the two races was rapidly changing into a possible storming of the city. Raziel watched the giant ladders appear from the trees again and immediately they forced the ladders up against the walls. Swarms of Goblins rushed up the ladders as the scattered Elves readied themselves for the onslaught to come. The first of the Goblins crossed the edge of the battlements and were instantly knocked from the wall with arrows and spears. As the battle intensified on the wall, the creatures below altered the trajectory of their catapults, hoping to hit the battered gate.

The Goblins hesitated for just a moment before letting the catapults release their powerful attacks. Out of the six siege weapons the enemy possessed, only two of their attacks met their targets. Four boulders struck the strong stone wall while two of them found their mark, turning the weakened gates into a shower of wooden splinters. The door broke in half, sending huge pieces of wood and stone in on the Knights and even knocking one from his horse.

Raziel lowered his shield to look over the edge, finding the gate fallen and his Knights left as the only form of buffer between the hordes outside of the city and the Elves within. Once the gate had been destroyed, both armies seemed to hesitate, both watching the remains of the gate collapse in on itself, neither one ready to make the initial charge into battle. Once the dust had settled, the wall of Ogres rushed towards the gaping cavity created by the catapults. The Knights pressed their horses together at the opening, preparing to defend the bottleneck the gate created. The commander pointed to the Knights desperately.

"Hold the gate! Do not fall back!"

He shook his head to himself, knowing that even with the might of the Knights below, they wouldn't be able to hold them off forever. He blocked another arrow with his shield and stepped back as another ladder landed at the top of the wall. Waiting patiently, he delivered a powerful overhead swing down on the Goblin at the top of the ladder, braining him then pulling his sword back for another attack. Three more Goblins fell to the same fate before the Elf was forced to drop back away from the ladder. His Elves had been scattered into pockets of resistance but they stood their ground, refusing to give the city up without putting everything they had into defending it first.

"Commander! Commander what do we do? Orders sir?" one Elf cried out as he dodged an arrow.

Raziel cut one last Goblin from the ladder and turned to the Elf. "Hold the wall. Do not retreat! Archers keep firing!"

The orders seemed simple but the creatures were starting to swarm the battlements. Raziel stabbed one after another but his progress was slow. He ducked left and slammed his shield into one creature's chest, finishing it off with a quick thrust of his bloody sword. Seeing the loss on the battlements, Raziel turned to the Knights below and was pleased to see them fighting the Ogres off. The bottleneck created a narrow area where only five or six of the creatures could squeeze into and it gave the Knights and archers room to kill anything that came in front of them. Though they were fighting and holding, Raziel reluctantly decided it was a lost cause, seeing the ladders flooded with Goblins and Hobgoblins.

"Fall back to the keep! Everyone back to the keep!" he ordered morbidly, shoving one creature off the battlement from behind.

The Elves held the walls long enough for Raziel to retreat back through them and then the rest of the soldiers followed, using the archers already at the keep to hold the Goblins back far enough. The Knights fought madly at the battered gate, trying their best to hold the flood of enemies off until the bulk of their numbers was safely inside the fortress keep. With a handful of Knights and soldiers still outside fighting, Raziel ordered the castle gates closed and braced, praying to be forgiven for sentencing those Elves to their deaths.

The screams and sounds of battle slowly died out below and the Elves within the heavily fortified keep peered over the walls, watching as the flood that had once settled outside of the city made its way in. The catapults the Elves had used were now out of reach, lost forever to the enemies who began turning them around to use against the keep. The sight of his own siege weapons being used against him made Raziel sick to his stomach. Lines of archers took positions on the outer walls and suddenly the creature Uljic appeared, seemingly untouched from the battle.

The gate to the keep was stronger than the one at the outer wall but even with its reinforced construction of wooden beams and metal braces, it would only be a matter of time before the enemy penetrated the city even further. Feeling that victory was out of their reach, Raziel sat down and leaned against the stone wall, letting out a breath that he had held for what seemed like forever. One of the Knights arrived from the lower levels of the keep, his tunic and armor stained red with blood.

"Commander? Commander Raziel are you alright?"

"I'm fine. Will the gate to the keep hold?"

"For a time yes. Sir, we need to prepare. It will not be long before they find a way to scale these walls and break the gate down. What have we left?"

"Left… it is a sad thing to see. We started this siege with close to a thousand Elves and now we're less than three hundred. No catapults, two ballista on the keep walls, and no morale or hope in any of our forces. A devastating blow has been dealt to us in more than one way."

"Morale, my Lord, can return. Show them you believe. Show them we will not give up, we will not go quietly. We may not have the numbers we started with, but we are fighting all the same. If they see you haven't given up, it will be easier for them to have hope as well."

Raziel looked at the Knight and realized every word the Elf had spoken was true. If he walked around defeated, so would his soldiers. There was still a chance to hurt the enemy, to give them a reason to remain at Mihlann instead of moving on to Swanhaven or Pentegarn. If the Elves gave up, all that they had fought for so far would be lost in seconds. Raziel extended his hand to the Knight who helped him to his feet. With a nod, the commander turned around to the Elves on the upper walls, ordering them to gather.

"Alright, listen up and listen good. The enemy has the city, not our keep. We hold this keep until every single one of us is dead. The longer we fight them here, the longer it will take for the army to move north into the other lands. Are you with me

Elves?"

The Elves were quiet, but slowly a cheer from the wary and tired soldiers could be heard across the walls and in the keep. Raziel turned to the Knight and nodded, realizing that the soldier had probably just saved the heart of the Elves that remained alive. Sheathing his sword, Raziel followed the Knight into the keep as the soldiers prepared for the next wave of attacks guaranteed to come. He leaned his shield against the wall and collapsed into a chair at one of the tables in the war room to rest for a few minutes. The Elves began readying the defenses for a new type of siege, one with taller walls but fewer soldiers to defend them. Some of the Elves still felt the desperation they arrived in the keep with, feeling that no matter what happened, they had no chance of surviving. The keep would be their tomb, even if they only survived days or if they made it weeks, nearly every Elf there knew that time was something they were quickly running out of. As the Elves prepared, so did their enemies and Raziel knew that before nightfall, bloodshed would return.

Erzel walked through the halls of Tvan followed by a glowing orb similar to the one Ectle had conjured. It hovered a foot above and behind the Elf granting daylight in the underground world. Some of the Dwarves in the castle seemed almost insulted by the magic light, skulking away into their usual dim torchlight. Erzel stepped past the guards holding the throne room door open and looked upon the Elders of Tvan and the group that had followed him with the exception of Rhen. The wizard reached out and wrapped his fingers around the ball of light, extinguishing it slowly. The torches regained their superiority in the room and the Dwarves seemed more comfortable.

"Glad you could join us Erzel, I was about to send for you." Ardis said with a nod as he stood from the table.

"Good timing I suppose," Erzel replied. "So what is it I can do for the council?"

The Elder Dwarf sat once more, leaving the group standing without so much as offering them a chair. Ardis and Odar remained seated as the other two Elders left the table to tend to their own affairs. Ardis slid a few candles closer to the map that he had laid out on the table and motioned for them to come closer.

"Odar and I believe we may have found a suitable task for your skills and background. To our west you see a small port village here. We've lost any communications with that area and trade routes have been cut off. Possibly Goblins, more likely a mixture of everything Valsera has to offer. There is a small mountain fortress here that overlooks the valley and ocean but it too has not been heard from in quite some time. I fear that the enemies are mounting an attack by shipping an army into this port. Whether they pose a threat or not, I seriously doubt it."

"So... you want me to ride to the port and see if it is still even there?"

"Not exactly. You see, this fortress can be reached by the ocean as well as by entering this narrow river here and following it down to the mountains. From there it is merely a few hours walk. If you still want to serve us, I would ask that you take your group to that city and if it remains in the hands of our Dwarves, you will be head of it. A Lord over the fortress."

"What sort of defenses does this fortress have?" Thorgrim asked, reviewing the positioning and natural earth formations depicted on the map.

"Nestled among the cliffs, a very strong wall formation, the very location makes it more than difficult to assault or lay siege to. Right now there is a force of between thirty and forty Dwarves defending it, give or take a few. It is not a very battle prone area but it does have its uses," the Dwarf said calmly, looking from the wizard to the Elf.

Erzel looked at the map quietly as he pondered the position of the fortress and its value to the Dwarven lands and how it could be used against the enemy. On the map he noticed the spot marking the port. The two were not far apart. Overall, it was not a very bad offer. If babysitting a fortress was all the Dwarves had to offer, he wondered if he should take it and leave the Princess in Tvan. Then again, the King of the Wood Elves had requested that he not leave her side.

"I never realized there was a port this far north. How long has it been there and how long ago was it when you lost contact with the Dwarves there?"

"The port has been there for as long as I can remember and we lost any sort of contact with them about... hmmm, I'd say four weeks ago."

"Is there a reason why you haven't sent a force of your own to see what the problem might be?" Kail asked suddenly, catching what appeared to him to be a flaw in the story.

"It hasn't been a priority. We've much that must be done but if Erzel would like to help in some way, it could be a valuable service. It is not something that must be done mind you, it is just an offer."

Erzel looked down at the map again and looked at the route through the ocean that eventually cut back down through the mainland to the mountains where they would find the fortress and its occupants. The opportunity of a ship and a general direction in which they should travel almost coincided with Ectle's theory of the Dragon Isles so well that Erzel wondered if the wizard had somehow influenced the Dwarves to appoint the task to the group so he could persuade them to join him in searching for the Dragons. He looked up at the wizard out of the corner of his eye, wondering if the thoughts he was having were possible. Ectle was once again talking with Ardis about the libraries and the records he had found in them.

"Ardis, I would accept your offer without hesitation, but I would like the opportunity to speak with my group before I make any hasty decisions. Would you mind if we meet back here in an hour or so? Give us time to talk things over."

The Dwarf gave a slow nod. "I see no harm in that. Take your time lad as time is something you have plenty of. We will be here when you've decided what you would like to do."

The Elf thanked the Dwarves and followed the group out of the room, twisting and turning through the halls until they came to the room where Erzel was staying. He pushed the door open and everyone gathered round as he stopped on the wide balcony outside. He gave a suspicious look to the wizard, trying to decide the best way to ask what he wanted to know.

"Ectle... just curious, but have you the ability to influence people to say and do what you want?" he asked, forgoing subtlety.

"At times perhaps. It is not an easy task to accomplish though. Why do you ask?"

"Well, it seemed a touch odd that the Elder Dwarves are asking us to complete a task that would also give you the ability to pursue even deeper your seemingly mad studies of these Dragons. Did you not claim you could plot a course that would intercept their island? And would you, having a ship and crew, be able to reach it if you used this influence on us?"

The rest of the group watched as the Elf and the wizard talked back and forth, not quite sure what the argument was about or who was in the right. "Well, I could do that. However, I do not recall using my abilities to sway their decision to offer you a post that requires a trip around the coast in the ocean. My respect for the Elders prevents me from making such a move on their free will."

Erzel looked down at the stone floor, feeling somewhat foolish about his suspicions. He knew that Ectle had not an evil intent, but his deep fascination with a race that was not proven to exist did unnerve the Elf slightly. He kicked the edge of the railing, cursing himself for being so quick to judge the wizard.

"Forgive me Ectle, I should not have judged you so. I just thought the events seemed too perfect to be a simple coincidence. I suppose I should ask the lot of you what you think about our current position and our options."

"Don't really matter to me what you decide to do Erzel, I'm gonna follow you," Rathe blurted out, clapping the Elf on the back.

"Good... what about the rest of you?"

Kail and Nimir gave simple nods to show they agreed and Thorgrim merely grunted at the question. Ectle looked at the captain with a new light in his eyes, as if he had a great many questions to ask.

"Erzel... what about Rhen? Did you not swear to never leave her side until she was safely home in Swanhaven?"

"Yes but I..."

"How do you think she is going to react when she finds that you are planning on leaving her here while you go defend a fortress in the mountains."

"Well I wasn't..."

"You weren't planning on taking her with you were you? I could not imagine moving her from the safety here to simply ensure she did not go without you."

"Ectle... if you would just..."

"... and if I was correct in the location of the Dragon Isles, would you take her there?"

"Ectle... stop talking!" Erzel shouted. "One, I don't know what I am going to do yet, two, I have no idea how to tell Rhen, and three, how did those damned Dragons get into this argument again? Seriously, are you sure you didn't mess with those Elder Dwarves and make this a journey of your own interest?"

"Fairly sure master Elf. Very well, I will leave you to decide what to do and how to explain it to the Princess. We will meet you in the throne room once you've finished," the wizard replied with an expressionless face.

Ectle and the rest of the group except Nimir left the room to return to their rooms or to the throne room. When Thorgrim left the room, Rhen caught the door before it could close, walking in quietly, almost eavesdropping on the conversation on the balcony between the young Dwarf and Elf.

"So... how do you plan to tell her Erzel?" Nimir asked, looking out at his home city with a new love. He had never before spent time inside the great fortress of Tvan.

"Tell me what?"

The two turned and found Rhen standing in the doorway between the bedroom and the balcony. Her beautiful red hair seemed to shine in the dim light thrown at them by the torches and candles. Nimir walked slowly past her, giving a slight nod to the Elf as he left the two to have their conversation in private.

"Tell me what?" she repeated, taking a few steps closer.

"Princess, I didn't expect to see you quite yet. Are you well?" he asked, trying to find a way to tell her the news about their possible departure.

"I am, and please stop avoiding my question Erzel. What is it that you have yet to tell me? I am a big girl, I can handle whatever it is that has gone wrong. Was it news from home?"

"No. Here, sit down," he said, pulling a chair up next to the balcony. He did the same, sitting beside her. "Alright, the Elders of Tvan have offered me a duty to help them while we are here under their protection."

"That is great Erzel. What is it?"

"Well, it is a fortress at the edge of the mountains that the Dwarves use to watch their western lands. It needs fortification and they wish to give me that task. It will not be a very safe area and it is possible that the port city even further west has already been overrun by Valsera's forces. Because of that... it may best if... well, if you remain here while my forces and I carry out this task."

Rhen looked at him incredulously. "I know you are not about to say what I think. There is no way, no way you are going anywhere and leaving me somewhere else. Might I remind you of the vow you made my father back in Pentegarn?"

"Yes Rhen, I remember that vow all too well, but I was not meant to stay under the mountains. It unnerves me, makes me feel uneasy at all times. I was a soldier before this, and it is a soldier that I long to be now."

"Then take me with you!"

"You know I can not. Rhen, you will be safe here, and when my duty is done at that fortress, when I have gathered the information needed and fortified their position, I will return to Tvan, I promise."

Rhen got out of her chair and looked at Erzel sadly, not knowing whether to believe what she was hearing or not. At the moment, it seemed like a cruel joke to her that someone she had grown attached to was about to leave her behind. It wasn't supposed to happen like this. He wasn't supposed to go.

"Never make a promise that you can not keep, captain."

The Princess turned and left Erzel sitting in his seat on the balcony, his head swimming in a sort of disbelief. He knew it would hurt her to find that she would not be joining them on their mission, but it was the first time she had ever addressed him as "captain". The formality caught him off guard and all at once he realized how cross she was with him. Instead of just being sad, she was hurt and angry. Erzel pushed the two chairs back to the table and fumbled for his next choice of actions. So far, things had not gone so well.

While walking back to the throne room where the Elders and most of his group would be, Erzel rolled the journey around his head, remembering the stay in Murm, the night in the woods hiding from the Goblins, and several other events that had most likely pulled the Princess and himself closer together. Perhaps she felt deeper for him than he had realized and by leaving her in Tvan, Erzel had broken her heart. He was a soldier, and knew that the wound was one that would mend with time.

The same Dwarves pushed the doors open as he approached and admitted him into the throne room once again where he found everyone had returned with the exception of Thorgrim. Erzel trudged on through the room, unhappy with himself and not looking at the members of his group as he made his entrance. Ardis and Odar nodded to him as he sat down across from them and the rest of his companions gathered around him, waiting for the Elf to address the two Elders. Ectle stood the closest, as if he was desperate to know the decision the captain had chosen. Erzel turned in the chair and stared back at the wizard, his eyes probing the man for a moment.

"Ectle, will you join us?" he asked quietly, motioning to the chair next to him.

The Elders looked at one another and then at the Elf as the wizard took his seat next to the captain. The wizard waited, looking at the Erzel with confusion befitting the sudden events.

"What can I do to be of service?" he asked, a hint of confusion in his voice.

Erzel looked at the wizard cautiously. "Are you certain… that you can accurately predict where to find that island?"

The Dwarves were at a loss for what the two were talking about but the wizard showed a look of beaming happiness. The words the Elf had just spoken showed a rejuvenated interest in the matter. "Yes, I can. It will take a little time and I will have to get to work immediately, but I believe so."

"Good, get to work."

"Excuse me, could you please let us know what it is you are planning, considering you are within our city borders," Ardis asked quietly with a bit of an ill tone.

"Very well. I am sorry to say this but I must decline your offer to make contact with the fortress to our west. I know I asked for the task, but another matter has presented itself and I must say, it appeals to our interest in a far greater manner."

Odar, who had not made a sound in a long time slapped his hand on the stone table. "Well, what is this interest of yours? Perhaps it is our interest as well."

"I am not at liberty to discuss that as I do not quite understand the situation fully myself. Ectle is the main architect behind the idea, so I would prefer he explains it when he gets the chance. The Princess will remain here and I will ask that you continue to offer the ship and crew to have at our disposal."

Ardis and Odar looked at one another and nodded. "Done."

All Eyes Upon the Elves

The nightfall at Mihlann did not bring with it a very peaceful time for the Elves. No more than an hour after the sun had disappeared behind the mountains, a massive offensive was launched against the keep. The Elves used every means they could to hold the Goblins back and were easily successful, finding that the Ogres and siege weapons were not even used during the attack. Overwhelming numbers of Goblins and Hobgoblins swarmed the walls using newly constructed ladders and ropes. At one point, they managed to get to the battlements of the keep but were easily turned by the Elves with their renewed strength and courage. Bodies fell from the walls and piled in the streets and courtyards as the enemies refused to draw back.

Several hours passed and the Elves traded their tired and wounded for fresh soldiers from within the keep, replenishing their numbers the only time they would be able. When the Elves pushed the last of the creatures from the walls, the catapults were moved a little closer, positioned so that with a little altering, they could eventually be used to break the gates. Raziel looked down at the street that led from the outer wall to the keep, watching numerous masses of soldiers moving into position for the next attack. Since they had fallen back to the keep Raziel had not seen a sign of Uljic, but with the enemy continuing to move on the keep, he could only assume that Uljic had not been killed in the volleys of arrows that had blanketed the city.

Raziel looked out across the smoldering city with a heavy heart, watching as a full battalion of Wood Elves appeared from the forests to their north and engaged the Goblins at the edges of the enemy formations. The archers picked off dozens of the creatures before they could mobilize to strike the Elves. When the charge was issued, Raziel watched helplessly as Ogres and Goblins closed from both directions, crushing the Elves in a pair of coordinated attacks. What was left immediately fell back into the forests, trying to get away to send for help. Soldiers gathered along the battlements to watch their Elven brothers in battle and see them fall in the end.

"Where did they come from my Lord?" one asked, watching the Wood Elves trying to defend themselves.

"Probably a battalion stationed on the edge of their lands that ventured far enough south to realize we were under siege. Sadly, they were not prepared to deal with the numbers we face."

"I can't believe it... the Goblins within our walls didn't even turn to help those outside. It's like they don't care their comrades are being killed while they try so hard to get into our keep."

"Valsera's numbers have never cared about anything other than their own self gain. If they lose ten thousand soldiers but take one city, Valsera will be pleased. It is a sick way to win a war."

"Tell me about it. Throw enough of your own soldiers at a city and if they all die, just send another army. I wonder how many soldiers he has at his disposal in the southlands," a Knight asked as he approached.

Raziel watched the last of the visible Wood Elves fall out of sight as the Ogres charged through them. "Fifteen minutes and the entire Wood Elf battalion was destroyed. They weren't prepared. They had no idea."

"Looks to me like they are tired of waiting on the gate to fall, look."

The Knight pointed to the catapults that were slowly being wheeled into the streets and aimed at the gate. Only three could fit but the three were enough to break down the wooden structure with little effort. Elves notched arrows and drew the bowstrings back, preparing to fire on the mass of soldiers gathering in the streets below who in turn were readying to scale the walls with huge ladders and long ropes tipped with hooks.

As the soldiers of the south turned their sights to the keep once more, Ogres began filling in behind the walls of Goblin soldiers, waiting for their chance to get in an attack on the last gate between them and the Elves. Raziel sheathed his sword and pulled a spear from the rack on the wall, looking down at the soldiers as the ladders began to rise into the air. He looked to his left and right at the last of his soldiers and nodded.

"Fire at will!"

Archers across the walls began blanketing the ground with volleys of arrows, causing two of the ladders to fall back to the ground. Goblins fired back, but their aim was not as good as the Elves and only a handful of their targets were hit. The remaining two ladders continued to rise, their speed hindered by the added weight of countless Goblins clinging to the ladders, hoping to be the first to strike the Elves. Archers tried to pick the creatures off but were unsuccessful. The huge ladders crashed against the walls and Goblins were flung from the tops into the mass of Elves, swords and axes swinging wildly. Raziel ducked under the body of one such enemy and watched as three Elves ran their blades through its chest, letting it slide to the ground in a bloody heap.

Standing at the edge of the battlement, Raziel barely had time to move as an arrow whizzed by his head, taking a chunk out of his ear and causing him to fall back in pain, blood dripping down the side of his head. He hefted the spear and threw it as hard as he could, striking a Goblin that had just made it to the top of the ladder, sending it bouncing down the ladder to the ground below. He grabbed a second spear and when he turned, the enemy had closed to within a few steps, a bloody axe lifted above its head. The commander dodged to the right and a Knight appeared behind the Goblin, cleaving its head with one hard swing of his sword.

"Commander, more ladders coming. They're going to swarm us over if we don't fall back inside the keep!"

"No! We fall back no further. I'm tired of running. Stand your ground!"

The soldier turned back to the wall and continued to drop the creatures arriving up the ladders. Things were looking bleak as the Elves who had been well disciplined and precise with their actions were now reacting desperately against the massing number of Goblins that had managed to penetrate the keep. One of the Elves at the wall turned and shouted at Raziel, pointing out into the city.

"Catapults!"

The words echoed in the Elf's ears and for some reason, everything around him was silent. He couldn't see the catapults, but seconds after the soldier warned him of the danger, a massive stone boulder struck the upper battlements, sending soldiers of both sides flying in every direction. The wall crumbled onto the Goblins below as a second boulder struck the upper defenses.

"Why do they not attack the gate?" one archer asked as he crawled to the captain.

"I don't know. Fire back!"

The ballista that had been manned at the two corners of the keep battlement was deserted, allowing the enemy easy access to the walls. The commander threw his spear at a random Goblin and ran for the closest siege weapon, grabbing it around the shaft to release the monstrous bolt. He didn't bother aiming but instead jerked the mechanism, watching the bowstrings snap forward, hurtling the projectile out into the city. Some of the enemy were lucky enough to scatter but several Ogres and Goblins took the full force of the attack in a shower of dirt and rock as the spear struck the edge of a building.

Before he could grab a second spear to use in the ballista, six Goblins rushed across the battlements at him, their weapons drawn and ready. He ripped his sword from its sheath and brandished it drastically, dodging the first three enemies and cutting the fourth's head from its shoulders. The last two stabbed and slashed but out of the group, only one landed a blow, the head of a spear in the Elf's hip. He cried out in pain as he struck the creature down. Elves arrived around him to finish the creatures as a third boulder struck the castle, shaking it violently.

Raziel stumbled forward, leaning against the wall as another powerful lurch nearly caused him to fall to the floor. He looked at the wall where the two initial ladders had become eight, allowing dozens of Goblins into the keep every second.

He looked down in time to once again see a mass of Ogres carrying a gigantic battering ram towards the gate with no oil to use against them. His shoulders sank slightly and he looked to the Elves behind him.

"Fall back to the Heart of the Keep. Everyone, to the Heart of the Keep!"

The Elves began falling back once more under the shower of boulders and wall of angered Goblins. Raziel started towards the main entrance to the keep when a creature to his left caught his eye. It stood alone on the wall, noticeably different than the Goblins and Ogres. Uljic had arrived. Raziel turned to face him, his sword dripping the blood of the many slain Goblins he had met in battle. Uljic took three long steps towards the Elf and drew a curved sword from a long leather sheath at its waist. The battle around them had started to end as the Elves that were left alive fled into the inner corridors of the castle, leaving some outside to fight for themselves. Unfortunately, it also trapped the commander on the battlements.

"Well master Elf, you're all alone. Ready to give up?" Uljic suggested evilly.

"I will die fighting you and your soldiers before I ever give up. I wouldn't give you the satisfaction of breaking my spirit."

"Have it your way."

The odd creature pointed to the Elf and a line of Goblins converged on Raziel, their weapons ready to spill his blood. The commander hid behind his shield with his sword poised to strike and the second the first of his enemies came into range of his weapon, the Elf delivered a powerful overhead strike, splitting the creature from the head to the chest. Wrenching his sword free he swirled and swung again and again, using his shield almost as often as his sword. After felling the fifth Goblin he turned to Uljic with an angry glare streaking across his face.

"Are you such a coward that you choose not to fight me? Come on, show me you are more than just talk you coward!" the Elf taunted, chopping through an opponent's arm cleanly.

"You will die soon enough."

Another Goblin charged and another, their relentless assault beginning to wear the commander down. The last of the opponents dropped to its knee and thrust its spear forward in unison with Raziel's sword stroke and though the creature was instantly beheaded, its spear met the weak spot in Raziel's armor. Thrust just below his waist, the spear pierced him easily, making him gasp in pain as he shook the weapon free. He gave another look to the creature and was met with the sharp sting of an arrow.

To the left of Uljic, a Goblin archer fired, striking the commander in the left shoulder which caused him to drop his shield. Standing nearly defenseless with blood dripping from his many wounds, Raziel brandished his sword hatefully at the creature that appeared too afraid to face him in open combat. Only after his opponent was injured from several attacks did Uljic approach to fight the Elf.

"You're a coward... a coward." Raziel muttered weakly, his voice cracking as he pulled his energy together to try to defend himself.

Uljic raised the curved sword and swung at the Elf who ducked backwards, feeling the two swords meet with a hard stroke. He returned the swing but with less effort and was easily blocked and the creature kicked him in the spear wound, making Raziel fall to one knee. He struggled to drag his wounded body back away from his opponent; the loss of blood was making him weaker by the second.

"You're not at all the fight I thought you would be Elf. I am very disappointed," the creature hissed delightfully as he watched the bloody Elf struggle to regain his footing.

Raziel swung twice, missing each time as the creature gave little dips and bobs of its head. The sword streaked through the air with only inches to spare but it felt like feet as Uljic's reflexes showed how advanced his skills in battle really were. Goblins had huddled around the two. With a last swing of his sword, Raziel managed to land a small cut across the creature's bicep, revealing a dark red streak of blood.

The gash seemed to almost please the enemy, amplifying his bloodthirsty nature. He rapidly approached the Elf and delivered a swing so powerful that Raziel was knocked off balance and fell to the stone floor. Uljic took a step across the Elf and delivered another swing straight down which the Elf managed to block at the cost of having his sword knocked from his grasp. The blade skidded across the battlement and Raziel reached out, his hand grazing the shaft of an arrow which he desperately plunged into the calf muscle of the creature.

A painful roar filled the air and Uljic reached down, punching the Elf across the jaw twice and wrenching the arrow from his calf in a sharp twist, his blood streaming down the leg. He lifted the wounded leg and brought it down on the Elf's chest with a powerful stomp, bringing blood to the commander's lips. With the Elf completely unable to defend himself, the creature stepped away, holding his sword in the air as a show of victory over the Elf. Goblins and Hobgoblins alike cheered as Uljic took his time killing his opponent. He turned back to Raziel and grabbed him by the front of his armor, jerking him up off the ground in one swift motion. Dangling in the air, the commander's eyesight blurred and colors ran together. Enemies and allies bled together as one and he blinked several times, struggling to clear his eyes. From below the keep, Ogres and Goblins alike cheered their leader on, pleading for the Elf's death.

Uljic sheathed his sword with his free hand and reached back, striking the Elf across the face. Raziel's head snapped backward and rolled down, his chin resting against his armor. Two more sharp strikes to the face and Uljic seemed to tire of the game. He lifted the Elf with both hands and walking to the edge of the battlements. His jagged sneer was the only thing the Elf seemed to be able to focus on.

"Let's see if Elves can fly," it called out to the Goblins, earning an uproar of laughter and more cheers.

Uljic twisted to the side and threw the fading body of the Elf over the edge of the keep, watching as he plummeted towards the soldiers below. Raziel could vaguely make out the shapes below him but could tell the ground was moving towards him faster than it seemed possible. The commander of Mihlann covered his head but the actions were useless as he met the earth below with a bone shattering thud. Ogres and Goblins converged upon him, stabbing and hitting the remains of the Elf to ensure his death. The creature turned to the Goblins.

"Mihlann is ours. Clean out the castle! Leave no one alive!"

Tanis sat on his throne, a saddened look on his face. His Queen sat next to him with her hand on his, trying to find a way to comfort him. News of the destruction of Mihlann and the loss of their soldiers had reached the King of the Wood Elves and it brought with it the overwhelming burden of deciding what to do next. Sending soldiers back to Mihlann would only add more to the casualties but if he did nothing, the enemies would soon lay siege to Swanhaven. The city that his people had called home for many years was now in danger of being taken from them.

"Tanis, please dear, tell me what we should do. The longer we wait to act the less time we will have if the armies are already on the move."

"I know. What am I supposed to do? If we stay there is no telling what will happen here in the forests. If we retreat to the ancient fortress then we abandon our High Elven brothers to hold the lands on their own. What would you have me do my Queen?" Tanis asked, raising his head for the first time.

Narissa rubbed his shoulder and bit her lower lip, not entirely sure what she was supposed to say. "That is not a choice that I can make. Elendil's armies have always been capable of holding back the swarm. It wouldn't feel right to leave without his council. That is why I dispatched riders to Pentegarn at the first hint of news of the slaughter at Mihlann."

Soldiers passed through the throne room, gathering their numbers and continuing through the castle. The King and Queen sat nearly alone with a handful of royal guards and even though there were dozens of Elves passing in and out, the two ignored them. One soldier approached the throne, kneeling before the two and bowing his head respectfully.

"Yes, rise."

"My Lord, we've word that the armies that raised Mihlann have not moved further. They seem to be refortifying the city for their own uses and scouts reported that a massive group of reinforcements arrived shortly after the city was lost. Valsera's armies are making their presence very obvious."

Tanis shook his head slowly, sickened by the thought of even more soldiers to back the already overwhelming numbers the enemies possessed. "Thank you, please, leave us."

The soldier turned to leave and the King walked down the steps that led to his throne, his Queen only a few steps behind him. They crossed the room slowly, neither one sure what they should say at the time. The last time Valsera's armies pushed this far north, all of Swanhaven had been destroyed and the Wood Elves were forced to rebuild their home. The thought of having to do it again was disheartening.

"Tanis... if we leave for Eglarest now, we will have more than enough time to fortify and prepare in case the enemy presses further. Eglarest will never be broken," Narissa said softly, touching Tanis on his shoulders.

The King of the Wood Elves nodded. "You are right Narissa. Perhaps we should abandon Swanhaven before it is too late. I will send word to Elendil to let him know that our army will follow our people to Eglarest and from there we will offer whatever support we can. I don't know what to expect when we get there but I hope we will be safer."

Narissa nodded and kissed the King on the cheek, turning to leave him as she headed to their room further up inside the castle. The rest of the city already knew that the Wood Elves were planning on leaving for Eglarest as soon as they possibly could, but the thought was not one that anyone seemed to take lightly. Leaving their homes again was depressing to even consider, but it looked to be something that they were going to do regardless. Outside of the throne room there were wagons and carriages all being loaded with supplies and equipment for the trip to the ancient fortress. Families packed only what was needed as much of the necessities were already stored at the castle.

Tanis dismissed the guards and crossed the room twice more, his pacing having no effect on whether or not he should leave for the fortress. A large group of Elves, mostly families with children had already left for Eglarest earlier that morning and now it was the bulk of the army and the remaining Elves that had to follow. In all, close to eight thousand Wood Elves remained in the lands and with the numbers they possessed, it wouldn't be difficult to defend the fortress of Eglarest.

The King lifted his sword from the stand next to his throne and pulled it from the ornately decorated sheath. It wasn't the type of weapon you generally saw a Wood Elf use but it had a history. The sword had belonged to Tanis's father when the Elves had first begun settling in the area and once he passed away, the blade was passed on to Tanis. It was a rather short blade, edged on both sides and tapered to a point. The hilt and pommel were both carved from bone and wrapped in black leather, which made it odd considering all other swords the Wood Elves carried were wrapped in brown leather with simple steel guards. He looked down the blade and gave it a few quick swings, testing it carefully. A knock at the door made him sheath the weapon and he turned.

"Enter."

The door opened and a single soldier walked in, giving a slight bow to the King. Tanis returned the gesture with a nod and waved his hand. "Yes, what is it?"

"Sir, the royal carriage has been prepared for you and the Queen. Shall I carry your belongings down for you?"

"No thank you, I will be riding on my horse. I prefer the view from the saddle as opposed to one of the walled transport. The Queen however may wish to ride in the carriage. I shall ask her."

Tanis left the throne room and made the quick trip to the upper rooms where the Queen of Swanhaven was packing away clothing for their stay at the fortress. She tied the top of one travel sack closed and started packing another. The King knocked on the door even though it was his bedroom as well as hers.

"Oh… Tanis you startled me." she said, turning to the open doorway.

"Forgive me. I wanted to ask in advance. Will you be riding in the carriage? I will ride up front with the soldiers so I will not be in the carriage with you. What would you prefer?"

"I will not be riding in the carriage Tanis," she replied flatly.

"Ok then, on horseback I suppose?"

"Yes, right beside you. If we are to leave the city I want our people to see that I am not hiding in the carriage and that I am out amongst them. Plus what happened to Rhen makes me wary of carriages."

Tanis nodded at her answer, knowing all along that she would more than likely not want to be cooped up in the carriage for the duration of the trip. Narissa was a strong Queen and preferred being out in the world with those serving her. Unbeknownst to the King she had already sent word to the stables to have a mare ready for her when the Elves began to leave.

Servants grabbed the bags for the Queen and Tanis packed some of his more important items. He strapped the King's sword to his hip and loaded down a servant with a sack of scrolls, maps, and important books. He let the door to their room close as he stood in the hallway watching the room disappear. He felt a tear emerging but fought it back, leading the Queen back to the throne room. The racks of weaponry and armor that had dotted the walls were gone, packed away in the wagons and carts and most likely already on its way to Eglarest.

"This is the right thing to do Tanis, even if it heart breaking," Queen Narissa said as she watched the King stroll heavily to the balcony.

"I know. So often the right thing to do affects us in the worst ways. Sending Rhen away the first time was disheartening. Doing it the second time when she left for Tvan nearly killed me. Now we abandon our homelands. What will become of us, I am not sure."

"No one can be sure Tanis. All we can do is make the best of the situations we are given. We should really consider moving down into the lower courtyards while the caravan is here. Something tells me that we will be back one day."

Tanis nodded and led the Queen down the stairs that led to the grassy courtyard that stretched through the trees. A mass of soldiers waited for their leaders around groups of horses, allowing the families and common Elves to leave ahead of time with the bulk of the soldiers.

"We are ready to leave my Lord. Your horse my Queen," the Knight said, holding the reins of the steed.

"Thank you soldier. Do not despair, we shall return one day to our beloved city, I promise."

Between the soldiers and common Elves, close to eight thousand Elves were in route to Eglarest. The numbers were nowhere near what the High Elves possessed but they would not go quietly into the night. On top of the eight thousand Elves headed to Eglarest, another twelve hundred waited at the city, stationed there permanently in times of war.

Narissa rode next to Tanis, leading the mass of Knights through the trees and out into the clearings. The line of Elves stretched as far as the King and Queen could see, disappearing over hills and around bends. Wagons, carriages, cart and horses carried the rest of the race to their last hope of survival, a fortress nestled at the edge of the sea on the cliffs, surrounded by sparse forests and the added bonus of isolated geography.

Tanis turned to his Queen, a renewed smile on his face. "What suddenly has you in such a decent mood Tanis?"

"Well, by leaving Swanhaven behind and traveling to Eglarest, we will be that much closer to Rhen and the others. Perhaps we could have them bring her to the fortress and remain with us after all. What do you think?" he asked the Queen.

"I love the idea Tanis, but we need to get there first before we send for her. If there were to be any dangers between Eglarest and Tvan, she would be in more danger than it would be worth to have her by our side again."

The words were harsh to believe, to think that his daughter was better off without him but she was right. If rouge groups of the southern army had moved north, having her brought to the city could possibly put her in greater jeopardy than just letting her stay at the city of the Dwarves.

"Let's get moving dear. We've quite a long ride ahead of us. If we keep moving we could be there in two days time."

In the Belly of the Beast

True darkness seemed to stain the lands around the castle of Nomaria. The tainted and scarred fields that reached the foot of the stone walls were as dark and barren as the night sky, harboring no signs of life with the exception of Valsera's mighty armies. Campfires numbering near the stars in the sky covered the lands that led to the gnarled forests to the north, giving an impressive appearance to the number he commanded. The castle itself stretched into the sky, its towers stabbing at the clouds above and the walls reinforced heavily to withstand any attacking army. Through the time the army had labored, the fortress had become larger and larger until it finally looked more like a dreadful mountain in the distance.

Within the castle were broad passages and immense rooms that housed some of his more deadly soldiers. Inside the castle stayed his deadliest soldiers, the Slayers, amazingly strong creatures that existed only to find and kill Dragons. For fear of retaliation from the Dragons and their forces that had survived long ago, the sorcerer armed his castle with as many of the Slayers as he could, hoping that behind the fear that they delivered, he would be safe.

A throne of rock and skulls sat centered in the room and on it was the strong form of Valsera, ruler of the southern armies. His form was hunched over in the seat, staring at the floor as if he expected something miraculous to happen in front of him. He had black hair that draped to his shoulders and deep scars across his chin and the right side of his face. His attention was so drawn to the spot on the floor that he did not even bother looking up as the massive throne room doors swung open and a band of

Goblins entered. They stopped a good distance from the throne, none of the group willing to venture near the motionless sorcerer. Finally one of Goblins was pushed from the group and staggered forward nervously.

Valsera looked up from his deep trance and stared the small creature down, his eyes probing for any emotion it had. The Goblin immediately dropped to its knees, pressing its face to the stone floor. The others followed the first, bowing the moment Valsera's eyes met them. The sorcerer stood and took a single step from the throne.

"What news have you that you felt important enough to disturb my moment of meditation?" he asked in a deep voice.

"Sir... please... do not be angry... I..."

"You what!"

"Sir... the Elven city has been taken. Mihlann burns my Lord," the Goblin stammered.

Valsera stopped at the bottom of the throne only a few steps from the creature, his emotion not wavering. He was dressed in sturdy black armor and a long cape dragging behind him. He stopped and leaned against his dark staff, gripping it with both hands as he leaned a little closer to the Goblins. His eyes were completely black and hollow, looking darker than the darkest night. With his brow furrowed the sorcerer suddenly allowed a smile to cross his lips.

"Mihlann has fallen? Is that what you are telling me?" the sorcerer asked, looking the creature in the eyes.

"Yes... my Lord."

"Finally! Have you more to say Goblin?"

The creature shook its head, keeping its eyes on the floor to avoid the stare of the sorcerer. Valsera turned his back to the creatures and started toward the back of the room where a monstrous yet crude map covered the entire wall. "Then be gone!"

The Goblins turned and hurried out of the room as if they were being attacked, trampling one of their own in the process. The sorcerer stopped next to the map that gave a depiction of what the lands above his castle were like. He studied the map intently, noting where Mihlann had been and looking at the lands immediately north of it. Everything pointed to one option if he decided to continue moving north. He was going to have to send his armies through the Pass of Merwold. It was the only area wide enough for an army of great size to move through without taking weeks to do so. The other options would mean the thickest parts of the forests or a small path that led around through Swanhaven.

Valsera moved down the map with his eyes, noting the areas around Qwaz where the next largest section of his forces was waiting. The sorcerer raised a finger to his temple, closing his eyes and taking a deep breath. He nodded his head and rolled it around, cracking his neck loudly and taking another deep breath. He opened his eyes and followed the movement from where his army at Qwaz was located to the Pass of Merwold and then on past deep into the Elven lands. It would be a quiet invasion right through the front door with the largest bulk of his armies leading the way. Footsteps behind him caught his attention and the sorcerer turned slowly, starting at a tall Lizardman.

"Yes? What is it?"

"My Lord... the southern tribe is ready to move at your order. Where will you have us go?"

He turned around, prepared to snap an answer when an idea struck him. He paused, looking at the monstrous reptile. Yet another addition to his growing army. "Indeed... very well, I have a task more than fitting for you and your tribe. Join with the Goblins moving north to Qwaz and follow the forces north to the Pass of Merwold. We will invade the northlands."

The Lizardman gave an almost hollow look to the sorcerer, as if to question whether or not to believe the orders. Its tail slid across the stone floor behind it and it looked up at the map.

"Is something wrong? Was it not clear enough?"

"Master... the Pass will be heavily defended by now. Would it not be wise to move out through the east and..."

"Silence!" the sorcerer yelled. "It was not a debate you overgrown pond scum, it was an order. Your soldiers will join the force moving north tomorrow and enter their lands where I said to enter them. Now... was that clearer?"

"Yes... master..."

The creature turned and walked out of the room, its head

lowered from the verbal attack of the sorcerer. Valsera turned from the map and slowly walked through the throne room. He circled the throne, looking it up and down before continuing on to the huge hole leading to the outer balcony and walls. The sorcerer stopped at the railing and looked out across the desolate lands. Below, in the plains and fields were thousands upon thousands of Goblins and Ogres building siege weapons and forging armor and weapons. The mass of soldiers in the northern part of the fields were mobilizing and preparing to move north to join the armies that massed between the ruins of Mihlann and the city of Qwaz.

Valsera rolled his staff in his hands and looked as far as he could see in every direction. He stared to the north where his armies were massing, preparing to surge forth into the Elven lands. He knew the loss at Mihlann would have angered the Elves and retaliation would be swift. Greed was pushing him to move further into the lands, taking more from them. An evil smile crossed his face and he chuckled. He knew he would be moving more soldiers into the pass than the Elves expected and his sheer numbers would overrun the area. All they needed was time.

From behind the sorcerer came a figure dressed in plated armor and a solid helmet with narrow slits for eyeholes. The creature stopped behind the sorcerer and stood rigid as a statue, waiting to be addressed. Valsera turned and raised his eyebrow at the sight of the Slayer.

"What is it?"

The Slayer took a deep breath, hissing slightly as it exhaled. "My Lord, we are ready for you. The prisoners have been prepared."

Valsera turned and followed the Slayer off of the balcony and through the throne room. He walked proudly, moving through the empty halls with one thing on his mind. He wanted power, as much as he could get as fast as he could manage. For as long as he had been fighting to take the northern lands, Valsera had been struggling to gain more power to strengthen his magic.

Deeper in the heart of the castle the Slayer and Valsera came upon the monstrous dungeon door. Six more Slayers stood guard at the doors and pushed them open as the leader approached them. Valsera entered the dungeon alone and the doors closed behind him, locking the sorcerer in with the prisoners and three more Slayers. He stopped next to the three Slayers and looked into the cell.

"The prisoners are ready my Lord."

In the cell on their knees were two prisoners, one Human and one Elf each stripped of their gear and armor with the exception of their pants. Their hands were bound behind their backs and both stared up at the Slayers and the sorcerer. Valsera walked into the cell and stopped right in front of the Human. His right hand slowly rose and stopped above the mans head, the fingertips straightening and beginning to glow. The light shifted to a green and intensified, engulfing his entire hand and wrist as the sorcerer grinned evilly.

Valsera shoved his hand down on the Human's head, grabbing his skull and watching as the pulsating green light began to seep into his hair and skin. The Human opened his mouth to shout, to scream in pain but sound never left his lips. His eyes rolled back into his skull and his body shook violently until Valsera released his grip on the man. The body fell back onto the stone floor lifeless. The sorcerer turned to the Elf and repeated the process, digging his nails into the Elf's skin as the green light disappeared and once again the victim fell back to the floor dead.

"The easiest part is over with," Valsera said, looking at the two dead bodies spread out on the floor.

The sorcerer leaned his staff against the wall and stepped up to the two bodies, looking down at them. Their hands remained bound even in death. Valsera pressed his hands together and closed his eyes, his lips silently forming a spell he had fought so hard to perfect. As he pulled his hands apart a dark blue light formed between them, pulsing softly and fighting to remain visible. The sorcerer spread his arms wider, watching as the fading blue light dropped down across the two bodies and slowly disappeared.

His muttering continued as he began to focus all his energy into the spell. The light disappeared completely and Valsera slowly opened his eyes, looking at the two bodies just waiting to see if they moved. The lifeless bodies remained lifeless and the sorcerer slowly grew impatient. Valsera reared back and kicked the Human body in the side and turned towards the Slayers behind him, his eyes glaring angrily. He stormed past the soldiers and kicked the doors to the dungeon open.

Having spent months on the spell, Valsera grew angry at its imperfection. He had gone through dozens of prisoners, trying desperately to discover the correct method to raising the dead. He had killed them in every feasible method, used different races, different genders and even trying fresh bodies over aged ones. So far, no results.

Valsera stormed up the stairs on his way back to the throne room, his temper flaring viciously as he moved through the castle. He threw the doors to the throne room open so violently one of them splintered. The sorcerer walked straight up to the throne and threw himself back into it. He watched the door hanging precariously from its hinges swing slowly back towards the gaping hole that the doors usually covered. As the door on the right finally came back to the other, a pair of Goblins entered slowly, their eyes flickering fearfully at the sight of the angered leader.

Valsera looked up at the two Goblins and grit his teeth, staring down the two. He reached back with his right hand and a swirling ball of fire appeared in between his fingers. He flung it forward, striking the first Goblin in the chest and bringing him to the ground engulfed in flames. The second Goblin turned to run, making it to the door before it suddenly found that it could not move. The Goblin hovered in the air being pulled back towards the sorcerer, struggling to break free the whole time. As the two found themselves eye to eye Valsera began tightening his fist and at the same time strangling the Goblin. Its eyes slowly rolled back into its skull and just before death the sorcerer angrily flung the creature across the throne room, watching as the body crashed against the wall and collapsed to the floor.

The lights around Qwaz flickered softly as another full army prepared to move on the Elven lands. The monstrous numbers waited in the fields and twisted forests around Qwaz as the rest of Valsera's armies in the south began moving north to combine their armies. The sea of Goblins and Ogres were a sight to behold for anyone who came across them. The army was divided with the veterans defending the city. The few thousand soldiers involved in the battles above the borders were nothing compared to the forces waiting to be released. Qwaz had once been a beautiful city under the care of the Humans but with their defeat and having been driven from the lands, the city had become a ruin.

The army began to disperse, the masses of Goblins leading the way with formations of Ogres and Lizardmen mixed in with them. The sound the army made moving across the fields rumbled and echoed through the forests and lands around them. Tens of thousands of soldiers moving together created the largest single force to ever cross the southlands. As the armies moved on the northlands they left the city of Qwaz vulnerable and open. Who would ever make it past the army they thought. No force could break the army and assault Qwaz, they were sure of it.

Secrets Aboard the Dwarven Ship

*E*rzel sat in the library with Nimir to his right and Ectle across from him as the wizard reviewed his findings and explained what they meant. A new map was produced, one exactly like the first he had shown except this one had dark lines drawn onto it representing the route the island was believed to take. Erzel kept his skepticism in check as they continued through a list of things that seemed important, even though they were not sure of anything that had to do with the island.

"Alright, what do you think so far?"

"Once more, I am not sure what is fact and what is fiction amongst all this mess. The island has a shroud of mystery that accompanies it wherever you go. No one who actually knows anything about it first hand seems to exist."

"Either that or they never made it back," the Dwarf added, an almost fearful tone in his voice.

"There is that point as well. We have no idea what sort of dangers await on the island. Not counting the overwhelming abilities of a Dragon, we do not know what other sorts of creatures wait for us," Erzel noted quietly.

"Risk and reward go hand and hand Erzel. It would not be worth the trip if it were so easy to find."

"And they wouldn't have gone to such lengths to prevent people from finding it if they had wanted to be found."

Ectle rolled his shoulders and breathed slowly, finding the conversation was getting them nowhere fast. "If it pleases you Erzel, I can go with a small group of volunteers from Tvan. It does not have to be something you and your group need concern yourselves with if you find it not worth the time."

The Elf nodded to himself, taking the words of the wizard in slowly. He had long been a nonbeliever of the Dragon race but Ectle's persistence was strong, giving the myth a sort of life. Just when he felt he could turn the venture down and remain in the city along with the Princess, Ectle breathed new life into the cause. Quests had always driven Erzel and the only difference here was the fact that they would be headed for something they truly were not sure was there.

"No... no Ectle, we are more than willing to accompany you to the island. I feel that until their existence is proven, I will continue to speak of them with a touch of skepticism. No offense to you of course."

"None taken captain. There is one thing that I do not have figured though."

"What's that?"

"How long before everyone is ready to leave?"

Erzel stood from the table with Nimir right behind him. "Well, we will go and check."

The two walked the halls in search of the rest of the group that had agreed to accompany them on the adventure, everyone except for Rhen. They found Kail and Thorgrim out in one of the large courtyards, relaxing and taking in the rest they had earned. Erzel watched the Dwarf run a sharpening stone across the blade of his axe several times, the sound seeming to keep him in a slight trance. The ranger leaned against one of the stone pillars, watching the Elf and Dwarf approach.

"Where is Rathe?" Erzel asked as they stopped, looking around the open courtyard.

"Food," Thorgrim replied, not taking his eyes off the weapon.

"Well then, I have something to discus with the two of you anyway. I will find him afterwards."

Thorgrim leaned the axe against the wall and looked up for the first time. Kail left the pillar and joined the group, leaning in next to the Dwarf. "Go ahead, what is it?"

"Ectle and I have worked things through and decided that we are leaving to try and find the Isle of Dragons. The question lies with how many of you plan to come with us and when can you be ready to leave?"

Thorgrim looked to his right at the ranger just visible in the flicker of the torchlight. A simple nod was all he received. "This is gonna sound real odd coming from a Dwarf, but I can't wait to get back to the surface world. I've been away from these underground cities for too long and I just can't adjust."

Erzel nodded and looked to Kail. "You too?"

"The same, it is odd here. No sun to judge the time. No trees and no wind. I could not live here."

"Very well, I assume that if we can be ready tomorrow, Ectle will want to leave by then. Of course, sooner is an option. Now if you will excuse me, I will see if I can find Rathe."

Nimir followed the Elf closely, navigating the intricate maze of tunnels and corridors to the lower levels where the kitchens and dining halls were located. The smell of meats and baked bread filled the passages and though Erzel had not been hungry, the smell was making his stomach growl. After dropping down the last flight of stairs, the Elf turned his head, somewhat surprised to see Nimir still following him.

"Nimir… you do not have to follow me everywhere. I told you that what happened in the forest was my duty. You are not indebted to me."

"Thank you master Elf, but I have nothing more to do. I am truly grateful and I was taught that once a deed so great has been done, one must return the favor, one way or another. Plus, I would kind of like to go with you."

"What, on the ship? Nimir we are soldiers. We've trained for these sorts of expeditions for a long time. No offense, but a former miner does not really have the background I am looking for when taking on such a dangerous task."

The Dwarf kept walking, determined to change the Elf's mind. "I will take care of myself and whatever happens to me will not be on your head. If I am to die out there, at least it is somewhere other than here. I have longed for a life elsewhere and this is the chance. Please reconsider master Elf."

Erzel pondered for just one moment and sighed. "I take it you would not just simply sit by happily here if I leave you. You understand that my concern is to my friends and having to look after someone will put strain on my duties to protect them if the situation arises. If we encounter danger, you will be expected to hold your own. Is that something you can promise?"

"If it gets me away from here, I can do it. I promise you."

The dining hall was enormous but appeared nearly empty. It was still a while before the next meal would be served but a few people had gathered for something quick before returning to their duties. Six tables away was the hulking form of Rathe who appeared to be easily devouring a heaped plate of meats, potatoes, and bread. He waved to the two and the Elf and Dwarf joined him.

"You want some? They cook ya whatever ya want."

"No thank you Rathe, I'm sure we will be fine. I spoke with Thorgrim and Kail earlier about the findings of Ectle and that he expects to leave as soon as possible, tomorrow at the latest. They are going with us, are you?" Erzel asked bluntly.

Rathe wiped his face, looking from the plate to the Elf. "Leaving tomorrow?"

"Well, tomorrow at the latest. If Ectle had his way, we would be leaving right now. Can you be ready to leave that soon or not?"

"Yeah, I'm going. What about the Princess?"

"No, she will be staying here."

Rathe gave a look that bordered between confusion and surprise, wondering how the Elf had managed to get her to remain in Tvan while he took the group somewhere else.

"Don't worry about it Rathe, I have that under control. Just be ready by midnight tonight, in case Ectle wishes to leave earlier than I am guessing."

"Ok."

Erzel was back in the higher reaches of the castle, walking through the halls outside of the throne room. When he arrived the guards opened the doors and announced him, closing them the moment he walked through. The Elders, with the exception of Divos, sat around the table in deep discussion, seemingly unaware that the Elf was now standing a few feet away. Erzel cleared his throat and the Dwarves looked up from the table, acknowledging him for the first time.

"Erzel, we didn't see you. What can we do for you captain?" Ardis asked, folding his hands across a scroll on the table.

"Good Elders of Tvan, I have returned with news of our expected departure. I have spoken with all of our group and it is clear that we will be leaving within the next twenty four hours. I assume the ship and crew will be made available within that time period?"

"Yes Erzel, they will be. May I ask a question."

"Of course."

"I see that your group has chosen to venture off to the north but to what destination I am unsure of. I do not ask where, but the other Elders and myself would like to know what will come of the Princess of Swanhaven."

Erzel nodded to Odar. "She will remain here. My group will accompany me with that of the ship through the sea and we hope to return at a later date to Tvan. She will be safer if she remains here. I assume that will be accepted."

"Of course. We only hoped you had not planned to take her with you. The sea is a dangerous place for someone like her. We will look after her well while she stays. I believe Ardis appointed a young lady to assist her. Human girl, but very nice indeed."

"Thank you my Lords. I will go and prepare for the trip. Send word if you have a need of me."

Erzel left the throne room, tired and sore from the countless hours he had spent talking with the wizard and the Elders. Sleep had not been at the top of his priorities but now he was determined to try to rest while he could. He passed the Princess's room and stopped, remembering the events that had taken place only a day earlier. Fearing she was still hurt and cross with him, the Elf continued on to his room where he collapsed on the bed without undressing.

Morning arrived with no visible evidence as Erzel woke

to the same torchlight and candles as when he had fallen asleep. He rolled on the bed and tossed the cover off of him, looking around the room to get a better grip on where he was. Turning to the side of his bed, the Elf rubbed his eyes and stood, stretching to help wake his tired body. A knock on his door opened his eyes and he walked to it, pulling it open slowly. Standing in the door was Ectle with a face that seemed to asked the question of why he wasn't already awake.

"I'm up Ectle, I'm up. Where is everybody else?"

"Kail and Rathe are in the dining hall, Thorgrim and Nimir are somewhere in the city, and I have not the slightest clue where Princess Rhen is. She wouldn't answer the door when I knocked so I did not continue."

"I have not seen her since I told her she would have to stay here while we ventured to the island. I know she was angry with me but her safety comes first. I hope that she can forgive me one day."

"She will Erzel, she will. Come, let us eat before we go. If I calculated the days right, it may be as long as week before we can cook a hot meal."

The Elf and wizard strolled through the halls and made their way to the dining hall to join Rathe and Kail. Once again, Rathe had a plate heaping with food while Kail ate smaller portions. Sitting next to Rathe made the ranger look small. Ectle sat down across from Kail and Erzel took the seat to his right, taking a piece of bread from one of the many platters spread across the table. The breakfast looked more like a banquet, but to the Dwarves it was the way almost every meal was served. Pitchers of strong ales and wines were passed around the group but only Rathe seemed to be drinking. Throughout the meal, Erzel kept an eye on the entrances, hoping to see the Princess arrive for breakfast, but she never did.

"Don't worry Erzel. I need your concentration here so please, focus. She is fine," Ectle whispered to him.

Though Rathe ate twice as much as everyone else at the table, it took him only minutes longer to do so. He set the ale back on the table and leaned in his chair, rubbing his stomach in wide circles. "That was good. These Dwarves damn sure know how to cook, I'll give them that."

"Wait, so you are actually full?" Ectle asked in a sarcastic tone.

"Yeah, I am. What, you not gonna eat too?" Rathe asked in a similar tone, eyeing the wizard.

"Rathe, perhaps you should lay off the ale a little bit if you are taking the ship with us later. No one likes a drunk on a boat, especially one as big as you."

"Is that supposed to mean something Erzel?" the big man asked, turning in his seat to face the Elf.

"Only that you are bigger than the rest of us and a little testy when you've been drinking. There will be plenty of time for drinking later on."

Rathe pushed the ale away and shrugged. "Fine then, when we leaving?"

"When Thorgrim and Nimir get back we need to have a parting word with the Elders before we go. Once that is out of the way all we have to do is take our gear to the ship and we are off."

"Odar and Ardis did confirm that the crew and ship were ready last night when I spoke with them so I guess the only thing we are waiting on is us," Erzel added as he pushed his finished plate away.

"While we wait for the two Dwarves to return, let us go and see this ship."

Tvan was unique in many ways: The fact that it was ruled by four Elders instead of a King, it was mostly under the mountains where the rest of the world never saw it and also because under the mountains was a deep channel that led out to the sea. The Dwarves had their own port under the mountain and used it regularly to transport their goods and supplies to other areas. The port was manned mostly by Humans but the Dwarves did have a hand in things, supplying soldiers and guards to the shipyards.

Erzel, Ectle, Kail and Rathe made their way through the small cluster of buildings that led to the ports where close to fifty ships bobbed and rocked in the water. A small group of soldiers approached, stopping them before they reached the docks.

"Where are you folks headed?" one Dwarf asked.

"We're here to look at the ship we will be taking north later. There should be a crew prepping it as we speak."

"Are you Erzel?" the same Dwarf asked, stepping up to look closer.

"Yes, this is Ectle, Kail and Rathe. I presume Ardis or Odar informed you we would be here today?"

"Yes, go ahead. Watch yourselves on the docks, water is a bit chilly."

Erzel and the others walked past the group of Dwarves and started down the first of the docks, looking at the different ships and boats one at a time. Once they reached the end of the dock and didn't see their ship they tried the next. After their third try, they located a ship with a Dwarven crew on board. It wasn't a large ship, one mast and ten rowing slits in the side. The oars rested above the ripple of the water, waiting to be used. Erzel watched them carry barrels and sacks below, probably food and water for the journey.

"Morning!" he called to them.

"Ah, morning sir. What can I be doing for ya?" one Dwarf asked, stepping up to the ladder from the dock.

"Are you the crew taking us out to sea later?" Ectle asked, stepping in beside Erzel.

"Yes master, we are. Are you ready to leave already? We have much we have yet to prepare. It may be another hour or so before we are ready."

Erzel held up a hand to slow the Dwarf down. "No, we are not ready to leave yet. We just wanted to see the ship that we were going to be taking. Carry on as you were."

The Dwarves returned to their work stocking the ship and getting it ready to leave while the group looked the ship over. It looked to be very dependable, not like some of the older vessels that were docked in various other areas. Rathe looked down at the dark water, kicking a stone over the edge and watching it splash with a small ripple effect. He took a step back away from the edge wearing a very ominous face.

"What's wrong with you?" Kail asked, looking over the

edge to see what had spooked the fighter.

"Uh guys, I don't know about this one. I mean, I want to go but I uh..."

"Rathe, what is wrong?" Erzel questioned, noticing his odd behavior.

"I uh, I can't swim."

The group was silent, not sure to believe him or if he was having a drunken moment of stupidity. Finally, it was Ectle who broke the silence, with laughter. "Oh dear me Rathe!" the wizard roared. "You charge head first into every battle, fight anything that looks at you cross, never been scared of anything before in your life and you can't swim?"

"I fail to see the humor," the fighter said through gritted teeth.

"I'm sorry, I really am. I just figure that if we ever met something you were afraid of it would have seven heads, razor sharp claws and breathe fire."

"I killed one of those the other day..." Thorgrim teased, enjoying the newfound fear in the fighter.

"Well when we meet it I will be sure to remind you who was afraid after I've killed it," Rathe said quietly, taking another step back.

Erzel stepped between them, his hopes to end the argument as quickly as he could before the two separated themselves permanently. "Ok, perhaps we should head back to the castle. We still have much to do before we can set sail, isn't that right Ectle?"

"Of course. Let's go. We can continue this later when we're all on our way to the Dragon Isles. Perhaps I could dunk you in a few times during the voyage to help you learn a few manners master Rathe."

The big fighter walked a ways ahead of the others, muttering to himself the whole trip back to the castle. Upon arriving he went straight to his room and slammed the door, avoiding any confrontation with the rest of the group. Seeing his reaction, Erzel turned on Ectle before entering his own room.

"You are going to have to make amends with him Ectle. I can't have him sore with you the entire voyage, cooped up on that ship with nowhere to go to avoid the humiliation you handed him. Surely you can see the anger you've brought and a simple apology is the best way to start. Do it for us."

"Very well Erzel, for the sanity of the rest of the group, I shall go and talk with Rathe but one day he is going to have to get rid of his boyish nature and grow a good sense of humor."

Erzel entered his room and closed the door, pulling his armor and gear together and spreading it out on the bed. Removing his robes he slid his shirt on and then the chain armor. The chain was cool against his skin as he fastened the hooks and secured the mail armor. He pulled his boots back on and secured his swords to his waist and the quiver of arrows across his back, carrying his bow in his right hand. The black chain mail was accented with the blue tunic and though it did not have the crest of the White Eagle on it, Erzel had the faint feeling like he was back with his soldiers. The captain pulled a pair of brown leather gloves over his hands as he left the room, walking towards the throne room to join the rest of the group. As he entered, he saw everyone but Rhen. Saddened, he trudged to the table and leaned his bow against the wall, taking a seat next to Kail.

"Good to see everyone here. I suppose you are planning on departing very soon?" Ardis asked, leaning back in his chair.

"Yes, we hope to. I'd like to thank you for your patience and for allowing us to carry out this duty while leaving the Princess here under your protection. I assure you, we shall return as soon as possible," Erzel replied gratefully.

"I assume you have been down to see the ship and its crew, so by all means, whenever you are prepared to leave you may do so. However, I strongly advise you to watch the shores very closely. Goblins and their fellow soldiers have been seen roaming about and we've no telling what grip they have on the seas. If you encounter a force while sailing, there may be very little you can do to prevent them from boarding, as the vessel is not a military ship. I wish you the best," Ardis said as he stood from the table, followed by the rest of the Elders.

They shook hands and the four Dwarves left the room and Erzel's group did the same. On their way back down the halls, Erzel stopped Ectle behind the rest of the group, pulling him off to the side for a moment.

"Ectle, I want to try to say goodbye to Rhen. I will meet you at the ship in a few minutes."

"As you wish Erzel. Give my regards if you see her."

Erzel nodded and parted ways with the rest of the group, walking the last staircase to the rooms where they had all stayed. He stopped in front of Rhen's door and raised his hand, knocking firmly and praying she would answer. Just when he was ready to turn and leave he heard footsteps and the door opened a crack. Out stepped a young Human who closed the door behind her quickly.

"Good afternoon, I would like a word with the Princess if I may."

"Are you the one they call Erzel?" she asked timidly.

"Yes I am."

"The Princess has requested that no one bother her, you least of all. She said that she regrets she will not see you off but her heart aches so and she could not watch you leave without her. I was instructed not to allow anyone in."

Erzel bit his lower lip and sighed, knowing that he was not about to go against the wishes of the Princess. If she did not want to see them off, he would respect that wish.

"Will you at least give her a message for me?"

"Of course sir, what is it?"

"Just let her know that I am truly sorry for not allowing her to accompany us to our destination, but my duties were to see that she is protected and safe, and here is where she will be safe. I will be back, I promise, and then I will apologize in person. Thank you ma'am."

Erzel turned and left the Human standing in front of the door, guarding it as if her life depended on its secrecy. He felt horrible that he had hurt her but in truth, he had sworn he would see her safely to Tvan and that no harm would befall her. That duty had been performed, and as long as she remained in Tvan, she would be safe. Taking her into uncharted lands, across un-tamed seas would be a risk he was unwilling to accept. Erzel rubbed his head as he hoped that the hostilities he had created would not persist once he returned to the city of the Dwarves.

The docks were more alive than before as he strolled past the guards and up the dock to where the rest of the group was storing their weapons and supplies. The Dwarves had taken positions at the oars while the group looked about the ship. Kail extended his hand to Erzel who took it and jumped down into the ship, ignoring the stairs completely. He looked back up the tunnel that led to the city and sighed. Knowing their journey could last days, or even weeks, and he would not see the Princess. Saddened but focused, he turned to the crew.

"Alright, let's get moving. The sooner we reach the open ocean, the sooner the winds can catch the sails and move us faster."

As the crew rowed, Nimir and Thorgrim joined in to help the Dwarves, taking the last two spots without argument to help the Dwarves. The cavern they entered was wide enough for two ships to use but they stayed in the center, using the torches on the bow of the boat to guide them through the dark tunnel. In all his years out in the world, Erzel had never known that the Dwarves had an underground port city complete with a tunnel for ships to move to and from the outer world.

"So Erzel, did you speak with the Princess?" Ectle asked, walking up beside the captain who stood at the very front of the boat.

"No I didn't. I met the Human girl in charge of her care but she claimed that Rhen would not see us off. She was still hurt from me not being willing to bring her along and would most likely not recover until we return to Tvan. I feel so ashamed Ectle, I hurt her and I had never meant to."

"Sometimes you must hurt the ones you love to protect them, as odd as that sounds. Her safety depended on the Dwarves and their cities built deep underground, far away from the turmoil of the outer world. She will come to see that this was for the best Erzel, I assure you."

"I hope so. Living with the disappointment will haunt me for the rest of my life. I will try to make amends the moment I am able."

Ectle left him to his thoughts, joining Kail and Rathe near the mast as they watched the walls around them, marveling at the size of the channel. The big fighter looked from Erzel to Ectle and raised his eyebrow. "What's wrong with him?"

"There was a minor disagreement between Erzel and the Princess. It seems that she had her heart set on joining us for this journey but Erzel refused to allow it. Since that moment, she hasn't spoken a word to anyone."

"It was in her best interest to remain in Tvan," Kail whispered to the wizard.

"Yes, well love often overrules what the mind knows to be true. She knows she is safe in Tvan but she will not have Erzel by her side. The young Princess has had her first taste of heartbreak, and I am sure that though he possesses a rigid exterior, Erzel is feeling the pains as well."

"Love? Between the captain and Princess? Somewhat of an odd combination, don't you think?"

"He saved her life when she believed no one would be able to. For the rest of their lives she will feel that attraction, no matter how he feels or reacts to her."

"Love is a weak feeling. All my life I've lived knowing that love is a feeling that brings the toughest of men to a point of weakening. When you love someone, your judgment is conflicted and you will most likely be set up for unwanted pain."

Ectle rubbed his knuckles for some odd reason. "That is an interesting way of explaining things Kail. Perhaps it shows why your emotions are so well kept in check. Hurt in the past perhaps?"

The ranger looked up as the flash of daylight invaded the cave, muffling the weak torchlight. Their eyes felt the power of the light that they had not witnessed in some time and it took several minutes to be able to even make out details around them. As Kail regained his sight he looked to the side at the wizard.

"Perhaps, though I don't really see how it is important now. We've more important things to think about."

"It is nice to see the outer world once more. The underground was getting a little… dark," Rathe added nervously as the ship bounced through the waves.

The Dwarves at the oars rowed steadily, propelling the ship further away from land as they moved out of the channel and into the open sea. The thick forests behind them hid any possible signs of life in the shadows. The salty spray of the sea met the captain's face, giving him a chill that ran up his back. Straight ahead there was nothing but open water for as far as anyone could see and behind them, shrinking slowly, was the only home he had ever had. He steadied his feet and rocked with the motions of the boat to keep from loosing his balance.

No more than three hours into the voyage Rathe was clinging to the railing of the ship, his face green as he fought off the sea sickness. Every so often a rogue wave would hit and the ship would rock violently, shaking the mighty fighter and turning his face four shades of green. The rest of the group seemed to be fine, having very slight bouts of sea sickness but nothing that crippled their ability to stand on their own two feet.

Feeling bad for the big man, Ectle sat down on the bow of the boat and pulled three small vials from under his robes, each with a different shade of red churning within them. He poured the three together in a fourth vial, watching as the liquid changed from a dull red to a vivid yellow. He pocketed the vials and walked to the big man clinging desperately to the railing and knelt next to him.

"Rathe, here, take this. I promise you will feel much better afterwards."

The big man reached out and took the small vial from the wizard, looking at the swirling yellow liquid with a bit of apprehension. "What is it?"

"A simple tonic, just take it. It's not poison, I promise. Unless of course you'd rather spend the next three days losing your breakfast over the edge of the ship."

Rathe shook his head and took the vial, downing it in one gulp. No more than a minute after swallowing the liquid his face began to loose the greenish tint, becoming the normal blushed color it had always been. He shook his head a few times as a tingling sensation worked from his throat to his stomach, and then back to his head. The big fighter stood using the railing as a brace and looked over the sea as the sickness left him.

"Wow, Ectle that was… strong. What was that stuff?"

"Just a tonic that cures most simple little ailments. Sicknesses in the stomach, head, chest, muscles, simple wounds, and even some forms of infection. Three simple ingredients that really pack a punch."

"Magic medicine, I am grateful, and hungry."

"It will be a while yet before we bother with a meal Rathe. In the meantime, just make yourself useful and be a lookout. Watch for signs of anything out there, land, ships, anything."

The ocean began to take a toll on the group as most of them had not experienced time aboard a ship in their lives. Rathe seemed to be the only one having problems with sea sickness but the rest were not exactly enjoying the voyage. Only Erzel kept himself in reserve, refusing to move from the bow as the ship rocked with the waves. The Dwarves at the oars didn't seemed to notice the sea, having been used to moving the ships from port to port.

Night on the ocean brought with it a new kind of darkness, one that was not aided by the shadows of forests or mountains. In every direction, stars stretched past the horizon, inviting the group into a different world. A single torch a the front of the ship cast some light across the bow and the water in front, but for the most part, they sat in darkness, letting the sails push them closer to their destination. The Dwarves remained at their oars, some sleeping while they had the wind in their favor.

The stars gave light where the torch wouldn't and small meals that didn't need cooking were handed out to the occupants of the ship. Most consisted of dried or smoked meat, bread, and water or ale. They ate in silence as the ship rocked, the waves creating a constant slapping against the wood. Ectle handed what remained of his meat to Rathe who eagerly devoured the remains, finishing his ale in one long drink. Erzel sat down next to Ectle and looked at the map he held in his hands.

"So I never asked, but how long do you think the trip will take? How far before we are where we need to be?"

"It may yet be a while. We've just started our voyage and have only been on the ocean for a day. There may be five more, there may be less. I will know when I get there."

Erzel looked at the wizard in astonishment. "I thought you had it figured out Ectle. The whole idea revolved around the fact that you could predict where and when the island would be accessible to us."

"It isn't as simple as you seem to believe Erzel. Calculating when and where an island no one believes in will be is a little more involved than deciding how long it will take to march from Pentegarn to Tvan. I had little to go on and less to use as a reference. I did the best I could!" Ectle snapped, wrinkling the map.

"Calm down, I meant no harm. I just thought you knew when we could expect to find this mystical island. I will let you continue to work on it if you need time."

Erzel left the wizard and returned to his spot at the front of the ship where he would be alone. The sea was having an odd affect on much of the crew, causing them to prefer solitude to the company of others. Nimir left the oars and headed below to lie down, feeling that the trip was already draining him. A hard wave sprayed Erzel with cool water but he pushed the chill away, keeping his eyes on the stars and where the sun was supposed to rise.

When the crew was starting to think the darkness had a permanent grip on the sea, a dull orange glow could be seen on the horizon. It rose quickly, obliterating the black that had come with the night. Erzel cracked his eyes as the bright light invaded the water, catching him in the glare. Instantly, Ectle climbed to his feet and began looking in every direction for anything that hadn't been there the day before.

"See anything?" Thorgrim asked, joining the wizard.

"No... no I don't guess so. I am not all that surprised though, we've still a few days before we should be in range of the island's path."

"When is breakfast?" Rathe asked, scratching his head.

Ectle shot the fighter a narrowed look. "Is there anything else that you think about Rathe, anything at all?"

"Yes there is, but since there are no beautiful barmaids on the boat and no one to kill, that pretty much just leaves food. So... about the food?"

Thorgrim moved to the stairs and walked down to the

bottom of the ship, bringing up a few sacks of food that would be distributed amongst the other crew members. Nimir appeared behind him with a jug of fresh water still sealed with a small cork. They sat down around the oars and drifted as they all ate, watching the waves rock the boat from side to side. The Dwarves were silent, eating quickly and getting back to the oars.

"Guys, you don't have to be so intense with your rowing. Take a break, you've been rowing for quite a long time," Ectle offered as he took a bite of the bread which was sadly beginning to stale.

The Dwarves slowed down some but did not relinquish their grip on the oars, watching the ocean around them as they floated with the current and the wind guiding them. Erzel looked to his right and a prickle ran up the back of his neck. He watched the waves curiously, seeing an odd coloration that seemed to disappear and then reappear. He stood and stared off the edge of the boat.

"What is it Erzel?" Kail asked, noticing the Elf's odd behavior.

"I don't know... something in the waves."

The rest of the group seemed to flock to the edge as well, watching the same area but seeing no real sign of anything out of the ordinary. Then, as before, a strange shadowy coloring in one of the waves appeared near the surface and then disappeared just as quickly, bringing a hushed murmur to the group. Rathe looked at the wizard and then at the water.

"What is that Ectle?"

"I don't know Rathe, it's underwater. Whatever it is, it could very well be a threat. How many bows do we have on board?"

Ectle looked to the Dwarves at the oars. "We have three, and there were two more the Elf and the ranger stored before leaving Tvan."

"So five bows. Alright, get your bows and I will get ours in case they are needed," Erzel ordered as he started below.

The soldiers readied their arrows as the shadow disappeared once again, bringing a level of concern to the crew. Those who had not sailed before had never seen anything like it and those who had sailed had still never seen anything that matched the behavior of the shadow waves. With one last glimpse the shadow closed on the surface, breaking through the wave and revealing a tall grey fin. It cut through the water like a knife and then slid down into the waves out of sight.

"Shark! It's a shark!" Ectle shouted, stepping back away from the railing.

Erzel sighted down the shaft of the arrow as the marine beast turned towards them, reacting to the sound of the Human's voice. It cut through the water like an arrow shot from a bow. The fin broke above the water once more and the Dwarves readied their bows to defend their boat. It was a tense moment but when the shark came into range of the archers, it quite suddenly dove into deeper water, abandoning its apparent attack on the boat. The crew of the ship kept their arrows ready to fly, watching the ocean in case it decided to return. After more than ten minutes, the shark did not make a reappearance.

"What was that about?" one of the Dwarves asked, letting the bowstring slide slowly back to the bow.

"I don't know. Perhaps it was just in the area and heard us. After realizing where we were, it may have wanted to see just what we were," Thorgrim answered, setting down a long spear he had grabbed during the encounter.

"And when it realized we were not dinner it left out to find something easier to eat," Rathe added, staring at the waves for the first time since the shark had disappeared.

"First shark Rathe?" Ectle asked as he heard the fear in the young fighter's voice.

"Yeah, well, I ate one before. Pretty good but it was a little tough."

The last of Rathe's comments brought a chuckle to the crew aboard the boat as they stored their weapons and the Dwarves got back to the oars to propel them further away from the area where they had encountered the giant fish. Even though they were quite a distance away, Rathe continued looking over his shoulder.

"Rathe, seriously you need to relax a little. This ship is more than twice the size of that shark. It just wanted to know what we were, not attack us. They are not as foolish or stupid as many people think."

"I'm not worried about that one Ectle. What if there are bigger ones out there? Ones that would find this ship about the right size for a meal?"

"Knock it off Rathe!" Erzel ordered sharply. "We have no time for any paranoia on the ship. We are fine, we are going to be fine. Just sit down and keep your fears under check."

The fighter did as he was told and for a long time he was silent. As the sun peaked in the sky however, like magic he instantly knew that it was time for the midday meal. Thorgrim returned to the hull and brought back the rationed meals with a look of confusion on his face. He handed out the small meals and sat down next to Erzel, rubbing his hands before eating.

"Is something wrong?" the Elf asked as he took a bite out of the bread.

"I think someone has been sneaking food Erzel. This morning when I brought the meals up there was still half a loaf of bread in the first sack and when I went to get these, the sack was empty. Some of the meat is gone as well."

Erzel instinctively looked to Rathe who was eagerly devouring his food, already looking at the little that was left amongst the others. "What do you think? Rathe been sneaking around?"

"Perhaps, but I'd of thought he was too clumsy to keep from being seen by anyone aboard the ship. If he had gone below, someone would have seen him."

"Keep an eye on him Thorgrim, in case we are wrong."

The Dwarf moved across the ship to a spot where he could see everyone and watch where they went. He ate alone, keeping an extra close eye on Rathe though deep inside, he wasn't sure if the fighter was indeed the culprit. Even though the Human had finished eating and was always up for more food, he actually didn't seem to be eyeing anyone else as they ate. For the most part, he was relaxed, leaning back against the mast. Erzel too noticed the behavior and shook his head, not knowing what to believe at the moment.

One of the Dwarven rowers finished his food and left the group, walking towards the opening that led below. He caught

Erzel and Thorgrim's attention but the rest seemed not to even notice. The Elf shrugged to the Dwarf and took the last bite of his food. Though the bread was stale, it quelled the hunger that had taken his stomach by surprise. The Dwarf reappeared and moved straight to Erzel, carrying with him a short spear from the rack of weapons. The sight was a curious one.

"May I have a word sir?" the Dwarf asked, leaning in close.

"Of course." Erzel replied, waving Thorgrim over. "Go ahead, what is it?"

"We've a problem below sir. Come with me."

The Dwarf led Erzel and Thorgrim down below the deck to where much of the supplies were stored. There were several barrels of fresh water, sacks of bread and meat, racks of their weapons, clothes, blankets, and various other items. The Dwarf leaned on the spear and stared into the dark corner near the front of the ship. He turned his head and looked at Erzel, giving a nod to the area. Erzel stepped in beside the oarsman and peered to the darkness.

"What is it?" he asked in a hushed whisper.

"Something back there. It moved when I came down, I heard it," the Dwarf replied in an equally quiet whisper. "To the right side."

"Go up and ask Ectle to join us and then remain there. We will take care of this," Erzel ordered quietly, taking the spear from the Dwarf.

The time the two spent in the darkness below seemed to last forever before the wizard appeared at the top of the stairs, his staff at his side. Thorgrim stepped aside and the wizard moved in beside Erzel, staring into the darkness where the Elf was apparently fixated.

"What is it Erzel?" he asked.

"Quiet!" the Elf hissed. "There is something down here. In the corner towards the right of the barrels. If you can conjure one of those balls of light that are so useful I will move in and take care of the situation. We need to move quickly though, in case it knows."

Ectle nodded and Erzel readied the spear, hoping to finish

off whatever was hiding in the shadows before it had a chance to cause them any harm. The muttering of the wizard was barely audible but Erzel was ready, watching the corner. Suddenly the ball of light left Ectle's hands and shot to the corner, hovering near the ceiling. Erzel leapt as soon as the light illuminated the hull and landed on the other side of the barrels. He angled the spearhead down and prepared to thrust it but stopped short, shock working through his body. Ectle and Thorgrim watched as the Elf dropped the spear and reached down with one hand out of their view.

"Erzel? What are you doing?"

The answer came with quite surprising results as a hand appeared in his and then an arm. He lifted the form of a person off the floor and helped stand it upright, his face still reeling with disbelief at what had been dealt him. They watched the hooded form slowly reach up and pull the hood back, revealing its face. Ectle and Thorgrim suddenly realized why Erzel had been so shocked.

It was Rhen.

The Isle of Dragons

Erzel sat Rhen down above deck in the sun, giving an equal shock to the rest of the group who believed they had left her behind in Tvan. She seemed ashamed of her choice to hide on the ship to ensure that she did not get left behind but now that they were more than a day away, she knew Erzel would not make them take her back.

"What are you doing here Rhen? I told you this was going to be dangerous. I told you this was not a journey that a Princess should be making. If your father…"

"I am sorry Erzel. I just don't want to be left behind where I know absolutely no one. It will be ok and my father would understand my choice. It was, after all, my choice, and I am not a child," Rhen interrupted.

Erzel looked out to the ocean and then back to Rhen, still blinking the shock from his eyes. The Princess of the Wood Elves had been hiding below the ship for the entire trip, never making a sound and not moving from the spot where she hid. It also explained who had been in the sacks of food that Thorgrim had discovered to be empty earlier. She ran her fingers through her hair and looked back at Erzel, hoping he wasn't really all that angry with her.

"Rhen, may I speak with you privately for a moment?" he asked, leading her to the bow of the ship.

"What is it Erzel? Are you going to be mad forever?"

"No, I just thought, I thought you were mad at me. I figured you didn't come to the door back in Tvan because you were angry with me and didn't want to talk to me until we got back. You were on the ship by then weren't you?"

"Yes. I was mad at you and yes I was on the ship by the

time you made it to my door, but I am not mad at you now. I want to put that behind us Erzel, please. I am sorry I reacted that way but I was upset. I thought you were leaving me there all alone and I had no idea whether or not you would return."

"I... I am sorry too. You realize how dangerous things are going to be? We don't have enough time to take you back to Tvan and make it to where we need to be to intercept the island. I suppose you are coming with us."

"Thank you."

"Have you eaten yet Rhen?" Kail asked, bringing bread and meat wrapped in a cloth to her.

"No I haven't, and thank you Kail. Would you mind if I sit Erzel? Being cramped under there in the dark has really made me feel weak."

Erzel helped her to the floor and sat next to her as she ate the food that the ranger had brought. Nimir arrived with a mug of water and she happily accepted it too, drinking it quickly. The oarsmen went back to their area and began rowing once more, propelling the ship along faster and kicking up a breeze as they rocked through the waves coming their way. Even though close to an hour had passed since Erzel had found Rhen to be the stowaway that was sneaking food, he still couldn't take his eyes off her. Something told him to be happy she was back around him but another feeling urged him to be firm with her. She had put herself in harms way. Ectle arrived a while later to examine her, finding that though she was hungry and a little sleep deprived, the Princess was in fine health. The sea had not affected her the way it had Rathe and a good thing it was, cooped up in the hull of the ship.

Time on the ocean was hard to tell but amazingly nightfall was fast approaching. The sun dove towards the distant waves of the horizon, casting an orange red glow across the water. The Princess was now wrapped in a blanket and huddled close to Erzel as they rocked with the ship, watching the sunset together. It was perhaps the closest the two had come to romance. When the sun finally disappeared into the ocean, the torch at the bow was lit and the group huddled under blankets, trying to preserve their body heat. The further they traveled, the cooler the air seemed to become.

Erzel leaned forward and rubbed Rhen's shoulders, trying to add a little more warmth to her chilled body. "Are you ok Rhen?" he asked, keeping his voice down so not to worry the rest of the crew.

"I'll be fine Erzel. It is just cold, that's all. Are you still mad at me?" she asked.

"No, in some strange way I am glad you are here. Even though being here is a very dangerous and foolish move on your part, I will not continue to chastise your decision. It took a level of courage to make such a choice."

"Thank you."

Rhen opened her eyes in a different but somehow familiar room. She looked around the stone room and realized that somehow she had made it back to the dream where she had first met Alora the Dragon. She looked to her left and then to the right, finding the monstrous Dragon sitting upright staring at her with large eyes of wonder. It gave a gentle nod to reassure she was safe.

"Is this another dream?" she asked, looking around the room.

"Yes and no dear Rhen. Just like before, you are here only in your sleep, but this is very much real."

Rhen walked across the room, feeling much braver now that she realized that the Dragon would not harm her. "So why am I here this time. We are trying to get to your island but it is slow going. Is there something to speed this journey up a little?"

"Have patience my dear. Soon enough you will find your way to us. I must warn you, it is only I who knows of this voyage you have taken. There are many of our kind here, but few would ever approve of your kind finding us. One must use caution on the island as there will be tests and obstacles you and your group must get past before you can see us as we are."

Rhen became worried. Had she known that dangers still existed once they reached the island she would have warned the group of the imposing dangers. As it was, none of the them knew anything more than the island was where they would find the race of the Dragons. "Can you not help us great one? Can you not help us get to you faster and in a safer way?"

"This is a task I have appointed to you and your followers. If you are meant to find help here amongst this race, you must first prove your heart is true and your intentions are good. Only then will the rest of my kind accept you as one worth assisting in your struggle. If you can not help them through this they shall not make it. Sadly, I have lived my life and my future appears bleak and empty. If I am to help your kind, it would grant me a form of honor as I have no way to continue my kind. It pains me to tell you, for I am the last of the Blue Dragons."

Morning came and went as nights and days began to run together. Five days on the ocean and stress was beginning to show between some of the crew, mainly Thorgrim and Rathe. Several times the two had to be separated and sent to different ends of the ship to keep from harming one another. Sensing the escalating tempers between them, Erzel consulted the wizard once again.

"How much longer do you think we are going to have to wait Ectle? With the addition of an extra body our food and water stores are running low, the crew is starting to fight amongst themselves and it is getting colder. Is there no way to accurately say when to expect something to happen?"

"Well I could predict, but the accuracy is going to be off. However, if you want a prediction, I would say we can expect to see something in the next few nights.

"Well then, we'd better start keeping a close eye out. I would hate to come all this way and miss it in the middle of the night."

The Elf gave Ectle a pat on the shoulder and returned to where Rhen was huddled under a pair of blankets. Her eyes were barely cracked when he sat down beside her, touching her on the shoulder gently to wake her.

"Are you ok?" Erzel asked, watching her stir.

"Yes, I'm ok. How much longer does Ectle say we have

before we reach dry land?" she murmured, not yet fully awake.

"He estimated tomorrow evening, perhaps a little longer."

A simple nod was her only response as she laid her head over on Erzel's shoulder. He started to lean away, afraid it was inappropriate but stopped himself, seeing how sleepy she was. Rhen curled her knees up closer to her and pulled the blankets tighter to her chest after a shiver danced up her back. She looked to the right at the Elf captain and gave a week smile, showing her exhaustion for the first time during the voyage. Erzel smiled and the two rekindled the bond that had been threatened in Tvan by his leaving her behind.

Rhen smiled. "I'm glad you're back Erzel. I missed having these conversations. Do you remember that night in the gardens in Pentegarn?"

"Of course, very well in fact. The mist from the fountain, the beauty of the flowers, the stars. I remember that night in detail."

"I'll never forget it. My first night in Pentegarn and my freedom granted away from those horrid Humans."

The night was beginning to approach and Kail lit the torch at the front of the boat. A low fog had arrived with the night, making the torch almost useless except to see around the front of the deck. Ectle tapped his staff on the bow of the boat, impatient with the imposing fog as it had just started and threatened to hide his vision of the sea. He looked through the fog and into the darkness beyond it but found the area dense and impenetrable.

"Any luck sir?" one of the rowers asked, staring up at the wizard.

"Luck?' Ectle mocked. "I don't believe in luck but to answer your question, I do not see anything in this fog. No sign of land yet."

Thorgrim looked to the north and south, finding nothing but water and fog in every direction. He gave up and pulled the axe from his belt, running the blade across a sharpening stone slowly. After the third stroke however, the wizard reached down and took the weapon away from him. Ectle ran his hand down the blade and handed it back to the Dwarf, leaving the blade flawless. Thorgrim looked at the blade and slid it back into the belt. Obviously the noise had disturbed the wizard.

Night had taken the sky completely and the fog was beginning to ease off when Ectle finally decided to sit down and rest for a while. Just before he left his post however, the waves against the boat became choppy. He could hear them stronger out further in the sea beyond the torchlight but couldn't see why. Eagerly he rushed to the side of the boat, scanning the water. Ectle raised his arm into the air and snapped twice, sending two white streaks into the air through the light fog.

As the lights erupted in the sky above, the wizard could suddenly see the outline of land in the distance. He repeated the actions again and this time he was sure that he could see the rocky edge of shore. Ectle turned to the rest of the ship with excitement rushing through his body.

"Land! We've drifted close to land!" the wizard yelled, firing off more of the flares to illuminate the shore.

The crew rushed to the bow of the boat and stared out at the rocky shore, happiness running through them. Thorgrim nudged the wizard softly. "You know Ectle, the ship has been anchored for the past two hours to ensure we didn't drift off course during the rest. We are not drifting anywhere."

Ectle looked down at the Dwarf and then fired another stream of light into the darkness, showing a sandy area in the flash. He whirled around and with a wave of his hand the anchor rose from the water, locking against the ship. With the ship loose of the sea floor, the waves began pushing it away from the shore.

"To the oars! We can not afford to miss this! Row towards the flares!" Ectle yelled as the Dwarves grabbed the oars and rowed with all their might.

The boat rose and fell with the waves as the crew forced it through the water as fast as they could. They needed to land the ship before the island drifted out of their reach. Just before the ship reached the shore, Ectle leapt from the bow of the ship to the sand below, clearing what was left of the water between the two. As the ship was being pulled up onto the sandbar, the wizard carefully explored a little further from the beach.

"Ectle... where are you Ectle?" Rathe called out into the darkness.

"Here!" he called, waving his hand to create one of the many glowing orbs he had conjured before. The ball of light floated towards Rathe, showing him the location of the wizard and the grounds to cover between them. The crew secured the ship as Thorgrim and Rathe joined the wizard, looking around the dark area. Thorgrim carried a torch with him but the light it gave off was muffled by the magic glowing orb. Ectle scanned over every tree, stone and bush as the reality of finally finding the island set in. He nodded to the forest and the orb floated off above the trees, illuminating the area below.

"Where would you advise making camp Ectle?" Erzel asked as he approached with Kail, Nimir and Rhen.

Ectle turned slowly. "Camp? We need to explore and see just what this island is like. Now that we are here, we should get right to searching for the Dragons."

"Uh, you are a wizard. Can't you just use one of your many spells to find them?" Rathe asked, still watching the orb float around as if it had a mind of its own.

"That was the first thing I tried when we arrived but apparently there is a power here that eclipses my own. I have yet to penetrate the shields in place that must serve as a buffer against curious wizards trying to find their lands."

"Your magic doesn't work on the island?"

Ectle opened his hand and the ball of light floated back to his palm, hovering inches above his skin. He held it out for Rathe to see. "Obviously my magic works on the island my oblivious friend. Somehow there are powerful shields in place against magic from the outer worlds."

The group looked over the dark shadows of the forest as Ectle realized that searching the monstrous island in the dark would be suicidal. If the island was home to the mythical Dragons, it would be dangerous enough during the day. He nodded to Thorgrim who turned to start pulling a camp together. Erzel and Rhen slowly strolled down the edge of the beach back towards the ship, his sword bumping against her hip as she stayed close to him. They sat down in the sand with the rest of the others.

"So, what do we have left to eat?" Rathe asked eagerly.

"Not very much," Thorgrim replied. "Some salted pork, stale bread, and a little dried fruit. We definitely need to find something else to eat come morning or things will get a bit difficult for us," the Dwarf said handing the broad fighter his portion of the small meal.

Two of the Dwarves finished their meal rather quickly and grabbed their weapons, heading to the edges of the light of the campfire to keep the first watch. The rest of the Dwarves headed to the ship to look after it through the night in case it decided to set adrift for some reason. As he lay down, Ectle looked around the beach one last time. He knew that when morning came, they would be thrust into an unknown world.

Erzel opened his eyes to the first touches of sunrise, looking at the island for the first time with the help of the sun. Rhen was still curled up next to him sleeping soundly. Ectle and Kail were already awake and sat around the remains of the campfire, looking at the sunrise. He stretched and tested his shaky legs, walking over to the two around the coals.

"Morning, how long have you guys been awake?"

"Not too long. We were waiting for the sun before we woke everyone. Now that you are awake, feel free to go ahead and get the Princess up."

Erzel leaned over the Princess and gently rocked her, watching as her eyes cracked slightly. She sat up and brushed the dirt from her dress, happy to see the morning sun once more. "Good morning Erzel."

"Good morning. Do you feel well enough to travel?" the captain asked, standing and securing his swords in their sheaths.

"Yes. Is it time to leave already?"

"We need to cover as much ground as we can before the sun sets again. The sooner we get moving into the forests, the more likely we are to find suitable shelter, food and perhaps even the Dragons that we set out to find in the first place."

Rhen reached up and Erzel helped her onto her feet, watching as she knocked the couple of leaves from her hair and the sand from her dress. She gave a slight wiggle that caught Erzel's attention instantly, even though he tried to look away. The rest of the group was around the campfire gearing up for the hike into the forests and unknown beyond them. They strapped their weapons and supplies on and started towards the trees, eager to see just what there was hiding on the island.

From behind came the Dwarven rowers, carrying their bows and spears with the plans of joining the expedition. "Master Ectle, shall we come too?"

The wizard turned around to address the Dwarf. "No, I would prefer that you and your crew remain here with the ship in case it decides to leave without us. There is plenty of food in the surrounding forests and fresh water so as long as you stick together, you should be fine. Now, we must depart. Keep the fire burning."

The Dwarves stood in the clearing of the beach and watched as the group started off into the forest. Rathe and Thorgrim followed Ectle with Nimir, Kail and Erzel hanging back with the Princess. They picked their way through the trees, finding that the progress was very slow going as no one had ever been through the areas. They continued to hike up into the hills and then crossed over into a deep valley, careful to keep their footing as they navigated the steep terrain. As they came upon a fresh running stream, Rathe threw himself down into the water, drinking deeply of the cool liquid.

Ectle knelt down next to the water and broke the surface with the bottom of his staff, an evil smile crossing his lips. "This water is poison," he mentioned quietly.

Rathe choked and spit what he had not swallowed back out. Fear crossed his face as he looked up to the wizard for help but found a wide grin instead.

"Sorry, I was simply trying to lighten the mood. It is fine to drink," Ectle said, bringing a cupped handful of water to his lips.

The Human seemed hesitant even as the wizard satisfied his own thirst. At last he returned to the water and was joined by the rest of the group. Once they had their fill of the water they refilled their skins in case water became hard to find later in the journey through the forest. Taking one last look around the forest, Ectle gave a weak wave to the group.

"Alright, thus far I have managed to get us tired and that's about it. Anyone care to offer suggestions on which way to start off?"

Thorgrim looked left and right with an obvious shake of his head. "Well we ain't going back the way we came so might as well just keep going the way we we're going. Eventually we will come across something."

"Yeah, like the other side of this cruddy island," Rathe added sarcastically.

Thorgrim looked at the oversized fighter with a stern glance. "Shut it Rathe. You could've sat back there on the beach and complained to the rowers."

"Perhaps, but then I wouldn't have had the chance to be a pain in your ass Thorgrim!" the man replied with a sneer.

"I'll give you a pain in the ass!" Thorgrim yelled, drawing his dagger from his belt and taking a few quick steps towards the Human.

Ectle and Kail stepped between them and the wizard lowered his brow to the Dwarf. Thorgrim slid the weapon back into his belt and started off in the direction he had suggested. Rathe started off in chase of the Dwarf but Erzel grabbed him by the collar, jerking him down to eye level so he could be sure the man understood.

"Listen close Rathe. We may be away from home with no throne or crown, but in the presence of the Princess you will maintain a sense of dignity and honor in your words or I will cut your tongue out. Have we an understanding?"

Rathe nodded and the Elf released him, watching as he hurried off in search of the Dwarf. Ectle shook his head with a laugh, knowing the seasoned Dwarf would tear the Human apart if provoked to that point. It was Rathe's lack of experience that threatened to cause trouble.

The hike through the forest was quiet as the seven companions searched for anything that could give them answers about where they were and what they were looking for. The trees thinned and thickened randomly as they kept moving. Ectle kept his eyes trained on the forest around him, watching the trees and thicket around them. Up ahead the trees suddenly thickened to the point that no sunlight shone through them. As Ectle looked around the group he found that the trees in every direction seemed thicker than he remembered.

"Hold it here. Answer me this. Is it just that I've seen nothing but trees for the past three hours or are these trees growing thicker?"

Thorgrim and Rathe stopped to look around with Kail and Erzel doing the same, finding that the way they had just come was almost completely blocked with the thick mass of trees. The path they had emerged from had grown together with such speed that the group took a few steps away. The seven grew restless as any sign of escape in any direction had been cut off. They backed together in a close circle, watching the forests around them carefully.

"Uh... Ectle, these trees are alive," Rathe whined as he drew his monstrous sword over his shoulder,

"Trees are always alive you fool. These trees are special... they're..."

The Dwarf was interrupted by a low groan and creak behind him. The group all turned and faced the same direction, finding one of the tall trees making more noise than the rest. As they watched, it took one long step towards them, causing Rathe to take several backwards away from it. The wizard on the other hand remained motionless, watching the monstrous tree creature take two more steps towards them. When it was close, Ectle raised his hand across his eyes to block what little sun was coming through the tree tops. The tree and wizard stared at one another for a few minutes before Ectle decided to speak.

"Um... greetings. We've come not for trouble my large friend. We are here to find the ones who call this island home."

The tree looked at each one of the group, taking its time on deciding whether or not there was any truth to what the small man spoke. A second, even larger tree stepped out into the small clearing. It moved around the group slowly and stopped next to the first tree that had approached them. They spoke in groans and creaks, their actions very deliberate and they referenced the group with low sweeps of their limb like arms. Ectle looked back at the others with a nervous glance, not sure what to expect from such a creature.

The first tree gave a loud groan and the second stepped back, leaving Erzel's group and the first of the tree creatures alone in the center. Ectle took a step forward as the tree leaned down slightly. It turned to the right and pointed further up through the trees towards the crest of the hill. It didn't speak, but its actions were obvious enough. Ectle respectfully gave a bow to the tree as it uttered a low groan, sending the rest of the trees back through the forests. As they cleared out, gaps soon returned, showing them a path once more.

"What the hell was that?" Rathe asked, suddenly looking at the Princess. "Uh... sorry Rhen."

"My guess would be that they are the first line of defense against intruders. It is interesting that they allowed us passage with little resistance," Ectle answered, watching the trees disperse.

"It is odd that they let us pass so easily. I wouldn't have thought they would have just let us pass if they were the guards," Rhen noted as the last of the trees disappeared.

"I'm sure there will be much more we will be up against. After all, if these tree folk are the first line of defense, whatever comes next will most likely be stronger."

"Stronger than a thirty foot tree with an attitude?" Thorgrim asked as he eyed the forest.

"Why don't we find out?"

The wizard took the lead, his staff ready in case of an unexpected attack. Rathe stayed right on his heels, his sword still drawn from the previous encounter with the trees. The group climbed up a gradual incline for what seemed like half an hour where the trees were beginning to become sparse. The top of the incline flattened and stretched out for a good distance, scarred by large rock formations and outcroppings. The rocks grew taller as they stretched away and soon their tops were as tall as the tops of the trees, hiding further areas from the groups view.

"Come on, we need to keep moving. Out here in the rocks we are a bit more exposed and it is more dangerous. Stick close and let's move quickly."

They moved across the ground and through the rocky landscape at a brisk trot, moving around the formations and not stopping to see what kind of differences this part of the land possessed. Ectle disappeared around a corner and as the rest of the group caught up with him, they found the wizard standing completely still in awe.

Twenty yards further away the ground dropped off suddenly, stretching straight down for close to fifty feet. The shocking part was that another twenty feet past the base of the drop was a solid wall that stretched for what was estimated to be one hundred feet. It shot up into the air from the bottom of the trench, hiding the area beyond completely from view. In either direction the sight was the same. Ectle stepped to the edge of the trench to examine the new challenge closer. Rathe had found a large boulder and leaned against it to rest while they worked on a solution to overcome this new problem.

"So... we went from a giant tree soldier to a hundred foot tall wall. Any words of wisdom to help out here?" Thorgrim asked the wizard.

"Go sit down and let me think for a minute. Every problem has a solution, but sometimes it takes a while to uncover the answer."

Ectle sat down at the edge of the cliff and stared at the wall looming in front of him. He racked his brain trying to see the most simple route past the obstacle. The first thought that came to mind was to blast the wall with a fireball or other powerful magic to break through but he knew that was too easy and the Dragons would surely have protected it against magic as they had against his ability to see across the island in his mind. He stood and ran his fingers through his hair, struggling to think.

Erzel and Rhen walked up to the edge, looking down at the ground below. Down near the base of the wall he could see ruined sets of armor and faintly, the skeletons of the bodies that had originally worn them. People had found the island before, but not made it further than the wall. Rhen picked up a stone and tossed it down to the trench below, watching it bounce down to the edge of the wall.

"I guess this would be so much easier if we could just all fly huh?" Rathe asked in a voice that seemed to taunt the wizard.

Thorgrim leaned over and punched the fighter across the shoulder. "Shut up Rathe, we've had enough of your foolish jokes to last this trip."

Ectle looked up to the top of the wall for a minute and then whirled around to face the two. "Wait, say that one more time!"

"You see? Ectle agrees you should knock it off with your jokes before…"

"No Thorgrim, not you. Rathe said he wanted to fly over the wall so that is exactly what we will do."

The group looked at the wizard with disbelief spreading across their faces. For the first time ever, Rathe had an idea that someone agreed with. Even the fighter wasn't sure he had heard Ectle correctly. Ectle didn't bother to explain but quickly looked through a bag that he produced from under his robes. He dug through it, producing a collection of vials and small sacks. He lined the vials up around him on the ground and began mixing the ingredients into three small vials. The liquid was a greenish color but after he corked and shook it violently, it turned to a cloudy yellow color. The wizard tossed one to Rathe, one to Erzel, and one to Kail.

"What's this?" Rathe asked, holding the liquid up to the light.

"That my friends is what will get us all over the wall. It is a tonic of flight. When you drink it you will be able to soar above the wall. The only problem is that I have just enough of the ingredients required to make these three."

"So… we split it?"

"No Rathe. If you share it you will not have enough flight time to make it to the other side without a dangerous fall. As for myself, I can use my spells to fly, but casting them on everyone would physically drain me. You will be in charge of carrying Thorgrim during your flight. Erzel, you carry Rhen and Kail will carry Nimir."

"Hold it!" Thorgrim burst in. "You think I trust him enough to let him fly me a hundred feet into the air and not drop me? No way! Think of something else."

"There is nothing else! We have to get across and this is our way. The sooner we get to where we need to be, the sooner we can find what we came here for. I need you with me Thorgrim and we both know you don't want to be here left alone. On top of that, you can not carry Rathe, so it is your only option right now."

Thorgrim looked around him and realized that he was outnumbered in the matter. Everyone else was preparing for the flight except him. Grudgingly, the Dwarf gave a nod as he knew the words the wizard had spoken were true. As he agreed, Rathe pulled the stopper from the vial and raised it to his lips. It had a sour smell but the fighter turned in up and drank it quickly, trying to keep it from touching his tongue as he swallowed.

"How do you feel?" Ectle asked the three who had taken the tonics.

Erzel rubbed his eyes. "Yeah, I feel chilled all over and my body feels light. Am I supposed to tingle all over?"

"Yes, now get ready to go because the tonic will not last forever. Rathe, grab Thorgrim and let's get going."

The wizard kicked off of the ground and shot up into the air with Erzel and Kail right behind him, their companions in their arms. Rathe held the Dwarf under the arms and locked his wrists on his shoulders. The wind rushed past him as they rose to the top of the wall and got the first peek over the edge at the land on the other side. The ground opened into a massive field that stretched for no less than a two hundred yards in every direction. In the distance they could see the wall curve back around to form a circle, completely enclosing the interior lands of the island.

To the far right of the clearing was a mountainous region and at the foot was an odd looking castle. It was basically five pointed towers that stretched several hundred feet into the air. The four outer corners were about fifty feet shorter of the middle tower which was also a good bit wider than the others. They were all joined at the base by a wide fortified stronghold. Another odd sight was the complete lack of guards or a presentable army.

Ectle touched down with his staff ready and his eyes alert in case anything unexpected happened. Erzel and the Princess dropped in to his right while Kail and Nimir landed on his left. Just as the wizard turned back to check on the progress of the last pair, Rathe came down behind him. With the added bulk of the Dwarf he crashed violently into the ground. Thorgrim bounced twice and came to a rest at the wizard's feet. The Dwarf pulled himself to his feet and started towards Rathe with his fists balled. Rathe backed up a step.

"Sorry Thorgrim, I don't fly around very often and your weight..."

The Dwarf pointed angrily at Rathe. "My weight! Don't you ever touch me again you overgrown spastic moron!" he interrupted.

Rathe lowered his gaze as the insults flew his way. When the Dwarf had finally calmed down the seven companions turned and looked across the field at the castle for the first time. As before, there were no soldiers, no guards, and no army to speak of. For the most part, it looked completely vacated. For an Isle of Dragons, there sure seemed to be very few of them.

"Well, we're here Ectle. What do you have in mind now?" Erzel asked.

The wizard started off briskly towards the odd fortress, his robes whirling behind him as he strolled swiftly away from the group. Everyone ran to catch up and when they were halfway across the field a great shadow fell across them. Everyone dove into the tall grass, disappearing in the thick broom straw and watching as the huge shape of a bird soared across the sky. It dropped in behind the towers and they watched a second bird appear from the same direction as the first. It circled the fortress as well and then dipped out of sight. From their positions in the fields they thought the birds looked a lot like giant eagles.

"Well, maybe those were the guards... or the army," Rathe whispered as he watched the area where the birds had come from.

"Perhaps..." Ectle replied, crawling through the tall grass

to get closer to the castle without exposing themselves to the eyes above. "We need to move out of this field and maybe in the fortress we will find our answers. Those were definitely not Dragons."

"Something else…" Rhen added quietly.

Ectle looked up. "What is it?"

"The wall, it disappeared. I can see for miles and the wall isn't there any more."

The Princess was right. After landing in the field and hiding in the grass, the group realized that the wall that circled the castle and lands was no long evident. Instead, the area seemed to stretch for miles and miles without the slightest hint of a wall.

"Perhaps it is another form of their magic barriers, to make the lands seem small but once across the wall, the terrain changes," Erzel noted, looking around them.

They crossed the field as quickly as they could and found themselves at the steps of the castle. Ectle and Kail took the lead with a nervous look around the area. The others followed at a safe distance, their weapons ready, watching the sky, castle, forest and fields for any sign of trouble. The wizard started in the doors, finding a long hallway filled with statues. The seven made their way down the hall with their eyes wide and alert.

"Hold on a minute… did you hear something?" Ectle asked stopping in the middle of the hallway. The top of his staff was glowing white as he and the rest of the group turned around.

A soft scraping echoed behind them. As they looked back towards the entrance, the first four statues stepped down off of their pedestals and began a slow march towards the intruders. Everyone retreated further down the hall and as soon as they did, two more of the statues came to life, joining the others. The statues prepared their weapons and continued their slow march toward the group.

"The further we retreat, the more of the statues come to life. Ectle… any ideas?" Rathe asked, hefting his sword to defend himself.

"I don't have all the answers Rathe, just cut its head off and see if that works."

Rathe charged up the hall, dodging a low spear and swinging with all his might. His sword met the statue with a loud clang and its head cracked from the neck and rolled down the hall. The torso and legs stopped moving completely as its head rolled away but only seconds later it took another step up the hall towards the fighter. Rathe retreated back to the group until Ectle stepped between the two.

The wizard extended his arm and a raging ball of fire left his fingertips. It rocketed up the hall and met the headless statue with a violent explosion that shook the area. Chunks of rock went flying in all directions and dust filled the area as the group watched to see how much damage the wizard had done. From the settling dust came a hand which grabbed the floor and drug the ravaged torso across the floor, continuing towards the group. Behind it came the rest of the statues. The group realized it would take more than physical attacks to stop the guards.

"Well, obviously we're not going back out the way we came so we have to move deeper. Come on, they're slow so perhaps we can find another exit before they get close enough to do any harm," the wizard said, only half believing his own words.

As they moved swiftly down the hall, the rest of the statues were coming to life, creating a vast army of slowly moving stone soldiers. They came to a point where the hall branched off two ways in opposite directions with a great door directly in front of them. Thinking that the door led into the middle tower and with the statues closing in on them rather quickly, Rathe forced it open and the group hurried inside, closing the statues outside in the hall. The group hesitated inside, seemingly all shocked into immobility at the sight that was before them. Inside of the middle tower they found themselves looking at a vast stretch of land containing a mountain range, lake, grassy field and forest.

"Impossible..." Thorgrim gasped, staring at the land.

"It would seem best to not assume we know anything about this island. Apparently it is very possible. This is magic beyond my comprehension," Erzel murmured, looking around them.

The land was more than real. There was even a breeze blowing through the tall grass of the field, making the vegetation bend and sway. If it were only a mirage or fake vision used to throw off intruders, the breeze would not feel as cool nor the water sound as inviting. Erzel and Nimir took the first steps into the new fields, sheathing their weapons to show they meant no harm to anyone who might be watching. On the side of the mountain was a very noticeable cave entrance far larger than that of the Dwarves and obviously not carved naturally from the elements or time. Ectle pointed to the area and nodded.

"That is where we should head first. It looks too inviting to be a simple cave or crevice. Come on."

The sun danced within the blue sky, giving off heat which only strengthened the belief that this was not merely a vision. Erzel and Ectle were climbing the hill a few yards ahead of the rest of the group when a noise to their right made them both stop. They were fifteen yards from the cave entrance when something moved in the forest to their side. Instinctively, the entire group armed themselves.

"Quiet, we are not alone," Ectle whispered, his fingers twitching as he prepared a spell silently.

Kail drew his bowstring back and sighted down the arrow as he moved the tip from tree to tree in search of the target that had made the noise. Rhen huddled behind the soldiers in the center as Nimir and Thorgrim stayed close to her in case they were attacked. Just when things were quieting down, another loud pop to their left drew their attention. Erzel moved back down to the group with Ectle next to him. The moment Erzel reached Rhen, a blue flash of light left the trees, streaking through the air and hitting Kail's bow just above his hand, splintering it to pieces. From the trees appeared three Knights, all dressed in plated armor of silver and gold with wide shields across their bodies, their swords drawn back to attack. To the right of the three Knights appeared a fourth, dressed in similar armor and carrying with her a crossbow. They didn't speak, but advanced several steps on the group, their weapons glimmering in the sunlight. Ectle flicked his wrist forward and a blast of white light left his fingertips, streaking towards the attackers.

Just before reaching them it seemed to fizzle and disappear, leaving the shining Knights unfazed. A fifth appeared and with him came a figure dressed in armor but wearing a long blue robe across his plated suit. In his right hand was a long white staff which he kept erect as he approached the group.

"Who are you to attack us in such a way?!" Ectle shouted at the man carrying the staff.

The opponent stopped and waved his hand, bringing up a strong gale wind that nearly knocked the group from their feet. His power was amazing and even Ectle felt his spells would do little to intervene with the skills of this wizard, but seeing his companions being battered by the winds, the wizard whipped his staff around and created a shield that broke the winds around them.

Seeing his winds rendered ineffective, the wizard sighed, shoving the staff forward and amazingly, he split the magic shield in half with nothing more than a flick of his wrist. Ectle fell backward onto the ground, bouncing when he landed. The wizard didn't move after hitting the ground and Rhen knelt next to him, placing a hand on his forehead. His skin was cold and he was without any sign of life. Rathe took a running start towards the wizard but only a few steps from his opponent, the wizard raised his staff and the big fighter stopped suddenly as if running head first into a solid wall. He stumbled back and knelt, shaking his head.

As the group fell back together, the opposing wizard gave a wide wave of his hand and their weapons were suddenly wrenched from their hands and belts and suspended in the air above them. Even the arrows in their quivers magically floated away, hovering in the air with the tips all pointed at the group.

"Erzel... he's unconscious."

"That's ok Princess, I don't think he'd want to be awake to see this anyway"

A Gathering of Armies

Elendil slammed his fist against the table, knocking scrolls and maps to the floor. A glass of water turned over and ran across the tabletop, dripping to the floor below as the King shook off his fury. He threw the letter that he had just received and turned back to the Elves in the room. "They've raised Mihlann to the ground... to the ground!"

"My Lord... please calm down. Surely we have time to launch an offensive to retake the lands or at least put battalions in place to defend the lands we still control. If we move now, maybe there is something we can do about it," Aric replied, trying to calm the distraught King.

Elendil punched the table once again before throwing himself into the throne, an exasperated look on his face. The King avoided the gaze of the other Elves as he stared out the window. His grip on the arms of the throne made his knuckles white, his teeth clenched tightly. His thoughts were a jumbled mess of anger, confusion, and fear.

"My Lord?"

Elendil turned. "Yes Aric, what is it?"

"I know that things are not exactly the way you would prefer them to be at the moment but we must consider the next course of action. How would you wish us to proceed?"

"Proceed... with our fortresses and cities being taken so quickly I am not sure what to expect. Where would one start?"

"One suggestion..." Aric noted. "Perhaps you should consider moving part of the massive army to the Great River northwest of Mihlann. From there you can control nearly all of the border and what is not of your land, Tanis and the Wood Elves will protect."

"Only one problem with that idea Aric, the Wood Elves have retreated to their fortress to the north. They should have already reached Eglarest so their soldiers will be of very little support in this matter. I do however like the idea of moving an army to the river in case they are moving north."

The idea seemed to stick in the King's head and his face lightened somewhat. He picked up a piece of paper at his feet and looked at the map, following the river on the map. The distance that needed to be covered was made possible by the fact that the area of river to the west was three times wider and deeper than the area to the east. If they planned on defending the shore, the Elves could mass around the Pass of Merwold, a stretch of shallows that connected the southern portion of the Elven lands to the northern lands. The area that needed to be held was roughly a quarter mile wide. Other than the pass, the terrain of the land made the rest of the river nearly impassible. Elendil noticed the plan was a long shot, but it could work if things were put into place quickly enough.

The other problem with the pass was that on either side of the river were wide shores that allowed for massive numbers of soldiers to approach and assault at one time. Though it was not easy to cross the water in any other area, the Pass of Merwold would prove a difficult area to protect all the same. It would take a massive force of soldiers consisting of archers, Knights, footmen and siege weaponry. Elendil looked up at the Elf for the first time since his explosion.

"Aric, what did you have in mind for the river? What will it take to guarantee that you can hold the river banks against the horde to our south?"

"To hold it permanently? My Lord that would take catapults, ballista, an ample number of soldiers."

"How many soldiers?"

"Two... three thousand."

Elendil raised his eyebrows. "That would be all of Erzel's Order. You are talking about a massive movement of our forces to the Pass of Merwold. Are you sure of these numbers?"

"You want my guarantee my Lord and with this number

I can give you that assurance, that nothing shall invade from the south by way of the Great River. With the enemy held at bay there, it will take fewer soldiers to guard Pentegarn. So what are your orders my King?"

Elendil looked to the Elf curiously, finding the Knight's willingness to return to the battlefield to defend his homelands compelling and admirable. Aric had never had much use for castles or luxury and had made his life in the woods and land surrounding the kingdom. Elerith walked to a gigantic map on the far wall with Aric following him. They looked together at the area that was to be protected. Aric knew in his heart that he could protect the Elven lands with the number of soldiers he had requested.

"Use whatever resources you need to ensure the river remains in our control. I suggest you leave with your forces as soon as possible. Inform me when you are ready and if there is anything more you require in preparation."

Aric bent at the waist in a bow to the King, turning to the door when it suddenly opened in front of him before he reached it. Through the doors walked three soldiers of Pentegarn and a very short creature carrying with it a rolled parchment. Elendil looked down at the guest who barely stood four feet tall. The soldiers dropped back to the door, leaving only the King, Aric and the shorter person. Elendil took a few steps towards the man and nodded.

"What can I do for you?" he asked, looking down at the creature.

"Most gracious King of the Elves, I am a messenger from the King of Domari, leader of the Gnomes. His lands reside further east across the sea but recently we have received word that our settlement here in Nalawren was destroyed and its people killed off without mercy. His highness would like to know why and to make an offer."

Elendil extended his hand to the table and followed the Gnome, taking his seat at the throne. "It is with a sad heart I must tell you that the conqueror Valsera has unleashed his furies on our lands. The settlement you speak of was many days south of us and had little chance against his legions. We are putting together an offensive to counter his sudden attacks," the King said with a nod to Aric.

"His highness was outraged that our people were so brutally executed and such evil is rampant. We are simple farmers, not warriors, but my King has sent thee a letter to better show his intentions."

The Gnome unrolled the parchment that he had tucked under his arm and stood up straight, preparing to read it aloud. Elendil looked at the shorter man with a sense of amusement, not realizing just how short the Gnomes really were. He stopped the Gnome and reached out, taking the parchment so he could personally read it himself.

To his most graciousness,

I send this messenger to offer thee my services after receiving news of how my people were slaughtered most recently. I know not this creature that has plagued your lands, but his hostility to our race hath forced me to intervene. I hereby pledge the entirety of my army to serve next to yours as you see fit. They shall arrive shortly after this message reaches you.

Eludrial, Gnome King of Domari

Elendil read the letter once more and then rolled it, handing it to Aric who in turn read it to himself. The light of his eyes gleamed as he realized that the number of soldiers he had asked for had just jumped significantly. He set the parchment on the table and nodded to the King who raised a hand to the Gnome.

"Apparently your King has decided to send his army to help us in our struggle. Though it is not that I am ungrateful, but I must ask. How many soldiers does your army consist of?"

"Gnomes rarely fight good King. We are peaceful and spend all our time farming and tending to livestock. War is of little importance to us. Our army was no more than five hundred, but after enlisting the Gnomes who would help despite their lack of military training, we managed to bring close to twenty five hundred. Most are bowmen as it is the only weapon they have ever used, routinely for hunting."

"So few of your people are trained soldiers, correct?"

"Nothing compared to your armies good King. We are a simple race. A mere thousand soldiers at best."

"I see," Elendil said quietly, rubbing his chin as he thought about the uses of such a small army. "Well I assume that if they are archers that they are proficient with the bow. So using them from a distance would be an option."

"Oh yes good King, we are very well trained with what we do use to defend ourselves."

"Well then, we shall await the arrival of your soldiers to help in our efforts to rid ourselves of Valsera. In the meantime, I invite you to stay here in Pentegarn for a while to regain your strength and rest up for the voyage home."

The Gnome nodded. "I thank you. I must return to the coast tomorrow to meet the ships and lead them to where you would have them join your army. Only then will I be able to return to Domari and to the Gnomes."

The soldiers walked the Gnome out to a room where he could rest, leaving the King and Aric to talk once again, now that things had changed slightly. They both walked silently to the map hanging on the wall and looked at where the Gnome had come ashore and where the rest of the Gnome army would be expected to arrive.

"With the extra numbers of Gnomes, I am more confident that we can hold that pass. They may not be the most skilled in battle, but an arrow shot from even an amateur bowman can be lethal. Valsera will never have expected to find the Gnomes taking up arms against him," Aric noted, beaming over their new odds.

"It will be a very unpleasant surprise for him indeed. He will not think that we mean to hold the Pass of Merwold, or that we would dedicate this force to hold it. This will be a triumphant victory, or a devastating defeat. Only time will tell."

Aric stepped out into the maze of hallways that made up the depths of Pentegarn in search of soldiers to help him pull his forces together. When he walked out of the castle he found a group belonging to the Order of the White Eagle and stopped them, finding one from the Order of the Golden Lion amongst them. They huddled around the Elf, listening closely.

"Alright Elves, listen up," he ordered in a loud voice. "We've orders to move all of the Order of the White Eagle and one battalion of the Order of the Golden Lion to the Pass of Mer-wold as soon as we can mobilize. We will be joined by other soldiers once we arrive and we can expect a heavy offensive from Valsera and his armies. We shall be taking with us several cata-pults and ballista so prepare for the journey and spread the word. Inform your commander that I would like to speak to the head of the Golden Lions."

The soldiers all left to spread the word. With several thousand soldiers to inform and prep for battle, Aric worried that it would be a considerable amount of time before they would be leaving for their destination. To add to the confusion, no one knew just how fast the armies of the southlands were moving or if they even were. Through all the years of conflict and war, Erzel had always been by Aric's side but now the captain was gone, leaving his army in the trust of his closest friend.

Aric stepped into the room where he had stayed for the past weeks and looked out the window at the massive movement of soldiers in the city below The siege weapons were notice-ably visible in the outer courtyard as they prepared to move them south to the battle zone. He pulled his sword from its sheath and looked down the blade, finding it straight with the exception of a nick in the top. Otherwise, the blade was near perfect. The leather that wrapped the handle was worn smooth but still felt soft in his hands. He gave it two quick practice swings and then slid it down into the sheath once again, hiding the glimmering blade away from the world. He left the room and headed down to the banquet hall where soldiers and townsfolk were eating a late lunch.

He sat down near a group of the Order of the White Ea-gle and a plate was immediately handed to him. He took it and pulled several items to his plate, starting in on the food before it had the chance to get cold.

"Feeling alright sir?" one soldier asked, seeing the Knight's feisty appetite.

"Fine thank you... just a little nervous, and hungry. Everyone else feel well?"

The soldiers chatted quietly amongst themselves and nodded. "As well as can be sir. When are we leaving for the Pass of Merwold? The soldiers are anxious for the chance to repay these evil creatures."

Aric nodded as he chewed. "Tomorrow... not sure yet," he replied as he swallowed.

He finished the light meal and decided to walk out to the outer wall and watch the sun set with the rest of the soldiers. The mixture of red, orange, and yellow bleeding into one another painted an amazing picture on the distant sky. It was natures way of entertaining the rest of the world as it gently passed from one day to the next.

A day had passed since the King and Aric had decided that the Pass of Merwold would be the staging ground for another battle, one to hopefully hold the southern armies in check. In that time, almost eighty percent of the soldiers preparing to leave were ready and geared up for war. Supply wagons and the first initial section of the army stretched across the fields in a long line as they continued to the pass. In the rear, teams of horses and Elves rolled the collection of six catapults and four ballista out of the city gates. The tremendous number of soldiers and horses marching south was indeed a sight to behold. Their march echoed across the fields and into the trees as the Elves looked to defend their border reaches once again. Aric stood next to the King in the courtyard, watching the army move out.

"I have to admit Aric, I wasn't expecting you to move out to battle this soon. At the earliest, the day after tomorrow. I am impressed."

"Thank you my King. If we were to wait too long they may move through the pass without being challenged in the least. This will give us ample time to prepare for their arrival. No harm in being ready."

Elendil nodded in agreement. The sooner they arrived at the Pass of Merwold, the longer they would have to prepare and set their surprise for the enemy. A sturdy defense was what they were building on, and without it, there would be very little they could do to hold off the waves of Goblins and Ogres.

"What do you plan to do my Lord?" Aric asked.

"I ride to Cisalia to straighten out our Human neighbors. With any luck, we will not have to see them in battle. All the same, be careful out there."

"Well, the best of luck to you and your plans my King. I will send updates from the pass as they are needed and if anything drastically changes."

Aric pulled himself up into his saddle and took the reins of his horse from a waiting servant. He gave a nod to the King and fell in beside a group of Knights riding out into the fields. When all was accounted for, the army consisted of a thousand Knights, close to a thousand archers, and eight hundred footmen. These numbers did not count the teams manning the catapults, ballista and supply wagons. Also with the army were blacksmiths, carpenters, masons and general peasants. With the war looking to last quite a long time, it made sense to fortify the area with whatever means they could.

"Do you believe in this mission sir?" the Knight beside Aric asked.

Aric sat quietly for a while without responding, a flood of thoughts invading him all at once. He did believe in the mission, but he also thought that it might be just sending another army to their doom. He shook the thoughts away and turned to the soldier. "Of course I do sir Knight. What good would I do if I did not believe in this mission? To abandon hope before ever reaching the battlefield would be more than foolish. There is always hope."

Even though the Elf sounded very convincing, the Knight beside him was still unsure. Even with the four thousand soldiers backing the massive movement, the odds had not seemed to favor them in many years. In the last few weeks, the armies in the south had struck powerful blows to the Elves and their lands but now was the chance for them to strike back. The recent losses in the south had made the Elves wonder just how strong the Goblins had become.

The line of soldiers stretched back into the forest and out of sight. The bulky siege weapons were making good time behind the teams of horses as they remained with the marching Elves. With the timing of their march through the forest, Aric guessed it would be no more than two days before they reached the Pass of Merwold where the army of Gnomes would join their numbers. The river was the key. Hold the river and it would secure the entire northern reaches of Nalawren, until Valsera could find a way around them.

Elendil was dressed in his ceremonial armor and surrounded by his most elite of soldiers, Elendil's Winged Knights. He looked at the map on the wall at the area where Aric's forces were headed and then to the lands between Pentegarn and Cisalia. He knew that if the Humans decided to stand against them that he would have no choice but to fight them, and it would be all too easy to crush the struggling Human race. All he wanted was to ensure that they sided with the Elves, once again.

Elendil walked down to the stables where the Knights were mounting up and preparing for the ride to the Human city. He mounted his horse and took the reins with a nod to the stable boy.

"Thank you lad. Alright Knights, we ride to Cisalia. The Humans have been suspicious of treason, of abandoning the alliance that has existed between us for many years. We ride to secure that alliance and to ensure that the Humans remember their place amongst the races."

The fifty Knights he brought with him rose into their saddles and secured their weapons, preparing for the journey north to the Human realm. No Elven army had ever entered Cisalia but now it was time to make an impression that would not be forgotten so easily. The King leaned back in his saddle and stretched, adjusting to the mount as it had been quite a while since he had ridden. The first few Knights rode out ahead of the rest of the group and then came the bulk of everyone else, Elendil leading the way.

The Dragon Courts

The cells where the group had been taken were pitch black, giving no chance for them to get any bearings or idea as to where they were. The floor was cold stone and the air was stale, much like a dungeon would be. Erzel sat in the corner alone as each person was in a different cell apart from the others. He had no way of knowing how long he had been in the darkness, but the cold was hard to get used to. It penetrated his skin to the bone without wind or ice. He shivered, knowing that the others were sharing the same discomfort. To his right he heard someone move in their cell and he crawled slowly towards the noise.

He ran his fingers across the wall as he used them to "see" where he could not. The stone that confined them was cold like the floor but he continued towards the shuffle that started once again. Between the cells was a small section of bars. They were just wide enough for one to get their hands through but good for nothing else. At best, a prisoner could speak with the others next to him. He heard a distinguishable muffled cry and at once he knew Rhen was next to him.

"Rhen? Rhen is that you?" Erzel whispered, touching the iron bars with his fingertips.

"Yes… Erzel? Are you ok?"

"I'm fine I think. I blacked out earlier but I think I am fine. Are you hurt?"

He heard yet another cry and wished he could comfort the Princess but knew he could do nothing to help. "No… I don't think so. Erzel, they're all gone."

Erzel looked around the dark room where he though the other cells would be, realizing that he did not hear anyone else in the rooms with them. He banged his fist on the wall, hoping to wake someone up. "Rathe... Kail... Thorgrim... Ectle... someone answer me!" he ordered.

The silence that greeted him brought uncomfortable feelings. He knew that the one who was responsible for their capture was more powerful than he could imagine, and that if this new enemy wanted to do them harm, there was little Erzel could do to stop them. He felt empty, like for the first time during all of this he was alone to face things he could not understand. All at once he remembered Rhen and the Princess brought him back to reality.

"Where did they take the others?" he asked desperately, running his fingers through the bars.

"I don't know. They came in pairs and each time they took someone different. The last to leave was Nimir, who didn't even put up a fight. I don't want to know what they are doing to them out there Erzel... I just want to curl up and disappear."

Erzel gripped the bars and pleaded with his own brain for something to comfort the distraught Princess. "Rhen, everything is going to be ok. I do not know how I know that, but I do. I wish we had more time to talk, more time to spend with one another. I took those feeling for granted and now I fear that time will not be kind for us."

"What feelings are those?" she asked, her timid voice almost inaudible.

"The ones that make me..." he trailed off, swallowing. "I do not know what will happen to us here, but I do know that it may be the last time I have the chance to tell..."

"Erzel, I care for you more than anyone else," Rhen interrupted. "I've loved you since the day you pulled me from the ruins where your enemies held me. The time we've spent together on these trips and this journey has only strengthened those feelings."

Erzel sat silent in the dark, not sure how to sum up how he felt to the young Elf next to him. It was a little more complicated than love, but the heart of his feelings did contain some measure of compassion for her. It was more difficult than he could have imagined to describe those feelings. He felt fingertips touch his at the bars, the only form of warmth in the room. He found he couldn't speak, but reached further through the bars to her arms.

The captain ran his fingertips down her hands and lost the feeling of her arm for a moment. He felt the soft fabric of her dress and under it the warm, round form of her breast. The Princess squealed softly, grabbing his hand and pulling it into her own, squeezing his fingers tightly. Erzel struggled for an apology, having not meant to touch her in such a way.

"I'm sorry... I didn't mean to... I was just..."

His hand was pulled a little higher and he felt a wet kiss on the back of his hand, stifling his stammering completely. He sat in the darkness, staring at where the Princess was sitting and believing that even in the blackness that surrounded them, he could see her form. He pulled his hands back through, bringing hers with them and leaning down to them. He gently kissed the palm of each hand and then the backs, smelling her soft skin as she ran her fingers across his cheek.

The moment was amazing, one that Erzel had never dreamed would come true. He knew that any moment could be their last and it pained him inside because there were so many things he had never made a part of his life. He had never known love or a family. Sitting next to him in the darkness was a someone with similar feelings and dreams, none of which seemed possible at the moment. She squeezed his hand tightly and a tear dropped onto his fingers.

Sudden light drenched the cells as the far door opened and figures marched in carrying torches. They opened Erzel's cell and the Elf stood quickly, unsure how to defend himself against the strangers in the bright light. He took one step forward and a sudden bright white light shot from the hand of one silhouette, wrapping itself around Erzel's wrists and securing them tightly together to keep him from fighting back. Swords were drawn and Erzel abandoned the idea of fighting back, giving a sad look to the area where he had heard Rhen earlier.

Silence gripped them as the Elf was led away, leaving Rhen all alone in the cell. The amazingly thick darkness returned and she curled up in the corner, rubbing her arms and sobbing softly. She felt safe with Erzel in the cell next to her but now that she was completely alone, the Princess felt desperately afraid. She felt a tear streak down her face and drop to her neck.

At some point she must have passed out because when her eyes opened again she found the room light with torches and filled with a handful of the Knights she had seen earlier. In the middle of the five Knights was the wizard that had captured them, his face void of emotion. He nodded to the Princess and spread his hands, showing that he was not armed and had no intention of doing her any harm. Her experiences with wizards taught her to know that even if they appeared unarmed, they were still dangerous.

"Do not be afraid Princess of Swanhaven, you are not in danger. As long as you seek not to harm anyone here, you shall be treated with respect. Tell us, how did you come to our lands?" the wizard asked.

"How... how do you know who I am? Who are you people?"

"We know much more than your races would believe. We are the protectors of this realm. We care for the lands, dispose of intruders and serve the remaining Dragons as they see fit. My name is Yanosh."

She looked at the wizard as she moved up to her knees, unsure if what the man spoke could be true. She raked the hair out of her face and bit her bottom lip softly. "Dragons?" she asked timidly.

"What else would you have been searching for? You and your group of soldiers did not simply arrive here by chance. This realm has an interesting way of attracting unknowing adventurers to us in the hopes of finding gold, jewels or even the Dragons themselves."

Rhen braced herself against the wall and pushed herself up onto her shaky legs, hoping not to fall back to the floor. She took a weak step towards them and then another, watching as most of the Knights left the room. Only two remained; one hidden behind plated armor and a low cut helmet with small slits for the eyes and the other wearing similar armor but no helmet, her wavy brown hair flowing down to her shoulders. In her arms she cradled a crossbow. The wizard waved his hand and the last two Knights left the room.

"Come with us Princess. We have much to discuss and the rest of your group is already there waiting for us to arrive. We mustn't keep them waiting."

Rhen followed them without a need for guards to walk her. She didn't think of running or that escape was even possible. Without the help of the rest of the group, it would be like running through a forest of darkness while blinded. She had no idea where she was or how to get anywhere else. Once out of the room she found herself in a wide hallway filled with statues and paintings depicting different races and classes. She stopped next to one carved from what appeared to be marble and admired it. The base was a cluster of stones and rocks which eventually changed into the claws of a Dragon. She followed it up to the proud face of a massive Dragon, standing as if it were real.

"Princess, we must continue on. Please do not delay any longer than necessary," the wizard said, hardly stopping to catch her attention.

She looked at the statue even as she walked away from it, waiting until the last second to turn her head back to the hall in front of her. Rhen felt out of place and scared, even though the Knights and wizard had posed no real threat to her wellbeing. She followed them through a network of curving tunnels and halls until a monstrous pair of doors appeared in front of them. The doors were amazing, close to thirty feet tall and wide enough for a group of soldiers ten wide to walk through shoulder to shoulder. The awe it inspired in her was taken with no surprise by the wizard who waited patiently for her to follow them further. When the doors cracked open, Rhen took the first step tentatively, afraid of what might be lurking on the other side. The light was much brighter from rows of impressive torches that illuminated the entire room. If the doors had caught her attention, what was behind them brought her to a dead stop, her heart caught in a small flutter of fear and amazement.

On the left side of the wall was the entire group she had arrived with, their hands and feet bound with similar bindings that Erzel had been taken with. They were not guarded, but all held their heads high no matter the situation they were in. On the right side of the wall though was a huge row of benches that no man or woman could find a use for. Centered in the benches was a tall podium of similar size. She was led to the group and stepped in next to Erzel without any sort of binds or restraints.

"Are you ok?" she asked, smiling as soon as she saw him.

"Well, as best as we can be. Did they harm you Rhen?" he replied, happy to see her again with the light to help him. A blush formed on his face as he recalled what had taken place between the two of them earlier in the cells.

A smaller door behind them opened and two lines of Knights entered, their armor the same as the ones who had captured them. In all there were maybe twelve, all armed and without expressions upon their faces. The wizard and his two Knights joined them, standing the closest to the prisoners. Rhen looked down the line at the ones she had called friends, finding Ectle had an extra form of restraint around his throat and mouth.

"What did they do to Ectle?" she whispered to Erzel.

"As best as I can tell they realized that even without his staff he could use his magic so they cast some sort of spell on him. Now every time he speaks it shocks him. It keeps him from doing anything to free us."

The room was larger than it appeared from the outside, stretching upwards into a dark area. The walls were solid granite and the floor was marble, polished smooth with a beautiful shine. A few statues stood on either side of the podium, each depicting a different Dragon in a different pose. A few smaller statues of Knights and soldiers were scattered against the wall around the room. The Princess looked back at Erzel and smiled, happy to be around the Elf again, even if she had no idea where they were or why they were there. Movement behind her caught her attention.

Rhen looked from the Knights behind them to the group to her left, wondering why exactly they were being held in this room. The answer came to her as the gigantic doors to her right opened. Everyone other than the Knights and wizard turned to see what was coming next and immediately they were all shocked at the sight. The doors spread wide and from the gaping hole came the head of a huge Gold Dragon. It walked slowly, its talons curved against the stone floor and stepped up to the benches. The Gold Dragon was roughly twenty feet long from head to tail and it ignored the group as it walked past. Two more followed behind it and took seats with the rest of the Dragons. A minute passed and then a fourth appeared. It was the same color but much larger. It didn't waste time in examining the group but instead moved straight to the podium and stood on its back legs like a Human might, curling its long tail in around its feet.

Everyone was in shock, staring at what they had fought so hard to find, something that at times they hardly believed in. The Dragon looked over the seven prisoners with large eyes, scanning them for anything it might find interesting. The doors opened once more and this time it was Silver Dragons, totaling twelve that entered, taking their places in the seats below the Gold Dragons. They were much smaller, hardly fifteen feet tall but still a deadly appearance. The doors closed again and this time the Knights moved about the room, standing in front of the Dragons in a long line between the creatures and the group.

The Gold Dragon at the podium leaned its long neck down towards them, looking them over. Its lips parted. "You are here for crimes against the Dragon race including suspicious behavior, invading our lands, and criminal intentions. How do you plead?"

Everyone in the line looked at one another, seemingly amazed that the Dragon could speak their language. Erzel took a timid step forward, feeling that since Ectle was currently unable to explain their situation, he would have to do so. "Great one, we have no intentions of criminal behavior and we meant not to invade your lands. We've come a great distance in search of your help."

The Dragon turned its head to the other behind it, whirling back around to look at the Elf. "Who are you?" it asked bluntly.

"I'm... I am Erzel, captain of the Elven armies of Nalawren and commander of the Order of the White Eagle. I would however like to make it clear that in this matter, the wizard you have restrained has more information you may find pertinent to this current situation."

The wizard of the Knights took a step forward and pointed to the wizard who remained bound by the wrists and around the neck and mouth. "Know this wizard, if you decide to try to bring harm to anyone in this room, the consequences will be severe. I suggest you answer what questions are asked of you and give me not a reason to strike you down. Are we clear?"

Ectle gave a distinct nod and the opposing wizard waved one hand, pulling the restraints that were around Ectle's neck and mouth away. Ectle shook his head and cleared his throat, stepping in beside Erzel and staring up at the Gold Dragon.

"Well young wizard, what defense have you against these accusations?" the Gold Dragon addressed Ectle.

"Well great one, it was I who found where to be to intercept this island. This group accompanied me and we had no intentions of causing any harm to anything on this island. Our lands are being…"

"You've already caused damage in the east hall where our guards first spotted you. If I am correct, a ball of fire was used against the sentinels who stand watch over our entrances. Perhaps you remember the damages we speak of?" one of the smaller Gold Dragons interrupted, the voice clearly female.

"Forgive me, but in that moment I felt the need to protect my companions was of greater importance. Had I of known that action would put us in this predicament, I would have acted a little differently perhaps."

There was a creak to the right and the massive doors opened once more, seeming to surprise even the Dragons of the court. Their heads turned towards the noise as a lone Dragon entered. Rhen recognized it at once as the same Dragon from her dreams, the one that had addressed herself as Alora. The great Blue Dragon was similar to the smaller Gold Dragons but her size was impressive all the same. She was leaner, and very muscular while the others seemed to possess more bulk and sheer size.

The Dragon gave a look to the young Princess and though they were not certain, the group swore the Dragon winked. It stopped between the head Dragon and the prisoners, facing the rest of the court. Waiting to be identified, the rest of the court spoke in hushed whispers, looking at the sudden intrusion by their fellow Dragon.

"What is the meaning of this interruption Alora?" the Gold Dragon asked, a hint of irritation in its voice.

"My Lord of Dragons, I have come to ask to represent this group in your court as they are not familiar with the proceedings or method of these interrogations. I fully understand the penalties should they be sentenced under my defense."

The Dragon turned to the council behind him and spoke silently with the rest, receiving mixed responses of nods. The other Dragons seemed apprehensive about having a Dragon defend intruders from an outer world but they seemed to have no opinions against the matter. The head of the Dragons turned back to the Blue Dragon and nodded silently.

"I will give you a moment."

The Blue Dragon turned back to the group and stepped passed Erzel and Ectle, lowering her head to Rhen who instinctively took a step back. "Do not be afraid little one, I am here to help."

"You can talk too? Why have you not before? Everything you said was... well it was in my head."

"It was but a dream. Understand that I will do all that I can to help you and your friends. Sadly, I moved against our laws by bringing you here, but have faith."

The great Blue Dragon turned around and faced the Gold Dragon and its council, her head high to meet their gaze. The council began taking their positions once more and the court continued. The Dragon interrogating the group now turned to Alora, its eyes fixed on hers.

"I take it that you are aware of why they have come to our shores?"

"Yes my Lord, I am well aware of why, and of how they managed to find this island with such ease."

The Dragon hesitated. "Will you present your knowledge before us?"

"Gladly my Lord. The youngest one here known as Rhen

had a vision many moons ago, a vision involving a Dragon to assure her that our existence was a sure thing. That vision helped her to pursue us with the help of the wizard who already possessed great knowledge of our existence."

The council suddenly erupted in a chorus of both disbelief and anger for the sudden admittance to sacred laws being broken. The Knights moved in between the Dragons and the lone Blue Dragon on the floor as the uproar grew louder. The armored wizard stepped towards Ectle to ensure there were no surprises. The Gold Dragon suddenly pounded its clawed fist on the stone podium, silencing the mass of fellow Dragons.

"It is against our laws for a Dragon to expose itself to the minor races. I demand to know who would do such a thing!" the Dragon ordered, its temper flaring.

Alora took one step forward, keeping her head raised. "It was I great one. I am the Dragon who contacted the Princess of the Elves and if a punishment need be served, I will gladly take that punishment and all the blame for this crime myself."

"You dare to break our laws so carelessly Alora? At what cost did you believe that this was worth doing? Explain yourself!"

"Forgive me my Lord, but it was a choice I found all too easy to make. All of you know the situation that I have been placed in. My kind sadly has no future for the last of the Blue Dragons other than I have been killed. Knowing that my kind is doomed to extinction, I chose to send out word to this group in the hopes that my last actions will help preserve another race from their destruction."

The council became quiet as the last few words of the Blue Dragon echoed throughout the room. The silence soon gripped everyone as they pondered what she had said. The words were very saddening. The Dragons knew the ill fate of the Blue Dragon but until that moment they had not realized how painful the Dragon felt about the matter. One of the Silver Dragons stood from the stone bench and looked down to Alora, its face tortured with the reality of what Alora was truly feeling.

"Your pained loss does strike us deeply Alora as there is nothing we nor anyone else can do to change this future. The law you have broken has been broken with the purist of intentions and not to bring harm to our race."

The Gold Dragon looked from the Silver Dragon to the Blue Dragon with an odd expression on its face. The disbelief was very apparent. "What do you mean no harm to our race?! We have been exposed! The laws held most sacred to us have been broken! Forgiveness should not be given so freely!"

The Dragon's voice boomed throughout the room, making the group step back away from the angered creature. Even Alora seemed to lower her head as the leader of the Dragons scolded her loudly. The room fell silent as the two Dragons stared at one another, unsure of what would happen next. Alora raised her head higher, showing she was less afraid than it appeared.

"Regardless of your intentions, you've committed a crime against your own kind. Would you not expect another who acted the same to be punished?"

"Another would not have as much to lose, great one. Choose to act as you will, but my choice to act as I have will not change. If those who remain will remember me for anything, I want it to be that I was not afraid to help those weaker than us. I have nothing more to add."

The Gold Dragon drew back from the podium and with the others who filled the benches, exited the room. Erzel and the rest watched, confused as to what was taking place between the Dragons. The tension was obvious, even after the Dragons had left. Alora curled her long tail around behind her and turned toward the prisoners, looking first to Rhen and then down the line. Erzel took a step towards her, making sure to watch how he approached the beast.

"May I ask a question?"

The Dragon looked upon him with wide eyes. "Of course, little one."

"Why have you decided to take up for us? It isn't that I am ungrateful for what you are trying to do Alora, but I found it surprising that you are willing to risk your wellbeing to help us."

Rhen walked in beside the Elf, moving closer to the Dragon and extending her hand to her strong foreleg. She touched the

Dragon, finding that she was not covered in scales like the Gold and Silver Dragons but rather with a tough leathery skin. The Dragon watched her intently, not moving a muscle as the Princess moved back to the group.

"As I said, my legacy is ending. In a few hundred years, I will be gone and all that made up the Blue Dragons will disappear with me. With no chance to save my race, I decided to save yours instead. There was no question as to whether you and your races were worth helping. If Valsera manages to conquer your lands, he will control the largest of nations. Very little would be able to stop him from sweeping across the lesser lands. More depends on us getting help to your lands than you realize."

Ectle walked up, cautious of the Dragon just as Erzel had been. "Where did they go?"

"The council will decide whether or not you pose a threat and if you are here to start any problems with our race. If you are not, you will be allowed to go free but if you are found guilty, you will be imprisoned until the Dragons can decide if they want to send you back or sentence you to death."

"Death! Oh hell no!" Rathe burst out suddenly.

The Knights behind the Dragon and around the group suddenly readied their weapons, startled by the fighter and his sudden outcry of anger. Ectle took a step up to the fighter and put a hand on his shoulder, calming him quickly before there was a need for the Knights to intervene. Alora looked from the Princess to the fighter whose sudden outburst caught everyone's attention. Ectle approached the Dragon and gave a courteous bow.

"May I address you as Alora?" he asked.

"Of course master wizard."

"Well, granted I just barely understand how we arrived here, or by what forms of magic brought us. When we did arrive, we were in a lowland area with a strange castle but when we entered it we were forced into another door, we found ourselves in an entirely new land. How is that possible?"

"It is one of the simplest explanations, and a very easy concept to grasp. That doorway that our guardians forced you into is in fact a doorway to a different world. It was the easiest way to protect our kind against intruders. As well, we are able to monitor everyone who makes their presence on the outer island."

"So that is why your Knights were able to make such an effective attack on us when we entered the land within the doorway. You knew we were coming," Erzel added, stepping in beside the wizard.

"Likely. We know everything that goes on in the borders of the island. Once you cross into the forests where the trees move about, we are able to watch every move you make. Incidentally, I was impressed with your manner of crossing the great wall. A great many failed once they arrived at that obstacle."

"Thank you, however it was not my idea. Rathe accidentally came across the concept of flight as a mere form of sarcasm," Ectle replied modestly.

The doors to the right opened and the groups of Dragons that had left returned, taking their seats throughout the room. The Gold Dragon in charge was the last to appear, taking his spot at the podium with a glance at the Blue Dragon Alora. The Knights resumed their positions around the room and the group with Erzel lined back the way the Dragons had designated they stand. Erzel and Ectle were the only two up front with Alora. The Dragons quieted and the silence that filled the room was almost unbearable.

"Alora, allow us to address the intruders on their own behalf. Step to the side," the Dragon ordered.

The Blue Dragon did as she was told and the seven from Nalawren stood together in a straight line, waiting for the Dragon to continue. The Dragon took a few minutes, looking at each of the group one at a time. He stopped at the Princess and stared intently at her, as if looking through her to the Knight behind her. After looking them all over, the Dragon took a step around the podium and stepped down into the floor in front of the group.

"My council and I have discussed your presence here on the island in depth and though I find myself against you being here, the majority of the Dragons have decided you pose no threat to our well being. As such, you will be permitted to remain here as you so choose, under the supervision of the Celestial Knights," the Dragon said sternly, turning to the Blue Dragon. "You are free to go Alora."

Joy ran through the group as they realized they had just avoided the punishments the Dragons had planned to use against them. The wizard waved his hand and the ties that bound the group suddenly dissolved and disappeared. The Silver and Gold Dragons filed out of the room without another look at the group, leaving only Alora and the Celestial Knights in the room with them. Alora lowered her head next to Rhen who carefully touched her on the side of the neck. She wasn't sure how to thank the creature, but it was understood between the two of them.

The Celestial Knights departed with the exception of the wizard and the two Knights that had remained by his side. The one on his right removed his helmet and sheathed his sword, nodding slightly to the group. To the left was the woman with the crossbow who wore no helmet. She cradled her crossbow in her arms, seeming to hold it as if it were the most important item she owned. Alora stepped to the side and let the three approach the group.

"Welcome to the Isle of Dragons. Now that you have been deemed suitable to remain, you may accompany us to sleeping quarters for rest. Whenever you are ready you may join us outside," Yanosh said as he turned.

The three left the group alone with Alora and for the first time through the entire ordeal, all seven were allowed to admire the Dragon without fear of being detained by the Knights. The Dwarves seemed to shy away from the Dragon, not sure if staying around something that size was the smart choice. Alora nodded to them and departed in the same direction the rest of the Dragons had left.

Finding they had no need to stay in the room, Erzel and the group left, finding the three waiting outside just as they had said. The wizard walked ahead of them with the man beside him and the woman beside Erzel and Rhen. Rhen glanced at the woman to the left.

"Have you a question dear one?" the Knight asked, catching the Princess as she looked away.

"Well, not really. I just hadn't expected to find a woman serving as a Knight. It was just a little, surprising, that's all. Do many woman of your race serve in Knighthood?"

"There is another besides myself. We are trained just as well as the men and fight for the same cause. Do the women of your lands not fight for their homes?"

"When we must, yes. It is not common to see women on the battlefield in Nalawren though."

The Knight nodded at the thought, realizing that not all cultures chose to pursue the same methods of battle as the Celestial Knights. She walked with her eyes on the Princess, wondering what sorts of thoughts were swimming in the young one's head.

"I do have another question. When we arrived in the inner lands of the island, we found ourselves in the fields. While there, giant birds flew over and disappeared behind the castle. What are those?"

The Knight laughed to herself. "Those are Warbirds. They are the trusted companions of our Celestial Knights. It is similar to how your races use horses in your lands. We use Warbirds."

It was a short walk to the towers of the Celestial Knights. They left the tunnel where they had been kept and walked down past where they had been ambushed the first time. Roughly ten minutes of walking in the forests brought them to the small fortress that the Knights called home. It was similar to the one they had encountered on the surface but as they walked through the doors, they found no stone guardians. The other Knights that had been in the room were now at the fortress. The group walked the marble halls, admiring the tall arches that allowed radiant sunlight to penetrate the rooms.

Two Knights opened the doors before them and the group followed the wizard and his Knights in. The room spread wide, having within it many tables and chairs as well as numerous arches that allowed in more light. The wizard took a seat at the top of one of the large tables and waved his arm to the group, bidding them to do the same. As they approached, the group saw their weapons spread across the table, each of their own items at a certain chair. Each member of the group took the chair where their weapons sat and looked through their belongings.

"I trust everything is in order? Nothing missing?" the wizard asked, conjuring a platter with chalices and pitchers of drink.

He took one of the chalices and set the platter on the table. With a wave of his hand, the platter slid silently down the length of the table, hesitating in front of each person long enough for them to take one for themselves.

Erzel rested his drink for a moment. "It appears everything is where it needs to be, thank you. I do point out that formal introductions have yet to be made."

"Of course, quite well put. I am Yanosh, leader of the Celestial Knights. To my right is Lavian, my second in command. She's quite the marksman with that crossbow. Lastly, to my left is Galador, the leader of our Knights. He has been by my side for countless years. The rest of the Knights are here and there, perhaps you will get to know them at a later date."

Erzel nodded. "I am Erzel, this is Rhen. Down the line is Ectle, Thorgrim, and Kail. On the other side of the table are Rathe and Nimir. Now we've been introduced."

"Well put Erzel. Seeing as how you and your group will be staying a while with us, perhaps it would be best suited if we show you to your rooms for the evening. I imagine that you and the others are quite tired after this ordeal."

The others collected their weapons and gear and left the table. Erzel nodded as the group got up to leave under the escort of the two Knights who had earlier opened the doors. Erzel, Ectle and Rhen remained at the table with Yanosh and the others. They took another few drinks and the wizard cleared his throat, looking at the three who had remained.

"So, have you more questions?" he asked, almost knowing the answer before he did so.

"More than you might expect. So many that I really am not sure where to begin. Something tells me that our encounter here on this island is less than just chance," Ectle stated bluntly.

"Alora chose to bring you here Princess, and though it was against the laws set by the Dragons and their kind, she found it to be the most logical option. You can thank her for the so called chance encounter."

Ectle nodded to himself, seemingly believing that things were making more sense. For the other two however, it was just as confusing as it had been earlier. They remained quiet as the wizards talked back and forth, learning more about the situation they were now in and the best way to profit from the encounter. It turned out that Yanosh was far more powerful than Ectle, but his most powerful of spells were not used to cause harm, but to help those around him.

"So how long have you and your Knights been here on the island and what drove you to refuge with the Dragons?" Erzel asked when a silence between the two emerged.

"Quite a long time. I can not give a certain time, as I have no way of knowing myself. Longer than it seems possible. We, along with the Dragons, came from a distant land where Valsera first launched his assault. Much like yourselves, we were weak against the best of his armies but we fought him with everything we had. One of his most deadly servant soldiers has yet to be unveiled to your people. They are the reason we were forced to abandon our homelands and retreat here to survive," Yanosh replied, looking away from the group. "The Dragon Slayers or to us simply Slayers."

"If I may ask... how were the Dragon Slayers deadly to your forces? I wouldn't have assumed you and yours would be affected by their abilities," Rhen joined in.

"Ah, the worst of memories. True it is that the Dragon Slayers are most effective against the race of Dragons, but their weaponry is just as deadly if not more against the other races. Most use tainted swords and bows that not only cause great harm, but also poison and even rot the flesh of those who come in contact with the blades. They are a shattered race, defiled and the remnants of the group that was first conquered by Valsera. They are now forced to serve him until their death or his, whichever comes first.

Erzel turned in his seat and looked at Ectle for the first time in the conversation, his eyes quite nervous at the thought of the soldiers that the wizard spoke of. He turned back to Yanosh. "Why have we not seen creatures as powerful as this in the many years that we have been fighting Valsera's horde? We have fought Goblins, Ogres, Hobgoblins, Lizardmen, and even Humans rallied from a far off land."

"He has yet to be defeated in a manner that will have him send out his strongest of soldiers. When he finally defeated us in our lands, the Dragons and my Celestial Knights had just wiped out the largest of his armies and pushed them back to the wastelands in the south. When we arrived to finish them off, hundreds of these Dragon Slayers were waiting for us. They nearly annihilated all of our forces in one battle, forcing us to flee or suffer the loss of our races. Once we left, what remained of our past and our legacy was destroyed forever."

Erzel and his companions lowered their eyes, realizing that in seconds they had just witnessed the destruction of the Celestial Knights. With all that remained of their race centered on the island, Erzel realized they had lost just as much as the Elves were in danger of losing. He nodded in understanding to the Celestial Mage, knowing that if they could not get help from the races on the island, their races back in Nalawren would unfortunately meet the same fate.

Lavian stood from the table and nodded to Erzel and the others. "If the three of you would like to follow me, I will show you to your rooms. It will soon be late and I presume we could all use a little rest. Yanosh, Galador, goodnight."

Erzel and the others left the table and followed the Knight out into the hall and up a tight spiraling staircase to the level that held the sleeping chambers. She showed Ectle to one room and then led Erzel and Rhen to theirs. When she stopped at the room for the Princess, Rhen stepped in. "You won't have to show us anything more. Erzel is my personal guard and I would prefer that he remain by my side, even in my sleeping quarters. Thank you for your hospitality thus far Lavian."

"Very well. If you have any further needs, I would be happy to oblige you and your guard. Goodnight."

Where the World Really Stands

*E*lendil sat on his horse staring out at the gates of Cisalia. Behind him was the entire royal guard known as Elendil's Winged Knights. Of all the soldiers included in the armies of the Elves, the royal guard was the most powerful. They wore full plated armor from head to toe and the horses on which they traveled were armored in a similar manner. The noticeable difference between them and the rest of the armies was the helmets. The group got its name from the curved eagle wings on either side of their helmets.

The King spurred his horse ahead with the fifty soldiers riding in unison right behind him. They crossed the plains that led to the city rather quickly and when they approached, the gates were slowly pulled closed. The force of Elves came to a halt outside the city, waiting for the city to open for them once more. The guards on the wall watched the force of Elves arrive.

"Who goes there?" a voice called down from the wall.

"I am Elendil, King of Pentegarn and ruler of the High Elves. Open these gates at once!"

The gates remained closed for a few minutes as the soldiers seemed to discuss the Elf's claim. From the distance even someone who knew what the King looked like would probably not recognize him. Finally the seam between the gate broke apart and creaked open slowly. Even before the gates were opened, the King and his Knights rode through the opening. Humans scattered as the horses carried their masters deeper into the city. Elendil stopped his horse and one of the soldiers took the reins and steadied the animal so the Elf could climb down.

"King Elendil... what do we owe to such an unexpected visit?" the head of the guard asked as he and the Humans bowed.

"Lead me to your King sir. We have a lot to discuss and time is of the essence," he replied in a stern voice.

The soldiers looked to one another with nervous glances as they parted for the Elves to move further into the castle. Most of the soldiers stayed behind at the mouth of the castle but a handful followed Elendil inside. People moved to the side as the group strolled through the hallways with the Human in front. Elendil didn't even slow down at the doors to the throne room, hardly giving the guards time to open the doors in front of him. The people in the room seemed to freeze during the unexpected intrusion. The Human King Calyn stepped down from the throne towards the Elf.

"Who are you and what are you doing intruding into my city?" he asked forcefully.

Elendil boldly pushed past the two Humans standing between him and the Human King, standing face to face with Calyn. The Elves behind him quickly blocked off the Humans in the room and sealed the doors, making sure no one would interfere with the plans of their King. The Elf King squared off with the Human King of Cisalia, staring him down angrily.

"I am the reason you and your pathetic Human city still stands to this day. I am the one who defended the border while what was left of your race betrayed us and dared to side with Valsera and his ilk. I am the one you are going to have to answer to Calyn."

Calyn took a step back, his hands shaking from the confusion that was slowly setting in. He stuttered as he tried to find an answer to the sudden verbal assault by the Elf. The guards in the room found themselves pinned against the wall with the tips of swords pointed at them.

"How dare you side against me after I have protected you this long!"

The Human King fell to his knees, pleading for his life. "Please Elendil, I've not a clue what you speak of. I have not joined the side of the enemy!"

"When my soldiers came to you for help, you denied

them any sort of assistance and turned your back on the alliance we have kept for so many years. You spat on our alliance when you turned your back to us!" Elendil yelled angrily.

"I had no intention of breaking an alliance. I had much to deal with at the time and fighting a battle that was not of my making was out of the question," Calyn replied as he stood once more.

Elendil looked around the room at his soldiers who still had the Human guards held at bay. Luckily, the alarm was never raised and the soldiers outside of the throne room had no idea what was taking place. He looked back at the King, his hand resting on the hilt of his long sword as if he had planned to use it. Calyn found himself unarmed, and without a soldier to protect him. The Elf King rounded on him, his eyes narrowed and dangerous.

"For the record, the Princess of Swanhaven was recovered swiftly by my Knights and with the combined efforts of King Tanis's soldiers. Had we not acted as we did, the Princess could have been lost forever. What would you feel if something like that had happened? Would you even show remorse?"

Calyn was still reeling from the apparent shock, leaning against the table to get a better grip on what was happening before him. Never had he been spoken to in such a way, and this from a King. He lowered his gaze as he no longer felt worthy of looking Elendil in the eye.

"I am glad to hear that she is safe, and you have my apologies for the foolish decision I have made."

"I do not want your apology Calyn, I want your allegiance."

Elerith waved his hand to the Knights who lowered their weapons, allowing the Humans a chance to breath. The King looked at the man, waiting for a response. Calyn was hesitant, not sure what he was agreeing to. Going to war with Valsera again was something he had never wanted to have to do, regardless of the alliances of the past.

He sighed, nodding to himself. "Then you have it. How you see defeating the masses in the south is beyond me, but if I do not join your forces, there will be nothing left for my people in the end."

Elendil nodded happily, a smile on his face. "So you finally see how things are supposed to be? I am glad. If you wish to prove your loyalties to us once again… start now. Get back down on your knees."

Calyn reluctantly dropped back down to both knees, looking at the floor. Elendil drew his sword from its sheath and pointed it to the Human's chest, raising his head a little. "Upon the pain of death, do you Calyn of Cisalia swear your loyalties to the old alliances? Do you pledge your armies to our cause and support the war efforts with all you have?"

Calyn looked up at the King standing in front of him, a serious nod to seal his answer. "I do. What shall I do Elendil?"

The Elf King turned and motioned for his soldiers to stand at ease, finding the Humans breathed easier when the Elves didn't have weapons pointed in their direction. He grabbed a chair from the table and took a seat, beckoning Calyn to join him. Elendil reached his hand out to his left and one of the soldiers produced a rolled map. The Elf King unrolled it and spread it on the table, using chalices to hold down the corners. Calyn looked over the map, finding arrows and numbers written on the parchment in different locations.

"What is all this?"

"A map Calyn. This is obviously the Great River just above the borders between our northern lands and the southern lands which Valsera controls. As we speak, some three thousand plus Elves are on their way to the Pass of Merwold to hold it against the southern invasion, inevitably the last defense before their armies spill onto our home soils. This mass here in the east represents a new addition to our alliance. The Gnomes of Domari have pledged the entirety of their armies, some two thousand Gnomes to back our three thousand Elves. As you can see, we have an ample number to do our part. Now surely you can figure out what I want done."

The Elf and Human looked at one another for quite a long time without so much as a blink shared between them. The wordless pause was a common understanding that Calyn had finally come to respect, knowing full well what the Elves needed and what he was expected to do. He handed the map back to Elendil, leaving his hand extended until the Elf took it. Elendil stood from the table and nodded to the Human King.

"I am truly glad to see the old alliance remade Elendil. Forgive me for ever doubting what could be accomplished if our forces were combined."

The Elves filed towards the door but Elendil turned back to the Human King. "We have not accomplished anything yet Calyn. Just show me you believe in this alliance. Show me you've earned this second chance."

Across the lands of the Elves the great fortress of Eglarest was bracing for a rumored attack that seemed inevitable, even though the slightest sign of an enemy never appeared. Scouts made regular rounds every day for a mile in every direction from the fortress but no sign of enemies was reported and all the soldiers returned safe and sound. Tanis and Narissa spent most of their time in the fortified throne room, waiting for word from the other races, anxious to see what had happened in the south since their departure from Swanhaven. One scout had been sent to the city of the Wood Elves, but had yet to return. Patrols of archers and spearmen relieved other soldiers on the walls and in the towers, making sure that everyone was rested.

"How do you think things are going below Pentegarn?" Narissa asked, looking out the small window at the ocean in the distant east.

"There is no telling. We've no reason to say things have gone wrong, but then no news to say everything is fine either. If Pentegarn had fallen, we would know by now."

"What about Rhen? Do you think she is alright in Tvan? Can we not send for her, to have her with us?" the Queen pleaded.

"Narissa my dear, we must think about what is best for her. If it were true that we are under a threat from some enemy somewhere, the last place she should be is here where she would be in danger. Tvan will never fall. When the rest of the cities fall, the Dwarves will remain."

Narissa caught the glimmer off the ocean and turned her head, blinking several times to clear her eyes. She had truly never been this long without her daughter and every day was a new form of torment. She often walked through the halls wondering if the Princess would be around the next corner or in the next bedroom. She tapped the tabletop, wishing she could convince the King to at least consider her request. An idea came to mind, one that might be a decent compromise.

"What if we just send her a message? Just to see how she is and let her know that we still think about her daily. We could just keep touch with her and make sure that she knows everything is alright."

Tanis stood next to the thrones, staring at the floor with a confused look on his face. The idea wasn't horrible and it didn't necessarily mean that the Princess had to know where they were. "I suppose that would be acceptable, assuming we leave out telling her that we are here in Eglarest. I don't want her trying to come here if we can help it. Go ahead, write her as you wish."

The Queen brightened and hurried out of the throne room to her personal chambers where she could write in private. Tanis didn't give it a second thought, knowing that if he allowed her some small communication, things would not be so sullen around the fortress. A guard walked into the throne room with a bow to the King.

"Yes, what is it?" the King asked, looking at the messenger.

"Sir, I have returned from the northern cliffs with news of the enemy. They were sighted about a day to the north. Not Goblins, though they carry Valsera's battle standard."

"Then what were they? Hobgoblins... Ogres... Lizardmen?"

"No my Lord, Human. They appear to be a very primitive form of Humans, using bronze armor and weaponry and having nothing in the form of mounts or siege weapons. To be honest, they look simply out of place, as if from a different land."

"It is not unbelievable. Valsera has stretched his grasp across many lands and has more than likely conquered many different races. Making them his slaves and armies only seems the next step. How many of them would you estimate?"

"Between four and six hundred. Not a large army but enough to create a problem."

A few minutes after the messenger arrived in the room to report on the odd Humans to the north, a second scout arrived, out of breath and his face beaded with sweat from an apparently strenuous run. He stopped in the arch of the doorway, breathing deeply before entering. Walking up next to the first scout he gave a quick bow and nod to Tanis.

"My Lord, I have news from the east. The ocean is dotted with ships aiming to make landfall within the next day or two. As best as we can tell, they are Goblin warships, each capable of carrying a hundred soldiers. Given the number spotted off the coast, they could have upwards of two thousand soldiers landing after nightfall."

"Are you sure the ships are of Goblins?"

"Yes my Lord. They are sailing dangerously close to the coast and fly their clan banners. We've already seen one run aground on the shallow reef near the shore and it was evident that those struggling to swim to shore were Goblins. What do you make of this my Lord?"

"I can not be sure. Perhaps Valsera is massing an army here in the north to keep us occupied while he wages his war against the borders in the south. Then again, he may know we are here and is sending these armies at us to try and take the fortress. Sadly for him, Valsera has sent far too few."

The soldiers nodded, waiting for their orders.

"Alright, here is what is going to happen. The both of you are to leave with messages, one for Elendil in Pentegarn, and the other for the Elders in Tvan. Warn them that Valsera has moved a number of his forces north in the unclaimed lands between Tvan and Eglarest. Also warn that ships are being used to transfer his armies above the lines we were holding in the south. This may be the start of his invasion. I do not know whether you will be able to get back to Eglarest before an attack is staged, so keep your eyes open, and your ears alert."

The two messengers bowed to the King, turning together and leaving the throne room. They went directly to their horses and started off towards their destinations. Tanis watched the mighty gates break open and the pair moved out across the barren area in front of the fortress, speeding off and breaking into different directions at the start of the forests that distantly surrounded the Wood Elves and their shelter.

Tanis rubbed his hands together, wondering what was in store for the Wood Elves and their fellow races. Tanis knew that the numbers that had been reported were not nearly enough to break the walls of Eglarest. He walked across the room and took his seat in his throne. It was his favorite place to think.

At some point he dozed off because when he opened his eyes again, he found the room darker. The sun was dancing with the mountain peaks, just starting to disappear behind the tallest of them. An Elf with a torch appeared, lighting the other torches that hung from the walls in the room. The torches flickered to life, casting an eerie sort of light around the walls. Tanis thanked the Elf and stood from his throne, stretching and rubbing his eyes. His crown was slightly ajar so he straightened it and proceeded to find his wife. Tanis walked into the bedchamber and found Narissa at the desk where she had apparently been attempting to write the letter to Rhen. Her head was down on the desk and her body rose and fell faintly as she slept. He decided not to wake her as it was the first time since they had arrived that she had slept so soundly. He looked over her shoulder at the piece of parchment, finding it blank. The thrill of making contact with her daughter had been overwhelming, but the spell of exhaustion was stronger. Tanis retrieved a blanket from the bed and wrapped it around her shoulders to keep her warm while she slept. He turned around and left the Queen where she sat, walking out onto the small balcony to the back of their room.

He looked off in the direction of the forest where the Elves claimed the forces of Humans had gathered. All he could see of course was the forest and the tops of the mountains of Tvan. For some reason he was having trouble imagining an army of Humans armed in such an old fashion. Bronze had never been a choice amongst the Humans of Nalawren so wherever they came from was obviously different from the Elven lands in many ways.

He looked down at his chest, seeing the solid plate over his chain armor, knowing that when compared to bronze armor, his was far superior.

As for the Goblins, they had always been armed weakly and wore almost nothing in the form of armor. When they were armored, it was usually weak leather or rusty chain. The Elves and Humans took more pride in their defenses, wearing chain and plated armor at all times. He looked down to a group of Elves on the outer wall, finding their discipline far greater than his enemies and their unruly armies. Though he had yet to see the Human soldiers to their north, Tanis was hardly worried about their threat. He walked back into the room and headed to the lower levels of the fortress, looking to make sure the soldiers were aware of the armies headed their way.

A Blossomed Love

Erzel sat alone on the edge of the balcony, looking out across the tops of the trees at the world he had never before seen. He marveled at how large a world it was, considering he had entered a small castle and then another doorway to find it. That was one thing he just couldn't seem to get straight in his head no matter how hard he tried. What kind of magic was able to hide an entire world inside a castle no bigger than Mihlann? It was amazing, but it was not the only part of the Dragon Isles he couldn't quite understand. The rooms were larger than the tower that supported them and in each they found an enormous basin built right into the floor that worked as a wash room. It was large enough for two or three people. It seemed that behind each door was another marvel the group from Nalawren had never seen before.

Erzel looked back into the room where Rhen was sleeping, watching her chest rise and fall under the soft, white sheets. She turned her head in her sleep, facing away from him now. Her hair curled around the pillow, hiding her shoulders. She tossed again and Erzel wondered what it was that she was dreaming. Her lips moved, as if talking without the sounds. Her hands moved on the covers and she whimpered, making Erzel change from wondering what she dreamed, to wonder if he should wake her. Rhen suddenly tossed to the right and cried out, a mournful sort of cry that brought the captain from the balcony to the bedside.

Her arms shot violently from the covers and Erzel grabbed her wrists, keeping her from hitting herself as he struggled to wake her. She moaned fearfully and then after his continuous shaking and pleading, the Princess opened her eyes.

"Rhen, are you ok? What was happening? What were you dreaming?"

"I don't... I don't know. It was horrible. I can remember the Dragons dying, one by one falling to something I couldn't see," she said between sobs, wrapping her arms around his neck.

Erzel took a second to think, rubbing her shoulders softly to try and calm her nerves. She shook in his arms, still scared of what she had dreamed. He reached one hand up into her hair, rubbing the back of her head and back at the same time. "It was just a dream Rhen. Maybe you saw what they went through in their lands, what Valsera put them through. You are safe here though, so do not worry."

Her sobbing lessened and she pulled her head out of his chest, looking Erzel in the eyes. She ran her hand across her cheek and wiped the tears away, looking to the balcony where Erzel had been. She looked back at him and at once, the memory of what had taken place in the prison cells of the castle came back to them. She remembered what he claimed, how it made her feel and how he had touched her in what they feared would be their last minutes together. Their eyes looked one another over, rekindling the feelings that had blossomed in the darkness.

Erzel gave a weak smile, not entirely sure of what he had said in the darkness earlier, but knew from her look that it had been more than he meant. Rhen pushed the covers back, revealing she wore only her short nightdress. Erzel turned his head. She drew a little closer, keeping their eyes locked on one another. Erzel felt frozen as her lips drew nearer, feeling that he needed to stop her but at the same time, not having the power to do so. He watched her eyes close as she was only inches away. Just when their lips came to meet, a knock on the door ripped them from their moment, bringing them back to reality once more. Erzel pulled back, looking at the door.

"Erzel, we need you in the council room. Come quickly."

Erzel reluctantly stepped away from the bed and walked across the room towards the door. He looked back at Rhen atop the blankets, her hands folded across her lap. Through the sadness she forced a smile and nodded.

"I will come back as soon as I can Rhen. Get some rest," he said turning.

"Erzel…"

The captain stopped as he pulled the door open, not turning to face her. "Yes?"

Rhen looked down at her hands and swallowed, shaking her head. "Never mind, I will just see you when you are done with them."

Erzel closed the door behind him and followed the Knight to the council chambers where most of his group had gathered. He walked into the silence with an expression of curiosity on his face, hoping to have his questions for the disturbance answered. He took a seat next to Ectle and tapped his fingers on the table. Yanosh looked to the captain, his eyebrow raised.

"Have I interrupted something Erzel? You seem mildly perturbed."

"Nothing of great importance I assure you. Is there a problem or something that needs our attention?"

"In a way, yes. The ship that brought you here has departed. They either felt you would not return, or you were already dead. In any case, you have apparently been stranded on our island indefinitely."

"Indefinitely? Surely there is another ship on this island. How sure can you be that the ship left us here?"

"Like we stated before, we know everything that happens on this island. If someone is here, we know it. When someone leaves, we hear it. When someone dies, we feel it."

Erzel looked around the table at the rest of the group, finding that they seemed less than concerned with their current predicament. Rathe, though childish as he had always acted, almost seemed to enjoy the news. He was kicked back, leaning his chair back against the wall with his hands behind his head. Erzel blinked and looked to the next few, finding that only Kail seemed to have any sort of worry on his face.

"Am I the only one who finds this a minor setback?" the captain asked, looking at everyone once again.

No one answered, and Erzel felt the first signs of panic

set in. The island was amazing, but to have no option but to stay with no way off was a bit of a shock. He was glad that Rhen was not around to hear the news. The thought of not being able to get back to her parents and her home would definitely upset her. Erzel stood up from the table and leaned against it, looking around at everyone.

"Well, I guess someone needs to tell Rhen. I hate the thought of being stranded but if I know the Princess, she will take it especially hard. If you will excuse me, I have to take care of a few things."

Erzel did not try to hide his discomfort from the rest of the group. He knew how Rhen would react to the news of their being stranded on the island and he was less than pleased to have to break it to her, but it had to be done. The Elf walked back through the halls in a sort of daze, trying to find the right words to explain to the Princess that there was no way off the island. Nothing was coming to him.

When he looked up and found himself at the door where he had left the Princess, he realized he still had no idea how to tell her. He felt the urge to just be forward, to come straight out with the truth. He pushed the door open and looked inside, finding the room empty. Erzel walked in and checked the bed, the washroom, and the balcony, all of which were empty. He leaned against the railing of the balcony, wondering where the Princess had gone. He looked down to the forest and by chance, he saw a cloaked figure sneaking into the trees. Looking closer, he saw a dress and felt that perhaps the Princess needed a walk.

Erzel hurried back through the room and down the hall, pulling the door closed behind him. He took the stairs two at a time, hoping not to lose her. When he reached the outer gates he knocked them open and ran out into the clearing, turning and rushing towards the trees where he thought he had seen the Princess enter. He wove through the trees, using what little light was left in the day to find his way through the brush.

"Princess?" he shouted, looking around the trees. "Rhen, where did you go?"

No answer. The captain pressed on a little further into the forest, calling for her every few minutes. He could not think of why she would suddenly take off into the woods of a land she was not familiar with. Whatever the reason, he was dead set on finding out. The news from earlier about their being stranded on the island seemed to float away from his mind at the time, put aside until he knew what was going on. Erzel hurtled a down tree and landed on the other side, kneeling in the moss for a break. He could hear running water and walked towards it to get a drink.

The stream ran down through the forest, twisting and winding its way out of sight. He put his hand to the water and brought the cool water to his lips, drinking quietly as he looked around the forest. After feeling somewhat refreshed he stood and continued down through the tress, following the stream as he went. Soon the water reached an edge and cascaded down into a sparkling pool below. Feeling he had taken the wrong direction, Erzel walked down the hill towards the bottom where the pool shimmered.

As he started down the hill, he noticed a small set of footprints ahead of him leading through the trees. After studying them closely, he followed them towards a thick stand of trees that separated him from the pool of water. He followed the footprints until they disappeared behind the trees. Erzel looked through the trees out into the clearing where he had spotted the pool of water. He peered out between a pair of large oaks, spotting movement near the water.

"There you are…"

The trees ended at last and a wide clearing took their place. At the end of it was the large pond where the waterfall cascaded down into the shimmering water. He saw the movement at the edge of the water and he realized it was indeed the Princess. He could see the green dress on the ground next to her and all that remained was her short nightdress. She pulled the nightdress up above her thigh as she stepped into the cool water. She walked in further and as the water reached her thigh, the captain left the cover of the trees and started out into the clearing. She kept her back turned to him as she stepped deeper, letting the silky fabric float on the surface of the water.

"How deep are you planning to go before you come back?" he asked, walking up to the edge of the pond.

Rhen didn't turn when she heard him but instead took another step towards the waterfall. "Just deep enough to get you to come out of the trees. I was wondering if you'd even seen me go," Rhen replied, turning her head to shoot him an all too obvious glance. "Are you going to join me or are you planning on standing there instead?"

Erzel stood rooted to the spot, her words echoing in his head as he tried to take in what they meant. Only in his dreams had such a thing happened and he was cautious to pursue the Princess. He looked down at her as she turned away from him again. Erzel was used to the shy and unsure Elf he met back in Pentegarn. He unfastened the harness holding his swords across his waist as well as his belt, pulling his tunic over his head. He pulled the restraints of his chain armor and slid out of it, letting it fall to the ground in a heap next to his boots. He took his first step into the water, following her towards the waterfall.

He caught up with her just as the water reached her stomach. The material of her nightdress was floating around her, lifted higher by the level of the water. He caught her from behind and pulled her closer, wrapping his arms around her stomach and taking in the scent of her hair. Rhen ran her hands up the front of her dress, bringing them back down to Erzel's where she gently caressed his fingers. She pulled them apart and slowly turned in his arms until their eyes met, his hands resting in the small of her back. She reached up and touched his chest, tracing her fingers across a scar that stretched just below his collarbone. He looked at the scar and gave a weak smile, remembering it vaguely.

"What happened?" she asked, touching it again.

"Long ago, when we saw the first assault on the borderlands. Valsera's soldiers were advancing on a small group of us left behind to see the villagers out of the area. We were hit from three different directions and almost everyone who stayed behind was killed. I tried to fight back so the others could get clear of the area, but I too was struck down like the rest of my soldiers. It was very vague after that. I do not remember who came to help, who pulled me from the battle, or who revived me. All I have to remember it by is this scar."

Rhen touched the scar again and Erzel tightened his arms

on the Princess, trying to push the memory out of his head. Her touch brought him back to the waterfall and the forest surrounding it. She traced her fingers from the scar down his chest, admiring the toned muscles. She looked up to his eyes, drawing nearer to him as he did the same to her. Their faces became closer, the distance between them inches that felt more like miles. She closed her eyes, and when their lips met for the very first time, her body gave a shiver.

The kiss seemed to last an eternity and when they parted, she smiled, glad to finally know how it felt to kiss the one in her dreams. She took a single step back into the deeper water, lifting the bottom of her dress up out of the pool and over her head, tossing it towards the shore. She ran her fingers through her hair and then down her body, watching Erzel as his eyes followed her hands. At first he had the overwhelming urge to look elsewhere out of respect, but realizing it was what she wanted, he kept them fixated on her.

Erzel looked from her eyes down her body, taking in the beauty as it arrived inch my inch. In the moonlight, he could see the curves of her body, her breasts firm from the chill of the water, her bellybutton dancing with the surface of the pool. He took a step towards her and she took another away, giving the impression that a chase was about to take place. About the time that the water reached an inch or so under her breasts, Erzel caught her from behind, pulling her close to him.

He kissed the back of her head, running his lips down her hair and as she turned her head their lips met again, sending yet another shiver through her body. He ran his hands down her shoulders, across her breasts and down to her hips, holding her close to his body. She kissed him deeply as he reached down into the water, locking one arm under her knees and the other across her back, picking her up out of the water and carrying her towards the shore.

The water dripped from their bodies as he carried her out onto the ground, laying her down in a large area of soft moss and thick ferns. Her hair spread all around on the ground behind her and he hesitated, staring at her beauty. Her hand met his and she pulled him closer to her, kissing him savagely as lust had taken over. He pulled away a little, surprised and shocked at what was happening.

"Erzel, it's ok... please don't look at me that way."

"I'm sorry... I just wasn't expecting..."

"It's ok..." she repeated, taking his hand again and pulling him back down to her lips.

The chill in the air brought her chest erect and Erzel couldn't help but stare, flattering the young Elf. She blushed and wrapped an arm around his neck, pulling his lips back to hers again. Her heart fluttered and skipped as he softly kissed her ears and neck, working down her chest. As he shifted over her, she raked her fingernails up and down his back, bringing the same chills to his body. His lips caressed her firm nipples before rising to her lips once more. They moved as one, and as his body settled against hers, only the stars and moon remained to witness their growing love.

Some time in the night Rhen opened her eyes, finding Erzel asleep beside her with his arm around her waist. She curled up against him, pulling her dress up close to her body to add some sort of cover for her bare skin. His breathing was deep as he slept soundly with the one who loved him by his side. She blinked several times, looking at the area around them and stopping when she found a stand of plants around the pond in full bloom. Moonflowers, standing in the full light of the moon and just as beautiful as the ones she had encountered back in Pentegarn. She ran her fingers across his hands, feeling him shift next to her and bring his arms a little higher to hold her closer.

They snuggled in the ferns and the moss, not wanting to part from one another after becoming so close. Erzel cracked his eyes and looked around, leaning closer to her to kiss her neck from behind. She smiled, turning her head and looking at him out the corner of her eye. The moment they shared was silent, but an amazing amount of emotion was passed in that silence. Erzel leaned down but at the angle he was only able to kiss her cheek. When he leaned back, both Rhen and Erzel jumped. Rhen grabbed the dress and pulled it across her chest and hips to cover her from sight. Erzel lifted himself onto his elbow and looked into the clearing. Walking silently towards them was the huge form of Alora, moving through the moonlight with grace and poise.

"Al... Alora? What are you doing here?" Rhen asked, calming down a little when she realized the Dragon was the same that had befriended her.

"Just walking in the moonlight. Might I ask, is that how your kind shows your love for one another?" the Dragon asked, settling into the grass a few feet away and curling her tail up comfortably.

Erzel and Rhen looked at one another, wondering how the Dragon knew what had taken place at the waterfall or if she had seen it. "Were you watching the whole time Alora?" Erzel asked, touching Rhen on the shoulder.

"No, but like the mage told you, we see and feel everything that goes on within these lands. Do not worry, only myself and Yanosh were awake to know what happened here tonight."

Rhen breathed a sigh of relief, hoping that word of what happened wouldn't spread through the group and the rest of the soldiers. She reached up and took Erzel's hand in hers and kissed his fingers, looking back at the Dragon. "Yes, that is one of many ways our kind shows love."

Alora lowered her head to the ground, resting her chin against the soft grass as her large eyes scanned the two Elves. She took one large breath and gave what appeared to be a smile, stretching her wings into the sky. She brought them back down and curled them up against her body.

"Are you going to sleep?" Erzel asked, looking at the Dragon.

"Perhaps. Mostly I am here to watch over the two of you until you can return to the castle."

"If I may ask, under who's orders?" the captain asked politely.

Alora tilted her head to the side, looking intently at the Elves. "It was in my own interests to see you safely back to the castle master Elf. Do not resent my intentions Erzel, I want only to be sure that she is kept safe."

Erzel nodded, feeling foolish for his approach. He looked up the body of the Dragon, admiring how her muscles were toned and strong, but her form was still lean. She stood from the grass and turned towards the forest, peering up towards the stars above them intently.

"Do you mean to leave us now Alora?" Rhen asked, brushing her hair back out of her face.

"No dear one. I will however allow you your privacy to dress before returning to the others. From what I gather of your race, many are shy and prefer not to be watched throughout many of the actions you carry out daily," the Dragon said as she walked away from the two Elves.

Rhen quickly got to her feet and pulled her green dress on over her cool body. The fabric slid down her body as Erzel watched intently, unable to take his eyes off the Elf and her beauty. He followed her actions, fastening his armor on and then his tunic, hooking the belt and swords around his waist and leaning down to the ground. He picked up the soaking wet nightdress, holding it out so Rhen would see what she had forgotten. The Princess turned and took the dress from him, squeezing the water from the silky fabric. She half folded it and let it fall across her arm.

Erzel leaned down and kissed her on the cheek, finding the Dragon had returned once more, watching the two Elves share their moment. The emotion was not uncommon to the Dragons, though their way of expressing it was somewhat different. Intrigued, she continued to watch them until the two Elves turned and joined her at the edge of the grass. Alora nodded to them and quite suddenly took flight, soaring into the moonlit sky and out of sight.

"I take it she is not gone. If she arrived to see us safely to the castle, then she will probably stay up there to make sure that is where we are going. She kind of startled me," Rhen admitted, looking into the sky where the Dragon had disappeared.

"Me too. It would seem like something... uh... someone that size would have made more noise upon her arrival. At least we are relatively safe here on the island. Come, let us get back to the castle where we can find a proper bed to sleep the night through."

The two Elves walked through the dark forest, finding the patches of moonlight that streamed through the treetops enough to see by. They walked side by side, their hands clasped together in a warm embrace. Erzel stared through the trunks and brush, watching the forest for any other signs of life but amazingly, they were the only ones moving anywhere in the dark. Soon they could see the torches above them on the hill, guiding their way back to the castle.

"Well, we're back. Are you ok Rhen?" Erzel asked, seeing her walking a little slower than normal.

"Yes... I'm fine Erzel. Just a little tired and sore. Falling asleep on the ground was not exactly comfortable, but I will be fine."

He led her in slowly, her hand still clasped in his own. They did not see Alora as they entered so they figured that she knew they were safe and returned to the caves of the Dragons. Erzel led her up the tower to the bedroom and helped her into bed, hanging the damp nightdress on a rack near the window to finish drying. As he turned to walk out onto the balcony, Rhen reached up and caught his hand, stopping him before he could get any further.

"Erzel, don't go. Please, come lie down with me."

The captain walked round the bed and climbed under the sheets slowly before he even realized what he was doing. As soon as he settled in next to her, Rhen snuggled in close to him, burying her face up under his chin. Her lips met his skin again, working up to his lips. He wrapped his arms around her and she laid her head on his chest, drifting off to sleep quicker than he expected. Her breathing was slow and soft, bringing him to the edge of sleep himself. Before he closed his eyes again, he looked down at the Elf with him, taking in her beauty one last time.

Tragedy on the Isle of Dragons

*E*rzel sat under the large shade tree with Rhen's head resting against his chest. After the events two nights before, their concerns with getting home seemed to dim and they spent more time enjoying each others company. She stirred only briefly, making Erzel look down at her. He ran his fingers through her hair, making sure to brush her ear with each stroke after finding out how sensitive they were. The water from the creek below them gave off the soft rushing sound that surrounded them. Erzel leaned his head back against the tree and took a deep breath, wondering just how long they had been on the island, and how much longer it would be before they had a way off. As peaceful as it was, he almost missed the unpredictable nature of Nalawren.

Rhen stirred again and this time she sat upright away from him, looking around the trees and forest where they had stopped to rest. She reached back and touched the hilt of his sword that sat against his side, running her fingers down the handle and then off to his stomach.

"Why exactly do you continue to carry those while we are here on the island? The mage and his Knights have everything safe and the Dragons are the ultimate soldier. You should feel safe."

"It is just normal for me. I've hardly gone a day without a sword or bow with me. When you live in lands where war tears the world, it pays to always be prepared. It's not that I don't feel comfortable here, but I'd rather just be on the safe side if I can."

Rhen gave an understanding nod and looked around again, stretching and getting to her feet. Erzel waited until she was standing and joined her, leaning against the tree as his foot came back to life after their extended rest. She leaned against him to kiss him lightly on his cheek before walking off towards the creek. Erzel started after her, dragging his foot as it still had yet to find life. When he finally got the feeling back in his foot, Rhen had already washed her face and was starting back through the woods toward him, a smile on her face. He wrapped his arm in around hers and led her out of the trees, squinting as the sunlight glared in his eyes.

As the two Elves looked at one another, Erzel saw a large black shadow cross them, circling back around. They looked up into the air, finding the form of a large Dragon dropping lower towards them. As it got closer, they looked at Alora. She landed in the clearing with a rush of wind that made them shield their faces. Erzel looked at her as she approached.

"Rhen, Erzel, you must accompany me back to the fortress for your own safety."

Erzel looked to Rhen and then back to Alora, confused and concerned. "What is going on Alora? What happened?"

"There may not be much time. We have to move now. Climb on and I will take you. It will be much quicker this way."

Erzel helped Rhen onto the Dragon's back and climbed up to join her. Alora nodded and turned her head around to see Erzel and Rhen. "Hold on tight young ones, this is going to be windy."

Alora stretched out her neck and with a powerful beat of her wings she shot up out of the grassy field, climbing higher into the clear sky. Rhen's hair whipped around her face, obscuring her view of the blend of colors that was the ground below them. She closed her eyes and wrapped her arms tighter around Erzel's waist, burying her face in his back. Erzel closed his eyes as Alora rose higher and then dove across the tops of the trees towards the mountains where the Dragons resided. She tucked her wings close and dipped low between the trees, aiming for the monstrous cave. Before reaching the cliff face she extended her broad wings to catch the air and immediately slowed her descent. Erzel and Rhen lurched forward as the Dragon landed at the front of the tunnel.

The two Elves sat precariously on her back, unsure whether or not it was safe to climb down. Erzel gripped the wing next to him and dropped to the ground, waiting for Rhen to do the same. As she dropped, Erzel reached up and caught her, lowering her to her feet where she stood quietly. They both looked up to Alora and watched as she nodded and turned towards the tunnel.

"Go ahead, I will follow you. The Celestial Knights and our Dragons have met in the great council room. I believe your group is already there as well."

Rhen took Erzel's arm and walked next to him up the monstrous tunnel with the great Dragon right behind them. For her size, Alora's steps were remarkably quiet. Had Erzel and Rhen not already known she was there, her presence could have been mistaken as a simple echo of their own footsteps. They followed the tunnel around the many curves, ignoring the passages that branched off in other directions. Dead ahead was the council room where Alora claimed the others had congregated. Erzel could hear heightened voices from behind the cracked doors and released his grip on Rhen's arm, pushing his way into the room. As he did, those within the room quieted, looking at the two Elves and the Dragon.

Along the far wall were racks of weapons, which is where most of the Celestial Knights were staying. The few Dragons that were already in the room seemed to be along the outer walls with the exception of the head Gold Dragon who sat upon a large throne at the back of the room. Ectle, Kail, Thorgrim and Rathe hurried towards the two, their faces all bearing a look of fright. He did not see Nimir or Yanosh but Lavian approached, her crossbow held firmly in her hands. She too appeared concerned and more alert than usual about her surroundings. Erzel stopped next to her and rested his hands on his sword, an eyebrow raised curiously.

"Will someone please tell me what is going on?" he asked, looking from his group to the Celestial Knights and finally to the Dragons.

A number of the Silver Dragons turned towards the Elf, revealing the body of one of their own lying on the floor, lifeless. Erzel took a few steps towards them to see what had happened, but the great Gold Dragon stepped in between the Elf and his fallen. The Dragon lowered its head and looked at the Elf with a face that showed a great deal of anger and sorrow.

"This is your fault Elf!" the Dragon roared angrily, shaking the room.

Erzel took a step back, shocked at the accusation. "What are you talking about? How is this my fault?"

"Not you, the Princess. She's the reason they are here. Now my kind has paid for your presence."

Erzel looked at the Dragon without a clue as to what was going on. He looked at Ectle and at Yanosh who had just arrived. He walked towards the Celestial Mage. As he stopped in front of the groups, Yanosh held up a hand to keep from being pummeled with questions right off the start. He waited just a second, and then nodded, permitting Erzel to continue.

"What is going on Yanosh? Why are we the cause of this?"

"I believe I know Erzel, but I need to be sure. Please, Rhen, come here for just a moment," Yanosh said, waiting for the Elf to approach. "What I am going to do is read through your thoughts. It will not hurt, but it may shed a light on this situation. Now please, relax and take deep breaths."

Rhen closed her eyes and took a deep breath as Yanosh reached up and pressed his hands against her temples, spreading her fingers around two different spots on her head. She reached up and touched his hands and together they closed their eyes. Yanosh rolled his head around in a small circle as visions and dreams flooded his head. He sorted the visions he was seeing and finally got to one that seemed relevant. He could see a dark room with two or three dark forms. They were scattered at different spots but in the center was a tall cloaked form, darker than the darkness that surrounded them. The form approached and reached down and touched the Princess on the temple, hesitating for a few seconds. It then withdrew and left the room, leaving the Princess sitting in the corner tied and unconscious.

Yanosh released his grip on her head and opened his eyes, looking into hers. His face was grim and though the memory was Rhen's, she could not remember it taking place. She swayed a little and Erzel quickly grabbed her under the arm to support her. The effects of the magic were a little draining but after a moment or two she felt fine. Yanosh turned and approached the Dragon King, giving a respectful bow.

"What have you learned?" the Dragon asked, watching the group behind him.

"This is truly disturbing great one. Without her knowledge, the young Princess was infected with a simple sort of spell to allow the caster to know exactly where she is at all times. Apparently, her capture was a part of a plan to get the information they needed to find you and your kind once again. Her rescue was planned, and once she was free, the visions of this island came again, which the enemy could access quite easily. Now that she is here, all they had to do was follow the visions in her head. They used her and this group to get to our island."

The Gold Dragon looked up at the group behind the wizard and slapped his tail against the ground, making most of the ones in the room jump. The Dragon was raging angry, having to refrain from causing harm to those who had arrived on the island. The loss of one of his kind sent the Dragon King into a fury. To keep from harming those it felt responsible, the Dragon turned and walked away. Erzel and his soldiers huddled around Yanosh, waiting for an explanation.

"What happened to the Dragon?" Rhen asked, peering between the other at the form on the ground.

"She was killed in an attack on the lands outside of these. We regularly patrol the outer beaches and forests to make sure all is well, but today was a day they should not have. For some reason we did not see them on the island, and when she flew over, they brought her down with arrows. Once she hit the ground, they used a combination of the bows and swords to finish her. One of the other scouts found her body and brought her back."

"What are they? Who is responsible for this attack?" Erzel asked angrily.

"They are a vicious race known as the Slayers. They are bred for a single purpose, to annihilate the race of Dragons. Valsera used the darkest of magic to infect the strongest of his followers, giving them the ability to withstand great physical damage and to use the dark magic themselves. They are here. We have lost the element of surprise and it is only a matter of time before they reach the outer castle and find their way in," Yanosh said quietly. "We are preparing for battle."

The last few words brought Erzel concern. "What do you mean? This island is home to the most powerful beings I have ever seen. How can you not defend your homes against these Slayers?"

Lavian and Yanosh looked at one another and then to the Elf. "You will see. We are meeting them in battle before they breech the outer fortress and reach the inner lands. Please, follow Kristian to the racks of weaponry. You will find that your current arms are next to useless against their abilities. Please, there is very little time and you can not possibly understand what we are now up against."

Erzel watched the wizard walk away and the new Celestial Knight approached, giving a low nod and waving his hand towards a door off to the right. Kristian led the group through the door to a long room with tall racks on either side, each rack containing every imaginable weapon in every design. The different weapons all looked normal, but the Celestial Knight assured them that each weapon was different and very powerful in its own way. All one had to do was pick it up and feel the power running through the item.

Erzel took different swords from the racks and was amazed to see that Kristian had been accurate. Each weapon was different. To his right, Thorgrim pulled a two handed war hammer from the rack, feeling his strength instantly double. Hefting the weapon in his hands, he felt like he could take on a giant and win without a second thought to the battle. Erzel did the same, picking through different swords until one almost began to glow in his hands. The blade wasn't more than three feet long, but it was sturdy and about four inches wide. The handle was long enough for two hands but the sword was light enough to be used one or two handed. The Elf ran his fingers up the edge of the blade, amazed at how sharp it was. He looked at Kristian and nodded, holding the sword up in front of him.

"So, how can we repay you for these weapons? We have

nothing to give and nothing to trade," Erzel noted with a worried tone.

"There is no need to concern yourselves with payment. We need you and your soldiers now, and if arming you with our weapons is what will help us, we are willing to do whatever it takes. Now, continue and meet us back in the council chambers," the Celestial Knight said, turning to leave the group with the room of weapons.

Rathe had pulled a number of different swords from the racks but in the end, he returned them all to where he found them, deciding to stick with his own. Kail took a weapon from the racks, choosing a long war bow to replace the one that had been destroyed in the attacks when they had been captured. He drew the string back and found that an arrow magically seemed to appear, shimmering light blue and disappearing once he let the string slide slowly back to the bow. The group looked at each other, as ready as they would ever be to face this new enemy.

Erzel led the group out into the council room in front of Yanosh and his Celestial Knights. The wizard nodded to everyone and looked at Rhen, his face expressionless. He approached her and put one hand on either shoulder, looking into her eyes.

"My dear Princess, you must remain in the Celestial Towers while this is dealt with. I will see that your protection is guaranteed while we are away. Who from your group is to remain behind with you?"

Rhen looked around them and shrugged. "I don't know. I don't want anyone to leave."

Yanosh lowered his eyes and took a deep breath as if preparing to scold her for being childish. Before he got the words out though, Nimir took a step towards the Princess. "I will stay with you Rhen."

The Dwarf took a respectful bow and stood by her side, looking at the rest of the group. From behind came the large form of Alora, her eyes scanning each of the group intently. She lowered her head in close to Rhen's and met the gaze of Yanosh. "I too will stay behind with the Princess. It was I who helped bring them here, and I will see that she remains safe while they are here."

The wizard nodded and waved his hand to the right where Nimir and Alora turned to leave the others. Rhen hesitated, walking swiftly to Erzel and throwing her arms around his neck, burying her face in his chest. She turned her head up towards him and Erzel kissed her softly, watching with a painful heart as she walked away to join the Dragon and Dwarf. As the three left the room, looks from both his group and the others caught his attention.

"What?" he asked under his breath.

"Well, I'm surprised it didn't happen sooner. You two have been attached for quite some time now. We should focus on what is in front of us though. Rhen will be fine," Ectle noted, walking off towards the Dragons. Erzel and the rest filed in and were soon being informed on what to expect and where to set up for the attacks.

"They are strong but thankfully their numbers seem to be fewer than feared. This must be a small force sent to infiltrate and kill off any they could before either being destroyed or succeeding in their task. We will take them in three locations. The first and second will be at the outer fortress that leads to our inner lands here. Erzel, you and your group will be located there as will Yanosh and his Celestial Knights. The use of Warbirds may be a hazard considering they have managed to already bring down one of our Dragons," the Gold Dragon said looking back at the Silver laying on the floor. "Use extreme caution Erzel as you've not fought anything like them before."

"What is the third location?" Yanosh asked, recalling the Dragon's initial statement of three different areas of attack.

"Our Dragons will take to the sky and attack once they have been engaged. If there is any way we can eliminate the threat outside of where your soldiers have engaged them we will. Our power would be destructive to your soldiers as well if you were to caught in the crossfire."

It made sense, but for some reason Erzel felt like the Dragons were afraid to meet the Slayers in battle, and this was their way of staying out of the fray. He avoided eye contact with the Dragon in case it could read his thoughts but at the same time he was tempted to ask why they didn't choose to defend their lands with more of their own. He sheathed the magic sword and stepped in beside Yanosh, looking at the Dragon bravely.

"We will meet them as you have noted and we will stop them from ever entering these lands with our lives if need be."

The Dragon nodded and turned its back to them, showing the two groups that it was time to head to their destinations and prepare to defend against the unwelcome enemy. Yanosh and Ectle led the way through the large doors and out into the clearings between the Celestial Fortress and that of the Dragons. The Celestial Knights broke away from the rest of the group, heading to the areas where the Warbirds were resting. Erzel watched the numbers of soldiers disappear in the trees and turned back to the two wizards leading them towards where the outer realms were located. Yanosh pushed the door open and the group filed in, looking up the halls at the mass of stone statues that sat undisturbed.

They were early, a good sign. Erzel and the rest spread through the hall, keeping an eye on the statues that had moved to attack them before. The mouth of the fortress opened into the fields and they looked out, wondering where the enemies were. The fields were empty and as far as anyone could tell, nothing was amiss. Yanosh and Ectle took the lead into the fields with Erzel and his group following closely. Erzel looked to Kail and nodded off towards the trees.

"One thing I'd like to know before we find ourselves in those trees, is how these creatures are going to get past those trees that stopped us before the wall. For that matter, how are they coming across that wall?"

"The Slayers are a confusing race master Elf. Very little is known about them but we are sure of one thing. They are here to kill off those they did not manage to before. Our duties as part of this island is to defend its inhabitants regardless of the danger posed towards us," Yanosh answered without turning around to look at him.

The group moved slowly out into the field outside of the fortress, spreading into a line and watching from side to side as they moved closer to the forest. They could not see the wall that had disappeared when they arrived and though it confused him, Erzel did not think to ask how a hundred foot wall simply disappeared once one crossed the top. The group moved slowly through the field, the dry grass raking their hips as they moved further towards the trees that Erzel did not recall seeing earlier. He realized that the island had an odd way of changing and trying to figure it out was a waste of energy.

"The wall was an illusion Erzel. It appears solid and very real from the outer face but within our lands, the wall simply doesn't exist," Yanosh said quietly, reading the Elf's thoughts.

"How often do you rifle through our thoughts Yanosh?" the Elf asked, eyeing the wizard suspiciously.

"Only as I see fit. I prefer that your mind is clear so you can focus on the task at hand."

Erzel took a deep breath and wondered how often the wizard searched his thoughts without his knowing. It certainly made him wonder how private his life really was to those around him. He felt the sword twist and bump his hip, bringing his thoughts back to the land around him. His hand slid down to the hilt of the weapon, his fingers tracing across the cool metal. The longer he stared at the trees in front of them, the more he wondered if the soldiers they were set to fight were as powerful as they had been made out to be.

The group looked up into the sky as a large shadow crossed over them. The Warbird streaked through the sky and cut back towards them, scanning the trees for any sign of the enemy. Two more of the giant birds appeared in the sky, following a similar pattern as the first and dipping lower with each pass. Two of the birds soon dropped low towards the group and landed roughly twenty yards in front of them. The Knights riding them dismounted and approached the wizard. Lavian and another Knight stopped in front of the wizard and gave a slight nod.

"Report Lavian?"

"Yes Yanosh. The forests appear clear and for the most part there is no sign of the enemy in the least. The Silver Dragon was killed on the other side of the forest so it would seem they should be here shortly. The rest of the Knights have taken flight and are scanning the rest of the island. What are your orders?"

"Send the others into the sky and continue your patrols. I would prefer you join us Lavian as we set up a perimeter and await their arrival. The Dragons should be arriving shortly once they feel the enemy has been located."

"Yes sir," she replied, waving the Knight back to his War-bird and sending her own back into the sky to keep an extra eye on things.

Lavian stepped in beside Erzel and nodded, setting her crossbow and eyeing the trees cautiously. The shadows crossed over them back and forth as the spread out through the field, hoping to wait until the enemy exited the trees to engage them in combat. The longer they waited, the more they realized that the creatures may not show themselves and that the soldiers may have to enter the forests. With a concerned look to Kail and Erzel, Ectle stepped up to Yanosh and cleared his throat.

"Where are they?"

"They wait… they wait for us…"

"Can you feel them?" Lavian asked, looking from the wizard to the trees in case the enemy showed itself.

'No, but I know they are there, waiting on us to make the mistake of coming in after them. That is exactly what we will not do, though. When the sun goes down they will come out. We will wait until then."

Everyone in the field looked uncomfortably at the trees and at one another as they noted the sun's position. Only a matter of an hour or two before the sun would be falling out of sight. Erzel drew his sword and checked the blade, finding it sharp and almost begging for a chance to spill blood. He looked to the rest of the group as they began arming themselves in a similar manner.

Rhen sat on the stairs leading up into the Celestial Towers. She stared off in the direction of where Erzel and his soldiers had disappeared. Her heart felt like it was breaking every second that she sat there without him. Nimir approached and knelt on the step below her, his eyes closed as he searched for the right thing to say to her about the situation. In all his experiences, he had not dealt with the emotion of love and heartbreak. He reached out and patted her foot, looking up into her eyes.

"He's going to be alright Princess, I'm almost sure of it."

She looked away for a minute and then back to the Dwarf. "Thank you Nimir. I know… I'm sure he will take care of himself out there. I just need him here… now."

The Princess hid her face in her hands as a tear appeared at the corner of her eye. Her red hair fell around her shoulders. Nimir looked away and moved as Alora slowly approached. The great Dragon moved slowly, watching the young girl grieve with a curious look in her eyes. She reached down with her tail and brushed the Elf's shoulder, making Rhen look up out of her hands.

"Dear Princess, grieve not for the Elf Erzel. The Slayers are a powerful enemy indeed, but the force against them is greater. Once we Dragons make it to the battlefield, the Slayers will fall, I promise you."

"How can you be sure?"

"We outnumber them and to add to that, they are on our land. They have no idea what is in store for them here."

Rhen stood up from the stairs and walked away from the towers, looking into the trees around her. She looked out towards the way they had come earlier and watched as a group of Silver Dragons took to the sky. They flew out above the trees towards the outer lands of the island. She watched as more left the land and followed the others, creating a line of Dragons in the sky. A glimmer of hope appeared in her eyes as she watched the last of the Dragons disappear.

"You see now dear Princess, we are quite capable of fighting off our attackers. Worry not, everything will be alright my dear."

Rhen took a deep breath and sat back down on the stairs next to the Dwarf and hung her head low, praying that they would all be alright. She remembered the way his hands felt on her skin, his lips against her neck and on her own. Another tear formed and she brushed it away. All the time she had been basking in the glow of love, she never would have dreamed that she would be hurting this bad because of it. Her love for Erzel was bringing out the fears that had been hiding within. For the first time, she truly believed that he may not come back.

Nimir looked up into the sky as the sun dipped lower, watching as the first streaks of purple stained the evening sky. The sun was fighting to stay in the sky as the darkness crept in, overpowering the radiant light from the glowing ball of fire. A soft breeze brought a sudden chill to the Dwarf and Princess and he turned back to her, nodding to the tower.

"Princess, we should head inside before darkness arrives. I'm sure Alora will remain here until they get back and in the meantime, we could at least make sure you are as comfortable as possible."

Rhen looked at the Dwarf in disbelief, having no idea how he could even suggest being comfortable at a time like this but after giving it thought she realized she was quite tired and the stairs were nothing close to comfortable. She pushed herself up onto her feet and nodded, looking in at the tower as the torches and candles suddenly came to life, illuminating the entrance and the hall within. Rhen walked into the mouth of the tower and stopped, looking back at the Blue Dragon who remained outside in the last rays of the sun. Alora nodded to the Princess and turned her head, moving off towards the bottom of the hill away from the Celestial Tower. Rhen walked in and Nimir pushed the large wooden doors closed, sealing the world outside away from the Elf.

"Is there anything I can do for you?" Nimir asked, giving a low bow to the Elf Princess.

"Come with me," she replied quickly, starting up the stairs to where the room she and Erzel had shared the nights before.

Nimir followed quickly, struggling to keep up as the longer legs of the Elf gave her the ability to take the stairs up to three at a time while the Dwarf was lucky to stretch two. The Princess arrived at the door and hurried inside, heading straight for the balcony as the Dwarf arrived at the door, his face a little red from the run up the stairs. He walked out to join her, looking at the sky as the last rays of light were finally drained away with the setting of the sun. Rhen was staring off towards the entrance to the fortress that served as a gateway between the inner and outer parts of the island. With the darkness arriving, she could not make out the land very easily.

"What... can I do... up here?" Nimir asked, catching his breath at last as he stopped and leaned against the railing of the balcony. He followed her gaze off of the tower across the tops of the trees to where they could see the temple that served as the doorway between the two lands.

The Princess did not respond. She gripped the edge of the railing, staring out into the dark with only the flicker of the torches on the wall behind her to see by. She pushed her hair back out of her face and dropped her fingers down her chest, feeling her heart beating wildly as her thoughts turned back to Erzel. She looked away from the balcony to the Dwarf and gave a weak smile.

"He loves me, doesn't he Nimir?"

The Dwarf raised an eyebrow. "Erzel? Of course my lady. Has he not shown you?"

Rhen did not answer the question but her thoughts immediately turned to the night next to the shimmering pool of water, his warm skin, his soft kiss. He had indeed shown his love for her, but she would give anything to feel loved by him again. She turned from the balcony and walked back into the room, waiting as Nimir made it to the door and opened it.

"Thank you Nimir. I am going to lie down. I feel exhausted."

"As you wish. I will keep you informed on everything as soon as I know something."

The Dwarf left the room and once the door was closed, Rhen untied the back of her dress and let it fall to the floor, leaving only the short nightdress covering her. She walked to the wall and stood in front of the tall mirror. She looked around the room one last time and turned back to the mirror, pulling the straps of her nightdress off of her shoulders and letting it fall to the floor as the dress had earlier. She admired her body in the torchlight and ran her fingers down her breasts to her stomach, letting them rake across the soft skin. Even in the dim light, her beauty was inarguable. She bent to the floor and retrieved the nightdress, pulling it on slowly and walking to the bed. She laid back on the top of the covers and once again her hands fell to her stomach, forming gentle circles and bringing a little smile to her face.

Erzel knelt in the grass and stared out towards the forest as the last ray of the dwindling sunlight disappeared. Even in the early hours of darkness the Slayers failed to emerge and show themselves. The group looked in the sky as the body of a Dragon flew silently above them. Ectle looked to his left at Erzel and shook his head, wondering what they were supposed to do now. Yanosh watched the trees and then turned to Lavian.

"Lavian my dear, we are going to have to go in after them. It appears they will not leave the cover of the trees with the threat of the Dragons looming overhead," the wizard said quietly, standing out of the grassy field.

"Agreed. How shall we proceed?"

"Ectle, take Kail and Thorgrim around the right side and work into the forest and Lavian will take Erzel and Rathe into the left. I shall enter somewhere in between those two areas and together we will flush them out. Beware, they are powerful creatures with strengths you have not encountered. Stay together, and stay alert."

Yanosh gave one last look back at the group and started towards the trees as the other six split and approached the forest from different directions. Erzel moved in next to Lavian with Rathe behind the two, their weapons all drawn and prepared for the second one of the creatures appeared. Yanosh disappeared into the trees and Ectle's group followed only seconds behind from their angle, leaving Lavian and her two companions out in the open. They hesitated for only a moment and with one last look up into the sky, the Celestial Knight pushed ahead with the two swordsmen right behind her.

The Elf ducked under a low branch and stared into the blanket of dark that spread through the trees, pierced only by sparse rays of moonlight here and there. They moved almost silently with the exception of Rathe who clumsily tripped over a root and stumbled into Erzel from behind. The Elf turned and grabbed the man by the front of his armor and pulled him down to eye level.

"Watch what you are doing Rathe!" he whispered angrily. "We're outnumbered and on unfamiliar ground with an enemy we know nothing about. Now is the time to straighten out and be a man!"

The fighter didn't reply as Erzel turned and rejoined Lavian. She walked silently, her crossbow pressed against her shoulder ready to loose its deadly weapon. They were about a hundred yards into the forest when a noise to their right made the three stop, their ears straining to hear more around them. Erzel's Elven ears scanned the darkness, picking up the slightest footstep in the brush, making him quickly tap Lavian and point off to where the noises were coming from. The three fell back into position and waited, Erzel on the right and Rathe on the left with Lavian behind but in between them. She sighted down the weapon and waited, scarcely breathing.

A louder pop to their right caught their attention and the fighter turned, his large sword drawn back to strike any who approached. The trees and brush moved apart and from the opening appeared Yanosh, his staff extended and ready to attack, Upon seeing the three he lowered the weapon and nodded. Having heard Rathe's stumbling earlier he turned and approached the area where the noise had originated. Lavian and Erzel stopped in next to the wizard, concerned and confused.

"Yanosh, where are they?" Erzel asked, clenching his sword a little tighter.

"They remain here Erzel, somewhere in these trees. I can feel them. I thought the noises moments ago would have been one of them but I see that it was only you three instead. I feel that coming into the forest may have been a mistake now."

"Why Yanosh? Have you a feeling of something to come?"

"Not exactly. The behavior of these creatures does not normally fall into this sort of fighting method. They are usually ruthless and unforgiving, choosing to attack the moment it is possible, but they are staying away from us."

"Perhaps they are scared?" Erzel added, looking around

the trees as the moonlight brightened the area. Suddenly he too could feel them in the trees.

"No master Elf, they do not know fear. Something is different. I should have felt it earlier but it wasn't until we were all in the trees that I realized what was going on."

"Which is?"

Yanosh looked at the Elf and the Knight for the first time with a hint of fear in his eyes. "A trap."

The last words brought silence to the group as everything set in. Lavian turned her head slightly, looking through the trees for any sign of movement but finding nothing out of place, she turned back to Yanosh. "Then we need to leave."

Lavian's words echoed in Erzel's ears but as they faded another noise caught his attention. It was faint, like ropes being stretched tight. It made no sense to him and as he turned to Yanosh to mention it, a snap sounded from the trees. The three turned to defend themselves but instead watched as Rathe was suddenly knocked back off of his feet, an arrow jutting from his chest. He dropped his sword and collapsed to the ground, a shriek of pain erupting from his lips.

Lavian whirled around and fired into the trees from which the arrow had come, seeing a blinding flash of light as the bolt struck a nearby tree. A dark figure stumbled away, retreating from the light but in its moment of retreat, it gave the wizard the chance to pick it out of the trees. He whipped his staff forward and from it came a bright ray of light that streaked between the trees. The beam bounced off a tree and immediately struck the fleeing creature in the back, knocking it to the ground. Yanosh took off towards the Slayer while Erzel and Lavian moved to Rathe's side.

"Hang on Rathe, you're going to be alright!" Erzel shouted, sheathing his sword and grabbing the man's hand.

The fighter writhed in agony, his muscles drawn tight as he shook violently on the ground. Erzel turned to Lavian who had dropped to one knee, crossbow pulled to her shoulder. Erzel grabbed Rathe's shoulder and pushed him against the ground, grabbing the arrow around the shaft and immediately letting go, his hand burned through his glove for some unknown reason. Erzel turned to Lavian, his hand throbbing.

"Lavian... help me get this out of him!" he yelled.

"Move!"

The Celestial Knight dropped in beside the fighter being tortured from the pain, casting aside her crossbow and wrapping her cloak around the shaft. She grabbed it with her gauntlet and gave a hard jerk. On her second attempt the arrow head slid out of his chest and she staggered back, tossing it away and retrieving her crossbow from the ground. Erzel looked at the arrow on the ground and quickly turned back to Rathe who was struggling to regain his composure. He reached up and gripped his chest where the arrow had been and gritted his teeth as the constant pain throbbed deep inside him.

"Rathe... answer me Rathe!" Erzel yelled, slapping the fighter across the face sharply.

"I'm a... what... happened?" the fighter stuttered, seeing the dark blood on his fingers.

Erzel looked back behind him as Lavian yelled something and fired off her crossbow. The bolt streaked through the dark and struck a shadow rounding in front of a tree. The blast of light sent the creature reeling, bouncing off a tree and falling back into the clearing where Erzel and Lavian were standing ready. The Elf quickly drew his sword and jumped towards the Slayer as it started to get to its feet. He saw another flash of light from the deeper part of the forest and wondered if Yanosh had managed any better against his opponent. The Slayer dodged to the right and lifted its sword to match Erzel as the two opponents circled one another for the first time.

Lavian pulled the next bolt from the quiver at her hip and locked it on the crossbow, drawing the string back and aiming at the Slayer but Erzel's path of circling the creature moved him directly into her line and she was forced to hold off the attack. The Slayer made the first move, a quick step towards the Elf followed by a fast overhand strike that Erzel easily sidestepped, moving out of Lavian's aim and giving her the clear shot. She released the bolt, striking the creature in the head with another blast of light that put it on the ground. Erzel leapt towards it and gave the Slayer a swift kick across the armored head.

As the creature rolled onto its hands and knees to get back to its feet, Erzel quickly brought his sword down, slicing through its neck cleanly and watched as the helmet and head fell to the ground. The body of the Slayer suddenly began to glow a soft orange as cracks appeared in its armor and all along its body. The orange light radiated from within its body out through the cracks and quite suddenly the body was engulfed in flames. Only seconds later it collapsed in a pile of ash and smoldering remains. Erzel looked down at Rathe and then to Lavian.

"We've got to get him out of here now."

Sheathing his sword he grabbed the unconscious fighter's hands, pulling him backward towards the area where they had entered the forest to begin with. Lavian remained in front, her crossbow ready in case another creature decided to make his attack on the group as they fled. Another blast of light from the deeper region of the forest assured them that Yanosh was still alive and fighting. Erzel pulled with all his might three figures appeared suddenly to their right. It was Kail, Thorgrim, and Ectle.

"Kail, help me drag him!" Erzel shouted as they stopped in awe at the sight of the big man's lifeless body.

Ectle joined Lavian as Erzel and the other two pulled Rathe's body out of the trees, stopping in the field a safe distance away. Ectle immediately dropped to the ground next to the fighter, running his hand across his brow and closing his eyes as if searching his body for the last signs of life. Erzel turned to Lavian angrily, remembering what had happened in the forest.

"What the hell was that?" he asked furiously. "What kind of weapon was that?"

She looked from his feet to his eyes. "It is one of their more sinister weapons. An arrow laced with the poisons of creatures from their world. It first brings on unbearable burning sensations that radiate out through the body. After that comes confusion and then the victim is paralyzed. I wouldn't give him till morning."

Erzel looked to the others and then back to the Celestial Knight. "Help him."

"I cannot. The wound is far beyond me."

From above came a rush of wind and three more Celestial Knights landed in the field around the group, their Warbirds waiting impatiently as the Knights moved in next to Lavian. Kristian approached Rathe's body and looked down, seeing the man dying, he turned to face the enemy. A Dragon crossed the sky above them and then disappeared back towards the rear of the island, leaving only a handful of the Warbirds and their riders in the air. Erzel looked up towards the edge of the forest in time to see another blast of bright light and then a figure stagger out of the trees. It was Yanosh. He hurried towards the group, his left arm soaked in blood and hanging useless at his side.

"Yanosh!" Lavian yelled, running to the wizard and examining the wound.

"Let it be Lavian, we need to move now. They're coming."

The Knight looked past the wizard, a chill running up her spine. "They're already here."

Yanosh looked at her and then turned slowly, finding that at the forests edge was a line of figures numbering ten and waiting ominously without a hint of movement among them. The wizard turned to face them, his good hand brandishing his staff while he struggled to regain his composure. Lavian, the other three Celestial Knights, Erzel, Kail and Thorgrim moved into a line opposite the enemy, mirroring their formation as best they could. Overhead, the Warbirds shrieked as their riders pushed them lower to the ground, making the Slayers look up at their other opponents. The field was far from an even match.

Lavian raised her crossbow and Kail pulled the bowstring back, watching the magic arrow appear, glowing blue and waiting for the chance to find a target. From the right side of the field came a rush of wind pushing lower towards the ground. In the light of the moon there appeared the body of a Dragon, its wings stretched out to slow it as it aimed for the Slayers. The creatures looked up at the last moment in time to see a bright torrent of fire erupt from the Dragon, engulfing the field behind the creatures and preventing their escape back into the trees. The fire roared high, giving the field new light and every detail was touched by the flicker of the flames.

The sudden aerial attack from the Dragon threw off the Slayers composure and they scattered, the two remaining ones with bows firing into the sky wildly with little aim. The Dragon disappeared higher into the dark sky, mingling with the stars and moon. As the Slayers watched for the Dragon to reappear, Yanosh and the rest of the able soldiers began a slow approach, keeping their intentions quiet for as long as they could while the enemy's attention was elsewhere. No more than a hundred feet remained between the two forces when the Dragon dove back towards the field, this time accompanied by a second. The first released another blast of fire that scattered the Slayers while the second dove lower, grabbing one in its claws and slinging it across the field before disappearing into the sky once more.

The Slayers fired off another round, this time striking the second Dragon in the back. The arrow jabbed in and the Silver Dragon faltered in the air, struggling to stay in flight as the pain from the tainted arrow spread. Yanosh watched helplessly as the Dragon dropped to the ground, crashing violently headfirst into the field at the edge of the forest. It lay motionless for a moment before it picked its wings up, testing them slowly. Fighting the pain the Dragon pushed up onto its feet and turned towards the Slayers, teeth bared and anger rushing through its body. Yanosh looked back at the Slayers in time to see another arrow leave the creature, flying straight for the wounded Dragon. It struck the creature below the jaw and almost instantly dropped it to the ground.

"Take them!" Yanosh yelled suddenly, sending a blinding flash of light into the middle of the Slayers to disorient them.

The last twenty feet between the two forces took only seconds and Erzel led the way, swinging his sword powerfully at the closest enemy, severing its head and watching as the body began cracking and burning. More bright flashes shot by him as Lavian and Kail released their bows, both hitting the same creature and sending it sprawling back onto the ground. The attack was so swift and unexpected that the Slayers appeared to have no way of defending against the fighters. One of the Slayers started back towards the forest, forgetting the flames and instantly falling back away from them. They were trapped and the Slayers drew back away from the enemies, the remaining eight ready to inflict great harm on those who dared face them so openly.

The Celestial Knights led by Kristian leapt suddenly at the right side of the line, their swords cutting the air as the Slayers ducked and dodged, using their own weapons to defend themselves. The sight spurred Erzel's followers to do the same, charging hard at the enemy and mocking the attack the Celestial Knights had mounted. The flames gave the battlefield a different feel as the soldiers did everything they could to fight off the creatures. A screech from above made Erzel and the Slayer he squared off against look up, finding a Warbird closing fast. The Slayer raised its sword but too late as the large bird crashed into the ground on top of the enemy, taking off again with the Slayer in its talons. The great bird climbed higher and just before it got out of sight, it let the creature go, disappearing as the Slayer plummeted back to the earth.

Erzel watched until it slammed back into the earth and burst into flames in the brush at the edge of the forest. To his right came another Warbird and the odds were finally beginning to level out. Yanosh pulled back out of the battle, doing his best to keep Rathe alive but at the same time trying to regain the use of his arm. The gash that ran down the length of his forearm was bleeding freely. He watched cautiously as the Slayers managed well against his Knights even with the addition of the Warbirds that made several dives and attacks at the creatures.

"Erzel! Wake up Erzel, the battle is over here!" Kristian yelled at the Elf, dodging a powerful swing from one of the creatures.

The Elf snapped back and turned to the Celestial Knight who was suddenly being attacked by two of the creatures at once. The archer fired an arrow which narrowly missed the Knight as he ducked under another blow from the sword. He ducked and dodged to the left and right as the speed of the attacks was getting faster. Erzel leapt into action as the creature with the bow notched yet another tainted arrow and drew the bowstring back taunt. He jumped towards the creature with his sword drawn back over his head, preparing to strike the enemy down but watched the arrow leave the bow. He brought the sword down as hard as he could, splitting the Slayer's head in half and immediately seeing the flash of light and heat from the dying Slayer.

He turned just in time to see the tainted arrow sink deep into Kristian's neck, snapping the Celestial Knight backward and dropping him to the ground dead. The Knight bounced against the ground and his head rolled to the side, a trickle of blood escaping his lips as a final gurgle was the last sound to leave his body. Erzel could hear a scream echoing across the battlefield and looked up trying to find its origin, not realizing it came from him. He gripped the magic sword and charged back into the battle with furious anger boiling inside.

As the battle began to thin out, the field was suddenly tilted off balance as the mass of Dragons arrived, filling the sky and landing in the field behind them. The last archer for the Slayers turned to aim but before it ever had the chance to fire the arrow a raging fireball struck it in the chest and sent it sprawling back into the flames. The shadows of the Dragons filled the sky and the Slayers tried regrouping, only to find a constant bombardment of fireballs and streams of fire from the most dangerous inhabitants on the island.

"Fall back to Yanosh, let them finish it!" Lavian yelled, firing one last bolt at the enemy before dropping back to the wizard. The other Celestial Knights carried Kristian's lifeless body back to the safety of the field as the Dragons began viciously pummeling the last of the enemy.

As the flames engulfed the largest part of the field, the last of the Slayers stumbled towards the group, its sword ready to strike a last blow. Kail and Lavian sighted the creature in and prepared to fire when a massive form fell on top of it, crushing the enemy to the ground in one powerful blow. The group looked up at the large form of the Dragon King as it lowered its head towards the dying Slayer. It bared its long teeth and roared, digging its broad nails into its chest and watching closely as the life left the enemy slowly and the flames began emerging from the cracks in its body. It turned and looked back at Yanosh and the others before leaping into the air and disappearing in the sky.

Erzel and Thorgrim slowly moved back into the mass of bodies as the flames began dying down, searching the bodies to make sure they were all dead and remained dead. The last of the bodies moved and Thorgrim raised the war hammer over his head and hesitated, watching the armored head move slightly from side to side. As Erzel approached the Dwarf dropped the weapon swiftly onto its head, smashing it in with one hit. The creature shuddered and erupted in flames, dying quickly. The Elf put his hand on the Dwarf's shoulder and turned him back to the rest of the group, concerned with the fate of Rathe.

Yanosh placed his hand over Kristian's face and slowly dropped his hand across the eyes, closing them and nodding his head in silence. He placed the Knight's sword on his chest and stood, turning back to Rathe who sadly had passed a few minutes earlier. The big fighter lay rigid as a stone, color drained from his body and blood dried around his chest from the horrid wound. Erzel turned his head away from the sight, trying to find something less traumatic to deal with. Sadly, the sight of the Silver Dragon near the far edge of the forest brought on another bout of sadness. It wasn't moving at all, which became a telltale sign that there was no life remaining in it. He sheathed the sword and walked away, still trying to take in the effects of the battle that were weighing heavy on him. He stopped outside of the edge of the fire where the forest met the field once more and knelt down in the grass, a tear streaking his cheek and dropping to the ground. A noise behind him made his head snap up and turn, finding the Dragon King approaching slowly.

"You fought well master Elf."

Erzel raised his head slightly to look the Dragon in the eye, his expression glum and emotionless. "Rathe... Kristian... the others... as well as we fought it doesn't change the fact that they are dead. It's my fault for bringing us here."

It was the first time the Gold Dragon had not responded with hostility towards the Elf and his soldiers. He took one more step towards the captain and looked past the Elf towards the body of the Silver Dragon laying lifeless. Several other Dragons had landed near it and were preparing to carry it back to the inner lands where it could be buried with the other that had been slain.

Erzel and the Dragon King stood side by side, watching the Dragons take flight with the body of their fallen in their grasp. Behind them the soldiers were carrying the fallen Celestial Knights and Rathe back towards the fortress that served as the gateway.

The Dragon King started to turn back towards Yanosh and the others but stopped, looking back at the Elf. "I believed you responsible for this event master Elf. My fallen were on your hands, but no longer. You fought with your heart to defend those who have lived here for countless years. I hold you at no blame. You should return to the Celestial Towers; the Princess is awaiting your return."

It was the first time he had thought about the Princess since he left the inner lands and the emotions flooded back to him all at once. He realized the Dragon was right and though the two had been at odds so viciously to start, they now had an understanding. Whether or not the Slayers were on the island because of someone in Erzel's group or not, Erzel had proven he would give his life if needed to protect those living on the island. He watched as the line of fighters disappeared, leaving only him and the fires in the field. He bowed his head and clenched his fists tightly, still remembering the pain of watching Rathe slip away.

"There is nothing more you could have done Erzel, it was sadly unavoidable. What we have done here has earned their trust."

He turned around to find Ectle standing in the field behind him, staff in one hand as he extinguished the flames around him with a wave of his hand. The wizard moved further down the field, smothering the flames with an invisible magic. Erzel followed silently, watching the flames die and change to smoke. He had questions he wanted to ask and things he wanted to understand but at the moment he had no way of asking what he wanted. Every time he felt the urge to say something he shut down and looked the other way. Soon the field was smoldering, leaving nothing as far as light with the exception of the moon and stars.

Rhen woke quite suddenly, sitting upright immediately as if someone had jerked her from her sleep. She looked around the room, seeing only the shadows given off from the flicker of the candles and the soft moonlight on the balcony outside. She kicked the covers off of her and slid out of the bed, wrapping her arms around her as the soft breeze gave her a chill. She stepped out onto the balcony and looked back across the landscape where the stars still controlled the sky, unwilling to release their grip on the world above them. As she panned around the forests and clearing she saw a Silver Dragon soar by in the distance, dropping in to where the entrance in the mountain opened. Her heart fluttered. She heard a knock at the door behind her and she turned, grabbing her dress up and quickly slipping into it.

"Enter," she said quickly, finishing the last few ties as the door pushed open.

The door opened slowly and Rhen stared hopefully, expecting Erzel to walk through. Instead, she found Kail and even though she was happy to see the Human, seeing him brought on two different emotions. To start she was happy to see that they were returning from the outer lands but on the other hand, she was worried that it was Kail coming to see her and not Erzel. She was afraid of the news that he was about to give her.

"Please... Kail please... do not come in here and tell me... he's gone."

He raised his hand. "No.. Rhen it isn't that."

"Then what?"

"He is alive but has yet to return. He and Ectle remained in the outer lands after the rest of us returned. He was visibly shaken by the battle. Perhaps you presence would help to bring him back to reality. If you would like, I will escort you to the outer lands."

"Let us go then," she replied quickly, starting out the door before Kail.

The Princess moved quickly out of the castle and down the trail that eventually led to the fortress. Kail opened the door for her and they moved down the long hallway where the statues watched their every move. When he opened the outer doors Rhen stepped out into the field with a shocked look on her face. The sight of the torched and smoldering field was definitely not something she had expected to see and Kail stepped in beside her.

"It appears devastating," Kail said quietly.

Rhen did not reply. Her simple nod gave him the only reassurance that she was even still alive as she stood rigid, rooted to the spot. Two figures moved across the forest edge on the other side of the field and Rhen picked up their movement almost instantly, her heart jumping as she assumed it was Erzel. She started through the grass towards the two figures, praying Erzel was alright. Kail was right behind her with his bow still drawn and ready in case the Slayers were not actually as dead as they appeared.

Erzel looked up in time to see the two coming across the field and stopped in his tracks, amazed that the Princess was in the field. He didn't move as she hurried towards him with Kail right behind her. She dropped to a walk fifteen feet away, catching sight of the bodies charred and smoldering in the grass. She stopped in front of him and stared at him for what seemed to the longest time without knowing what to say. She looked at Ectle and Kail who turned and continued down the field.

"When Kail came instead of you... I thought... I thought that something had happened... something horrible," she said quietly, struggling to keep her tears back.

"Something horrible did happen... just not to me. Rathe, Kristian, and two other Celestial Knights were killed in the battle. On top of that, another Dragon died because I led us here," the Elf said, angry with himself as he turned away from the Princess.

Rhen followed him and grabbed his wrist, stopping him so he would listen. "No, Erzel this is not your fault. Please, do not blame yourself. We never knew those creatures even existed. How can you be at fault?"

"I led us here! I let Ectle search for this island and find a way to get to it!" he snapped, his voice raised slightly.

Rhen took a step back, her eyes showing shock as the captain's anger got the best of him for the first time. He looked at her and lowered his eyes.

"Erzel... I love you," she whispered, turning her head away.

The captain almost felt as if he had been slapped. He reached out and took her hands in his, looking at her face in the glow of the moon. "I'm sorry Rhen. I have no idea what came over me. I just felt so overwhelmed what with Rathe and the others. This is too much at one time."

"That is alright Erzel. Are you hurt?" she asked, noting the blood on his arm and hands.

"No... no this is not my blood. Come, let us leave this field before the accursed remains of this battle sink us all into a despair," he said, looking at the bodies behind them.

He walked the Princess away from the carnage that had taken place earlier and followed Ectle and Kail to the fortress where the doors remained open, inviting them in. They passed the statues without a second thought of what had happened during their first walk through the hallway and minutes later were walking out into the open of the inner lands. Ectle and Kail waited patiently inside as they emerged, looking at each of the figures and starting off towards the caves where the Dragons resided. The sky was almost clear with the exception of one Dragon making rounds between the caves and the tower. Rhen watched the creature fly gracefully through the sky, its dark shape outlined only by the stars behind it.

"Is it over Erzel?" she asked, watching the Dragon disappear in the distance.

The Elf shook his head slowly. "I have no idea Rhen but if I were to guess I would assume that no, this is far from over."

"So long as Valsera remains in power, his followers will continue to spread to the outer reaches of the lands. The only option... kill him," Ectle added in a very grim voice.

"Perhaps there is some grand way you plan on accomplishing such a feat Ectle? As I remember, we have fought these wars for quite a long time and have yet to even see Valsera show his face. His numbers seem endless and his soldiers only get stronger. Kill Valsera... let me know when you figure out a way to pull that off."

The wizard did not respond and instead lowered his eyes, following them up the hill to the large cave mouth, nodding to a large Silver Dragon standing outside as a guard in case the threat was not completely over. The Dragon gave a subtle nod to Erzel and the others as they passed before returning its eyes to the trees and shadows within them. They walked silently through the cavern, following the flickering torches to the inner chambers where the two monstrous doors awaited their arrival. Erzel and Kail pushed them open and everyone walked inside.

Preparation and Celebration

The Pass of Merwold was one of only two feasible ways to enter the heart of the Elven lands and given the sheer number of soldiers in Valsera's armies, it was the most likely choice. The stretch of river spanned close to one hundred yards wide and the entire area was shallow enough to move soldiers and even wagons of supplies across with little trouble. The only other ways into the northern lands were roads and passes that were tighter and harder for larger armies to navigate. The pass was the best bet. The northern shore stretched fifty yards from the trees, giving plenty of room for defenses and earthworks to be constructed as the Elves awaited the arrival of the southern armies. The first of the Elves began filing onto the beach and spreading out across it, looking for signs of the enemy in the event that they had arrived earlier than expected. Thankfully, all was clear.

Aric sat in his saddle and stared out across the river to the other side. It was the first time in a long time he had been anywhere near the area and had forgotten just how wide the river was. With the constant defeats at the borders, the river had seemingly become the new border between the southern horde and the northern army. The Elf rested in the saddle and turned back to look at the soldiers arriving behind him. They pulled the row of catapults and ballista out of the forest followed by the supply carts. One of the soldiers approached as the carts were being unloaded and nodded to Aric, a puzzled look on his face.

"If I may ask sir, I'd like to know why there are hundreds of spears on those two supply carts. They are shorter than ours and we are well enough armed as is."

Aric nodded. "Before we left Pentegarn, the Gnome shared with me designs of a new siege weapon we could use to hold the pass. He called it a goliath, an intricate catapult capable of hurling twenty spears at once into the enemy numbers. We will begin construction on four of them and once the Gnomes arrive, their designs will come to life. It will be one more thing to help us hold our ground."

"Interesting... and what will you have us start with?"

Aric handed the reins to the soldier and dismounted, walking out towards the water. "Begin fortifications at the forest edge and have the carpenters and builders start construction on the goliaths. With any luck, we will have a good head start on everything and be prepared for them when they arrive."

Aric walked his horse out to the edge of the river and peered into the flowing water, his mind moving thoughts and ideas in circles as he began pondering different possibilities. He dropped the reins and walked out a few steps into the water and then a few more, testing the depth and the current as some of the Elves on the shore watched curiously. The newly appointed captain walked to the middle of the river and stopped, finding the deepest point in the crossing to be no higher than his waist. He started back towards the shore with an idea finally set in his mind.

"We need something in the water... something we can use to make their crossing even more treacherous."

"What do you have in mind sir?"

"Hmm... I am not sure. I am open to suggestions. In the meantime, I think it best if we position a few soldiers across the river to ensure their forces do not manage to sneak up on us. Do I have three volunteers?"

Three soldiers immediately stepped forth and saluted Aric, their horses waiting patiently behind them. They were lightly armed and would be able to move swiftly through the denser brush on the opposite side of the river. Aric nodded and led the three to the edge of the river and looked across, pointing to an area where the Elves would be able to move into the trees and wait. The three mounted their horses and started across the river. Their progress was slow as the water moved swiftly and the horses were forced to make their steps slow and careful. Aric turned back to the others and watched as the last of the supply carts arrived from the forest.

"Sir, the bulk has arrived. Many of our archers have taken positions on the hill within the forest just there," the soldier said, pointing to a cleared area where the hill overlooked the water. "From there they should be able to supply a ranged attack the entire time Valsera's forces attempt to cross. I believe that was the position for one of the goliath siege weapons you had mentioned."

"Very good. Begin construction at once and position them so we are ready. Make camp in the clearing we passed a few hundred yards back and use that for our soldiers while we construct the fortification behind that hill where the archers have taken position."

"Yes sir, at once," the soldier replied, moving back up the beach to the massive body of soldiers and workers, leaving only Aric and one of the upper ranked Knights of the White Eagle.

They watched as the massive number of soldiers on the beaches moved faster than could have been expected, erecting sturdy palisade walls out of trees cut to dangerous points, all jutting out towards the river. By the time the sun was setting the camp in the forest was in full operation and the first few walls on the beach were erected and already set with defenders. Regular patrols took routes from the furthest upper regions of the beach to the lower sections where the water was impassible without a boat. The initial pass where the armies were planning to meet was set under the heaviest guard with ample soldiers watching every movement on the opposite shore.

Aric and the head Knight sat in the monstrous tent at the camp, maps and notes spread on the small table between them. The scroll being given the most attention was a map with all possible routes across the river, the Pass of Merwold being the only one with the ability to move an army across in a timely fashion. If the enemy moved across any other area it would take weeks to get their entire force mobilized and ready for battle. Aric turned the map to the Knight.

"What are your thoughts on our chances for holding the pass Hamlen?" Aric asked the Knight.

"Very well sir," he replied. "Given the sheer size of the force under your command and with the added support of the Gnomes once they arrive, we should have less trouble holding than I originally thought. Not to mention these... goliaths."

"Yes... they will be a valuable asset to us if the enemy manages to cross the river in great numbers. Dozens of spears sent into the enemy numbers will be an eye opener and perhaps enough to make them withdraw."

"Withdraw, but they will not retreat. With Valsera giving orders they will rush at the northern shore until every last Goblin and Ogre have perished before they even think of disobeying the word of their leader."

Aric nodded, knowing that was the truth. Valsera didn't care how many of his numbers died so long as he got what he was after in the end. Everyone was expendable. The Elf looked at a different map. "I wonder. Reports show that Lizardman activity has all but stopped while the Goblins are flourishing. I could not believe that they had been wiped out completely in the last few battles. What is your take on their attraction to Valsera and his soldiers?"

"Fairly simple... the Lizardmen hate us and Valsera offered them the opportunity to get even for the battles in the past. I guess they want what every race that had no real chance wants..."

"... and what is that?" Aric asked without looking up.

"Revenge."

That word was more than enough to open his eyes. Aric looked around the tent and then to Hamlen, the word echoing in his ears. "Revenge... if they truly seek revenge then I wonder why their numbers have dwindled and disappeared, especially with Valsera backing them."

"An interesting question. If you are set here sir, I am going to make a round through the camp and check the river."

Aric nodded and the Knight left the tent, leaving the Elf alone with the pile of parchments and scrolls. He unrolled one and then set it aside, picking up a different one to read through.

The map was rough but it gave a decent idea of the lands below the pass and with it, the best guess as to which direction the enemy was coming from. The thickest parts of the forests created a funnel the army had to traverse to reach the pass. Scattered forces could easily move through the forests but an army as large as what was expected would never be able to move through the trees. Siege weapons and supply carts would have to go around the edges of the forests so if they had any chance of effectively assaulting the pass in a timely fashion, they would have to follow the clearest path.

The hundreds of torches threw a constant flicker of daylight to the encampment as the Elves moved supplies and weaponry to the edge of the forest so those at the river had everything they needed. A full battalion of Elves dug into the sand and waited, their swords and bows prepared for the first signs of the enemy. The darkness of night seemed to amplify the noise from the river, surrounding the soldiers with the rush of the water. The Elves waited patiently, hoping the Gnomes would arrive before the enemy reared its ugly head.

Tanis stood at the edge of the wall overlooking the vast field outside of Eglarest as the sun started to peek over the horizon in the distance. Early in the first hours of darkness the two armies of Valsera met in the field outside of the fortress and began an approach on Eglarest in an apparent attempt to besiege it. Oddly, as soon as the two forces came into range of the Elven archers, the Goblins turned and attacked the Human forces, waging a bloody battle against what Tanis had assumed were their allies. Initially the Humans held their own fairly well but with the constant attacks, the Goblins had overpowered and annihilated the strange Human warriors. With the battle between the two enemies coming to a halt, Tanis ordered the Elves into action. Archers fired dozens of arrows over and over again until what remained of the Goblins fell to the ground, dying in the same dirt as those they had just betrayed.

Tanis squinted to see the edges of the clearing, looking at the mass of bodies that stretched from one end to the other and yet not a single one was an Elf. It was the first battle that had taken place in the northern lands that had not claimed the life of an Elf. The King of the Wood Elves walked the edge of the front wall, wondering if the battle between the two forces had been some sort of a way to get the Elves off guard for the real force hiding somewhere, waiting for the chance to storm the fortress. He stared off at the trees and after a long time he felt sure there was no ambush waiting.

"Captain, send out a small group to check the scene more closely. See if they can tell where these odd Humans may have originated and maybe why they were attacked by those who appeared to be their allies."

"Yes my King."

The Elf rallied a small force together and they marched out of the fortress, their weapons prepared in case something unexpected happened. The Elves moved out past the edges of the field, spreading out and creating a solid line from one side to the other. They reached where the mass of bodies lay in the morning sun. The blood stained the ground all around the area and the Elves moved silently in amongst the dead, checking each to be sure they were dead. Every so often, Tanis watched one of the soldiers strike with his sword or spear, finishing off an opponent. After some time in the field it became apparent there was no surprise attack being planned. The soldiers moved out into the surrounding woods to scout as a second force left the fortress to search the bodies even further.

"My King, what are they looking through the bodies for?" one Elf asked as the soldiers began searching the dead in detail.

"Information. Perhaps one of the Humans was carrying orders from Valsera or maybe the Goblins. If we find something perhaps it will shed some light on the odd turn of events we have just witnessed."

"I see. What is your take on what happened my King?" the soldier asked.

Tanis leaned against the edge of the battlement and ran his hand across his chin, pondering the question and wondering to himself what the possible explanation for the events could be. The longer he thought about it, the more unsettling it became.

They were killing off their own soldiers on the doorstep of the enemy. It made no sense at all.

"My King?"

Tanis looked sharply around and then to the soldier as if being caught off guard. He looked at the field and the soldiers began filing back towards the fortress. When the soldiers were back Tanis finally breathed a sigh of relief. "I do not know where to begin with that assumption. Perhaps one of the two sides went against Valsera's orders and was punished."

"My King!" a soldier shouted, taking the stairs swiftly. "The Humans in the field were definitely much different from those of Cisalia or the rest of our lands. More… ancient, like a civilization that should no longer exist."

"Come with me," Tanis said shortly, turning and walking back towards the keep with the soldier behind him. The two Elves left the wall and moved to the throne room, taking seats at the long table and waited patiently as the Elf described the scene.

"They are very much Human. They were armed with bronze weapons and the armor is bronze as well, which is very brittle and overall useless against our weapons if we were to fight them. They do not have a single ranged soldier in their ranks, just axes and spears so they really had no chance of taking the fortress."

"You said they were more like a civilization that should no longer exist. How did you come upon that?"

"Well sir, the etchings in the bronze armor. It gave depictions of the lands to the farthest reaches south, the first ones rumored to have been conquered by Valsera. If they are true bronze soldiers then they would have been wiped out because the barbarians from that area would not kneel to Valsera and stood their ground. Sadly, they ultimately had no chance. The only thing I can think is that perhaps they were traitors who joined Valsera and were brought here to continue serving him."

"A befitting end if they were traitors… betrayed by those they trusted, but why? Why did Valsera order his own soldiers killed off no more than a hundred yards from our fortress?"

The soldier took a deep breath, pondering the question.

"We do not know if that was the order. I mean, maybe there was a measure of hatred still dwelling between the two and it finally boiled over."

"That is very possible. For now I think it best that we keep the fortress locked down and defenses on high alert assuming there is something else lurking somewhere in the southern lands. I will send out long range scouts to make sure the area is secure. You may go," Tanis said as he noticed the Queen entering.

The soldier stood and bowed to the King and then to the Queen before leaving the throne room. Narissa waited until the soldier had left before crossing the room and standing next to the table where Tanis remained sitting, his forehead wrinkled slightly from the curious turn of events. She laid a gentle hand on his shoulder and he looked up at her, a wavering smile on his face.

"What is troubling you?" she asked.

"The enemy in the fields. They chose to attack one another and ultimately kill one another off instead of laying siege to the fortress as we had assumed they would. An odd show of allegiance the two forces shared."

"Well, is it not a good thing that they killed one another? It reduced the battle that the Elves had to take part in."

It was very true. By fighting one another not a single Elf had been injured but the fact was still disturbing. Why did the two turn on one another and if it was happening at Eglarest, was it happening all throughout the rest of Valsera's forces.

"Yes, a very good thing, but it is just a strange turn of events to have witnessed. Perhaps it is nothing and I am making a big deal out of nothing Narissa but I just feel like I need to be concerned. What do you think?"

The Elf Queen pulled a chair in next to Tanis and sat down, looking at him deeply. She ran her hand down his shoulder and leaned down towards him, resting her head against his arm. He gently stroked her hair and closed his eyes, wondering what it was he was expected to do in such a rough time. Narissa picked her head up and looked at him again.

"I think you need a moment away from this war and misery that it is bringing. I think you would be good to relax even if it is just for an hour. It will help you see clearer and breath deeper. No matter what, this will be here when you get back but maybe, just for a little while you can escape from everything and see what it is like to let the world turn without your sword in your hand."

It was an interesting idea. He did not know how he was supposed to simply forget that the world was in complete devastation around them but somehow he believed it would change the overwhelming stress he had hanging over his head. The King followed Narissa out of the throne room down the hall to the larger balcony. They leaned against the railing, looking out across forest and the ocean in the distance. A soft breeze moved across the balcony and Tanis closed his eyes, taking a deep breath. He felt instantly better, the weight slowly lifting from his shoulders.

Debate Amongst the Dragons

*T*he fields where the horrific battle had taken place still bore the scars of the tragic event. The grassy field that had been torched was charred black and was no longer beautiful like the rest of the island. The bodies of the Slayers that once lay lifeless in the fields had since disappeared as dust in the wind. With the exception of the blackened fields, evidence of the battle was scarce. The fields and forests were empty as everyone had moved into the council chambers where Erzel's group had first found themselves in front of the Dragons. The Dragons lined the chamber walls where they had during the trial of Erzel and his group. The table in the center held Erzel's group with the exception of Rathe as the one to their right and left had the Celestial Knights and Yanosh.

All of the Dragons appeared in the chambers with the exception of a handful of Silver Dragons that remained outside on patrol in case the forests and fields were not completely cleared. As far as the Dragons and others could tell, the island was clear of any other forces. Those lost in the battle had since been buried and honored and now the council was in session about the future of Erzel and his group. The Dragon King stretched its wings wide in the room and settled back down, looking at the soldiers around them. The only Dragon not with the rest in the room was Alora who stood in the floor next to Erzel's group as she had during the trial.

Yanosh stood from the table where his Celestial Knights remained. The wizard approached the Dragon King, stopping in front and bowing to the Dragons. The Dragon King gave a nod in return and Yanosh prepared to speak to the mass of soldiers and

Dragons. The wizard looked at the group that had arrived from Nalawren and nodded.

"Let us remember those who have lost their lives defending our lands this past day. Their valor will live on. Now, we have a matter that needs to be discussed."

The wizard looked up to the Gold Dragon who nodded, watching as the wizard took his seat once again. The Dragon King looked over each of Erzel's group, pausing as his eyes met Rhen's. "The damage of our lands dealt by those intruders has been felt deeply. Losing our brethren in these past battles will leave a deep scar on us all. Sadly, we have an issue to address as the enemy has now located us. Princess Rhen, please approach us."

The Princess cautiously stood from the long table where she sat with Kail and Erzel and walked around the group, her eyes darting around the room. She was noticeably afraid of the Gold Dragon as the sheer size dwarfed her. To her right arrived Alora once more and she felt a little better, knowing the Blue Dragon would help her. She stopped and gave a low bow to the Gold Dragon, watching the Dragons closely.

"Princess Rhen, it was made evident that the Slayers that attack our lands were here by following you. You have been tainted by the corruption in the south of your lands and because of that matter, our lands are no longer safe. We have but one choice that I have thought long and hard over. We are forced to remove you and your followers from our lands at once. As it stands, Valsera could easily track and send more units and more will die needlessly."

Rhen's head was lowered and her eyes were locked on the floor, a tear on her cheek as she realized the death of Rathe, of Kristian, and all those Dragons were her fault. If she had stayed in Tvan where Erzel and the others had told her to stay, then Valsera would never had been able to track down the location of the Dragon Isles. It was all her fault. She looked up at the Dragon, trying to think of something to say.

"Great one, how exactly would you suggest we send them away? The ship they arrived on has deserted them and the one that brought the Slayers has as well disappeared. What would you have them do?" Alora asked, trying to step in for the Princess.

The Gold Dragon seemed to ponder the statement and turned to the Silver and Gold Dragons behind him. Yanosh stood from the table and joined the Princess, looking up at the council.

"May I address the council?" he asked, placing a hand on her shoulder.

"As you wish Yanosh."

"If we are to send them away, what prevents Valsera from seeing into these lands? I am able to tell that she has been tainted and the sorcerer can see her location but what I can not see is whether or not his vision remains once her presence is gone."

"Are you suggesting that once he has seen our lands he can continue to pry and watch our position?"

"It is possible, though I am not sure and I will not assume at this point. If he can continue to watch even if she is not here, then we lose the combination of their abilities mixed with our own. Next time he could send many more Slayers and other forces."

The Dragon looked at the wizard with a strange sort of confusion. He turned to the Dragon council behind him and nodded towards the door. He waited as the entire Dragon council exited the room and the Dragon King followed, stopping at the wizard and nodding, "We will return."

The Dragons all filed out of the room with Alora following the King out as well, leaving Erzel's group and Yanosh's Knights in the room. The large doors closed loudly. Rhen remained where she was, a tear still streaming down her cheek. She almost hated herself for going against Erzel's orders and hiding aboard the ship. Erzel left the table and replaced Yanosh's position with Rhen. He ran his hand up her back and wrapped his arms around her.

"Erzel, I'm sorry I did not listen to you. I should not have snuck aboard and followed you. I am so sorry," she sobbed, her tears reaching his tunic.

"Rhen, it is ok. Please, listen to me my dear. This is not all your fault and…"

"How is it not my fault Erzel? They only knew how to

get here because I am here. If I had just stayed Rathe would have survived, the Dragons would not have been killed... I'm a monster."

Erzel looked back at the rest of his group, hoping for some sort of help. He was not sure what to do with the Princess blaming the entire chain of events on herself. Erzel reached up and ran his fingers through her hair, trying to calm her. The Dragon was right but there was no way for the Princess to have known that she was being followed. The Celestial Knights joined Yanosh and the group stood around him, talking quietly about what the Dragon had suggested.

"Erzel, how are we supposed to leave with the ships gone?" Nimir asked as he approached the two.

"I don't know but perhaps the Dragons or Knights have an idea. Right now it looks like we are stuck here. If we leave here and the Slayers attack again, we will still be to blame but we will not be here to help them. Either way, another attack is a strong possibility."

"Erzel, we have an idea that may offer a possible solution." Yanosh said, looking past his Knights at the Elf.

The Celestial Knights and the wizard filed in around the table where Erzel's group waited to hear what they had come up with. Erzel noticed a gap in the group and even though Kristian had fallen, they honored him by leaving the space between their numbers as if he were still among them. Yanosh stepped up and placed his hands on the table, looking over the group.

"I think a solution has presented itself. If the Dragon King orders you removed from these lands and you have no way to go, our Warbirds can carry two and we can fly you back to Nalawren. It is not the most feasible plan but it is all we have at the moment unless you have something to add."

Erzel looked to Kail and then to Ectle, having nothing to say himself. Neither of them seemed to know what to say on the matter and the Elf simply nodded. "I have no idea what else we are supposed to do. If they move to make us leave, we have to leave. Would they allow your Knights to help us?"

Yanosh almost looked offended at the question. "The Knights are mine to command so whether the Dragon King and his followers choose to support us, I have the final say."

Erzel nodded, happy to hear that the wizard had complete control over his soldiers and that the Dragons did not sway his decision as much as the Elf thought. He touched Rhen's hand as the two realized that they were not completely alone in the matter. The groups sat quietly at the tables, anxiously waiting for the Dragons to return.

The door creaked and then swung open, allowing the first of the Dragons back into the room. The group sat quietly as the mass of Dragons returned to their seats behind the tall podium. Alora turned and stopped next to the table where Erzel and his numbers sat as the Dragon King made his way past. The Dragon stepped up to the podium and looked down at the Humans, Elves and Dwarves. His eyes held a stern glare as he finally spoke to the mass of soldiers.

"We have come to a decision. Though you have done a great service by helping us in protecting our lands, this council feels it best that you leave when an opportunity presents itself. As you have honored us by helping in this past battle, you may stay in the comfort of the castles until a suitable means of transportation is found. Now if you don't mind, we will retire to a more comfortable atmosphere to search these matters for a solution."

The Knights and Dragons stood and bowed as the Dragon King left the room, followed by the rest of the council. Yanosh turned to the group as most of his Knights left the room. He nodded to them and addressed Erzel and Ectle.

"We will go back to the castle and I believe I may have a way to transport all of us to where we need to be as well as help you and yours even further. Please, follow me."

The wizard walked at a brisk pace, having an excitement that seemed to glow around him. He turned a corner and disappeared down the hall with Galador and Lavian a few steps behind him. From behind them appeared Alora who nodded to them and then spread her wings, taking to the sky in a rush of wind. Rhen covered her face as her hair whirled around her and the gust threw up dust. The group continued to the castle and up the stairs to the large war room. Yanosh pushed the two doors open and the group entered, taking seats around the table. Yanosh waited for everyone else to be seated.

"Let us remember those who are not with us here today. Their sacrifice will not be forgotten," Yanosh said before joining the others.

Everyone at the table sat in silence, waiting for the wizard to start the meeting. Yanosh looked at everyone one at a time, stopping on the Princess for a few minutes, taking in the anger she had expressed at herself. She still felt that every bit of the attack was her fault.

"Princess, you must move past blaming yourself. This is not the time to point a finger at anyone for any reason. Now we must focus on a greater issue at hand."

"Which is?" Erzel asked.

"Getting you and your soldiers back to Nalawren. I know the Dragon King will allow you to stay for the time being, but each day longer will only frustrate him further."

"Well Yanosh, what do you have in mind?"

"Well like I said before, our Warbirds can carry two at a time. They are very strong and could have your forces back in Nalawren fairly quickly. Also, I know for a fact that Alora will be joining us when we make the trip back to your lands. It is possible that though most of the Dragons will not help, several may join our cause."

"Really?" Ectle asked. "Dragons may join our efforts?"

"Yes. Many have taken sympathy with Alora's state and the fact that she is the last of her kind. Knowing that she is willing to risk her life to help your group has given them the desire to help. I am proud to know they are glad to lend a hand."

The group around Erzel looked cheerful knowing that the Dragons were not completely throwing them off of the island without offering their help. Erzel looked from Yanosh to Ectle with a brow showing his confusion. Yanosh turned to the Elf and raised an eyebrow.

"Something wrong Erzel?"

"No, I do not think so. It's just that the Warbirds and your Knights are escorting us to Nalawren. Why are the Dragons going along? It is not that I am against the idea, but why the massive buildup?"

"Our forces will not be leaving Nalawren once we get you and your soldiers back. Once we leave this island, we are going to war with Valsera and his armies. We fought him once before and ran to survive. This time we fight to the death," Lavian answered, looking the Elf in the eyes.

The idea sank into the group and they realized that the Celestial Knights and Dragons that would follow them were coming to fight, not just escort. The thought of the Dragons descending on the battlefield was enough to bring a smile to their worn and tired faces. They had not realized that the members of the island were planning on fighting alongside the armies of Nalawren.

"You are sure? The armies in the south number in the tens of thousands, maybe even higher. It seems that the largest part of his armies are being kept in the south around Nomaria. If he sends his entire army north, there may be no way to hold them off," Erzel noted, remembering the loss of the borderlands.

Yanosh looked at Lavian and Galador and then to Erzel, nodding at the Elf. He gave a sly smile and the Elf looked to the left and right. "I have an answer to that Erzel and perhaps one that could turn the tide for your numbers."

There was a long pause on the table and Ectle finally broke the silence. "Alright Yanosh, what do you have in mind to deal with Valsera and his armies in the south? I'm sure that the rest of us would love to know what you have planned."

"Very well. Through the same method Valsera used to track Rhen's whereabouts, I can now do the same to the sorcerer. It will take some concentration and perhaps a little luck, but if we are able to know Valsera's location, we can assault him there with the Dragons and my soldiers. It would definitely catch him off guard."

The group was quiet as they wondered if what Yanosh claimed was actually possible. More importantly, they wondered how they would survive a battle against the head of the southern armies with such a small number of soldiers. Granted the Dragons and Warbirds were very powerful and could easily pose a threat to the armies of Goblins and Ogres but the Slayers were more than an equal match for the winged soldiers. Erzel and Kail looked back and forth as the idea started to sink in. Even though they could possibly assault the sorcerer, there was no guarantee they would ever make it out alive.

"I know it sounds impossible, but let me explain. Let us assume for one moment that we are successful in assaulting and defeating Valsera on his own ground. Killing their leader will ultimately send his armies into disarray and give your forces a chance to strike a devastating blow. I did not say it would be easy, only possible."

Ectle was the first to speak. "How long have you known you could locate the sorcerer?"

"Truthfully the idea struck me as we were leaving the council room earlier. I am sure that if it was a spell the gave him the ability to follow Rhen, then I can trace and use it against him. It is a chance at least."

"So the rest of your soldiers have not heard that you intend to assault the head of the entire southern army with just a whim of an idea? The Dragons who are willing to follow us back to Nalawren have no knowledge of the plan?"

"Well, perhaps I should be certain that I can locate the sorcerer before we plan to assault the southlands. With your permission of course my dear," the wizard added, nodding to Rhen.

The Princess looked to Erzel who nodded and she stood, giving the wizard a smile. The group left the table and followed the pair as the wizard led her through the war room and then to a small room off to one side. It had shelves all across every wall loaded with vials and potions of every color and size. In the center was a long stone table dotted with scrolls and books which the wizard moved. Yanosh motioned to the table and with a hand Rhen hopped up onto it, her legs hanging off the side.

Yanosh turned and began looking through the potions on the wall behind him, setting several on the table next to the Elf. It became apparent that Rhen was a little nervous about what the wizard had in mind but Erzel stepped in beside her, touching her hand to relax her a little. When Yanosh was finally done with the preparation he held a small vial in his left hand. Its contents were a dull blue and seemed to bubble slightly. He handed it to Rhen.

"Here you are Princess, please drink this and lie back on

the table. Relax, everything is going to be just fine, I promise."

Rhen took the vial with a nervous hand and raised it to her lips. She dared to smell it but found that the contents were odorless. With a deep breath she turned it up and swallowed, finding the liquid had a bitter taste. She pursed her lips and shivered as the taste finally began to ease.

"How do you feel.?"

"Fine... it tasted horrible."

"I know. Forgive me, I should have warned you. Alright, lie back on the table and relax. Take deep breaths."

The Princess did as she was told and the wizard waited patiently as she got comfortable. The Elf took one last breath and nodded. Yanosh backed the rest of the group up and walked from her feet up beside her, his hand hovering above her body by inches until he reached her head. He stopped above her and gently placed two fingers from each hand on her temples, closing his eyes and then opening them instantly.

"Relax Princess. You have to be calm for me to enter your mind. Take deep breaths and stare straight ahead at the ceiling."

"It won't hurt..." she started, biting her lip as she caught the middle of the sentence.

"No, you will not feel a thing, I promise. Ready when you are my dear."

Rhen struggled to slow her breathing as the thought of the wizard entering her mind gave her the chills. She didn't know what he would see as he pried into her thoughts and memories. Would he see the attack at the carriage or the intimate night in the woods with Erzel? The answers to the questions eluded her.

Yanosh waited until her eyes focused on the ceiling, staring past him. He began rolling his fingers in tiny circles on her temples, the circles very slowly becoming larger and the pressure growing slightly. At one point the wizard stopped and reversed his motions, the circles growing smaller and the pressure lessening. Try as she may, the Princess was struggling to remain calm. Flashes of visions appeared in his mind as he probed deeper, searching for what he needed.

Erzel took a nervous step forward as Rhen's eyes closed

but the wizard did not stop, his pace quickening as he seemed to suddenly concentrate. The group watched with curiosity, wondering what the wizard was seeing. With a last few motions the wizard finally pulled his fingers from her temples and opened his eyes, looking up at the group around the room. He placed a hand on the Princess's forehead and her eyes opened.

"Are you alright Rhen?" Erzel asked, stepping in beside her and taking her hand in his.

"Yes Erzel, I'm ok. Help me up please," Rhen replied, extending her hand to the Elf.

Erzel helped her to sit up and kept his hand on her shoulder to steady her. She rubbed her head for a moment and then looked to the side at the wizard. "What did you see?"

The wizard had his back to the group as he seemed to pace the small area between the two walls. He rubbed his head and almost seemed to be talking to himself. Finally the wizard turned to the group eagerly awaiting the information that Yanosh had extracted from the young Elf's subconscious. The wizard looked past them. "I need a map."

A rolled map of Nalawren was produced and the wizard poured over it, tracing several areas near Qwaz. He also focused on the rivers and the borders between the lands before looking up at the others around him.

"What is it Yanosh?" Lavian asked, looking at the wizard.

"I learned much more than I expected."

"What do you mean?" Rhen asked, fearful that he may have pried where he was not wanted.

"I know where Valsera is, I know where he is going, and that the armies of the south are about to move north in one full push. The numbers are so strong, stronger than any force I have ever seen in the battles before."

The group from Nalawren looked at each other, their faces showing concern at the news that was being handed to them. If Valsera was moving his armies north and the Elves were unaware, it would be a massacre. Erzel looked up at Rhen, knowing that she now worried for her parents and the rest of the Wood Elves. A tear appeared and she wrapped her arms around his neck, sobbing softly.

"There is more."

Erzel looked up. "What else is there Yanosh? We must get back to the Elves and warn them."

"Valsera is moving to Qwaz. He has a small force of these Slayers with him but mostly the city houses Goblins and Ogres. If Qwaz is without the largest number of his Slayers, we could deal a powerful blow to the sorcerer. Without those soldiers, our Dragons and Warbirds will clear out the rest of his army. This will be the only chance we have to catch Valsera off guard."

Everyone followed the conversation well, knowing that if the wizard had seen what he claimed, the sorcerer would be away from his army of Slayers that stood at Nomaria. The massive amount of Goblins and Ogres were a formidable opponent but against the Dragons they would stand little chance. The only issue was in the long run whether or not it could be carried out. Once inside of Qwaz, the Dragons and Warbirds would not be able to help them.

"We should probably give this a little more thought before we commit to it fully. This is not a simple matter and I really think we should give it another day before we know for sure if we should go," Ectle noted quietly, turning to leave the small room.

Most of the group left the room with the exception of Rhen, Erzel, and Yanosh who waited for the room to empty. The Princess was still sitting on the edge of the table, her poise returning as she recovered from the earlier event. Erzel gently rubbed her shoulders, reassuring her that everything was going to work out in their favor.

"I know we are going to be fine Erzel but if your forces and theirs go to fight Valsera, you might not come back. If you succeed in finding and defeating Valsera, how are you going to get back out? His armies will surely converge on the city and trap your forces inside. What will you do?"

Erzel looked at Yanosh and wondered if the wizard had an answer to the question Rhen had asked. "Is there a part of the plan that involves an escape?"

Yanosh looked back at the Elf and raised an eyebrow as if

pondering the question for the first time. His face made the two uncomfortable. "Well, honestly I do not know if there is going to be an escape. If we are going into Qwaz, we are going to kill Valsera. There is no guarantee that we will survive the assault but we will kill the sorcerer. After that it will be sheer luck if we escape to the surface to the Dragons and Warbirds. I know it is not a very promising plan, but it is what we have right now."

Erzel turned to Rhen who was in utter disbelief, her eyes wide and her mouth agape. She was obviously against the move now knowing that they had little chance of returning from the southlands. She took Erzel's hand and hopped down from the table, looking him in the eyes.

"Are you really going to go into battle somewhere you have little chance of surviving?"

Erzel looked at the Princess with eyes near hollow. He didn't know what exactly to say but he knew that if they succeeded in the attack on Valsera, things would change forever. If the leader of the horde was killed at last, there would be nothing to lead the massive armies. The hopes were that his numbers would then fall into disarray and collapse upon themselves. He turned to the door with Rhen's hand in his own, leading her out of the small room.

"You know, this would not be the first time I have led soldiers into battle with the odds stacked against us. I am confident in the skill of our group and we have the element of surprise."

"You assume you have the element of surprise Erzel. What happens if you don't?"

The captain lowered his gaze at the thought of having the sorcerer ready for them when they arrived to attack. If that was the case, it could turn out as a massacre for Erzel and the rest of his soldiers. He knew that Qwaz was crawling with Goblins and Ogres but their morale was easy to break. If the city had been reinforced with Slayers then it might be a different fight. The thought of going to their deaths was disturbing but he fought to keep from showing the Princess that he was worried. Erzel turned to Rhen and gave a weak smile.

"We are going to finish this, and in the end, you and your family will be home in Swanhaven. No wars to fight, no fellow

Elves to bury. When we are done, Nalawren will be free from Valsera's grip."

His words spoken to pick up her spirits, Erzel himself did not fully believe them.

Erzel stood in front of a tall stone marker, seeing the fresh earth below it. He slowly dropped to one knee and lowered his head in prayer. The battle hardened soldier brought his clenched fist up to his chin, a tear reaching his cheek. He opened his eyes and looked at the earth once more.

"I am truly sorry Rathe. You fought well, like the hero you were inside. We are headed back to Nalawren to finish off Valsera and his armies for good and the Dragons are coming with us. Your death rallied them to our cause and now they are fighting for us."

"Erzel?"

The Elf turned his head and looked back to find Rhen standing behind him, leaning against the wall.

"Rhen... I was just saying goodbye. I never thought we would be leaving one of our own behind when we left the Dragon Isles. He may have been rough to deal with at times, but he did not deserve to go as he did."

Rhen walked in closer to the Elf very slowly, not wanting to invade his privacy. She stopped behind the captain and put her hand on his shoulder, trying to calm him as another tear met his cheek. He had buried many soldiers while serving under the banner of the White Eagle but never one as young as Rathe. The fighter had much ahead of him and sadly would never have the chance to experience it all.

"It is going to be ok Erzel. We're going back to Nalawren and Valsera is going to pay for everything he has done."

"That is the plan... though I do not know whether or not Valsera will so easily be killed. He has survived this long and obviously his power grows. This may be a fool's errand."

Rhen dropped to her knees next to the Elf and wrapped her arms around his shoulders as she pressed her lips against his cheek. They sat together, staring at the grave marker for a long time, thankful to still have each other, as the Human's life had been extinguished so early.

Two days had passed since the idea of assaulting Qwaz with their small force had been brought to the table. Since then, Erzel and his group had adopted the idea as their best option for the salvation of the lands of Nalawren. All of the Celestial Knights had fully agreed to join the efforts which meant that the Warbirds would be coming as well. It was on the eve of the night that the group had laid their plan out to the Dragon Council. Surprisingly, the Dragons were in full support of the idea and offered their numbers to the attempt, realizing that if they helped to destroy Valsera's stranglehold on the lands, they as well would forever be free from his wrath. First Alora offered herself to the group, willing to carry two back to Nalawren. Then, several other Dragons stepped forth, pushing back their pride and offering their services to the cause.

In the morning after, Erzel and his group had almost completely prepared for the journey back to Nalawren. The Celestial Knights gathered in the large fields of the outer lands, their Warbirds waiting patiently behind them as they lined up to greet the group. Erzel and Rhen led as they approached Yanosh and stopped, the rest filling in the gaps. Erzel strapped the sword given to him by Yanosh across his back and wore his blackened chain mail under a crisp blue tunic.

The wizard stepped forward and clasped hands with the Elf, greeting them as the sun took full reign over the sky, "Are you ready for this Erzel?"

"As ready as we'll ever be, I'm sure. Such a sudden choice, but I know that if we are able to strike this blow to Valsera and his armies, we could liberate our home lands."

"The truth sounds very refreshing. Knowing that we would no longer be burdened by the constant battle nor threatened by the armies in the south. We could finally live peacefully as we did long ago before Valsera and his armies came to our shores," Rhen added, taking Erzel's hand in her own.

Galador and Lavian approached. "We are prepared to

leave master, whenever you are ready."

"Where are Alora and the rest of the Dragons who agreed to join us?" Erzel asked, searching the fields.

As the words left his lips, several large shadows crossed over them in the fields, blanketing them in shade. Everyone looked up into the sky, watching the enormous form of the Dragons crossing above them. The Dragons began dropping lower and lower until they landed in the field around the group. The last to arrive was Alora who walked up to Rhen and Erzel, her eyes rolling over each of them. She lowered her head to their level and looked them in the eyes.

"Good morning Alora. Are you ready for this trip?" Erzel asked, approaching the Dragon.

"Well prepared captain. Myself and the two Gold Dragons who have agreed to follow us to your lands have rested long and the journey shall be less than strenuous for us. Whenever you and your groups are ready, we shall depart."

Alora lowered her body to the ground next to Rhen and Erzel and picked her wings up, giving them access to climb onto her back. Erzel took Rhen's hand and helped her up onto the Dragon's back before climbing up to join her. Rhen wrapped her arms around him and pressed her face against his back. Kail and Nimir settled in on the back of one of the Gold Dragons as Ectle and Thorgrim did the same on the other. The Dragon King stepped in between the two and nodded.

"I see that everyone is ready to depart. I will not be joining you but as you can see, my council will be."

The Silver Dragons fell in around them creating a new total of eleven Dragons in all. The Blue and two Gold Dragons walked out toward the back of the field and waited as the Celestial Knights mounted their Warbirds. As the Celestial Knights took to the sky, it left only Yanosh in the field below. Erzel looked back at the wizard and watched as he suddenly began changing form. His arms grew and changed into long curved wings as his Human form disappeared, leaving the feather covered breast and a long tail. The wizard shook his new body and with a hard flap he took to the sky to join the others as a massive golden owl. The bird streaked by the Blue Dragon and her riders and took the lead, flying gracefully on the winds that led them closer to Nala-wren.

Rhen wrapped her arms tighter around Erzel's waist, her eyes closed and her face buried in his back but Erzel on the other hand was taking in every sight that he could, feeling no fear at all. The trees and fields below were a small blur as the winged beasts streaked through the sky, the wind whipping through Erzel's hair.

"How will you and the others find your way back to the Dragon Isles?" Erzel asked in a yell.

Alora turned her head to the Elf on her back and gave a disheartened stare. "I am afraid I do not plan on returning."

Erzel started to ask why but the Dragon turned her head back, giving him the impression that he was not supposed to know more about the situation. The Elf looked at the others, seeing that they were having no trouble with the flight so he gently patted Rhen's hand secured firmly against his waist. He watched as the group left the island. Having only blue ocean below them, they continued on to Nalawren.

Iron Wall at the Pass of Merwold

The once clean sand of the riverbanks at the pass had since been changed into a network of battlements and defenses. Up from the edge of the water the Elves had dug long trenches that spanned the entire length of the pass, working on fortifying them with palisade walls. The trenches were shoulder deep to the Elves and in order to assault the soldiers behind them, the Goblins would have to make it across and through the wall. Not only was the pass now scarred by the network of trenches and walls, but the hulking form of four nearly finished goliaths sat in the back of the beach, waiting to be completed.

Elves milled around the pass, finishing off small tasks as the meals of the morning were consumed. Camps further back in the forests and in the clearings were filled with hundreds of Elves preparing to move out onto the pass to begin their duties for the day. The guard traded off their shifts and the fresh soldiers moved down the beach, keeping a close eye on the southern shore. It had been several days since they had arrived and the timeline to when they expected to see the enemy was drawing near.

Aric leaned up against a tall tree with a plate in his hand. He had finished what little he could muster the urge to eat for breakfast and was staring off to the east, wondering where the Goblins would first be sighted and if by some freak chance they decided to completely avoid the pass altogether. Something inside told him that this just wasn't the case. The army would meet them here and the Elves would hold them, they had to.

"Sir, are you finished?" a soldier asked, reaching for his plate.

"Yes, thank you," the Elf replied, handing the plate over

and heading to the riverbanks.

The walk was peaceful and if they were not in a time of war, it would be a beautiful place to relax in nature. The forest above the river was thick and lush, hiding the sun from the ground below. Aric stopped as a group of Elves moved past him back towards the camp. They saluted as they walked and Aric gave a quick nod in return. He pulled a map from the pouch on his belt and unrolled it as he walked. The lands around his position were rugged and much thicker, making a movement of any army much more difficult than if they chose to move through the pass.

He looked down to the south of the pass, seeing the marker on the map for the city of Qwaz and the areas around it. The land had once been beautiful much like the rest of the Elven lands to the north but sadly they were now composed of gnarled forests and barren fields. Where grass had grown, now there was clay and rock. The trees had been forever changed, twisted and hideous from the corrupted evils that now called the lands home.

Aric shook his head, wondering if the Elves were victorious would the lands return to their original glory. Over time it seemed possible, but there was no guarantee that the Elves could break the stranglehold the armies of the south had delivered to the races. He also wondered if the Northern forces did emerge victorious, would any of the races ever want to settle in the south again. Cleansing and restoring the lands would take years.

The trees thinned and he stepped out of the forest, walking down the sloped beach to where the defenses had been built. The land between the trenches and the forest stretched quite a ways and it gave the Elves the ability to line archers behind the wall. Their formation up the hill would allow all of the archers the chance to fire at the same time, blanketing the attackers with hundreds of arrows.

Aric rolled the map and put it away again, looking at the defenses with a combination of pride and depression. The defenses would hold against the incoming enemies, but the beauty of the lands was now scarred by the trenches and walls that the Elves had built across the beach. To his right the Elves had wheeled in the catapults and ballista, lining them against the trees at the forest edge and arming them to be ready when needed. He looked down the beach when a commotion behind him caught his attention.

"They're here! They're here!" an Elf shouted, running from the trees.

Aric looked to the southern forests and drew his sword from its sheath, expecting to see the surge of Goblins swarming the river. Instead, the Elf looked upon an empty beach and river with no signs of the enemy at all. His confusion was very apparent as he turned round to the Elves appearing from the forests.

"Where are they soldier?!" Aric asked, his sword still ready.

"Sir?"

Aric took a long look at the soldier and realized her was not armed and seemed completely oblivious to the dangers of the imposing attack. Only then did Aric realize they were not under attack. He slid the sword back into the sheath and looked at the soldier with a face of foolish embarrassment.

"The Gnomes sir. They started arriving a few minutes ago at the northern reaches of our encampment."

"Of course, lead the way soldier," the Elf replied, still feeling foolish.

Aric followed the pair of Elves who had arrived back through the trees on their way to the encampment. He guessed the Gnomes would be arriving within the next day or so and it was a nice surprise to have them earlier. They moved through a massive buildup of Elf soldiers and into the front where the Gnomes were arriving still. Aric stopped at the edge between the Gnomes and Elves. Everyone was fairly quiet as the two races looked at each other.

The Gnomes were dressed in light leather armor for the most part while roughly one hundred had chain mail. All of the Gnomes in leather armor carried a curved bow and a quiver on their backs while the ones in chain were armed more like soldiers, small shields and short swords. They were a great deal shorter than the Elves and the difference between the two supplied some of the soldiers a measure of humor.

"It looks like an army of children," one soldier whispered behind Aric.

"My name is Aric, leader of this army. Who may I ask in charge here?" Aric asked, looking over the Gnomes.

The Gnomes parted and one Gnome appeared from the middle of the group. He was dressed in chain like many of the others except on his head was a small crown. He stopped in front of the Elf and looked up, his deep brown eyes staring down the Elf. It only took a moment for Aric to realize that the Gnome was royalty.

"I am Eludrial, King of the Gnomes. I lead them to this pass for those that Valsera has taken from us. We are here to serve"

Aric took a step back and gave a nod to the King, confused to have the King of a race telling him they were there to serve the Elves. He took a knee in front of the Gnome and extended his hand to the King who took it.

"We are honored to have your soldiers with ours in this Eludrial. We have begun building the goliaths that your messenger gave us the plans but we lack the last steps to finish the four siege machines. You are free to make camp and if you would like to join me Eludrial, I'd like to show you what we are faced with."

The Gnomes mingled in with the Elves and began setting up tents and bringing in supplies. The King and Elf walked down through the trees toward the river together, the Elf having to keep his pace slower so the Gnome could keep up. Aric looked back at the King and waited.

"How long have your soldiers been at the pass?" the King asked, stopping next to Aric.

"I'm not entirely sure now. Five, maybe six days now but they all seemed to run together after a while. We started our defenses as soon as we arrived and now we are ready for the armies invading from the south. Come, I will show you."

They broke the line of trees and walked out onto the beach, looking upon the massive defensive buildup. The Gnome King stood in awe, seemingly amazed at the sight of the deep trenches and long walls that stretched the sand. The catapults, ballista and goliaths lined the areas between the trees with two of the goliaths back a ways on the hill. A wagon filled with spears arrived and the Elves began unloading them next to the first goliath. They moved the wagon to each of the goliaths until all of the spears were out.

"Amazing."

"What is it?" Aric asked the King.

"The goliaths work. They were just designs that we had never actually built but here they are. I am impressed."

"Well we are about to see if they actually work. My Elves have finished the one on the far right and we want to test it before we use them in battle. I wanted to have the creators here to witness the first test of the goliath."

The Elves loaded the spears into the siege machine one at a time, taking their time to make sure everything was exactly the way it was supposed to be. They slid the last spear into place and stepped back, looking over at Aric and Eludrial. Aric nodded and waved for them to continue. A warning went out to the Elves on the riverbanks and they cleared out as the soldiers at the goliath prepared to fire. They aimed the siege weapon out into the middle of the river and when they were cleared, the Elf threw the lever.

The entire goliath lurched forward and the twenty spears shot from the weapon with amazing force. The spears sliced through the air and arched down towards the water. They met the water in a thunderous splash, leaving twenty spears jutting up out of the sand, blanketing the river just as they were expected to and Aric clapped his hands, happy to see that the siege weapons worked well. The Gnome King nodded to the Elf, just as pleased with the results.

"I can't believe it. They work!" Eludrial exclaimed, looking at the river as the Elves began to retrieve the spears.

"Now think about what will happen when four of them are unleashed on the enemy at once. It will bring down their charge before our forces ever have to engage them in battle. This will be a valuable weapon when the horde arrives."

Aric turned back to Eludrial, "Are you hungry? We ate earlier but it would take nothing for us to cook up a meal for you and your soldiers."

"A little perhaps. I would like to rest for a spell as it was quite a walk from the coast."

"Very true. I must admit I was not expecting your arrival. The messenger made no mention of you coming with the army but all the same, I am glad to meet the one who will lead his people beside mine. Come, let us get you fed"

"Thank you."

Aric led the Gnome back through the trees to the camp where meals were already being started to satisfy the hunger of the Gnomes. Smaller tents filled the northern part of the large clearing where the Elves had initially set up camp. The smell of crispy bacon filled the clearing as the Elves cooked for their new allies. The Elves had always been decent when it came to food preparation but as the Gnomes began preparing their meal as well, it soon became evident that the shorter of the two races was highly superior when it came to cooking.

Eludrial looked to the Elf and offered him a sample of the plate he held. It had on it the bacon and such from the Elves but the bread was lathered in a preserved grape jelly. Aric took a piece of the bread and bit a corner from it, chewing softly as the new taste invaded his senses. The Gnomes were masters at the crafts, which mainly consisted of farming, preserving and all around cooking. Feeling somewhat bad that they had so little to offer the King other than their basic meals, Aric thanked him and turned to return to the pass.

When he arrived Aric found three of the four goliaths up and ready for battle but they were having difficulties with the fourth. On the first test fire of the fourth weapon, the ropes that pulled the firing device back snapped and the goliath now stood useless. The Elves hurried to repair the siege weapon with stronger rope. As they drew it back this time, the ropes held and the weapon stood ready to fire. The Elf threw the lever and like the three before it, the spears shot from the machine and blanketed the river crossing. Aric nodded happily to himself, pleased to see the last of the weapons working and ready for the events to come. As it stood the initial charge of Goblins and Ogres would be met by close to eighty spears from the goliaths.

The Elves waded out into the river to retrieve the spears, one of them holding a spear aloft to show a large fish skewered on the head of the weapon. A round of laughs and some cheers erupted from the Elves in the water and on shore as the first casualty of the siege weapons was revealed. It flopped and shook as the Elf removed it from the spear head and tossed it to the shore where it was collected to be cooked later that evening. The Elves piled the spears next to the goliath and began rearming it once more. The four stood between the catapults and ballista and the siege weapons had a concave formation, the more powerful being the goliaths towards the rear.

Aric studied the trenches carefully and wondered where the weakest point would be once the waves of Goblins ascended on their defenses. The measures they had taken to defend the beach were the best they could muster with the little time they had. The wooden palisade wall was reinforced from behind and archers patrolled it regularly, keeping their eyes on the southern forest to prevent and surprise attacks.

It was a day after the arrival of the Gnomes when one of the scouts returned from the southern forests. He was tired and hungry but went straight to Aric with his news of the enemy. The Elf captain had joined the King of the Gnomes in the camp, talking about the events that were expecting to take place in the coming days. The Elf pushed through the camp and stopped in front of Aric, doubled over and breathing heavily.

"Catch your breath soldier," Aric said, noticing the Elf was one of those he had sent out to scout.

"Thank you sir... the south has begun to... come to life. Less than a day away I spotted the start of... their numbers."

"So they are on their way? How many?"

"No idea sir. There was a party out front of the main army between ten and twenty soldiers total. They pushed me out of the trees and I was forced to return."

Aric rubbed his chin. "What of the other scouts that were sent out as well? Any news from them?"

The Elves and Gnomes began to gather around as the

conversation reached their ears. The realization that the enemy was on the move towards them was creating a hushed whisper throughout the encampment. Before it seemed possible, the three thousand soldiers that were not on duty at the pass were aware that the battle was on the way.

"No word sir. I did not see them or hear from them before I was forced to leave the southern forests. The party of Goblins may have seen them."

"Let us hope not," the Gnome King said quietly, reminding the Elves that he was there.

Aric turned to the King and looked up into the air, his attention turned away from the rest of the soldiers around him. In his head he saw the map that was in the pouch at his hip. He pictured the river and the forests on either side and the soldiers of the north. He knew the southlands opened up to the thinner forests between the river and fields and once the scouting parties for the Goblins saw the defenses the Elves had built, they would be almost guaranteed to attack.

The air was growing cold as the Elf pondered the events to come. He paced away from the scout and King, seeming to talk to himself as he did. He waved his hands around and then turned back to the two and the Elves around them, the answers to his silent questions seeming to appear out of thin air. It was the time he had been waiting for since their arrival. It was time to mobilize the armies and prepare to hold the pass against the hordes from the south. The Elves of Nalawren depended on their success.

To the right appeared a second Elf runner, just as tired and sweaty as the first that had arrived. He on the other hand did not seem to be arriving from the mouth of the river as the first had but instead from the right side of the forests. The scout collapsed at Aric's feet and looked up at the Elf.

"I've seen them sir!" he blurted out, his face covered in sweat from the intense run. "Their numbers nearly trapped me where I hid. I was forced out to the right and had to come back across the river a mile west of the pass to keep from being taken."

"How many are there?" Aric asked, tapping the hilt of his

sword.

"I don't know. There were masses of Goblins and Ogres stretching across the fields in actual disciplined formations. There were thousands and that does not count the numbers still massed in the forests around the fields. They will be here soon."

Aric looked at the Elves around him and took a deep breath. This was the moment they had been waiting for. It was time to mobilize the army.

"Alright Elves, spread the word. All soldiers to the pass at once!"

The Elves began moving out through the camp, gathering their gear and weapons and beginning the march out to the pass where the defenses stood ready. Aric and Eludrial walked off toward the river together, the realization of what was about to happen on their minds. The camp and forests were a mass of soldiers scurrying around and preparing as the order had been given to move out in formation. The Elf and Gnome King stepped out onto the edge of the pass and looked upon the thousand Elves already set for battle, their bows ready to meet the arrow.

"I think it might be best to keep your numbers inside of the trees until they are needed, not show the entirety of our forces until we absolutely have to. Call it a surprise for when they cross the river," Aric suggested

"I like the way that sounds. I will give my Gnomes their orders and we will be ready to fight at once. I promise we will hold our own," the Gnome replied, looking at the trees.

Aric gave the Gnome King a bow and watched as he disappeared back to the camp to give out his own orders. The Elf stared across the river at the opposite side, knowing that soon it would be teeming with the vile creatures. The Elves would wait for them to cross the river and at no point would they leave the defenses of the northern pass. If they did the results could be disastrous. In the distance, somewhere in the forests of the south, Aric heard an Ogre horn sound.

"It won't be long now."

The Return to Nalawren

Tanis stood on the outer wall of the fortress and stared out at the mounded dead in the fields. The Elves had slain yet another patrol of the Goblins who foolishly thought that an assault on Eglarest would give them the position they needed in the northern lands. Underestimating the strength of the stronghold had disastrous effects on the Goblins as their entire patrol was annihilated in minutes by the elite archers on the wall and in the towers. The soldiers not stationed on the walls or in the towers had moved out into the plains outside of Eglarest, killing off the wounded and piling the dead near the forests. The thought of the mounded dead being seen by any more patrols would hopefully deter further attacks.

The scouts were returning from the northern reaches of the lands and the gates split to allow them in. The Elves moved up the stairs and knelt in front of the King, pausing long enough to be addressed. Tanis gave another look out to the fields at the soldiers laboring to clear the dead before greeting the Elves.

"What have you to report?" he asked as the two stood.

"Nothing to concern you my Lord. The northern ridges are clear and quiet. The path to the foothills of the Tvan mountains remain untouched by Valsera's forces and we can still use that to evacuate the city if the need arises."

"And from the south?" he asked the second scout.

"Mostly clear my Lord. There is a small collection of camps a few days south in the unclaimed lands but I was unable to come close enough to tell what race was camped there. As of right now, everything seems to be clear."

Tanis nodded and turned away from the two scouts to

look out across the fields in the direction of the Tvan Mountains, seeing the peaks above the forests and knowing that underneath the mountains were the many passages and cities of the Dwarves. As he looked over the wilderness in the distance, one of the Elves interrupted his thoughts with a question.

"My Lord, what will we do with their dead?"

"Pile them at the edges of the plains and burn them as a warning to any more of the southern army that decides to come our way. If they have an ounce of brains amongst their soldiers, they will not keep coming."

"Or at the least they could bring a force substantial enough to pose an actual threat," the second Elf noted, matching the King's gaze.

"With the armies of High Elves and Pentegarn below us I really doubt that they will spare enough of their forces to take Eglarest. If they separate their armies, they could end up weak against Elendil's forces. I don't see what they will gain by trying to take this position when the heart of the empire is Pentegarn."

"Have they done anything that has made sense yet? They let hundreds of their soldiers die over time instead of making one massive assault on the fortress like a disciplined army would do. If they ever realize that they outnumber us and could siege the fortress for months and months there would be little chance for us here."

Tanis shook his head suddenly in disbelief, not sure if he was hearing the soldier correctly or not. "What do you mean have no chance here? This fortress has never been breached in the hundreds of years that it has stood and I am not about to believe that it will happen now. We will fight down to the last Elf if we must."

"Of course my Lord. Have you orders for us then?"

Tanis saw Narissa emerge from a passage to the right on the wall and quickly turned to the two scouts. "Return to the forests and continue to keep an eye on the cliffs and lands to the south. As soon as there is a reason for concern, return at once so we may prepare."

"Yes my King," the scouts replied, bowing once more.

The soldiers on the walls moved aside as the scouts moved

back out into the fields and started off into the forests. Tanis turned and waited as the Queen approached and the two stood together, looking out over the field. It would have been a beautiful sight if not for the mounds of charred bodies and bloodstained grass in the fields. Where death had not scarred the landscape, small clumps of flowers gave color to the grasses. The King put his arm around the Queen next to him and took a deep breath.

"What is it Tanis?"

"Something feels out of place. That feeling where you know something unexpected is about to take place but you have no way of knowing what it could be. It has been plaguing me all morning."

Narissa reached up and gently rubbed the back of his neck. She knew he was under a tremendous amount of stress and no matter what he was feeling, the King would not complain. He closed his eyes and let his head hang forward as she moved down his shoulders. He turned and led the Queen back into the fortress towards his chambers. The guards opened the doors and the pair walked in, stopping in the middle of the large throne room.

"What troubles you so Tanis?"

The King looked at her for the first time since they left the wall. "I am starting to wonder if we have made the right move as far as leaving Swanhaven and our allies to the south. If we had stayed we may have been attacked and forced to flee but being here suddenly makes me feel like we have turned our backs on the alliance."

"Surely not my love. If they had moved on our homes, we would have stood no chance. At least here, we can fight back against those who would assault the fortress. Please Tanis, you did the right thing."

"Did I?" the King questioned. "Then why do I feel guilty?"

Narissa wrapped her arms around his waist and leaned against his chest. She was not sure how to explain that even though he had left their homes behind, he had done the right thing.

The sun was just beginning to reach its peak in the sky, overlooking the vast lands below. Soldiers across the walls of Eglarest lined the battlements, watching the forests as well as the lands close to the coast. There was nothing visible from where he was standing other than the trees and tops of the Tvan Mountains. If there was an army hiding in the forests, the Elves would never know it until they arrived on the fields. The King paced impatiently back and forth across the wall, wondering what he was to do. He still believed he had been wrong in abandoning the city of Swanhaven but to move back to it now would be suicidal. On top of his guilt came the concern for his daughter.

He looked up at the peaks of Tvan over the thick tops of the forests and wondered what she was doing within the city. Surely she missed him and her mother but to bring her to Eglarest would be putting her in danger once more, something he was not prepared to do. No news had come from the letter they had sent and the King worried that the messenger may have been intercepted by the enemy and now they would know where to find her. That weighing on his mind, Tanis knew the vast armies under the mountain could hold their own.

The King turned and started back into the fortress to get out from under the sun. It was surprisingly warm out even though the weather was taking a turn towards winter. He stood inside of the stone pillars and looked out at the sky which was slowly being masked by low clouds. He noticed one of the towers to the far right of the gate was suddenly alive and active. The soldiers within appeared flustered, pointing out to the clouds and several left the tower to get an open view on the edge of the walls.

The King watched the soldiers as their behavior changed from curious to frightened, causing them to flee the forward towers and edges of the walls. Tanis ran back out of the fortress to the wall, grabbing one of the soldiers by the arm as he looked to where everyone seemed to be watching.

"What is going on soldier? Why are you fleeing?"

"Sir, something in the clouds! We saw it come low and then disappear back into the clouds just as quick. Something is flying through the clouds towards us!" the Elf cried out fearfully, pulling free of the King and hurrying into the fortress.

Tanis stared where the soldier had been claiming the sight had taken place but he saw nothing. No creature in the clouds, no disturbance at all. He started to doubt the claim but with so many Elves on the battlements terrified and fleeing, he realized it couldn't possibly be a figment of their imagination. Several of the Elves had notched arrows and had the bowstrings pulled back, aiming into the sky as they waited for an attack from above.

Out of the corner of his eye, Tanis saw a large form drop from the clouds and streak across the treetops before turning off and disappearing in the direction of the Tvan Mountains. From his angle, it looked like an enormous bird.

"My Lord, my Lord did you see that?" one Elf asked, his arrow still notched as he followed the bird until it disappeared.

"Yes, keep ready. I have never seen a bird that size and we will not let our guard down. Get back to the walls!" he yelled at the soldiers who had fallen back in fear of the unknown.

Soldiers timidly moved back out onto the walls and once again lifted their eyes to the sky. The clouds were thickening, making it difficult to see anything in the sky but the Elves continued to scan back and forth. The alarm had been sounded and the army within the fortress flooded the walls and towers, drawing arms against the invisible adversary. Tanis looked to his right and saw Queen Narissa emerging from the tunnel to the inner wall and immediately turned and moved towards her.

"Go back inside Narissa!" the King yelled, pointing to the heart of the fortress.

"What is going on Tanis? Why was the alarm sounded?"

"Get the Queen inside and keep her there! Lock yourselves in the throne room now!" the King ordered the group of soldiers to his right.

The group quickly intercepted the Queen and steered her back into the fortress. The risk of having the Queen on the battlements during a surprise attack was not something Tanis would tolerate. With her out of sight and safe in the fortress, Tanis turned back to the sky. It seemed the clouds were starting to thin and the Elves on the walls were faced with a shock even greater than the one giant bird that had since disappeared.

From the far right the clouds split and a massive gust pushed them away, revealing a monstrous scaled beast. The Wood Elves that had originally been bravely willing to stand their ground now cowered in fear as three massive Dragons descended from the clouds. The beating of their wings stirred the fields below them as the three swooped from the clouds to the plains below. Soldiers along the walls fled back into the fortress, their courage failing them. The three Dragons were soon joined by more, of varying colors and sizes. As they landed in the grassy plains outside the fortress, Tanis dared not take his eyes from them.

"My Lord, what sort of trickery is this?" an archer asked, his legs uneasy as the Dragons landed.

"I have no idea. Soldiers stand your ground. I'm not sure what to make of this."

As the Elves who still dared to remain on the battlements watched, between eight and ten more of the giant birds arrived, landing in behind the Dragons and accompanied by a huge golden owl. The fields outside of the fortress of Eglarest were suddenly filled with Dragons and giant unidentifiable birds. Tanis moved out on the edge of the battlements and looked to the field where the creatures had landed. Now that the sky was clear of the Dragons, the Elves were moving back to the walls, a little braver as the monsters in the clouds had been revealed.

"Why do they not attack my Lord? What are they doing?" one soldier asked, his voice still showing fear.

"I do not know. I can honestly say I have never seen anything like this before."

A solder at the gate turned and yelled to the King, pointing to the Dragons in the fields. "My King! There are people down there!"

The soldier's yell brought more questions to the King but he quickly moved to the gate where the soldier pointed out the Dragons and just as the soldier had said, witnessed several figures drop from the back of the Dragons to the ground below. As well as the Dragons, he noticed that all of the monstrous birds also had a rider on each of them and they joined those dropping from the Dragons. The force in the field looked up at the walls while those within Eglarest stared back trying to decide what was going to happen.

"Tanis, what is going… on?"

The King turned to see Narissa standing just behind him, amazement spreading across her face as she caught sight of the Dragons outside of the city. Like most of the Elves on the walls, the Queen stood rooted to the spot, amazed at the sight of creatures that no one had ever truly believed in. Tanis turned and walked past the Queen on his way to the gate below. He took the stairs slowly, working through the events of the day in his head. He stopped as the Elves at the gate pulled the locks and defenses and pulled the gate open. The light filtered through the crack between the gate doors and the King walked out into view. Behind him came a mass of the armored Knights, following Tanis closely in case something was to happen.

The King was seen and a small number of the figures started towards him. The groups moved towards one another as the Dragons kept watch, staring down the walls and the soldiers on them. As Tanis moved into range, he realized one of the figures moving towards them was a female, an odd sight when it came to the beasts and soldiers that had arrived. The closer he got, the more familiar she appeared until the King stopped short. She continued to approach and as she did, Tanis fell to his knees in disbelief. It was his daughter.

Rhen ran towards her father as she saw him fall to his knees. She fell to him, her arms wrapped around his neck as the pair were reunited. The solders from each side had stopped as the Princess and her father greeted one another again, the King shocked even more than when he had seen the Dragons.

"Rhen… wha… what are you doing? What are they? Why are you not in Tvan?" the King questioned, his shock changing to a stern expression.

"It is ok father, I promise. The Dragons are not here to hurt any of us. They helped us when the Slayers arrived and helped us get…"

"Helped you? Slayers… what are you talking about? Why are you not in Tvan where I thought Erzel and his group were taking you?"

"They did... I just..."

"Rhen?!"

Rhen looked up as Tanis turned his head, watching Narissa as she pushed her way through the soldiers to get to her daughter. She fell in beside the King, her hands on her daughters face as she looked upon the Princess in disbelief. She touched Rhen's hair as if to test whether or not it was a dream.

"Rhen? Is it really you? How did you get here?" the Queen questioned as the three huddled together in the field.

The question sparked something inside of the King and he slowly looked up from his daughter to the soldiers standing behind them near the Dragons. He could see Erzel and Kail standing out in front of the rest and a rush of emotions arrived all at once. He felt the anger overtaking his joy for seeing his daughter again and he left the Queen and Princess together and started towards the rest of the group. His face was not hiding the anger and upon seeing it Erzel looked to the side at Kail, not sure what to expect.

"What do you think Kail?" Erzel whispered. "He looks upset."

"Very upset. We're behind you Erzel. Rhen is safe so perhaps he will not be as angry as it seems."

Kail watched the King of the Wood Elves stomp towards them and stop a few feet short, his face angry. "Erzel... why is my daughter flying with these... these... Dragons? Why is she not in Tvan where I told you to take her?"

"My Lord... it was not my decision to have her with us when we left Tvan. I made it very clear that she would..."

"I made it clear to you that she was to remain in Tvan and you were to protect her there!" the King yelled angrily. "Now tell me why she is not!"

The Celestial Knights behind the group had lined up to support the Elf. Even Alora took a step towards the Elf King, her eyes staring him down. Rhen left her mother and hurried to where Erzel was standing, getting in between her father and her love. Tanis's face showed surprise as he witnessed his daughter's actions. Things were quiet for a few minutes as the Elves looked at one another.

"Father, please calm down. Look at me, I am fine. Nothing has happened to…"

"Rhen, stay out of this!" Tanis yelled

Erzel took a step towards the King and Tanis raised an eyebrow, reaching to his hip as if preparing to draw his sword. The Elf stopped and eyed the King, not sure how things had gotten this far out of hand. He looked to the right at Kail who took a step in beside the Elf to try a diplomatic approach with the Wood Elf King.

"King Tanis, Erzel had no intention of placing your daughter in danger in any way. We did everything we could to ensure that her safety was priority."

"No offense to you and the rest of the group Kail, but this is an issue that none of you would understand. It was not your child in danger, it was not your promise that was broken, and it is not you that I am angry with. Stand aside, you play no part in this."

Kail looked at Erzel who nodded to the Human. The Elf looked at the King with an angered eye, offended that he was being yelled down by Tanis. He had protected Rhen even though she had not been in Tvan like the Wood Elves had believed.

"Tanis… the Princess boarded the ship without our knowledge and once we started out we could not turn back. I… we did not take her…"

"Obviously you had some sort of influence over her Erzel. Otherwise she never would have acted so recklessly. Stay away from her Erzel… you've already done enough against my orders. I thought you were trustworthy."

The anger that Erzel had suppressed was threatening to burst out into the open as the King continued to flood the Elf with his accusations. Erzel had not meant for Rhen to come with them to the Dragon Isles, and he had done exactly as he was told by getting her to the city of Tvan. Her desire to join the group once more through their adventure had nothing to do with Erzel's ability to follow orders. He did as he was told, she simply could not go without having the Elf with her.

"I don't have time for this my Lord. Your daughter is safe and now under your care. We have no time to stand here and argue over why she is here or if she is safe. We have somewhere else we need to be."

Erzel turned away from the King and a soft voice stopped him in mid step. "Erzel..."

He turned, looking at Rhen. "I am sorry Rhen, but you are going to stay here this time. I will come back for you."

The last words from Erzel seemed to enrage the King. Tanis reached for his sword and took a step towards Erzel from behind. His eyes were set on the Elf's neck and he pulled the sword free from the sheath. Things were moving in slow motion as the King advanced on Erzel who was not aware of the imposing attack. Ten steps remained between the Wood Elf and High Elf and suddenly a roar caught everyone off guard.

The Blue Dragon stepped in behind Erzel and lowered her head, her mouth opened, teeth bared, and a roar so loud that the entire fortress froze in fear. Tanis stopped and lowered his sword, his eyes locked on the Dragon as he realized that Erzel had quite a group of followers. The Dragon raised her head very slowly, her eyes probing the King as if to dare him to make the next move.

"You may be a King, but to me you are a threat. Lower your sword, you won't have a second chance."

Alora stretched her neck out above the Elf so the King and Dragon were eye to eye. The Wood Elf took a few steps back, his face flushed with anger at the sudden disrespect that Erzel and his group were showing him. No one ever dared to disgrace the King in such a way and the way he was being treated made him even angrier. Instead of exploding at the Elf and angering the Dragon further, Tanis took a step back next to his daughter.

As the Blue Dragon stepped back a little, the giant owl took flight and landed in between Erzel and Tanis, instantly changing from a bird to the wizard Yanosh. The wizard finally changed into his full Human form. He stood from his knee and looked the King of the Wood Elves in the eyes, seeing the amazement in his face.

"My Lord Tanis, this is not why we have come to Nalawren. The Princess was to be left here with you and your army as Erzel's forces combined with my own are moving out to assault

Valsera. We look to end this here."

"What are you talking about? You think this rabble of soldiers is going to just march into Nomaria and kill the leader of the southern forces? If it were that easy it would have been done already you fool."

"First off, we are much stronger than your simple Elves. Second, Valsera is not in Nomaria, he is in Qwaz."

"How can you know that?" the King asked, eyeing the wizard suspiciously.

One of the Knights approached from behind the wizard and stopped next to him, looking at the King with a small nod. "Sir, we need to get moving as soon as we can. Valsera most likely won't stay put for long."

"Yes Galador, mount up and let us go. King Tanis, we must depart. Look to your defense, in case things take a turn for the worse."

Yanosh and the Celestial Knight turned and moved back to the group as the rest of the soldiers began mounting the large birds. The wizard stood amongst the Knights and in seconds, he had taken the form of the giant owl once again, looking back at the King with his large, round eyes. Erzel's group had moved back onto the Dragons with the exception of the Elf himself. He stood alone, looking to Rhen, wishing he could tell her goodbye without the King knowing.

The Princess left her father's side and walked up to Erzel, wrapping her arms around his waist and pressing the side of her face against his chest. Erzel returned the action, and held her close for a few minutes, afraid to let her go. She looked up at him and let go, stretching up and kissing him on the cheek.

"Come back for me Erzel."

The Elf nodded and turned to the Blue Dragon who slid low to the ground so he could climb up onto her back. Erzel stared straight ahead as the Warbirds took to the sky followed by the owl. The Dragons followed and soon it was only Erzel and Alora waiting in the field. King Tanis stared up at Erzel with a face of anger but the Elf could not take his eyes off of the Princess. He smiled and nodded, reassuring her that he would indeed come back for her, no matter what the cost. He turned and patted

Alora on the neck.

"Ok, let us go Alora."

The Dragon stretched her long wings and with a powerful flap, she lifted from the ground, disappearing into the clouds with all of Eglarest watching. Rhen kept her eyes on the spot where the Dragon and her rider had disappeared for the longest time, her heart aching as she was truly without him for the first time. The King turned his daughter back towards the city and slowly they left the field.

The wind rushed by Erzel and Alora as they pierced the clouds and shot into the sky above. The group was far ahead of them in the distance but they would catch up. Erzel sighed into the wind and Alora slowed her pace slightly, twisting her neck around and looking back at the Elf.

"Do not be saddened Erzel. The Princess will be safe with her people. I know you love her, but you have to trust that she is not suited for what we are about to do. Keep your head up."

Erzel looked at Alora who nodded and turned back to the sky in front of her, shooting down through the clouds and skimming the treetops. She cut left and right and then shot back up through the clouds, enjoying the game she was apparently playing. Erzel finally looked up and gave a weak smile. The Dragon was right. Rhen was safe. She needed to be there with her family while he needed to lead his group to victory. He looked back over his shoulder towards where Eglarest was.

"Take care of yourself Rhen."

A Knight's Tomb

*A*lora slowly dropped out of the clouds and glided down to the ground below, landing in a small clearing in the forest. Several other Dragons and then the rest of group turned and came back to where the Blue Dragon had disappeared in the trees. As the rest of the group landed, Erzel shifted and dropped to the ground below, his eyes set on an area where the trees thinned a bit. He was not on guard, but the rest of the group looked around the area for some sort of opponent. The Elf turned back to the rest behind him with a face void of emotion.

"Erzel... what is going on?" Yanosh asked, looking to the trees.

"I needed to talk to someone for a moment before we move further. This is the first time I've come back..."

Erzel stopped in mid sentence and looked back to the trees, his mind wandering to the task he had set for himself. He took a step toward the trees.

"Come back where Erzel? Tell us what is going on. Who are you going to see?" the wizard asked, pursuing the matter.

Erzel stopped but did not turn back to the group. They could see his head drop as he took a deep breath. He turned his head back to the huddled soldiers and Dragons with hollowed eyes. "My parents."

The group looked at each other as the Elf moved down into the trees and just out of sight. He walked slowly, his eyes focused on the grown up path in front of him. It was almost impossible to tell there was once a trail as the forest moved in to reclaim it. He ducked under low branches and moved on through the forest. When he stopped, he heard footsteps and turned, finding Kail a few feet behind him.

"Kail?"

The Human nodded. "Are you alright Erzel?"

The Elf nodded, looking from the dense trail behind him to the Human in front of him. "I think so Kail. It has been a long time since I have been here, and it only seemed fitting to stop before we continued on. If we fail in the southlands, I would have never of had the chance to say goodbye. It should be done."

The fighter nodded in agreement, understanding that the Elf was right. "Would you like for me to let you go alone Erzel?"

Erzel looked at him for a moment, rolling the question through his head. He was not sure if he should go alone or not. It would not hurt to allow the Human to enter with him but at the same time he struggled to decide if what he was going to say was for others to hear. He looked at the man and nodded. "If it will not offend you Kail, this is something I should do alone. I do appreciate your concern though. You may wait here, I should not be very long."

Kail did not seem bothered and stepped back as the Elf turned and started into the trees once more. The walk was taken very slowly, as if dreading what he was going to say. Memories of his past flooded into his head. He could see the dense southern forests and by his side the tall form of his father, the deer from the hunt slung over his shoulder as they walked back towards town. He could see the swords of wood they used when his father trained him in the field close to the forest. It was a past he had long been without as he moved into becoming a true soldier.

Erzel pushed a limb away and stepped through the tall grass, wondering if what he saw ahead of him would even be remembered. He drew near, looking at the trees as they thinned and there in the side of a hill he saw a stone marker. It was weathered and worn but it was there. He reached out and ran his fingers across the front, looking past it up the hill a little ways. It only took a few minutes to climb the hill and at his feet he found a second marker. He knelt beside it and looked straight ahead, finding an area in the earth that had long been cut away. He stood and walked back where the hill now formed a ledge.

When he stopped Erzel found himself standing in front of a large stone wall that held the mountain back, protecting the ledge from the earth that threatened to collapse and reclaim the area. At his feet were two large slabs of stone, each covered in leaves and debris but they were there for any and all to see. He knelt and looked at the two slabs of rock, brushing back the earth that had begun to cover the two. At the top of each there were engravings filled with dirt and he struggled to clean them out, tracing his fingertips over the words.

"Mother... father... it's me... Erzel," he started, choking on the words. He could not understand how he thought it was going to be easy. "I know you can hear me and I came to apologize. I have not been what you set me forth to become."

Erzel turned and looked to the grave of his father, directing the conversation to the grave where he lay. "Father... you tried to make me see that war was a mistake that eventually hurt everyone but here I am, fighting every day. I have shamed you and for that I am sorry but the world was never as torn by war as it has become now. If you were here, perhaps you would feel differently."

The Elf shifted on his knee and turned to the grave at his right, sliding his hand down the stone and across the engraving. He had been to the graves many times before the wars but it had never hurt the way it did then. He dropped his head to the stone and kissed the engraving softly.

"Mother... I never knew your life. You were taken long before I was old enough to understand why but here we are. I hope that what I go to do has honor in it, that you would be proud of me whether we are successful or not. I may be joining you soon."

A soft footstep behind him made the Elf raise up and wipe the tear from his eye, turning his head to see a Knight standing behind him. Lavian stopped at the edge of the ledge and looked at Erzel, her concern apparent on her face. For the first time she did not carry her crossbow as she approached, choosing to leave it at the edge of the clearing. Behind her appeared Yanosh, his face equally concerned until he saw the pair of graves. The wizard and Knight knelt in respect and then approached Erzel.

"I was just... saying goodbye. You know, before we go to war in the south. I thought it might be appropriate."

"It certainly is Erzel. Allow me to assist you," Yanosh said, walking up to the top of the two grave markers.

"What are you doing?" Erzel asked, his tone fairly sharp as he watched the wizard slowly sit down at the top of the two stones.

"I will grant you the chance to say goodbye to them the way you would have preferred."

"You're not going to... going to bring them back... are you?"

"No, I do not have that kind of power Erzel. I can however show you them as a vision and you can speak with them one last time."

Erzel looked at the wizard with a face full of skepticism as he watched him place one hand on each grave. Lavian had since dropped back to the edge of the trees to allow them the privacy they needed. Erzel crossed his arms and waited, still annoyed with the lack of respect the wizard was showing his parent's graves. Minutes after touching the two graves, the large stones began a soft yellow glow, emitting a soft pulse as Yanosh focused his energies into his spell.

From the two stones rose two translucent forms, the light radiating from around their bodies as they hovered above the stones. Erzel's jaw dropped and he fell to the ground, his knees quivering as he stared at the shimmering form of his mother and father. The wizard had been right, he could indeed bring them forth. Erzel watched as his parents hovered a foot above the ground, looking down on their son who still could not believe what he was seeing. Finally his mother smiled and he realized it was real.

The Elf stood and took one step towards them, staring intently at his mother. She was just as his father had described her. Her face was a picture of happiness as her smile brought a warm feeling to his heart. Her blonde hair whipped around her shoulders, twisted by an unfelt wind. He looked to his father, still as strong and proud as he had been the last time Erzel had seen him.

"I don't believe this... you are here. Can you understand me?"

The two forms nodded but neither spoke. Erzel's smile faded slightly as he realized they had not replied. He looked at them and shifted. "You can't speak though can you?"

They shook their heads and Erzel understood, grateful for the chance to just see them. Thousands of questions needed to be asked and there were things he wanted to tell them about his life but he had no idea where to start. He looked at his father and then to his mother, deciding the most relevant questions were the only ones that should be asked.

"Are you proud of the life I have led? I mean, have I been the kind of son you would be proud of?"

Both of the forms nodded slowly and his mother reached up to her chest, pressing her hand to where her heart would be reaching out with her other hand. Erzel reached up to meet her hand but watched as his hand passed through hers with no resistance at all. He knew what it meant and touched his chest as well. It was the closest thing he had ever had to being told he was loved by his mother and it was tearing him apart.

The pair of glimmering forms were beginning to fade and Erzel knew that it would not be long before they disappeared again. He was struggling to think of what to tell them but there was no time. He didn't want to talk about the war or the turmoil. He didn't want to mention Valsera or the mission they were set to carry out. Then it was so obvious. He looked to his parents and knew exactly what to say to their smiling faces.

"I'm... I think I am in love. She's amazing, better than I could have ever dreamed of. Better than I deserve."

For the first time the form of his mother looked to his father and they shared a glance as if to remember their own love. His mother turned back to him and moved her hands over her stomach slowly, smiling to her son. Erzel raised an eyebrow and took another step forward as the light grew dimmer. Both his mother and father raised their hands as to say goodbye and then disappeared completely.

Erzel stood rooted to the spot, his face slowly losing the glimmer of happiness that had arrived with the sight of his parents. He looked to the wizard and watched as he stood slowly. His face showed how exhausted he had become, exerting his energy to bring the Elf one last moment with his former parents. The wizard used his staff to brace himself as he stood, walking between the two graves and stopping next to Erzel.

"It was all I could handle Erzel. I am sorry I could not keep them here longer."

"How did you do that Yanosh? I have seen spells that I could not believe all my life but that was something I have never even dreamed possible. I... I've never seen my mother before this day."

Yanosh nodded and moved off down the hill to where Lavian stood waiting for him. She took him under the arm and led the wizard into the trees, making one last glance back over her shoulder at the Elf on the hilltop. They disappeared and Erzel looked back at the two graves, still seemingly able to see the two forms hovering above the ground. He clenched his fists and dropped back to his knees at the bottom of the stones.

"I will be back one day and I will bring her with me. There will be peace in these lands and we will be able to live freely. I promise I will not forget you."

He made one last pass over the two stones with his hand and stood, following the hill down into the trees where the two had entered moments earlier. He walked through the trees and brush with a new glow radiating through him. He knew that if he was going to lead his followers to Qwaz and be successful he was going to have to be focused on the task at hand. No matter what happened, he had to believe the mission was possible.

Ahead he found Kail standing exactly where he had left him and the Elf stopped next to him, uncertain of how to tell him what had happened. There was no real way to explain it all to him so Erzel lowered his gaze and continued on past. They walked up to the clearing where the Dragons and his group waited. When he looked for the Warbirds and their riders he realized that they had already taken to the sky, apparent by the shadow that fell over them from above. Alora lowered her body and looked at Erzel.

"Are you alright Erzel?"

"I will be fine Alora. I needed to say goodbye to my parents one last time."

The Dragon turned from the Elf to the forest where he had come from, looking out to the trees. She could not see past the first few but it was suddenly very obvious to her that his parents no longer walked with them. She lowered her head and looked to the Elf as he got a hold on her left wing and pulled up onto the Dragon's back. He settled in and placed his hands on her neck, feeling her muscles tense underneath the skin. She turned her head and looked at the Elf again.

"Are you going to be alright?"

Erzel stared at the Dragon and finally nodded. "Yes Alora, I am fine. The rest are leaving, perhaps we should follow them."

Alora nodded to the Elf and stretched her wings out, testing them before giving a hard flap and jumping into the air. She rose from the ground in a rush of wind so hard that it threatened to push Erzel from her back. The sky above was clear and inviting as the formation of Dragons and Warbirds streaked by. They stretched in a line across the sky, the Warbirds and giant golden owl in the lead. The Silver Dragons flew lower than the rest of the Dragons, creating a shield between the ground and the Dragons carrying the group. They flew on through the sky, their destination ahead of them and their worries behind them.

Shroud of Darkness Over Qwaz

The army had long since left the city of Qwaz, leaving behind a force large enough to defend the city and its occupants. All of the army that had been moved from Nomaria to Qwaz had joined the movement and had continued north into the Elven lands. From the city the movement of Goblins, Ogres, and Lizardmen looked like a dark wave rolling across the desolate lands and out through what remained of the forests. From the sight, no northern army would ever be able to break the mass. They were like locusts, ravaging and ruining the lands they crossed as they set out to take the largest prize of Elven lands.

The dark banner of Valsera had been hung at the highest tower, signaling his arrival and the force that remained at the castle prepared to receive him. Their numbers pressed across the battlements and towers, straining to catch sight of the powerful ruler. The defenses of the city were mostly composed of Goblins on the walls but there were also a large number of Lizardmen. They were sure that their massive front pushing north was enough to hold back the Elves.

It was midday when the first of the Slayers appeared on the horizon, marching slowly across the barren fields towards the city. Behind it came more, approaching in lines of six and stretching at least twenty deep. The numbers at Qwaz could hardly make out any detail in the formations of soldiers but one thing was apparent. Halfway back through the numbers of Slayers came the only figure on a horse. He sat erect and proud, fearless with the mass of powerful creatures surrounding his every move. The army was nowhere as large as the ones that had been dispatched north but the sheer ferocity and strength of the Slayers was a match for the best of soldiers.

The Slayers spread in the front and the sorcerer on horseback moved forward ahead of their formation. His horse trotted up to the outskirts of Qwaz and the ruler looked up to the walls at the two massive towers that stretched towards the sky. Hundreds of Goblins stared down at the sorcerer as he dismounted his horse and handed the reins off to a lowly soldier. As he approached the castle gates, a form cloaked fully in black appeared and walked towards him. Valsera stopped in the open field and waited as it approached.

"Greetings Lord Valsera, welcome to Qwaz," Infus said, kneeling before the sorcerer.

Valsera looked past the creature to the city and then finally down to his general. The creature kept its gaze on the ground. "Rise Infus, I take it the city was prepared for our arrival?"

"Of course my Lord," the Demon replied, looking on Valsera for the first time.

Valsera started into the fortress with Infus right beside him. Every soldier and creature dropped to their knees and fell to their faces as the sorcerer passed. The sight of Valsera brought a mixture of amazement and fear in the soldiers of Qwaz. They moved in around him as he continued on, watching the ruler as he kept moving further. He moved up the stairway and spiraled up to the fortified throne room in the second tower. A pair of oversized Ogres stood at the front of the throne room and at the sight of the sorcerer they pulled the doors open, lowering their heads.

Valsera looked around the room curiously, seeing the bare stone walls and floor with an elaborate rock throne in the center. He walked around the room slowly, looking at the inside of Qwaz for the very first time.

"Is there something wrong sir?" Infus asked, following the sorcerer slowly with its eyes.

"I expected something... well something more. I suppose it will do for the time. Are the walls impenetrable?"

"Of course my Lord. Reinforced against siege weapons as well as protected by a surplus of soldiers. It doesn't really matter though, the Elves will never make it this far."

"Do not be fooled Infus. They may have fewer numbers

and be falling back, but as it happened years ago, they managed a turn around."

The Demon looked up to the sorcerer. "The Dwarves were the only reason the Elves were not defeated. Without them…"

"There is no without them Infus! The Dwarves are very much alive and still the greatest army in the north. It would spell defeat if they joined arms again. I want to know why they don't! Why do the Dwarves hide in their mountains? What will it take to bring them out?"

"You mean to attack the Dwarves?"

Valsera looked past the creature at the far wall with a desperate stare. The more he tried to explain his concern, the less the creature seemed to understand. It was obvious that Infus was best at killing and that was it. He looked at the Demon and took a deep breath.

"I will eventually. The thought is that I must know how long before the Dwarves arrive to reinforce the Elves. I want the Elven empire crumbling and in ruins before the Dwarves come to their side. Does that make more sense?"

Infus did not reply but gave a slow nod, staring the sorcerer down. Valsera moved up to the throne and looked at it closely. The rest of the room was plain and had nothing out of the ordinary in it but the throne was very impressive. Carved from one solid piece of stone and formed with an artistic touch. The feet of the throne were carved into claws and the arms were similar. Valsera sat slowly and looked straight ahead, finding the stone throne surprisingly comfortable. He settled back and looked at the Demon.

"Alright, what have you to show me Infus? I take it you have been working long and hard at the weapon you sent word of so let us see it in action."

"Yes my Lord."

Infus turned and walked to the door, opening it and giving a wave to the forces outside the room and then walking back to the center. The Demon stood straight and looked to the door as a pair of Goblins walked in with an Elf behind them, his hands tied and led by a rope. Valsera looked at the Elf with a sly smile, happy to see the captive at the mercy of his soldiers. The Goblins secured the Elf and left the room, leaving the sorcerer and Demon to do as they wished. Infus reached up under his robes and pulled a long handle out into view. It was no more than eight inches long but the Demon waved it through the air and it suddenly grew and thinned, becoming a long whip. It coiled on the floor next to him and as Infus raised it, the length of the whip suddenly glowed with light green flames.

Valsera's eyebrows raised as he saw the whip of flame, the weapon very impressive so far. The flames stayed along the length of the whip and also mesmerized the Elf as well who had never before seen a weapon like it. Infus reached back and snapped the whip, causing a flash of light green behind him. The Demon drew its whip back again and prepared to strike the Elf.

"Hold your attack Infus!" Valsera suddenly ordered, leaving the throne.

Infus stood with the flaming whip ready to strike as the sorcerer moved past and stopped in front of the Elf. With a wave of his hand, the restraints on his wrists and neck fell to the floor. The Elf looked at the sorcerer, shocked as Valsera pulled a sword from the rack on the far wall and tossed it to the Elf.

"If this weapon is as powerful as you believed, you should have no trouble besting an armed opponent. Now, continue when you are ready," Valsera said, sitting back in the throne and watching as the Demon circled the Elf.

It was apparent that the Elf was outmatched even without the new weapon the Demon was wielding. The Elf drew the sword back and waited as Infus snapped the whip above his head, making him duck. The Elf tried to stay out of range of the weapon but the whip was unpredictable. The Elf ducked another strike from the whip and stepped forward prepared to attack. Just before he could swing Infus took a step and leapt through the air, landing behind the Elf and whirling back around to face him. The Elf turned and raised the sword.

Infus snapped the whip forward, and struck the Elf across the face, leaving a deep gash from his ear to his chin. Blood ran down his chin and the Elf drew back as the Demon struck again, leaving a deep gash down the front of his shirt. The Elf gripped his chest and the cloth became wet with his blood. The Elf turned to flee, thinking that the only chance he had was to run but as he did, the whip caught his feet and jerked them out from under him. The Demon stepped up to the Elf and kicked him in the side as it drew its sword, lifting it above the defenseless soldier. One quick stab through the chest and the Demon finished the Elf, looking up at the sorcerer on the throne.

Valsera sat with his hand on his chin, slightly impressed with the show that the Demon had given. Infus twisted and snapped the whip, watching as the green flames disappeared and the whip retracted into the handle. Infus tucked the weapon away inside of its cloak. The Demon stepped up in front of the sorcerer as the Goblins arrived to drag the body away.

"Worthless Elf," Valsera scolded, watching the Goblins. The dead Elf did not reply, they almost never did.

The guards closed the door and left Valsera and Infus alone once again. The sorcerer stood and left the throne, looking over the room and the puddle of blood on the stone floor. He stepped over the pool of blood and moved to the far wall.

"What do you think of the weapon my Lord?" Infus asked, pursuing the sorcerer across the room.

"Very impressive Infus. It will be useful in the battle."

"Which battle would that be?"

"The one that I am about to start Infus. I am looking to the north of Pentegarn in the untamed lands. There we have an option to either sandwich the Elves in and surround them or we can move on the Wood Elves at Eglarest. I want you to take the Slayers north and create a war on their own lands."

"Where would you prefer we attack sir?"

"The Princess is in Eglarest with the rest of the Wood Elves. With our attack on the island a failure, taking the rest of the Slayers to the fortress and besieging it will give us a great advantage. Keep them busy while we ravage the middle lands of the High Elves."

Infus stood still, staring ahead at the sorcerer as the Demon received its orders. It was something Infus had always been good at, causing pain. He looked around the room and took a step towards the ruler of the south.

"What route shall we take?"

"Ships," Valsera replied without a second thought. "Take as many as you need and move the mass of Slayers to the north. Make landfall somewhere in the untamed lands between Pentegarn and Eglarest. From there, I suggest you take Eglarest but do not move near Tvan. Enrage the Dwarves, and we may fail."

Infus turned to leave the room, stopping near the doors and looking back at the sorcerer on the throne. "Should I send you prisoners to tune your skills on my Lord?"

Valsera nodded and the Demon left the room, letting the large doors slam. Infus traveled through the halls and moved down to the lower levels of Qwaz, pushing past the Goblins that stood as guards at the dungeon. The rooms in the dungeons were small and packed with Elves and Humans, withering and dying from the length of time spent in the cramped dungeon. Infus looked over the rooms and reached to the door, pushing it open with ease. The contents of the room was all Elves with a single Human in the corner.

"Take them to Valsera," the Demon hissed, staring at the prisoners.

A mass of Goblins shuffled into the room and ordered the prisoners out at the tips of their spears, the sharp points inches from the skin of the Elves. The six prisoners trudged through the halls with between twelve and fifteen of the ugly creatures forcing them forward, Infus leading the way. One of the Elves made a quick turn and a grab for one of the spears, kicking the Goblin back from the group. As the Elf turned, Infus met him with a wide swing of its sword, slicing cleanly through his neck.

The body slowly crumpled to the ground, the spear bouncing against the stone floor. The other prisoners were obviously not thinking about trying something bold. The Goblin retrieved the spear and they pushed on down the hallway. The death of their fellow Elf broke any morale they might have had as they were forced to the top of the tower. The Goblins at the doors pushed them open and entered in front of the prisoners. Valsera looked over them and smiled, happy to see a group on which to strengthen his skills.

The Goblins surrounded the prisoners from behind but Valsera waved his hand, nodding to the door. The guards were hesitant to leave the sorcerer alone but the ruler of the southern armies lowered his brow and pointed to the door again.

"Leave us!" he ordered menacingly.

The Goblins almost fell over one another as they hurried to the door, trying to get out of the room at once. The prisoners moved towards the back of the room at the point of Infus's sword. As the prisoners lined up shoulder to shoulder, Valsera examined each one from top to bottom. At long last he grabbed the Human by the front of his shirt and pulled him into the center of the room away from the Elves. He shoved the Human back and picked a long spear from the rack where the sword had been drawn earlier. The sorcerer turned and raised the weapon as the Human raised his hands.

"Hey... wait I don't..."

Valsera hurled the spear forth, striking the Human in the chest and sending him back across the floor. The sorcerer crossed to where the Human lay dying and grabbed the shaft of the spear, pulling it free with a hard jerk. Looking down at the body, Valsera began the string of odd chants and the light formed on his hands again. The body absorbed the magic and suddenly the Human's fingers twitched. The reanimated corpse shivered and looked from side to side at the room around it as if never before seeing it. Valsera looked at the body as it slowly got to its feet, standing rigid and staring straight ahead at the sorcerer. Infus took a step towards the sorcerer and stared at the reanimated corpse, amazed that the spell had worked.

The Elves against the back wall shrank back further, afraid of what had just happened. Valsera reached out and snapped his fingers, watching as the corpse collapsed to the stone floor in a pile. As the life quickly left the reanimated body, Valsera turned and looked at Infus.

"I learned that the only way to reanimate the dead is to use a corpse not previously touched by magic. So many times before, the slaves were killed with magic, and raising the dead would not work. Now I have it all figured out. To prove my point... I'll do it again, once after magic and once without."

The sorcerer raised the spear from the ground and hurled it at the Elves, striking one in the chest and watching the Elf as he died. As the Elves scattered, Valsera shot a bright red bolt of light, striking one of the Elves in the back. The two bodies lay crumpled on the ground and Valsera stopped at the one still harboring the spear, performing the same ritual as he had earlier and just as before, the body came to life. He walked to the second one and repeated the process but his time, nothing happened. The Elf's remains lay smoldering on the floor from the horrid spell.

"Very interesting... what made you think of this my Lord?"

"Just a thought."

Another snap and the new corpse fell to the ground next to the others. Valsera looked to the remaining Elves who had crowded towards the door. "Take them back to the dungeon. Perhaps I will use them later."

"Yes Valsera."

Infus pushed towards the Elves and drew its sword, forcing them out the door and into the hall. The doors slammed with such force that it shook the room. Valsera watched as the Goblins arrived once more to remove the bodies piled on the floor and walked up to the throne to rest. He could see blood on the stone floor but he looked away, not caring in the least. Something in the back of his head was bothering him but he shook his head, forcing it away. He raised his hand and his staff floated from the far wall to his hand.

The sorcerer grew restless and as he waited his mind worked, putting the pieces of his plan together. Infus would take the strongest of the army north and move on the fortress of Eglarest. It would be the most unexpected move for the armies in the south.

Infus and a group of the Slayers arrived in the throne room. Valsera slowly sat back in his throne and looked at the group. The Slayers all took a knee in front of the sorcerer and Infus stepped up to the bottom of the throne stairs. It gave a low nod and turned back to the Slayers. The Slayers stood from the floor and formed a half circle around the sorcerer and Infus. They stood staring at the two, waiting for their orders.

"I take it you are ready to move on the north, Infus?" the sorcerer asked, staring into the hollow darkness within the

Demon's hood.

"Yes, my master," Infus hissed with a low nod.

Valsera nodded and gave a weak smile. "You will take the largest part of the Slayers north to assault the fortress Eglarest where the Wood Elves have fallen back. You will move to the coast and board our ships instead of crossing the land. With this, they will not have scouted your approach and you and the Slayers will wreak havoc on their pitiful defenses."

"When shall we leave?" Infus asked.

"The eve of tomorrow. I have another matter to discuss with you before you leave. I do not want you to leave before we have it taken care of. For now, gather whatever forces you will take and prepare for tomorrow's departure."

The Slayers turned to leave the room but Infus remained, waiting to hear what the sorcerer had to say. As the Demon waited, it soon became apparent that it was not a matter that would be discussed at the moment. He gave a bow and turned to the door, following the Slayers out. Just before leaving, Valsera stopped him.

"Infus, shut the door…"

The Demon did as it was told and turned back to Valsera. The sorcerer stood and left the throne, meeting the Demon in the center of the room.

"Yes master?"

"There is a matter that needs to be taken care of before you and your forces leave. There is a swell of dissent in the ranks of the Lizardmen. I've heard they are less and less willing to follow the orders given to them. This will not do."

Infus gave a vague nod. "What would you have me do?"

"Quell their uprising before it takes form. A large part of their forces are stationed here as defense with another group moving north with the armies I sent out against the Elves. Kill all of them."

Infus stared at the sorcerer from the hollow darkness within its hood, not entirely sure that he had heard the sorcerer correctly. Valsera was ordering him to kill their allies, a strange move when he wanted to swarm the Elven lands. Infus took a step back and looked at Valsera again.

"Kill them all even if they have not turned against you my Lord?"

"I do not want to give them the chance to rise up against me. If they are thinking it, they could be planning it. If we wait until they try to rise up, it could be too late to do something about it. We will not wait. Take the Slayers and show the entire army what happens when they show disloyalty."

The Demon gave a nod and turned to carry out the orders even though it did not fully agree with them. Infus moved down the halls and gathered the Slayers in behind it as they moved down to the courtyards and the open fields. When they arrived, the number of Slayers tripled and suddenly the Demon held an impressive army all its own. Infus stared out at the camps of soldiers across the fields and picked out a large group of Lizardmen at the far side of the field. The Demon started towards the creatures the sorcerer had ordered destroyed.

The Slayers followed in lines behind the Demon and it did not take long before the Lizardmen noticed the force moving towards them. Feeling that something might be wrong, they armed themselves and waited. When Infus stopped in front of the Lizardmen and the Slayers filed in behind, forming a concave around the Demon and Lizardmen. One of the Lizardman stepped up to the Demon and stared into the hood. The Lizardman started to speak but Infus stopped it immediately, drawing its sword and the whip at the same time. The Slayers followed the movement and Infus took a step forward.

"Your traitorous nature has condemned you and your kind," Infus said, igniting the whip and whirling around.

The whip shot out and caught the Lizardman around the neck, severing its head from its shoulders and sending the body to the ground in a heap. The other Lizardmen looked on in horror as the Demon continued with the whip, killing another of the reptilians. The Slayers charged into the Lizardmen. Rows of the Lizardmen fell at once before they finally started fighting back. They were strong but were out matched by the superior endurance of the Slayers.

Infus stabbed and swung on every Lizardman in sight,

felling them one after another until the Slayers swept past, killing off most of the creatures. The last of the Lizardmen fell back into the gnarled forests in an attempt to get away from the sudden and unexpected onslaught. Infus stabbed one of the Lizardmen on the ground, making sure it was dead. It had only taken minutes and in that time, close to forty Lizardmen were slain with only five or six escaping into the forests. The massive armies of Goblins had begun to move in on the action and Infus wondered how they were going to react.

"Stop where you are!" Infus ordered, the Demon's voice thundering across the field.

One of the Goblins stepped forward, looking at the bodies of Lizardmen on the field. "Why did you kill our allies, Demon?"

"They were guilty of plotting against our Lord Valsera. This is the punishment for those who dare stand against Valsera. Keep that in mind and clean these bodies out of the field."

The Slayers followed Infus back towards Qwaz without a word. They did not have to be ordered to do anything as they seemed to share a link with the Demon. The Demon had only to think of what needed to be done and the Slayers followed without a second of hesitation. The Slayers spread out in front of the city and stood guard, watching as the Goblins cleaned up the bodies of the Lizardmen.

Infus walked through the halls on the way back to the throne room, still not entirely sure why it had killed off the Lizardmen without proof that they were treasonous. The two Ogres at the entrance to the throne room hurried to open the doors, letting the Demon in. It moved up to the throne and stopped at the foot of Valsera, kneeling silently.

"It is done my master."

"That did not take very long. Were they all taken care of?" Valsera asked, rapping his fingers on the arm of the throne.

"A few did escape back into the forests but I do not think they will be a problem again. It was a powerful example to have them killed in front of the rest of the armies. What else would you ask of me my Lord?"

"A few escaped…" the sorcerer noted, repeating the Demon's words.

"Yes, but I do not think it will be an issue. They fell so quickly that any of those who escaped will not return."

"Very good then. Prepare the Slayers for tomorrows departure. Gather the armies of Goblins and get them ready to move north in behind the last army that was sent. Consider them reinforcements."

"Yes my master, at once."

The Demon nodded and turned to leave the room. The sorcerer sat upon the throne and stared around the room, happy that his orders had been followed so quickly. The slaughter of the Lizardmen would send a message to the rest of the forces that if they were to stand against him, they would fall. Even though the Lizardmen had been killed, there were still quite a number in the swamps to the east and south of Qwaz. Even so, he did not consider them a threat and his sights were now fully on the lands below Pentegarn. Something was bothering the sorcerer and he scratched the back of his neck, wondering what it could be.

The gnarled forests were thick and twisted, much like the armies that roamed through them. Not only did the forest hide the creatures of the south but it also masked the arrival of the Dragon force. The group dropped from the sky and landed wherever they could throughout the trees. Alora curved her wings and dropped into the forest slowly. The tips of her wings brushed the trees as she landed and she pulled them in tightly to her as Erzel looked for any sign of the enemy.

Yanosh landed and morphed back into the form of a man, looking back at the rest of the group. They were all dismounting from the Dragons and Warbirds and Erzel approached the wizard, his eyes darting frantically through the trees.

"This is nothing like the lands of Nalawren," Erzel whispered, looking at the trees and seeing the grotesque differences.

"Very true Erzel. Now, we are going to have to know what is going on around the city before we fly in and try to find Valsera. If we attack without knowing what is there, this could be a very quick defeat."

"I agree. On top of that, we will not attack until dark. Otherwise we might as well fly in and surrender. There will still be a few hours before the sun sets."

Kail arrived in next to Erzel and looked through the trees towards where Qwaz sat. Most of the group had not seen the lands in the south since the corruption had swept through and changed them so drastically. What had once been the same forest stretching across the lands had now been changed to such a wasteland. It was saddening to see what the land had become. Even the grass was a dingy color, no longer the beautiful green that spread across most of the grounds in the north. Nothing was as beautiful as it had once been.

"This forest feels disgusting," Kail said as he looked around them.

"That it does. Like something that is clinging to life but just barely as it wishes for death," Thorgrim added as he joined the three.

"If we defeat Valsera, maybe the lands will go back to the way they used to be before his evil touched them. How soon would you like to send out the scouts and who will you send?" Erzel asked the wizard.

"I will go... if a Dragon or Warbird were to fly over it might be a little more suspicious."

"You don't think a giant owl is suspicious?" Erzel asked with a questionable glance.

Yanosh turned his head to the side and shot Erzel a warning look. "I am doing what I can with what I have Erzel. If you have another suggestion I would be more than happy to hear it from you."

Erzel looked down as he realized he had insulted the wizard which was not what he had wanted to do. "I did not mean it as an insult Yanosh. Forgive me. Whenever you are ready then, it would be best if we knew what to expect as soon as we can."

"Of course. If you will excuse me."

The wizard moved back towards the Dragons and Warbirds and began changing back into the huge bird. The owl stretched its long wings out and tested them each twice before jumping from the ground and flapping them powerfully. The owl disappeared into the clouds quickly, leaving the rest hiding in the forest as they pondered what they were about to do. No matter how they thought about it, the challenge they had in front of them was going to be extremely difficult to accomplish.

"Ectle, how do you feel about this whole ordeal we are about to attempt?" Erzel asked as the wizard approached.

"Of course I feel this could end disastrously but I am optimistic."

Thorgrim sneered at the wizard. "Ok, what do you really think?"

"Well, I seriously doubt that we will have the chance to confront Valsera if the armies here are as strong as elsewhere. On top of that, he is not a weak opponent even though we are taking him by surprise."

The mass of Warbirds ruffled their wings and rested as their masters milled around the trees. The Dragons with the exception of Alora had all dropped to the ground to rest before the night arrived. Knowing that they would soon be battling for their lives, the group took the time to rest and relax as best as it could.

Within the castle at Qwaz the remainder of the armies locked the city down and prepared for the night ahead. They were oblivious to the small attack force hiding in the forest and as the guard moved across the walls and settled into the towers, the sorcerer stood on a balcony alone. He looked across the forests and for the second time that day, something caused a shiver to run up his neck. It was a sign he had previously ignored but now brought on a swell of curiosity. He looked across the treetops once more but this time nothing came to him and he dismissed the shiver as a chill from the cool air. Somewhere inside though, something did not want to give up as quickly as it brought on another shiver. This time Valsera slammed his fist on the railing and turned back to the throne room.

"What is your trouble master?" Infus asked, approaching from the throne room.

"Infus... what perfect timing. Something does not feel quite right tonight. Tighten the defenses and keep all forces left at the city on alert. We sent the armies north right when something is changing here."

"Should I call the second force back master? I can send for them immediately."

"No... move everything to the walls. We will not be caught off guard by whatever is going on that has my senses running wild tonight."

"Of course master. I will have the rest of the forces moved out onto the defenses at once. Rest, nothing will breech the gate."

Valsera watched the Demon walk away and out of the room to pull the rest of the forces out into the defenses. The sorcerer walked back to the throne and sat back onto it, closing his eyes and taking a deep sigh. He was tired but concerned with the world on the outside and what might be waiting.

Hell From Above

Yanosh had landed in the small opening and stood waiting as the group gathered around him to hear what he had scouted. The wizard looked at the eager faces surrounding him and began to tell of what they are up against.

"It is not as I had expected. The city has a massive defense on the walls and in every conceivable tower and opening. There is no main army however so this may be in our favor as we are not walking through the front door. There are several places for us to drop and move into the city without being detected. Unfortunately, I have no idea where Valsera is so it will be anyone's guess where to start."

"How many entrances to the towers did you see?" one of the Celestial Knights asked.

"Two balconies on the left tower, one balcony on the right tower, and a larger entrance at the base of the two. Anything else is further down to the base of the city where the defenses are strongest. Something I was not very happy to see however were several Slayers in the lower courtyard of the city."

There was a hushed sigh amongst the numbers as they realized the Slayers were in amongst those guarding the sorcerer. The memory of what happened on the Dragon Isles flooded back and they knew that the battle was going to be that much harder. No matter which entrance they used, they were almost guaranteed to face the Slayers again on their own ground.

"Suggestions on where to start? With several entrances, we should probably pick one on each tower and hit them hard. Hopefully one of the two will be the right choice," Lavian added.

"The highest balcony should be one of the choices. If I

remember correctly the original throne room of Qwaz was there. Perhaps they kept the layout similar," Erzel noted, remembering the layout of the fortress. "Sadly, there is a chance that the throne room now sits in the heart of the fortress."

The group shared a nod as they realized that the fortress could have easily been changed to better suit the Goblins and their master. If they had, finding Valsera could end up being just as hard as killing him. For the time, they all clung to the hope that the fortress still held the same layout and the sorcerer would be caught completely off guard. The plan seemed to have so many small loopholes that the slightest mistake could spell disaster for the entire mission. The window of opportunity was small, but at least there was still a window.

"Curious, what will the Dragons and Warbirds do once we are in the halls of the fortress other than wait for our need to evacuate," Erzel asked, turning from the group to Alora.

"We will give you the distraction that you need to keep their attention elsewhere. With the walls and towers so exposed we will be able to cause great losses to their defenses, especially if they don't expect us."

"The Warbirds as well?"

"Yes. Those who are not joining us within the fortress will take to the sky and fight against the defenses that Valsera has in place. If we are lucky, the attack from the sky will keep his forces completely occupied while we do what we have to do. Getting out may be a problem," Yanosh said as he took a seat on a fallen tree.

"Why?" Thorgrim asked bluntly.

"Well, if we get inside and manage to find Valsera and kill him, we then must find our way back to the entrances and hope that the Dragons or Warbirds will be able to reach us. Once they attack the outer walls and defenses there may not be a time where we are clear to get back into the air. It is just a thought of course."

"There are so many risks involved here that to weigh them all would be insane. We need to focus on what we are here to do. Get into the fortress, find Valsera, and kill him so he can no longer push the armies north against us," Ectle said, his tone impatient as he began pacing.

The group was as ready as it could be but at the same time, none of them really wanted to make the first move. The sky was painted with purples and reds as the sun was only minutes from disappearing completely. They had agreed to take to the skies once the sun had left and the time was approaching quickly. All of the Celestial Knights with the exception of Lavian sat around the clearing, resting for the event to come. Erzel's group all sat with the wizard as he pondered the chain of events that needed to take place for their attack to be successful.

When the last of the color finally disappeared from the sky, Yanosh stood and looked around at the rest of the group. Whether they were ready or not, the time to move was now. Everyone in the woods started pulling themselves together, stretching and waking as they realized that the time had come. Alora stretched her wings as far as the trees would allow and turned her head to Erzel and Kail as the two approached.

"The time has come?" the Dragon asked, a beam of moonlight shining in her large eyes.

"Yes. I must ask you Alora, how are you this calm when it appears that you are forced to face the one responsible for your near destruction?"

"Revenge master Elf. What happened long ago still brings us pain to this day. The chance to bring down the one responsible for the loss of our kind will give those we have lost the justice they deserve. I am ready whenever you are."

The rest of the group moved towards the other Dragons and the Warbirds that would carry them into the heart of the battle and began mounting up. Off to the side Yanosh quickly changed into his owl form again and looked around as the rest of the soldiers settled onto their mounts. They sat quietly on the beasts that would take them into the battle as Yanosh stepped out of the trees and looked up at the dark sky above. The owl looked from star to star with a curious eye before turning back to the rest of the group behind him. A nod from the Dragons and the owl shot out of the trees and into the sky.

The rest watched for a moment before the numbers of Warbirds began taking off one at a time. The Celestial Knights fell into a line and circled the area where the Dragons were in the trees as they moved higher and higher. The first of the Golden Dragons took flight with Thorgrim and Nimir, followed shortly by the second carrying Kail and Ectle and then by the entire flock of Silver Dragons. Erzel reached out and touched Alora on the neck. She turned around and looked at the Elf.

"Are you ready Erzel?"

"As much as I will ever be. This is not something one can prepare for in such a small amount of time."

The Dragon nodded and left the ground with a single flap of its wings. They climbed higher into the sky, catching sight of the others who had left before them and falling into line with them. The castle was visible in the distance and the line of winged soldiers were moving towards it. It was what they had been talking about, though now it seemed to be a disaster in the making. The many torches of the city cast light all across the battlements and walls, showing that the task would be even more difficult than they had expected. The first of the Warbirds streaked by the tops of the towers and disappeared on the other side where the torchlight no longer reached. The rest followed and Erzel kept a close eye on the walls as Alora drew nearer.

Alora shot up high into the clouds and paused as the Gold Dragon carrying Kail and Ectle stopped next to her in the sky. The two shared a nod and Alora closed her wings in tight to her body, diving at the balcony that stood out from the left tower. Erzel turned and saw the Gold Dragon do the same and the pair sliced through the sky.

Seconds stood between the tower and Dragon as Erzel gripped the beast tightly, the wind threatening to push him off. At the last moment she flung her wings open and suddenly slowed in midair. Alora reached out and grabbed the railing of the balcony and came to a stop just long enough for Erzel to drop from her back to the stone floor below. Alora dropped from the railing and disappeared, allowing the Gold Dragon to do the same. Kail and Ectle fell together, landing at the same time and like before, the Dragon disappeared.

"Ready Erzel?" Ectle asked, gripping his staff and staring into the room from the balcony.

"Yes… for now."

The Elf watched a Warbird streaking towards them and the three on the balcony moved back against the walls. The Warbird hovered above them and from the saddle dropped Lavian, her crossbow ready. She rolled when she hit the floor and Erzel gave her a hand up to her feet. Shouting from the walls below caught their attention and the four dared a look over the edge. The soldiers down below were all scurrying around the battlements, pointing to the skies.

A whistle could be heard in the air as the Blue Dragon dove at the battlements, her body a streak against the dark sky behind her. She opened her mouth as the walls came into range and a brilliantly bright flash of lightning raked across the top of the battlements, sending Goblins falling to the ground. Right behind her was the Gold Dragon who followed up the attack with its own raging torrent of fire that left the top of the wall near the gate smoldering in ruin. As the two circled back around for another attack on the wall, Erzel turned back to the others.

Movement inside the room brought them back to their task and the four moved in against the wall on either side of the entrance, struggling to hear over the attack on the walls below. Erzel drew his sword from over his shoulder and nodded to the rest, daring to peek around the corner. He quickly pulled back away from the opening and held up three fingers for the others to see. He stopped and struggled to think of a way to tell them that the three were Slayers but nothing was coming to mind. Finally he ran his finger across his throat and mouthed the word.

Lavian and Ectle nodded and the Elf turned to Kail, whispering the news to the man. With Slayers in the room, there was a good chance that they were guarding something or someone of importance. The group heard another blast of fire hit the battlements below and the footsteps grew closer. The Slayers would stumble onto the group but this time they would have the surprise they needed. One more step and they acted as one, turning the corner to attack.

The three Slayers stood in the opening of the room, stunned at the sudden sight of the group in the castle. Kail and Lavian focused on the one on the left, firing their bows and striking it at the same time, sending the creature to the stone floor. As they reached for their own weapons, Erzel brought his sword around, slicing cleanly through the neck of the one in front. The third turned and ran back into the room but Ectle stepped up and with a wave of his staff conjuring up a long rope that caught it around the feet. The Slayer fell to the floor with a crash, dropping its weapon.

As they walked into the room, Kail and Lavian finished off the two that had been stunned as the third was already engulfed in orange flames. They walked into the room very slowly, their weapons ready and eager to spill blood. They scanned the room from one wall to the other but they saw nothing other than the remains of the Slayers near the balcony. They noticed the door against the far wall and Erzel glanced back at the rest.

"We're going to have to look elsewhere. He's not here and we can't wait for more Slayers to show up."

"We should move up the tower a little. There is one more balcony on this tower and if we do not find Valsera in that room, there is no way we will find him in time. If he is in the heart of the castle or in the other tower we will not have the chance to get to him," Ectle said with a sigh, rubbing the top of his staff.

The head of the staff emitted a bright light that illuminated the entire room. They looked to the door and Erzel took the lead, peeking into the hall as he pushed the door open. The Elf stepped out into the hall and waved for them to follow, moving towards the bend to his right. He didn't know why he felt like it was the right way to go but something was pulling him in that direction. The other four filed in behind him and they moved up the hallway together.

Thorgrim and Nimir stood on the edge of a large walk that wound around the tower and opened to a large doorway on the back side. Galador had left his Warbird and joined them, moving in front of the two Dwarves with his sword drawn and shield held in front of his chest. They looked into the sky as a Silver Dragon streaked by and made a dive at the wall below, its claws raking the wall next to an enemy as it shot off across the treetops. Galador nodded to the two Dwarves and moved further ahead, eyeing the doorway just around the corner. He stopped and held his shield back to stop the two as his eyes landed on a group of Goblins, their bows trained on the sky as they waited for the next enemy to pass over them. From his position he was not seen but Galador counted twelve, a formidable number for the three to handle. Galador turned back to the two Dwarves and sighed.

"What is it Galador?" Nimir asked as he saw the Celestial Knight's face.

"A full patrol of Goblin archers around the corner. They are set on the sky but I fear one step around the corner and we will be seen. Have a look."

Thorgrim stepped up to the corner and slowly peered around the edge. The Goblins had lined up against the balcony, their bows aimed to the sky and arrows ready to release. The Dwarf lowered his eyebrows and looked at the closest of the creatures with a burning hatred. The distance between them and the Goblins would not be possible to cover without being seen and none of them had a range weapon. Thorgrim looked to his belt and picked a small sword and looked around the corner again.

"We can take them Galador," Thorgrim said, hefting the enchanted war hammer in one hand and the small sword in the other.

"Are you sure? That's a lot of Goblins," the Celestial Knight asked, gripping his sword tightly.

"We can't stand here talking about it, we've got to do something, now."

Galador took a deep breath and looked around the corner one more time, seeing the Goblins looking skyward. For the moment they were distracted and it could end up being the only chance they had. Galador nodded to the two Dwarves and grit his teeth.

"Stay close."

The Celestial Knight charged around the corner, his shield leading the way. Thorgrim and Nimir followed, their shorter legs making it difficult to keep up with the man. Ten feet from the group one of the Goblins turned and found the three charging. It changed the aim of its bow and Galador raised the shield, covering the shot. Just before the Goblin could release it Thorgrim threw the short sword and caught the creature in the throat. The arrow left the bow and glanced off of the edge of the shield, hitting the stone wall behind them.

Galador lowered his shield and charged into the group, sending most of them sprawling across the battlements, the Dwarves bringing up the rear with a massive swing of the war hammer, knocking one Goblin to the ground below. The three fought back and forth with the Goblins until the last few retreated into the castle leaving the rest of their soldiers to die on the top of the wall. Galador turned and waved to the two, the front of his shield and armor smeared with the blood of the enemy.

"Come on! We have to keep moving before reinforcements arrive!"

Nimir followed the two but felt very out of place, knowing finally that this was not the place for one not used to war. He held his sword with both hands as he ran into the room behind the two, afraid to be left behind. The Celestial Knight charged through the hall and up a flight of stairs trying to catch the Goblins that had run. He got to the next corner and stopped, waiting for the Dwarves to catch up.

Thorgrim stopped next to Galador and looked up and down the halls as Nimir arrived, his eyes darting nervously around the hallway. The hallway was clear and the three moved further up through the castle. Two more curves and suddenly they stopped when they saw the hall in front of them blocked off by a mass of Goblins. Galador stepped into the middle of the hallway and raised his sword. Nimir turned and the tip of his sword slowly dropped lower. There was a large mass of Goblins in front of them and from around the corner appeared an Ogre and another six or eight Goblins. He bumped Thorgrim and pointed, revealing that their chances of getting anywhere were now gone.

Erzel, Kail, Lavian, and Ectle moved up the tower together, their weapons ready. The stairs ended and the hallway stretched to a large pair of doors. They moved together, Ectle watching behind them as they stopped at the doors. Lavian and Kail readied their weapons, aiming to the crack in the door as Erzel slowly pushed it open. The door was heavy but swung open quite easily, showing the inside of the room. The four stepped in cautiously, their eyes combing every inch of the room. Oddly, it was completely empty with the exception of a large stone throne in the center.

"Erzel, this room is empty too. Valsera must be in the heart of the fortress by now. We will never be able to reach him," Kail whispered, scanning the room once more.

"I can't believe this. The Slayers were guarding a room with nothing in it and now a throne room just as empty," Erzel noted, confusion apparent in his voice.

They looked out at the balcony and realized that the throne was the end of the line. If they were to get any further, they would have to fight their way into the heart of the fortress to find the sorcerer. Erzel looked back at Ectle, both knowing that the result of their current efforts had been a failure.

"We should leave before it is too late," Lavian whispered, seeing the look the two shared.

Erzel nodded, knowing that the heart of the fortress would be impenetrable for the four of them. With Valsera in the heart of the fortress, it would take a force greater than what they had to find and finish him. To top it off, with the Slayers and Goblins massing their bows on the walls the Dragons and Warbirds would not be able to keep attacking the fortress. Outside from the balcony they heard a loud explosion and the walls shook from the attack.

"Well... maybe we can draw attention on the balcony and get out of here before the Dragons bring the city to the ground," Kail said, walking out towards the balcony.

Ectle, Lavian and Kail moved out onto the balcony where one of the Warbirds arrived and then disappeared into the sky with Lavian on its back. Ectle looked to the sky and instead of the Gold Dragon that had dropped him, a Warbird arrived and Ectle carefully mounted the creature, clutching the restraints tightly as the Warbird dove from the balcony with amazing speed.

Kail and Erzel took a look back in the throne room and then back to one another. They knew the sorcerer was right there in the city somewhere but had no idea how to find him. They turned to see the giant owl streaking towards the two. They backed away and the owl landed in the open, shifting to the Human form quickly.

"Yanosh, we're too late. Valsera must have retreated into the heart of the fortress before we got here. This is the second room we've searched and…"

"Erzel… turn around," Yanosh interrupted, his eyes not meeting the Elf.

Erzel and Kail did as the wizard had ordered and were all surprised to find a man sitting on the throne behind them. Near the door came another surprise as a cloaked form arrived, blocking their escape. The soldier stopped when the man on the throne raised his hand, staring down the three on the balcony. The man was dressed in a black robe but underneath the group could see a hardened breastplate. He gripped a long staff and stared at the group menacingly.

"They were not here a minute ago Yanosh," Kail whispered to the wizard beside him.

"On the contrary my foolish friend, I've been here ever since you and your little group intruded on my throne room. The question is, what the hell are you doing here?" the man on the throne asked as he stood.

Yanosh took a step forward to confront the man. "We are here to punish you for your crimes against our lands. You have scarred them for the last time."

Valsera stopped at the bottom of the throne and looked at the wizard. "Oh really Yanosh? That would be an interesting thought, if it were possible. Why don't you surrender so I don't have to slaughter you needlessly. You can spend the rest of your days as my slaves instead," Valsera said with a smile, sarcasm flowing from his lips.

Erzel turned his head to the wizard, shocked and confused. "How does he know you?"

"I know plenty more than you think Erzel. I know where you have been, I know how you got here, I know that you left your precious Elf Princess with the rest of the Wood Elves. It shouldn't be long before my armies break their defenses. Oh, and you Kail, a homeless, shadow of a man that once was. You run from your past, from your nightmares. Do they know the truth?"

Erzel and Yanosh turned to the man, the question from the sorcerer stabbing at their minds. Valsera had already shown that he knew more than it seemed possible. Now there was an accusation against the man standing beside them, the man who had fought next to them. What did Valsera know about Kail that the rest did not.

"Kail, what is he talking about?" Erzel asked, the tip of his sword dropping slowly as he stared at the Human.

"Well, I suppose you don't know then? How sad. Perhaps we should pour over this matter together. Where should we start?"

Kail quickly drew the bow in his hand back and released, sending a bright arrow flying straight at the sorcerer. Valsera reached up and caught the arrow in midair, turning his head and looking at the projectile with an obvious sense of humor. He squeezed the arrow and it burst in his hand, disappearing as the remains fell to the floor. Yanosh sighed and looked from the sorcerer to the man next to him.

"Kail, is there something we need to know?"

The fighter shook his head, looking at the ground as he looked away. He took a step back from Yanosh and looked up at the wizard.

"This is taking too long... Kail was one of us," Valsera exclaimed, a smile on his face as he watched the two exchanging glances.

Erzel and Yanosh stared at the fighter, expressionless as the words from the sorcerer echoed inside of them. Kail looked at the two but did not say anything. He did not deny the accusation from Valsera and it was apparent that something was eating away at him. Yanosh narrowed his eyes at the man.

"Is it true?"

Kail took a deep breath. "Yes... and no, Yanosh."

Yanosh and Erzel took a step back away from the others

in the room, looking at the three with distrust growing in them. Kail took a step towards the two, his face clearly disgusted with what was revealed.

"It is not completely true. I was one of them, one of the assassins for Valsera, but I am no longer. I will serve him no longer."

"Assassin? You are an assassin for the enemy?" Erzel asked, not sure if he believed what he was hearing.

"No… no longer. I won't serve him! I could have killed you at any point, at the grave, in the forests! I could have killed Rhen on the island but she lives. Everyone is alive. An assassin for Valsera would not have let any of you live."

"A traitor to your master… how long will it be before you betray your new friends?" Valsera continued, digging at the man viciously.

Erzel looked at the man. What he said made sense. He had every chance in the world to kill the Princess and others including the Kings of the Wood Elves and High Elves. Knowing that he had at one time served the darkest sorcerer the lands had ever seen made it hard to completely trust him. Even if he hadn't performed as an assassin was expected, the Elf couldn't take his eyes off of the man. The room was silent as they struggled to decide if Kail was trustable.

Thorgrim gripped the handle to the war hammer, feeling the power flowing through his muscles. He knew it would amplify his strength through the fight but the numbers were too great for just his strength to overcome. He looked back at the Ogre and the handful of Goblins surrounding it. An idea began to form in his head and he looked the hulking beast in the eyes. The Dwarf leaned back a little and looked at Galador, knowing that the chance to act would soon disappear.

"Galador, we have to try to fight back the way we came," the Dwarf whispered.

"Are you kidding? That Ogre would wipe us out in two swings. There is no way we can beat it and all of these Goblins in one fight."

"With this we can," Thorgrim noted, hefting the war hammer.

The Celestial Knight looked at the weapon and then to the Dwarf, knowing that the magic of the weapon could in fact turn the tide in their favor. As soon as they tried to attack the group behind them though, the mass in front would charge and sandwich them before they had the chance to defend themselves. Nimir stood between the two, having no idea what he would be able to add to the battle. His proficiency with his sword lacked what the others brought to the fight.

"Nimir, move fast and try to defend yourself. We have little chance of making it through this, but just maybe, one of us can make it out alive," Thorgrim whispered.

The statement gave the younger Dwarf a chill and he tightened his grip on the sword. Sweat beaded on his forehead and he wondered if he would make it through the battle alive. Thorgrim and Galador turned to the monstrous Ogre, their weapons ready.

The Last Swing in Qwaz

The Dragons had scorched the battlements all across the fortress but the archers continued to appear, filling the sky with arrows. A bright bolt of lightning sent rock and wood flying in every direction at the top of the gate, knocking Goblins to the ground. Alora shot back into the dark sky, disappearing completely. The other Dragons made similar attacks, torching the faces of the fortress again and again until a well aimed volley knocked one of the Silver Dragons from the sky. It fell to the ground below, crashing head first into the field. The great beast did not move and the archers on the wall above fired another volley to finish it off.

Even as high as Alora had made it into the sky, she could see the Dragon become deathly still and knew that another of her kind had been slain. Anger surged through her body as she made yet another dive at the fortress, the wind hissing by her head as she dropped. She opened her mouth, feeling the charge of the lightning surging through her body as the top of the wall came into view. Just as she released the unbelievably powerful bolt of lightning, an arrow grazed her just below the right eye, leaving a deep gash.

Alora peeled away from the city, her face searing from the attack. She could feel the warm, wet touch of blood on her face and neck and she dropped down to the ground on the outskirts of the forest. She raised her right hand to her cheek, feeling the wound and finding though the gash was fairly small, the flow of blood was impressive. She shook her head and turned back to the battle in the distance behind her. Spreading her wings, the Dragon prepared to soar back into the sky.

The sky was filled with Dragons and Warbirds taking their shots at the soldiers on the walls and in the towers. Where the Dragons hit the fortress with torrents of fire and lightning, the Warbirds came in faster, using their strong wings and sharp talons to pluck soldiers from the walls and drop them from a deadly height. The Warbirds came in waves, three or four at a time from every direction. With the Goblins trying to protect themselves from attacks from every direction, they became easier to pick off.

After the third pass of the Warbirds, one of the monstrous Gold Dragons dropped in behind and knocked an entire row of archers from the wall. The eight Goblins bounced off the battlements and crashed to the ground below. Masses of Goblins were falling to the creatures in the sky but now there was a new foe on the walls. Slayers had arrived and the new menace posed a very real threat.

The Warbirds turned and dropped back towards the castle, catching sight of the Slayers for the very first time. The lead Warbird dropped low, its talons stretched out towards the enemy but it was in vain. The Slayers had drawn their bows back and now released, their tainted arrows cut through the sky faster than the incoming fighters. There was no time to react as the Celestial Knight in front took two of the arrows in the chest, knocking the soldier from his mount. He fell through the air and crashed to the ground just like the Goblins that had been plucked from the walls. The Warbird that had been carrying the soldier turned to see him fall and felt the horrible pain in its own chest. It's wings curled and the Warbird crashed into the wall of the fortress. Seeing the Slayers on the walls made Alora realize that the battle within the castle could be going poorly for their forces.

Yanosh stared past Kail at the sorcerer on the throne. The cloaked soldier moved in beside the sorcerer and stared at Kail, the hollow darkness under its cloak locked on the man. It rubbed the hilt of the sword just visible from the edge of its cloak, aching for a fight. Erzel looked past Kail to the cloaked soldier, his attention now grabbed by the weapon it possessed. He raised his own sword back up in defense, knowing that any second the room could be filled with battle.

"This is taking too long," Valsera said irritated.

Valsera gave a deep sigh at the moment of silence between the soldiers and the newly discovered traitor. He had hoped that uncovering the truth about the man would force the wizard and Elf to cast him out, attack him even. Looking at them now he wondered why the blood had not been drawn. The sorcerer gave an exasperated groan and lifted his staff, swinging it through the air. As if caught by an invisible force, Kail was suddenly slung backward through the air and slammed against the wall, sliding down to the floor.

Yanosh dropped back away from the two, his staff ready as he watched the man crumble to the ground on the far side of the room. He and Erzel stepped back towards the balcony with their weapons ready as the two opponents advanced on them. Valsera turned and looked at the soldier beside him and then to the Elf, a smile on his face.

"Infus, why don't you take care of the Elf. Yanosh is mine."

The cloaked creature turned and locked stares with the Elf, giving him a chill as soon as the creature turned. Yanosh moved away from Erzel to the right towards the fallen Human as Valsera moved swiftly across the room. The two squared off, both of their staves glowing as they prepared to strike. The room was silent as the two sides stared the other down. Erzel looked at Kail's body on the floor and then turned to the creature.

Infus reached to draw the sword from its sheath, holding it out at the Elf, daring him to make his own move. Erzel gripped his sword with both hands and took a step towards the Demon. The tips of their swords met and the two paused, as if giving the other one more respectful moment before the swing. Infus drew the sword back and charged, swinging wildly at the Elf.

Erzel used his speed over the Demon's strength, ducking and dodging the attacks with room to spare. Infus turned and slashed as the Elf brought his own sword up to defend, the blades clashing together loudly. Erzel pushed the sword back and made his own attack, thrusting the blade through the stomach of his opponent. Infus stood rigid and then brought a foot up, kicking the Elf in the chest. Erzel fell back, pulling his sword with him and watching as the sword slid cleanly with no blood or wound of any sort.

Infus took a step towards the Elf with its sword raised to attack but the Elf rolled to the right out of the way. The sword met the stone floor loudly and Erzel was on his feet, bringing his own weapon down on the Demon. Just as before, the sword passed through Infus's neck without a hint of resistance. The Elf backed away from the Demon, his sword held ready to strike even though it seemed pointless. The Elf looked to the right at the wizard with a face of fear.

"Yanosh? What do I do?" Erzel asked helplessly as Infus closed on him.

The wizard took a glance to the Elf, letting his guard down momentarily. Valsera thrust his staff out at the wizard and as Kail had earlier Yanosh was knocked backward. Instead of crashing against the wall though he slid across the stone floor, stopping a few feet from the wall. He narrowed his eyes and walked back to where he had been moments earlier. Valsera had not moved but watched intently as the wizard stepped back in front of him, his eyes glowing softly.

"You don't know what you're up against do you?" Valsera asked, his sneer giving the wizard a shudder.

Yanosh drew back his hand, a ball of fire slowly growing between his fingers. The sorcerer watched intently as the fire engulfed the wizard's hand. Yanosh hurled the ball of fire forward, watching as the sorcerer dove out of the way. The fireball struck the base of the throne and exploded, sending a shower of rock and debris all over the room. Yanosh covered his face as chunks of stone and wood sprayed across him. The wizard lowered his hand and peered through the dust, looking for the sorcerer. The cloud of dust hid Valsera.

Erzel dodged another swing from the Demon and backed away, knowing that he could do very little against Infus. Another clash of their swords and the Demon shoved the Elf back towards the balcony. He stepped back into the night air, feeling the cold wind on his back. He brought his sword up in defense as Infus approached from within the throne room. They squared off again. Erzel charged with his sword ready to strike the Demon once more.

Just when Infus came into range of the attack, the Demon ducked and forced his shoulder into the Elf's stomach. Infus grabbed Erzel by the front of his tunic and threw the Elf across its back onto the floor. Erzel's sword skidded across the stone floor, stopping against the wall. He arched his back painfully, his eyes blurred from the force of the impact. He pushed himself away, gripping his ribs from the sudden swell of pain.

"You never had a chance fools," Infus hissed, closing on the Elf.

Infus reached into its robes and produced a long handle. The Elf looked at the odd item as the Demon held it out in front. The green flames slowly leaked from the handle, growing longer and more intense. The whip snapped against the ground and Infus took another step towards the downed Elf. Infus drew the whip back and looked upon the Elf, the darkness within the cloaked hood holding a menacing glare. Just when the Demon prepared to strike with the weapon, a massive gush of wind blew across the balcony.

Erzel and Infus turned to the side of the balcony to find the wind pushed down on them from the wings of Alora. She reached down with her talons, gripping the railing to the balcony and stretching her neck forward with her mouth wide. The Demon took a step back, staring at the Dragon's sharp teeth. Infus turned to attack the Dragon with the magic whip when she reared her head back, energy surging through her. Alora threw her jaw open wider, a powerful bolt of lightning leaping from her mouth through the air.

The bolt struck Infus in the chest, the force knocking the Demon back against the railing. Infus's weapons fell to the ground as the Demon slammed against the edge of the balcony. Infus straightened and looked to the sword on the ground when a second bolt of lightning left the Dragon's mouth. The blast hit the Demon again but this time it was knocked clean over the railing of the balcony. It fell wildly to the stone wall below, crashing into the battlements violently.

Erzel pushed himself to his feet and walked to the edge of the balcony, looking down on the battlements where the Demon had fallen. Alora let go of the balcony railing and dove away from the tower, arrows chasing her through the air. The Elf watched and then froze as he looked down to the wall below. The smoldering form of Infus wriggled and then slowly stood. Even a bolt of lightning was not enough to bring down the Demon.

Thorgrim gripped the war hammer with both hands, his muscles taunt as he prepared to strike down the Ogre standing between them and the room from which they arrived. Galador gripped his sword and moved the shield over his chest, prepared to charge down the Goblins that stood around the Ogre. The oversized brute was the only thing that was really an issue. It gave a scowl, staring down the three intruders.

Galador and Thorgrim shared one last glance and the Dwarf charged towards the Ogre, the war hammer drawn back over his shoulder. His pace was brisk and ten feet away from the enemies he flung the war hammer at the Ogre, watching as it whirled end over end towards the enemy. The Ogre saw the weapon flying towards him but never had the chance to move out of the way. It smashed into the Ogre's chest and sent it stumbling back into the Goblins, sliding down the wall.

As soon as the Dwarf released the war hammer, he drew the mace from his belt, leaping at the first of the Goblins and swinging wildly. Galador was only a step behind, slashing wildly and smashing the enemy with his shield. They could hear the force that was behind them charging down the hall, pinning them. Thorgrim bashed the Goblins one at a time, pushing his way to the door. He could see the room and the balcony. The Celestial Knight cut one Goblin's head from its shoulders and pinned another against the wall with his foot, drawing back and stabbing it in the chest.

"Galador, look out!" Nimir yelled, turning to the hall behind them.

The Goblins were moving down on them but in front was a Slayer, its sword positioned to strike the Dwarf. Galador turned and knocked the sword aside, pushing the Slayer back with his shield. He turned and looked over his shoulder at the two Dwarves. Nimir was pulling his sword from the body of a Goblin and Thorgrim was poised to smash the Ogre with the mace.

"Get out of here while you can!" Galador yelled, raising his shield to the Slayer's attack.

Thorgrim and Nimir looked up at the Celestial Knight as the Slayer closed on him, the Goblins close behind it. Nimir looked at them and took a step back, not sure if he should run or not. Thorgrim retrieved his war hammer from the ground and shoved the Dwarf back into the room.

"Go. I am not going to run if I can help him. Get to the balcony and get out of here!"

Nimir took another step into the room and turned, fearing to look back at the scene. He picked up the pace until he had crossed the room and arrived on the battlements once more. He watched as a fireball struck the wall on the far left and the Dragon turned and soared upward. The Dwarf looked back at the room and wondered why he had abandoned them.

Galador swung at the Slayer's head only to miss time and time again. The opponent returned the attack with the same results, knocking a chunk of stone from the wall as the blade hit behind the Celestial Knight. They kicked and shoved back and forth in the small hallway, neither able to deal a deadly blow to the other. Thorgrim drew a dagger from his belt and threw it past the two catching one of the Goblins in the shoulder. It was all he could do at the time.

Galador brought his shield up to defend but the Slayer had expected the move and kicked it with all its might, sending the Celestial Knight back against the wall and the shield bouncing to the floor. Another stroke of its sword met the stone wall as the cheers and jaunts from the Goblins grew louder. Galador caught sight of Thorgrim out of the corner of his eye and wondered why the Dwarf had not left.

"Thorgrim, I said go!" he yelled frantically.

"But..."

"Get out of here!"

Thorgrim took a few steps back, still reluctant to abandon the soldier. As soon as Galador turned to face the Slayer, the creature moved to strike, delivering an elbow to the temple and then whirling, thrusting its sword into the stomach of its opponent. The Celestial Knight paused in the middle of his swing, the sword slowly sliding deeper through the plated armor and out the back.

The Goblins roared triumphantly as the blood dripped to the floor. Galador held his own sword above him, frozen from the intense pain surging through his body. His eyes were blurring and he knew that death had come. Galador dropped his eyebrows and summoned the last ounce of strength in his body. With a last yell, he brought his own sword down on the Slayer to the left of its head, sending a gush of sparks in to the air. He slowly slumped forward, dying as the Slayer burst into flames and together they collapsed in the floor.

Thorgrim stared at Galador's body, the enemy's sword still impaling him. The Dwarf turned and made a quick retreat into the room, slamming the door as the Goblins surged towards him. He felt the first of the Goblins ram against the door and he looked through the room for something to brace it. He grabbed a chair and shoved it up against the door, praying it would hold as he hurried towards the battlements. The door behind him splintered from the constant battering.

"Nimir! What are you doing?" Thorgrim asked when he saw the younger Dwarf standing at the battlements.

"The battle above has yet to stop. They haven't seen me here. Where is Galador?"

"He didn't make it," Thorgrim replied, looking back when the door burst open and the Goblins flooded through the room.

Nimir and Thorgrim turned to run but found that both the room and the path leading to the balcony now had a group of Goblin soldiers closing on them. The two Dwarves were backed against the railing, their weapons ready though they were greatly outnumbered. Thorgrim hefted the weapon and stared down the groups closing on them slowly. The two Dwarves pressed their backs together, each facing the enemies coming toward them. The wind grew and the Goblins suddenly fell back away from the two Dwarves. They turned and found a massive Dragon arriving, its claws stretched out as it grabbed them from the balcony. Nimir and Thorgrim both held onto the Dragon's feet, terrified as the Dragon dove out across the plains.

The Slayer archers in the tower on the far wall drew their bows back and aimed as the Dragon swept by, releasing their arrows and watching them streak through the air. The first two missed short but the third and fourth arrows hit the Dragon in the back between its wings. The Dragon fought to stay in flight but the pain from the tainted arrows were breaking her strength. She gripped the two Dwarves tightly, tucking them into her body as she finally gave in and fell from the sky, plummeting into the forests of the south.

Erzel picked up his sword and staggered back into the room where the sorcerer and wizard were still circling one another. Valsera stepped out of the thinning dust to face the wizard again, his staff glowing a deep red as he approached. The humor the wizard had shown earlier had since disappeared as he saw the remains of his throne strewn all across the room. The sorcerer stopped and lowered his eyes at the wizard, his mouth a thin line without emotion of any sort.

"This is going to end badly for you Yanosh. I give you a choice. You can surrender now and I will forgive this little act of lunacy. If you resist, I will destroy you and the rest of your precious Celestial Knights for good."

Yanosh pointed a finger at the sorcerer, cutting his eyes harshly. "I would never surrender to you Valsera! You've killed enough of my soldiers and forced us from our homes. If I give in now, I would insult all those you've killed and the lands you've ruined."

Yanosh had a ball of fire swirling in his hand and Valsera mimicked his move, summoning his own fireball to use against the wizard. Yanosh flung his fireball forth and Valsera did the same, watching as the two balls of fire met in midair and glanced off of one another, striking opposite walls and exploding, shaking the room violently. As Valsera recovered Yanosh summoned another fireball and flung it at the sorcerer who shielded himself and sent the attack to the wall once more. Yanosh threw another and the third roared towards the sorcerer with blistering speed.

Valsera did not dive out of the way but instead stretched out his arm and caught the spell. The ball of fire whirled in his fingers and slowly began to grow dimmer. Valsera grinned as he extinguished the fireball and looked at his hand where the fire had burned only seconds before. Yanosh grunted angrily at the sight and took a few steps back as he prepared for the retaliation that was sure to come.

Erzel stared at the fight in the room, praying that the wizard would be able to hold his own against the evil sorcerer. He gripped his sword and leaned against the wall, his side throbbing from the attack that put him against the floor earlier. He looked and saw Kail struggling to push himself up off the floor but his arms were weak and shaky and he collapsed again, disoriented and barely conscious. The Elf stared at the Human and wondered if he had told the truth. If not, why had Valsera attacked him? Erzel sheathed his sword and crept slowly into the room in the direction of the downed Human. He kept one eye on the pair in the center of the room as he finally moved in next to Kail who pushed himself up onto one elbow and looked the Elf in the eye. Kail sat amazed that the Elf had come back for him.

"Erzel? Why did you... come back?"

"Save your strength. Come on, let's get out of here before things get worse."

"Where... is the Demon?"

Erzel wrapped Kail's arm over his neck and started hobbling towards the balcony, Kail still barely conscious. "Don't worry about it, Infus won't be bothering us for now."

Kail could hardly manage to walk even with Erzel helping him along. His legs felt like they had a mind of their own, twisting and bending at odd times as the two finally made it to the balcony. Kail collapsed and Erzel dropped to a knee next to the Human. Kail looked up at the Elf and realized that what Valsera had revealed had not changed the alliance the two shared.

"Thank you Erzel," Kail muttered, still ashamed.

The Elf nodded and crept back to the opening of the balcony, staring at the two opponents as they began to circle one another. He looked to the craters in the walls where the fireballs had struck. The room that had once been a throne room was now covered with rubble and debris. The Elf stared at Valsera, wondering if he could help in any way as Yanosh seemed to be less and less in charge of the situation.

Yanosh took a step back and watched as the sorcerer's fingertips began to glow a soft red. The wizard quickly brought his staff up, forming a powerful shield similar to the one Ectle had used when they had met on the Dragon Island. It shimmered and slowly surrounded Yanosh as he prepared to act defensively. Valsera watched the shield grow and form a bubble around the wizard and gave a sly smile.

As the shield finished, Valsera thrust his hand out and from the glowing light erupted bright bolts of red lightning. They danced all across the magic shield Yanosh had formed, causing ripples to form on the surface. From within the shield, it was clear that Yanosh was struggling to maintain his spell. As the bolts of lightning hit the shield, it soon became apparent that they were growing stronger and the shield, weaker. Valsera grit his teeth and released another wave of lightning, draining the defensive spell even further.

Yanosh staggered and the shield collapsed on him, exploding violently and sending the wizard sliding across the floor. The wizard reached out and grabbed his staff beside him and looked up at the sorcerer who had yet to advance on him. He pushed himself up onto one knee and used his staff to support his weight. He was amazed that the spell he had chosen had been broken, making him wonder if he even had a chance. The sorcerer was well prepared for the fight and had brought Yanosh to the ground just as he had claimed he would.

Erzel reached over his shoulder and drew his sword from its sheath. He looked at the sorcerer and stepped into the room to see if there was anything he could do to help the wizard. Two against one had to be better odds. Yanosh looked to the left at Erzel and then back to Valsera, seeing the enemy was now outnumbered even though his power greatly eclipsed the Elf and wizard.

"Bested Infus did you? How did you manage that?"

Valsera asked as the Elf approached.

"Didn't seem to like lightning very much," Erzel replied sarcastically, lowering the tip of his sword and pointing it towards Valsera's chest.

"Ah... did he not? Well, how do you feel about it?"

From the tips of the sorcerer's fingers erupted bolts of bright blue lightning, curling and twisting across the Elf's body. Erzel dropped his sword and collapsed to the floor writhing in pain. The lightning arched across his body and sent the Elf into convulsions as the pain became unbearable. Yanosh stood from the ground and levitated a pile of rubble, sending it across the room at the sorcerer. The debris pelted Valsera and he covered his face to protect himself from the attack, breaking the assault on the Elf.

Erzel crawled away with his armor smoldering as Valsera turned to face the wizard once more, a deep gash on the right side of his face bleeding heavily. The sorcerer grit his teeth and clenched his fist, preparing to finish off the wizard who had so brazenly struck him. Valsera broke into a run, charging Yanosh with every intent to finish him off. The wizard lowered his gaze to the floor and closed his eyes, softly whispering the only spell he believed was left in his arsenal.

His staff began to glow an icy blue color, pulsing softly as the heartbeat in the wizard's chest would. Valsera was closing quickly but everything around the wizard seemed to move in slow motion. He dropped to one knee on the floor and brought the staff back, preparing to strike his opponent when in range. The top of his staff was glowing brighter by the second and the next step that Valsera took opened Yanosh's eyes. He found the sorcerer steps away and thrust the top of his staff forward, aiming for the his opponent's stomach.

Erzel looked up as the wizard's staff made contact with the sorcerer who instantly recoiled from the attack. It was too late. A blinding flash filled the room and flooded out onto the balcony, making even Kail shield his face from the intense light. The blue blast was so bright it brought the light of day to the balcony and the walls outside, catching the attention of Dragons, Warbirds and the enemy forces on the defenses below.

The Elf rolled and buried his face in his arms, pressing his body against the stone floor as he found the light also brought with it a chilling cold. As the numbness slowly left his body, Erzel lifted his face slightly to dare a peek at the room. The light was fading but all around him in the air appeared a haze that took on a glow all its own. The Elf pushed up off the ground and looked around, shocked when he caught sight of the sorcerer in the center of the room.

Valsera stood with his left hand shielding his eyes and his right extended down to where Yanosh had been kneeling. The sorcerer did not move at all and Erzel soon realized the reason why. The spell that the wizard had used had completely encased the evil sorcerer in a layer of crystal. The ice like formation was clear enough to make out Valsera's shape but strong enough to imprison him for good. Erzel walked to the cluster of crystals and laid his hand on the face of it, finding the stone as cold as ice but as sturdy as the strongest of stones.

It wasn't until he knew Valsera had been stopped by the wizard's spell that he noticed Yanosh was nowhere to be seen. Where the wizard had knelt was vacant and the Elf looked frantically around the room and out onto the balcony, seeing Kail leaning heavily on the railing as he too scanned the room.

"Yanosh?" Erzel asked timidly, looking around once more. "Where are you? Valsera is done, he has been finished at last. Where are you?"

Silence gripped the room and Erzel was faced with the real fear that the wizard may not have survived the explosion. Even so, why was there no body? Seconds ticked by and the Elf suddenly remembered the spell the wizard had used, and how his staff had pulsed as if it had a heartbeat of its own. He looked to the floor on the side of the crystal formation and his fears were answered. There, scattered in three pieces were the remains of Yanosh's staff.

Seeing it smashed, Erzel bent and retrieved the top of the staff. The shaft had splintered and burst about a foot and a half down. It was a grim answer to a question he had not wanted to ask. The Elf carried the top of the staff with him, retrieving his sword and sheathing it as he moved out onto the balcony with

Kail. The man looked at what remained of the wizard's staff and hung his head, feeling somewhat responsible for the turn of events.

"He is gone then?" Kail asked sadly.

Erzel looked down to the balcony floor and noticed the weapon that Infus had revealed lying in the open. The Elf crossed the balcony and stooped to the ground, retrieving the long handle and looking at it curiously. The handle was wrapped in black leather and the metal underneath was a dull black. The center of the metal was hollow, most likely where the green flames burst forth. He looked at the weapon and realized what he held in his hands could change the tide of a fight instantly. He tucked it to his belt and turned to the man on the balcony.

The sound of wind rushing through the air caught their attention and the pair looked up into the dark sky. The form of a Dragon was silhouetted against the stars and it dropped to the balcony. Alora reached out and skidded across on the stone balcony, landing beside them and looking into the room at the sight. She turned her head to the two and glared curiously.

"We will explain later Alora. Kail is injured. We have to get out of here before their reinforcements arrive," Erzel said, helping Kail up onto the Blue Dragon's back.

Alora took another look at the Human imprisoned in crystal and then turned her head back to Erzel. "Where is Yanosh?"

"He has fallen," Erzel replied, showing the Dragon the remains of the staff. "Now please, we have to hurry. Call all of our forces back at once."

The Dragon stretched her wings out and dove off of the balcony, catching the wind and soaring in a broad circle away from the fortress. Erzel held Kail on as Alora made a wide bank right, flying out over the forest towards the north. She opened her mouth and let out a loud roar, a sign to the others that the task had been completed. Erzel took a look back behind them, seeing Dragons and Warbirds leaving the air around the castle and falling in behind Alora and the two on her back.

"Alora, take us down into those forests," Erzel ordered, the images of Yanosh's last moments still fresh in his mind..

The Aftermath

*T*he forest was silent as the Blue Dragon landed softly in a small clearing safe from the reaches of the soldiers back at Qwaz. Erzel slid down to the ground and supported Kail as he dropped as well. All around them the rest of the Warbirds and Dragons were arriving but it was apparent that there were far fewer than before. Several of the Warbirds were missing riders and what remained of the Silver Dragons all seemed to have received at least one arrow on the assault. The Celestial Knights spread out and did what they could to tend to the wounds of their mounts and those of the Dragons. Ectle approached the Elf slowly, looking around the clearing at the numbers that remained.

"Erzel... so few have returned. Thorgrim, Nimir, Galador, several Dragons and Warbirds. Wait... where is Yanosh?"

Erzel looked at the wizard and found that the words did not come easy to him. Everyone seemed to be crowding in around the two and he knew that he could not keep it hidden any longer. He reached to his belt and pulled the top of the staff out into view, holding it up for everyone to see. A shocked awe gripped the clearing as beast and man stared at what was left of Yanosh's staff.

"Yanosh has fallen," Erzel answered bluntly.

Lavian stepped in between the wall of people and looked at the remains of the wizard. "How did it happen? What became of Valsera?"

Erzel looked around and lowered the head of the staff. "Valsera was defeated. The last I saw of Yanosh was a violent explosion of icy blue light that swept out of the room and across the walls. When the intensity of the explosion had lessened all that remained was a shattered staff and the sorcerer, encased in a cluster of crystals. Yanosh had disappeared entirely."

Lavian reached out and took the head of the staff from the Elf, examining it closely. She rolled it over in her hands and ran her fingers across the cluster of stones at the top. Even seeing the shattered staff that had at one time belonged to their leader was not proof enough in her heart for her to believe Yanosh was gone. She touched the top of the staff and a sudden flash made them all jump. It wasn't nearly as bright as the one that had imprisoned the sorcerer but it caught their attention. The Celestial Knight pulled her fingertips away suddenly and stared at the top of the staff.

"Lavian, what was that?" Erzel asked, staring at the crystals.

"They are still active. The crystals have not extinguished their power."

"So... what does that mean?"

No one spoke for a moment but Lavian looked up at the Elf. "It means that the spell Yanosh used is active. This crystal holds the key to keeping Valsera forever encased in the crystals that Yanosh used. It also is the key to releasing him."

Everyone in the clearing pushed in closer to get a better look at the item she held in her hands. Kail took a step in and Erzel shot a glance to the right, hoping that his trust was not misplaced. "Why not destroy it then? Be rid of it for good so he may never rise again?" the Human asked.

"No! That can never happen!" Lavian snapped, looking up quickly. "To destroy the crystals will break the spell and therefore release Valsera. This must be kept safe and out of reach of his armies."

"Wait, I thought Yanosh said that once Valsera had been defeated that the armies would fall into disarray. Why do his forces still hold together?" Ectle asked, looking back in the direction of Qwaz.

"Valsera is not dead. He is only imprisoned. The armies still have the will leading them even if the sorcerer is no longer there to order them. Yanosh only made it impossible for the sorcerer to fight alongside his armies which will be a heavy loss to them," Lavian answered, lowering the head of the staff.

Erzel looked around at the rest of the soldiers who all wore long, tired faces. He knew something they did not want to hear but it had to be said. "It will not matter that Valsera is no longer here to fight. Infus will take the armies and lead them with just as much hate and malice as Valsera had. The trouble is that Infus is invulnerable to a physical attack. My sword passed through the Demon over and over until it had the best of me."

"Yet you managed to survive... how is that?" Ectle asked suspiciously.

"Alora. The lightning was the only thing that bested the Demon. If she had not been there, I would not be here to tell you of what had happened."

Erzel looked up through the group and realized that several of his numbers had not returned. "Where is Thorgrim... and Nimir? Did they not make it back?"

The last Gold Dragon in the forest approached and looked down on the Elf, her large eye glaring at him. "In the swamps to the south. Their mount was knocked from the sky."

Quiet murmurs surrounded them as they looked to one another for an answer to questions that had not yet been answered. Erzel looked back behind him in the direction he presumed the swamplands to be. Right now every soldier in Qwaz was on high alert and probably combing the forests and plains looking for them. To go back would only invite another devastating slaughter. They did not have the energy, numbers or heart to go back into battle. Even he himself doubted ever reaching the two Dwarves.

"We must get far away from Qwaz and the armies that will soon be smothering these lands in search of us. We can not be here when the sun comes up. If what Lavian has said is true, we need to get the top of that staff as far away as we possibly can."

"What about Nimir and Thorgrim? Do you leave them to die?" Ectle asked angrily, confused at how the Elf could simply turn his back on them.

"I do not want to leave them Ectle but what choice have we? If we go back we will be victims ourselves and we have to get out of here with that!" Erzel raised his voice, pointing to the head of the staff.

Ectle stared at the Elf and turned away from him. He walked up next to one of the Silver Dragons. The Dragon lowered its head and Ectle ran his hand down its neck slowly, stopping next to the wing.

"Where are you going?" Erzel asked, staring at the wizard.

"Erzel, you can fly north and protect that shard of crystals but I will not abandon those two in the swamps for dead. I would rather die there myself than turn my back and walk away safely."

"Ectle, you don't stand a chance. The entire army of Qwaz is behind us not to mention the Lizardmen in the swamps. To do this would take an army and a lifetime of luck. Please, do not do this."

The wizard leaned down next to the Dragon's head and whispered so only they could hear. "You do not have to stay. Just fly me to where you last saw them and then you can rejoin the others moving north."

The Dragon nodded and turned back to the rest, staring intently on Alora and Erzel who seemed astonished that the wizard was going to fly back into the lands that they had just attacked. The Dragon turned its head and Ectle looked at the Elf one last time.

"Are you sure you will go north Erzel?"

The Elf took a deep breath and looked at the crystals in Lavian's hand. He gave a simple nod and looked up. "Yes. If we protect this then there is a better chance we could end this war. Their fate is regrettable, but there is no reason to believe they are still alive. Please Ectle, use your reason. This is far greater than you and I. Ignoring what the head of this staff means is foolish... madness even."

Ectle turned his head and patted the Dragon twice, holding tight as the beast shot into the sky. The group on the ground followed it until they could see it no longer and then turned their attention back to the forest around them. Erzel felt horrible. He knew the significance of the item they held in their possession but it threatened to destroy all he stood for. He would never have abandoned them before that moment but when he realized the power of the crystals and what they could do for the war, he knew that keeping them safe was the biggest priority.

"Lavian... is this the right thing to do?" he asked timidly, hoping she would reinforce his beliefs.

The Celestial Knight looked at the crystals and brought her finger to the top of it, watching as it flashed again. She looked up at Erzel and took a deep breath. "Erzel, this is all that is stopping Valsera from sweeping down on us. So long as this remains intact, he will never be able to lead his armies against us again."

Erzel nodded and turned around to the numbers that still remained. Kail was the only one left from their original group and he stepped in next to Erzel, placing a weak hand on the Elf's shoulder. The Celestial Knights moved out to their Warbirds and calmed them, getting ready to take to the skies again. Several of them were without a rider and Lavian looked at Kail.

"Kail, the Warbirds have to have a rider. This one lost its rider in the battle. Would you ride it?" Lavian asked, running her hand down the creature's neck. The Warbird looked to the left at Kail and lowered its neck for the Human to climb up into the saddle.

Kail looked at the creature with amazement. He walked in next to Lavian and reached out, touching the Warbird next to where Lavian's hand was resting. It turned its head and locked eyes with the Human as he ran his hand lower through the soft feathers on the back of its neck. The Warbird ruffled its feathers and looked up into the sky as Kail reached across the saddle and grabbed the restraint, pulling himself up onto the creature's back. The Warbird took a few steps away from the others and spread its wings, flapping them a few times before pushing off with its powerful legs and taking to the air.

"Where are they going?" Erzel asked Lavian.

"The Warbird will test Kail in the sky to make sure that the Human can handle its quick maneuvers and high speeds. So long as Kail does not interfere with its flight, the Warbird will allow him to ride without any issues."

"Interesting... I hope he does not fall."

Lavian and Erzel stared up into the dark sky and waited for the Warbird to return safely with the Human on its back. The clouds had started to disperse and stars began to show in the sky above. Though dull at first, they soon grew brighter and the forests were no longer as dark. The rest of the Celestial Knights had begun to climb onto their mounts and start towards the clearing in the treetops. Lavian looked to her own Warbird which stopped next to her.

"Are you ready Erzel? We should surely be moving on just as you said earlier."

Alora stepped up to Erzel and lowered her body to the ground. The Elf climbed onto the Dragon's back and watched the line of Warbirds take off into the sky. They disappeared quickly and soon it was only Lavian and Erzel not in the air. She secured the top of the staff in her belt and snapped the reins of the Warbird. She was gone in seconds and Erzel followed her example. He patted the Dragon softly and she shot into the air, her wings beating viciously to drive them higher and higher.

Erzel looked back over his shoulder to the lights given off by the smoldering city of Qwaz. Fires still flickered in the distance and Erzel knew that the armies would soon spread through the trees looking for those responsible for the damages done to the city. He bowed his head and said a silent prayer hoping that Ectle, Thorgrim and Nimir remained safe.

The night at the Pass of Merwold was one filled with waiting for the southern armies to make an advance on the river crossing. As it stood, the Goblins and Ogres remained on the southern edges of the pass, out of range but able to taunt the Elves. The archers had filled the trenches and stared down on the enemies, their bows ready for action the second they were given the order. Behind the trench of archers were rows of Elven soldiers, their spears and swords ready.

The siege weapons had been ready for the past eight hours, their spears and stones held back and begging for the chance to break the soon to be incoming army. Aric moved down to the front of the soldiers and stood on the edge of the trench, looking out across the sand and water. The stars and moon created a shimmer across the water and a glow to the beach. The soldiers stared across the water and watched as the Ogres moved several of their own catapults into the clearing on the southern shore.

Elves looked back and forth, wondering if they had a chance against the large siege weapons. They watched as it took two Ogres to lift one of the boulders into place. The arm of the catapult seemed to strain under the weight of the massive hunk of rock. One would have been frightening but the Ogres had armed five of the monstrous catapults. From the sight, it looked like just one shot from the weapons could devastate the trenches and anyone standing in them.

Aric walked in between the lines of Elves as he kept a sharp eye on the southern beaches. He had never been so close to the enemy without being engaged in battle. The feeling was strange. The Elves had been waiting for hours for the order to fire, their bows begging for the order to loose a cloud of arrows. Aric kept his soldiers as calm as he could, waiting for the sign that they had held long enough.

"Sir, why do we wait? The enemy is there and our bows will reach them easily from here."

"They are not moving any further. We were sent to hold the pass for as long as we can. Giving them a reason to attack by firing on them now will only shorten the length of time before they try to cross. The longer we keep them uncertain about our strengths and numbers, the longer they will sit and wait. With any luck, we may keep them in a stalemate until more reinforcements."

"A brilliant plan..." the Elf noted sarcastically.

Aric ignored the statement and looked across the pass at the flood of Goblins that was just now arriving on the opposite shore. They moved like a wave, filling any and every gap. Soon, the entire southern shore was filled with countless numbers of enemy. The sun was still several hours from appearing but the Elves were wide awake and ready for battle.

Only an hour before sunrise a group of Elves arrived with interesting news for Aric. The three Elves all looked past the Elf at the soldiers on the other side of the pass and then back at Aric.

They all wore a smile that could only mean good news.

"Yes? What is it?"

The Elf in the front nodded and looked back over his shoulder. "Sir, reinforcements just arrived."

"Pentegarn sent reinforcements?" Aric asked, astounded at how fast the plea for help had been answered.

"No Aric... not Elves. The Humans of Cisalia."

Aric stared at the Elf in disbelief when he heard that Humans were arriving to back up the Elves at the Pass of Merwold. The three Elves turned and one nodded up the hill towards the camp in the forest. Aric turned to one of the Knights behind him and left him in charge.

The three Elves escorted Aric up the hill to where the Humans were rumored to have arrived.

Even though they had told him the Humans were arriving, Aric did not fully believe it. As they crossed the crest of the hill inside the forest, Aric realized that they had told the truth. In the back of the camp were rows and rows of Human Knights mounted on horses and in front, one holding the banner of Cisalia. Aric walked through the camp and stopped in front of the Knight holding the banner.

"Greetings. Who is in charge here?" the Elf asked, looking across each of the Knights.

One of the horses to his right stepped forward, moving right in beside the Knight with the banner. The man looked down at the Elf and locked eyes with him. Aric looked upon the man and found him vaguely familiar.

"I am Calyn, King of Cisalia and head of this force."

Aric realized as soon as the words left the Human that he had offended the King. The Elf slowly dropped to one knee and lowered his eyes to the ground. He waited for what seemed like several minutes until he heard the sound of the King drop to the ground next to his horse. The armored boots gave out a ring as he landed and Aric looked up, finally standing once more. The Human nodded and looked off towards the pass and then back at Aric.

"Forgive me my Lord. I did not mean to offend you."

"We shall forget the matter. I take it that my forces will

still be useful in the pass?"

"Of course. The southern armies have been arriving all through the night and continue to grow. Our forces have not received reinforcements since the Gnomes arrived. They have added to our numbers, but I am not sure if it would have been enough," Aric said as he walked the King towards the large make-shift barracks that had housed Aric and his head Knights.

The King stepped into the barracks and looked around, finding humor in its crude manner. Aric had spread a large map out on the table and pointed out the area where the Pass of Mer-wold was located, looking up to the King. Calyn stepped in next to the Elf and looked at the area Aric was focused on.

"What is this Aric?"

"This is the pass, and this is roughly where the encamp-ment is now. I had scouts in the forests to the south and they re-ported armies massing all across the fields and forests. There are between two and three thousand soldiers that have moved onto the pass to the south and at least twice that still coming. There is no way to tell exactly how many there are."

Calyn gave a slow nod as he looked over the map, wonder-ing just how far back in the southlands the Goblin army stretched. A Knight from the army of Humans walked into the barracks and gave a slight bow to the King. Calyn excused himself and walked to the door with the Knight, talking softly with the man.

"My Lord, what will you have us do? Where should we position ourselves?"

The King rubbed his chin and looked out into the camp. "I want the bulk of the Knights in around their siege weapons and in the forests with the Gnomes. Whatever is left over move into position in the clearing with the Elves."

"Yes my King."

Calyn walked back to where the Elf was waiting and stopped, looking back at the map. "Now, where were we?"

"What was that about sir?" Aric asked.

"The soldiers were asking where to be positioned so I gave them the direction they needed. Now if you would please tell me what you have planned here."

The Elf looked at the King for a moment, finding the

man a bit to short tempered. He turned back to the map but for some reason he could not focus on the parchment. He ran his finger back down the map to the city of Qwaz where he assumed the armies were originating from. Further down the map were the wastelands and then Nomaria, all of which had the potential of numerous armies all capable of breaking the defenses at the pass.

He looked back at Calyn and noticed a group of Knights had walked back into the barracks and stood at the entrance watching the King and the Elf. Aric left the map and offered the King a seat, pulling one for himself from under the edge of the table. He sat and watched as the King looked over the map. The Human King looked up at the Knights and nodded, turning to the Elf and walking towards him. The air in the barracks felt thick as Calyn walked past the Elf towards the seat Aric had offered him. He took one last look at the Knights and then back down at the Elf.

Calyn quickly reached to his hip and drew the dagger sheathed by his side and grabbed the Elf by the back of his head. As quick as he had drawn the dagger the Human slid it up under Aric's neck, pausing to lean down next to the Elf's ear. Aric's blood ran cold and he scarcely breathed, having no idea what was going on. He saw the three Humans standing at the front door, blocking off any possible escape and any kind of help. The Human gave a laugh as he pressed the blade of the knife tighter to the Elf's neck.

"Let me guess, right now you are wondering how you didn't see this coming? Let me explain. You see, Valsera is going to come across this pass and sweep across your lands like a shadow. Nothing will be safe from him. The way I look at it, I would rather be his dog than his enemy."

"There won't be any room… for traitors."

"Oh I happen to disagree. You see, when this is over there will not be a single soldier left alive to report back to the King at Pentegarn. Everyone will die here. I am going to lead my Knights back to Pentegarn and tell your King that there was a horrible loss here at the pass and we narrowly escaped. Then, I will kill him."

Aric stared straight ahead as he realized that there was nothing he could do. They had been waiting for reinforcements and when they had arrived, Aric had no idea that they were there to support the army to the south. Calyn looked up to the three Knights and nodded to the door.

"Go give the signal. Let's get this over with."

Aric reached to his hip and drew his own dagger in a flash but as he did Calyn caught his wrist and jerked the blade across the Elf's throat. Aric felt weakened as the blood spurted from the gash and the weapon fell from his hand. The Elf fell forward onto the table and slumped slowly, dying as the Human wiped the blade clean. The Humans turned and left the barracks and Calyn looked at the Elf and the puddle of blood forming on the floor underneath the table.

The King took a deep breath and turned, walking to the doorway. Calyn stopped at the door and looked back at the table where the Elf lay dead and scanned the room. With one last glance he turned and left to watch the scene at the pass. The room was silent with the exception of the dripping of blood from the table. In the corner came a shuffle and behind a stand of barrels and a rack of weaponry came a Gnome, his eyes amazed at the sight of the dead Elf.

The Gnome had hid as soon as the others had entered the room and stood at the edge of the table, looking at Aric. He had heard everything and knew that the moment the Humans saw him he would be as dead as the Elf slumped over the table. The Gnome snuck to the edge of the barracks, peering out at the back row of Knights as they continued to move down towards the river. He looked around and started off away from the encampment, running to the north. Only one thing was stuck in his head and that was to get to Pentegarn before the Humans.

Behind him the Gnome heard the blast of a horn and knew that it was the signal for the combined effort of Goblins and Humans to attack the Elves. The Gnome ran as fast as he could through the forest, fearing someone would hear him but too afraid to stop. The sounds of battle suddenly erupted behind him and he knew that the betrayal had begun. He moved as fast as his small legs would carry him. The Gnome had left his weapons and gear back in the camp in his rush to get away and he was glad he did not have them to weigh him down now. The Gnome kept running until his feet were tangled in a low clump of roots and he fell face first into the dirt.

The Gnome turned and rolled on his back, reaching down and squeezed his ankle to test it. It was sore but he knew there was a bigger problem in front of him. He climbed to his feet and hobbled through the trees determined to keep going no matter the cost. The walk would take forever for the now injured Gnome, but he forced the thought out of his mind and pushed himself on. As the Gnome cleared the edge of the forest to the north, the sun broke the horizon, pushing back the shadows from the night before.

The smoke had just begun to clear on the Pass of Merwold and Calyn sat on his horse overlooking the massacre he had taken part in. His betrayal had been swift, knocking out all of the siege weapons in one swift blow before they could be used against the incoming Goblin and Ogre forces. His Knights had swarmed through the forests, slaughtering the unsuspecting Elven and Gnome archers and the catapults on the southern side of the river demolished the forward defenses as the Goblins flooded up the sandy beach.

The Goblins and Ogres were still flooding through the river and up onto the banks of the northern side. They had moved through the Elven camp, torching and destroying everything they came in contact with until nothing in the area was left unscarred. Though the betrayal was sudden and unexpected, the Elves did manage to do quite a lot of damage to the forces of Cisalia. The Humans started by slaughtering the archers and destroying the siege weapons but the center of the Elven army managed a strong counter attack, destroying the bulk of the Human army. Sadly their efforts were futile.

Calyn looked from the horse at a large group of prisoners surrounded in the middle of the beach by Goblins, Humans, and Ogres alike. The Elves and Gnomes remained on their knees with their hands locked behind their heads, disgusted and enraged at what had happened. One of the Knights approached the King and turned to look upon the mass of captives.

"My Lord, what do we do with the prisoners?"

Calyn looked down at the Gnomes and Elves with a glare of interest. Some of the prisoners looked up at the hill where the King sat. "What prisoners?"

The King turned his horse to the left and rode off into the trees. The Knight watched the King disappear. He walked down to where the soldiers stood holding the enemies at the tips of their swords and spears. Another Knight looked at him and turned back to the prisoners.

"What did he say?" the soldier asked, staring at the closest Elf.

"Well, apparently there were no survivors."

"As he wishes."

The Knight raised his hand and signaled for the soldiers to kill the prisoners. Those near the prisoners drew back their weapons and attacked, slaughtering what was left of the Elven and Gnome armies in a few minutes.

The bodies made monstrous piles on the edges of the pass as the Goblins and Humans stripped the Elves of their armor and weapons. Row after row of Goblin soldiers tore through the armor that had once belonged to the Elves, using what they could to replace their own tattered and worn armor. The sight was most discouraging as the grotesque Goblin soldiers turned into scavengers, mixing the elite Elven style of weapons and armor with their own.

Calyn stopped his horse in the center of the encampment that was now smoldering and a soldier took the reins. The King looked at a large group of his Knights that were returning from their patrol in the outer edges of the forest. They dismounted and all knelt in one motion. The King motioned and the Knights all stood.

"Has anyone made it out of the forest? There are no survivors, do you understand? I do not want a single one of their soldiers to make it away from this pass. Now get back out there and make sure nothing living passes your patrols."

The Knights quickly remounted their horses and rode

back through the trees the way they had arrived. The line of Humans disappeared and the King turned around and leaned against his horse, rubbing its neck gently to calm the beast. The horse pawed the ground nervously as the Goblins moved past to the forests behind the Human Knights.

Back at the river, the armies from the south continued to move through the pass, their numbers uncountable as they marched past the mounds of fallen soldiers. The Ogres struggled to push the monstrous catapults through the swift current and soon managed to bring them onto the northern side of the river. Even siege weapons the Elves had brought to hold the pass were now being repaired to use against the northern cities next to be invaded.

The Goblins and Ogres moved on through the pass as Calyn prepared his Knights to move back to Pentegarn. They all knew the plan. Calyn and a small group of the remaining Human forces would ride to Pentegarn and spring a tale of a horrible massacre at the pass that left the armies in ruin and how his soldiers had barely made it back alive. It would open into the perfect betrayal and give the armies from the south nearly free run through the Elven lands. Nothing was standing in their way as they prepared to take all of middle Nalawren in one massive sweep.

Promising New Life

The walls of Eglarest stood fully defended. The archers covered the walls and kept a sharp eye on the surrounding lands, waiting for the enemies that were rumored to be hiding in the surrounding forests. As soon as the Dragons and their group had left the area, Tanis had ordered the army of Wood Elves into the fortress and the gates were sealed and locked down tightly. The Elven soldiers prepared the catapults and waited, watching the fields. The King stood on the upper balcony of the keep, looking out at his defenses and the lands outside of the fortress.

His Queen approached silently and placed a hand on his shoulder, her gaze joining his as they stood rigid on the balcony. The two had not spoken much after the confrontation in the clearing. Tanis wanted his solitude. He had been shocked by the idea of his daughter being taken away to a far off place, that the Elf had defied his orders, and on top of everything else, that Dragons actually existed.

The Wood Elf turned and his Queen wrapped her arm around his back. "Are you alright Tanis?"

"Yes... and no. I am happy that Rhen is back home but I can not forgive Erzel for what he did. He took our daughter away from Tvan where she was safe and threw her into a world of the unknown. I can not understand why he would go against me."

"A Dragon though... I still can not believe that it was real. All those tales and all the myths have been proven and they are siding with him and his group. Things could have turned out a lot worse."

Tanis nodded, still not willing to forgive the Elf. From behind there was a faint set of footsteps. They both turned and looked at their daughter, standing alone and apparently distraught. Her eyes were red and swollen from the tears she had shed over the loss of her first love. She had spent the entire day thrown on her bed with her face buried in her arms, tears flooding from her eyes and her stomach hurting from the swell of grief.

"Rhen... are you alright?" Narissa asked, looking at her pale daughter.

"I feel strange. I keep hurting with Erzel gone. Father please, do not blame him for me being there. I went with them without their knowing it. Erzel never would have put me in danger, I know it."

"Rhen, I know you feel that those actions were all your own, but if Erzel had stayed in Tvan with you as I had told him, then there would never have been an issue at all. He defied my direct orders. There was nothing difficult about what I asked, escort you to the city and remain there where safety was guaranteed. I can not forgive him for openly defying me."

Tears began to form in her eyes again and she swayed on her feet. "Father please, he means so much to me."

Tanis turned and looked at his daughter somewhat angrily, his disbelief very apparent on his face. "What does he mean to you Rhen? I was looking to your best interest. What if those Dragons had not been interested in helping your group and instead decided you were enemies? Do you not see how foolish your choices were?"

"But I am fine! Look at me, I am right here and there is nothing wrong with me at all!" Rhen shouted, her fists balled and her face reddened.

The King and Queen were shocked at the anger that Rhen had just shown. They stood side by side as the Princess turned and stormed back into the keep. She hurried down the hall and through her door, flinging herself on her bed. She screamed into the blankets and pounded her fist on the bed in anger. Her stomach felt like it was being torn in two different directions from the swell of anger and heartache. She pushed herself up off of the bed and sat on the edge, looking out to the balcony with a desperate glance. In the back of her mind she wanted to run to wherever Erzel was to see him again but she knew the thought was crazy.

The door opened and one of the servants entered slowly, looking at the saddened Princess. "Are you alright my lady?" the Elf asked as she bowed.

"Yes... I think. I do not feel well. Is this how heartache feels?"

"I would not know my lady, I apologize. Tell me how it feels."

Rhen touched her stomach. "It feels like my stomach is being pulled away from my body and my chest is heavy. I keep feeling like I am going to be sick and my head hurts so bad. All I think about is Erzel. This is unbearable."

The servant crossed her hands in front of her own stomach and knelt in front of the Princess. She had no idea what to say and seeing Rhen in so much pain made her feel helpless. The two stared at one another until the Princess doubled over, feeling like she was going to be sick. The servant stepped back and waited until the Princess had rolled onto her back on the bed.

"My dear, what can I do for you?"

"I... I don't know. I think... I am going to be..."

Rhen rolled out of the bed and staggered out of the room. She made it to the edge of the balcony and doubled over, vomiting. She fell to her knees and shuddered as her body hunched over. The servant quickly dropped to Rhen's side and held her, helping her to her feet and back to the bed. The woman handed the Princess a towel and helped wipe her face and once the Princess was settled she immediately left the room.

Rhen could hear her in the hall ordering for the King and Queen to be informed of the Princess's sudden illness. She returned with the large washbowl filled with water to wash the balcony clean. The Princess sank back into the bed and took a deep breath, her head splitting.

It took five minutes at most for her parents to arrive but for Rhen it felt like forever. They stopped next to her bed and looked down on her, Narissa taking her hand as they watched the Princess turn pale as another wave of nausea swept over her.

"Rhen, what is going on?" Narissa asked, seeing her daughter in such odd shape.

"I... don't know mother... I feel so... sick."

Tanis turned back to the servant and ordered her to find more help as he saw his daughter losing color and curled on the bed. He had been angry before but now he was worried. The Queen rubbed her daughter's hand with her own, trying to comfort her as they waited for servants to return. The door burst open and six Elves entered carrying fresh water in bowls and clean towels. They moved to the side of the bed as the King and Queen moved out of the way. One of the servants soaked one of the towels in the cool water and draped it over Rhen's forehead. They did what they could to make her comfortable as one of the servants spoke with the King and Queen.

"My Lord, I do not understand. She was fine one moment and then suddenly sick the next. It came on so fast. She gets sick, her temperature runs hot and then cold, and she complains of pain in her stomach and head. I do know there is a healer in the lower levels. I remember seeing him a few days ago. He could possibly shed some light on the situation."

Tanis nodded to the servant. "Very well, leave at once and find him. I want him in here as soon as you find him and I want to know what is wrong with my daughter."

The servant left the room and hurried down the hall, taking the stairs as quickly as she could without losing her footing. She cut through the large courtyard and out into the open areas of the battlements. Soldiers moved aside as she hurried through the defenses, looking for the Elf she had seen days before. From the edge of the battlements she saw the Elf dressed in white in the open below and hurried down the incline that led to the ground.

She picked up the front of her dress and ran faster, stopping in front of the Elf and catching her breath for a moment. The healer placed a hand on her shoulder and helped steady the woman. "Are you alright?"

"Yes... the King and Queen... need your presence in... the Princess's quarters at once. She is very ill. They need to know... why," she answered, trying to catch her breath as she explained the predicament.

"Very well, lead the way at once."

The servant moved back through the fortress as she had come, the healer right behind her as they started up the stairs.

They burst through the doors and found the Princess the same as when she left. The healer stopped in front of the King and Queen with a low bow.

"Greetings my King and Queen, my name is Osslo. I have heard of the Princess's condition and I will do everything I can to help. I will need some quiet and less of a crowd."

"Whatever you need. Just help her," Narissa said as she turned Tanis away from the bed and out the door.

The healer dismissed several of the servants, keeping the sole Elf who had summoned him there. The healer reached down and gently touched the Princess on the shoulder, looking into her swollen eyes as she turned her head towards him.

"Who... who are you?" she asked, her energy nearly drained.

"I am Osslo, a healer from the lower forests of Swanhaven. They told me you were feeling very ill so I am here to help. Just relax and close your eyes."

The Princess did not find it hard to follow Osslo's instructions as picking her head up from the pillow left her dizzy and tired. The healer washed his hands in the bowl of water and pressed his fingers to her temples. He worked his way down her neck, chest, and stomach. He passed her stomach with his hands hovering over her hips and then back up. Every time he touched her stomach she seemed to grimace slightly.

"Is your stomach hurting you right now?" he asked, keeping an eye on her face.

"No... only when you touched it. I cramp every now and then..." she complained loudly, her face twisted.

Osslo touched her stomach again and raised his eyebrow, dropping down below her stomach and then up above it. He took a few steps to the top of the bed and placed a hand on her forehead. The grimace on her face lessened and disappeared as she slowly fell asleep. Her chest rose and fell softly as she fell into a deep sleep. She looked so peaceful now that her pain was gone.

The servant looked at the healer with a face of mystery as Osslo rewashed his hands. He dried them on one of the towels and looked at the Princess one more time, satisfied with her state of slumber. He turned and walked away from the bed, rubbing his chin as he pondered how to tell the King and Queen his findings.

"What have you found?" the servant asked, following the healer around the room.

"I should speak with her parents first. Would you please let them know I am ready to speak with them. Quietly, she is sleeping soundly."

The servant turned and left the room, finding the King and Queen standing right outside of the door. They walked in and closed the door behind them. The first thing they saw was their daughter sleeping soundly on the bed. She looked completely different from when they had seen her minutes earlier. They noticed the healer standing further off to the side away from the Princess and slowly they joined him. The Elf bowed and waved a hand to the balcony where they could speak privately.

"I think it best to let her sleep for now. We should keep our voices down so we do not disturb her."

"What have you learned Osslo?" Tanis asked anxiously.

"Well, I must say I had not expected to learn what I did. It seems that your daughter is not sick, but instead suffering from a mixture of things."

"Well... what is wrong and how can we help her?"

Osslo looked at Tanis and then Narissa. He took a deep breath. "She is suffering first from a broken heart. She weeps for the loss of someone, possibly a love. The pain is very strong inside of her and it is draining her of all her energy. As I calmed the pain in her, she instantly drifted off to sleep. She is exhausted."

Tanis nodded and crossed his arms, a wave of guilt sweeping over him as he realized Erzel had been the love she mourned for. He looked at Narissa and then back to the healer. "Go on."

The healer shook his head and took another deep breath. On one hand he knew he had to tell the King and Queen the news about their daughter but at the same time he did not want to be the one to reveal the truth. "Well... there is a very obvious matter that is causing her the sickness and pains that are sweeping her stomach. Apart from the heartache that she is suffering from, there is something more... interesting."

"Well, what is it?" Narissa asked impatiently.

Osslo finally gave in with a sigh. "She is expecting."

The two looked at the healer with faces of confusion. Something so simple should have registered easily but they seemed to be having a lot of trouble comprehending Osslo's words.

"You mean..."

The Elf nodded. "Yes... your daughter is pregnant. A mother to be and she has no idea."

Character Glossary

Elves

Erzel: High Elf, Captain of the Order of the White Eagle, charged with rescuing the Princess of the Wood Elves after her abduction and with leading the expedition to find the Dragons.

Rhen: Princess of Swanhaven, abducted on her way to Pentegarn, held by the Humans until rescued by the Elves. Sneaks onto the ship sailing in search of the Dragon Isles. She is drawn to Erzel.

Elendil: King of the High Elves and ruler over Pentegarn and all of the Elven lands that stretch across the center of Nalawren. Set with the task of defending the northern lands against the onslaught of Valsera's armies.

Tanis: King of the Wood Elves and ruler over Swanhaven and the northern fortress of Eglarest as well as the forests that surround the middle lands. Sends his daughter to Tvan and then retreats to the fortress Eglarest to wait out the war.

Narissa: Queen of the Wood Elves and mother of Rhen.

Aric: High Elf, Erzel's second in command in the Order and sent to the Pass of Merwold to defend it once the armies of the south begin moving on the Elven lands.

Elerith: High Elf left in charge of the borderlands once Erzel and his Order are pulled back to the city of Pentegarn. Has maintained the defenses on the border between the southlands and Elven lands for the past five years.

Raziel: High Elf in charge of the fortress city Mihlann and second defense of the borderlands should Elerith and his armies fail.

Thalun: Captain of the Wood Elves and sent to help Erzel and his forces recover the Princess once they learn who was responsible for her abduction.

Kail: Though only half Elf, Kail joins Erzel and his party to ensure the Princess is escorted safely to Tvan from Pentegarn. Very loyal to their cause even with a darker past that haunts him. Kail is an expert marksman with a bow.

Dwarves

Thorgrim: Adventurous Dwarf that joins Erzel's party. Has vast knowledge of the lands around Tvan and is a master with hand to hand weapons. He shuns the underground cities that most Dwarves love and prefers the adventures above ground.

Nimir: Originally a miner in Tvan, Nimir grows tired of the work underground and sets out for adventure above ground. Young and inexperienced, Nimir is saved by Erzel and Kail and pledges his life to the Elf.

Velex: Elder Dwarf of Tvan in charge of all diplomatic affairs.

Ardis: Elder Dwarf of Tvan in charge of the defenses on the surface and all soldiers that defend them.

Odar: Elder Dwarf of Tvan in charge of the defenses underground and all the soldiers that defend them as well as ruler of the main fortress within the Tvan Mountains.

Divos: Elder Dwarf of Tvan in charge of the massive mining community and the mines. He also handles all trade with other races and sees that the funds for their city never drop too low.

Humans

Calyn: King of Cisalia. Thought responsible for the abduction of the Princess. The King becomes angry after the Princess was recovered and plots darker things against the Elves.

Rathe: Incredibly large man who joins with Thorgrim as the group moves to Tvan. Even though he is a monstrous man, he maintains a boyish nature and seems more childish than manly. He enjoys torturing Thorgrim and does not miss a chance to get on the Dwarf's nerves.

Dragons

Alora: Dragon responsible for leading Erzel's group to the Dragon Isles by visions sent to the Princess in her sleep. She is shunned by her own race for helping the outsiders find the island but defends her decision. She is also the last of the Blue Dragons with no chance of saving her kind. Alora uses a powerful lightning breath attack and has taken to Erzel as he is very close to Rhen.

Wizards / Sorcerers

Valsera: Led the armies into the southlands and has yet to be stopped as he pushes further north with every battle. Valsera has begun researching the abilities of the darkest magic ever conceived including raising the dead and controlling them. Valsera has a tendency to be merciless and it soon becomes apparent that Nalawren is not the first land he has conquered in his quest for complete dominance.

Yanosh: Leader of the Celestial Knights who was forced to flee their homelands when Valsera attacked their lands in the past. He and his Knights have been in charge of defending the Dragon Isles ever since Valsera purged the lands. He has a swelling desire for revenge after what happened to his people in the past. One of the most powerful wizards to ever set foot in Nalawren.

Ectle: Final member to join the group taking Rhen north to Tvan. He is very powerful and has spent most of his life striving to find the Dragon Isles. Though he is the only one who still believes the Dragons exist he continues researching every scroll and book he can find about them, hoping for a clue to where the Dragons disappeared to.

Valsera's Generals

Infus: Demon summoned to serve Valsera and his armies. The creature has a rare ability of being invincible to physical attacks of any kind and becomes a nightmare to any who stand against it. Infus serves Valsera reluctantly.

Uljic: Little is known of Uljic though it appears as a cross between Goblin and Troll. Very strong and serves Valsera without question.

Slayers: Insanely strong soldiers serving under Infus. Extremely strong and more resistant to damage than most soldiers. Their weapons are poisoned, inflicting intense pain, and upon their death the body of a Slayer cracks and bursts into flames.

Celestial Knights

Galador: Head Knight of the Celestial Knights. He fled the homelands with the others when Valsera invaded. He and the other Celestial Knights craft the magically enhanced weapons that they use.

Lavian: Second in command under Galador. She is close to Yanosh and later to Rhen. Being one of the only two female survivors has pushed her to be a battle hardened soldier. She is very skilled with the magically altered crossbow she wields.

Kristian: The main Knight in charge of creating the weapons and armor used by the Celestial Knights. He is well versed in embodying the weapons with magical enchantments.

City Glossary

Pentegarn: Center of the lands of the High Elves, ruled by Elendil. Of all the cities in the lands, it is the largest, second only to Tvan. From a distance it could be confused as a mountain. To everyone inhabiting the city, it is impenetrable.

Swanhaven: Home of the Wood Elves nestled deep in the forests. It is ruled by Tanis and Narissa and has very little in the form of defenses as the Wood Elves prefer a more peaceful nature.

Tvan: Home of the Dwarves and hidden beneath the Tvan Mountains. The city never sees the light of day but houses an army so vast it would match that of all the other races. The Dwarves prefer to remain hidden in their mountains and dig for their riches. The defenses of Tvan stretch from the lands above ground to the heart of the mountains.

Cisalia: Last home of the Humans after they were forced to flee the southlands during Valsera's invasion. Ruled by Calyn, the Humans strive to remain out of the battles, preferring to let the Elves hold off the southern armies by themselves.

Qwaz: Originally the city of the Humans, Valsera swept over the lands and pushed them north, taking the city for himself and smothering it in the Goblins that served him. Once a beautiful and proud castle, it is now dark and falling into ruin. A staging point for Valsera's invasions.

Nomaria: Fortress city constructed by Valsera after the Chaos Wars ended. It serves as his permanent castle and from it he plunges himself into the dark magic from an ancient time. His darkest soldiers were created in Nomaria.

Mihlann: War torn fortress on the border that serves as a staging point for all Elven armies defending the borders. Raziel was appointed Lord over the fortress after the Chaos Wars ended and refuses to leave Mihlann no matter what evil comes his way.

Eglarest: Large fortress to the east of Tvan ruled by Tanis of Swanhaven. Since the Wood Elves at Swanhaven have very little as far as defenses, in times of war they tend to move north to the fortress of Eglarest to protect their people. The fortress has never seen a crippling battle.

Murm: Large trade city west of Tvan. It is a center for almost all trade and goods in Nalawren. Also, it is also the largest port city in all of Nalawren. The city remains neutral with a diverse number of races inhabiting the city.